UNBREAK
my heart

lorelei james

Unbreak My Heart
Rough Riders Legacy Book 1
Copyright © LJLA, LLC
Ridgeview Publishing

ISBN: 978-1-941869-69-7

Cover Design by: Meredith Blair – www.authorsangels.com
Cover Photo by: Sara Eirew Photographer – www.saraeirew.com
Interior Designed and Formatted by: BB eBooks Co., Ltd. – www.bbebooksthailand.com

Dedication—*to all my readers who worried that Sierra McKay and Boone West wouldn't get their happily-ever-after, and who waited patiently (and sometimes impatiently nagged me) for it the past four and a half years...this love story is for you.*

XOXO
Lorelei~

I BLAMED EVERYTHING on the fever.

Everything.

My nausea.

My surliness.

My weepiness.

My utter lack of reaction when he strolled into the exam room.

He gaped at me like I was an apparition.

I continued to stare at him blankly, as if it was no big deal he was here, right in front of me, wearing scrubs and a cloak of authority.

But the truth was I hadn't seen him for seven years.

Seven. Years.

I should have been in shock—maybe I was in *too much* shock. This definitely fell under the heading of trauma. Because on the day he waltzed back into my life? I looked worse than dog diarrhea.

I mentally kicked myself for not going to the ER. Or perhaps just letting myself die. Anything would have been better than this.

Screw you, universe. Fuck you, fate. Karma, you bitch, you owe me.

This chance meeting should've happened when I was dressed to the nines, not when I was sporting yoga pants, a ratty Three Stooges T-shirt, dollar store flip-flops and no bra. And the bonus? My hair was limp, my skin clammy, my face shiny from the raging fever I couldn't shake.

Wait. Maybe this *was* a fever-induced nightmare.

"Sierra?" The beautiful apparition spoke my name in a deep, sexy rasp.

Pretend you don't know him.

Not my most stellar plan, but I went with it.

I cocked my head and frowned as if I couldn't quite place him.

His expressive brown eyes turned hard. "That's really how you're gonna play this? Like you don't know me?"

I returned his narrow-eyed stare because I was too sick to fake an air of boredom.

"Fine. I'm Boone West. Your nurse," he said sarcastically. "I'm here to take your vitals."

I shook my head. My inability to respond wasn't from pettiness— I'd lost my voice the day before due to the fever. But my middle finger worked fine and I used it to point at the door as I mouthed, "Get. Out."

"Nice try. But keep your arm out like that so I can take your blood pressure."

My heart rate skyrocketed, so no freakin' way was he putting a blood pressure cuff and a stethoscope on me.

Boone moved in cautiously as if I were a feral creature. He smiled— not the sweet, boyish grin I once loved, but one brimming with fake benevolence.

My belly flipped, which pissed me off. And I wished projectile vomiting were my superpower instead of this uncanny ability to be at the wrong place at the wrong time, every time.

I jerked away from him.

"Look, Sierra," he said reasonably. "I wasn't expecting to run into you here. Not like this. Let me do my job and we'll talk afterward."

I shook my head so hard my vision went wonky.

"It's not like you have a choice."

Wrong. In full panic mode, I bailed off the exam table and hugged the wall, facing him as I crept toward the door.

"Whoa. Slow down. You came into the clinic because you're sick. You can't just leave."

My throat felt like I'd gargled with gravel, but I managed, "Watch me."

Then I threw open the door and booked it down the hallway.

But my fever had the last laugh.

My body chose that moment to fail me. Chills erupted as if I'd been plunged into a deep freezer, followed by sweat breaking out as if I'd been baking in the Arizona desert. White spots obscured my vision.

I swayed before everything went dark.

"SHE'S COMING AROUND."

I recognized that voice.

Doctor Monroe.

I peeled my eyes open and noticed I was back in the exam room.

"Hey girl. How're you doin'?"

Girl. She seemed to have forgotten that I was not a girl, but a twenty-three-year-old college graduate with the world by the balls.

"I need to poke around, so lie still." She lifted my shirt and started palpating my belly. For such a tiny thing, she pushed hard enough on my innards that I swear I felt her fingers poking the *inside* of my spine.

"Nothing out of the ordinary. Can you sit up?"

As soon as I was upright, the whooshing sensation started in my ears. My eyes burned but I could clearly see that Boone blocked the door. I gritted out, "He goes."

Doc Monroe got right in my face. "A patient who acts like they're trying to escape and then passes out in a waiting room full of people is hell on my reputation, Sierra McKay. Boone stays. You're lucky he acted so fast and caught you before you hit the floor."

"How did I…?" I gestured to the surrounding area.

"I carried you," Boone said. "You snuggled right into me. Strange behavior from someone who doesn't *know* me."

Goddammit. I hated this. I hated him. I leveled my best glare at his smarmy face.

He remained stoic.

Yeah, you were always good at hiding your emotions, weren't you, West?

"Sounds like you have laryngitis too," Doc Monroe said. "Boone, you didn't get her vitals?"

"No, ma'am. Under the circumstances, maybe it's best if you do that."

The doc looked at me with a raised eyebrow.

"He has to go," I croaked out.

"Sergeant West is here by government order, finishing the last few days of his training stint in rural healthcare that the army requires for medical personnel at his level."

She didn't have to explain that to me. In fact, I really didn't want to know *why* he was here.

Doc sighed and took my temperature, which tipped the thermometer at a toasty 103 degrees. She checked my eyes, my ears and my nose. She pressed her thumbs down the center of my neck and beneath my jaw. She listened to my lungs. Lastly, she shoved a tongue depressor in my mouth and shone a light in my throat while demanding I say *aaaaah*.

She patted my knee. "It appears you've got strep. But I'll send Sarah in from the lab for a throat culture to make sure."

No wonder I felt shitty and none of Rielle's natural home remedies had worked on me.

Doc Monroe poked the call button before she plopped on the rolling stool and typed on her laptop.

I stared at my knees, grateful I wasn't wearing a drafty exam gown that left me even more exposed.

To Boone fucking West.

Two knocks sounded on the door.

Boone stepped aside as the lab tech hustled in.

"One quick swipe is all I need," she chirped merrily.

I gagged when she jammed the long cotton swab into my throat and swirled it around.

Then she took a blood sample and said, "All done," with *way* too much fucking cheer.

She exited the room and Doc Monroe stood in front of me. "It'll be about fifteen minutes until I get the lab results. Why don't you lie down?" Doc pulled out the exam table extension.

After I curled up on my side, she covered me with a blanket. Part of me wished she acted cold and clinical instead of showing maternal concern.

The door shut with a soft click.

Everything ached. My throat was almost swollen shut so it hurt twice as much to cry. But the tears leaked out anyway.

"I'm still here," Boone stated.

Go away.

"Since you can't talk, you'll damn well listen."

He'd gotten bossier from his years in the military. But he must have struggled with whatever he wanted to say since he remained quiet longer than I expected.

"Of all the places in the country I could've chosen to complete this training assignment, I elected to do it here, in my hometown, because I wanted to see you again. Even when I suspected you'd kick me in the balls at best, or you were in a relationship with some undeserving douchebag at worst."

I hated that he admitted that his worst-case scenario was seeing me involved with someone else. Right then, I wished I had a hot, rich boyfriend with a big dick to flaunt at him.

"I don't know what surprised me more," Boone continued. "To find out that you actually changed your last name from Daniels to McKay—which is why, with all the damn McKays around here, I didn't know the *S. McKay* on the patient chart was you—or that you no longer live in Sundance."

Even if my vocal chords hadn't been raw and nonfunctioning, I wouldn't have responded. What could I say? He expected me to defend my choice to test my business skills beyond the Wyoming border? Screw that. He'd left for the very same reason. I owed him nothing.

"We're not done with this, Sierra. Not by a long shot."

His footsteps squeaked on the linoleum. The door opened and closed with a soft click.

I knew I was alone.

Nausea rolled over me. I closed my eyes.

I just needed fifteen minutes and this nightmare would be over.

WHEN DOC MONROE woke me, I didn't know where I was.

Then a cough and burning in my throat reminded me.

"You tested positive for strep," the doc said, helping me sit up.

Goodie.

"Two treatment choices. A ten-day cycle of penicillin in pill form or a shot of penicillin."

"A shot," I whispered.

"Good choice. You'll feel better faster. You want me to prescribe a cough suppressant?"

I shook my head.

"Rielle's opinions of western medicine have rubbed off on you."

My father's wife preferred natural remedies whenever possible. Most people attributed that mindset to her hippie-like upbringing. But the truth was before she married my dad, her financial situation dictated she find fast and cheap alternatives. She and I laughed that she'd rather be seen as a hippie than a cheapskate.

The doc pulled out a syringe and a vial of clear liquid. She attached one to the other and looked at me. "Drop your drawers. You get this shot in the butt."

Great. I hooked my thumbs in the waistband of my yoga pants.

Just then, three fast knocks sounded on the door before it opened a crack. "Doc, we need you right away in six."

"Dammit." She gestured to the needle in her gloved hand. "Get someone in here to do this."

That's when I knew the universe was giving me an opportunity for payback, because fifteen seconds later, Boone strolled in.

So the fever took control. Or the bad angel. Or the devil in my soul that Boone West put there when he left me with a broken heart.

"I'm here to—"

"Give it to me, right?" I said huskily in my best phone-sex-operator voice. I turned around. Peering over my shoulder, I affixed my gaze to his as I shimmied my yoga pants down to my knees.

He hissed in a breath.

I saw his struggle, the temptation to ditch decorum and drop his gaze from my face to my ass—which was completely bared by my thong.

My ass won out.

Sucker.

And oops—I accidentally shook my ass at him as I leaned over to rest my hands on the edge of the exam table.

"Hold still," he said tersely. He prepped the area with a cool swipe of liquid on my skin.

I clenched my cheeks together; I couldn't help it. Better that than him believing I broke out in goose bumps from his simple touch.

"Relax," he murmured.

Then before I fully prepared myself, he jammed it in.

A soft grunt escaped me.

He soothed me, gently curling his hand around my hip. "Just a little more."

I knew he was dragging this out. Big surprise that the bastard got off on causing me pain. The injection site started to sting, sending electric sparks shooting beneath my skin.

"Done."

Paper rattled and I looked over my shoulder to watch him press a circular Band-Aid over the tiny dot of blood. Then he slowly swept his hand over my butt cheek.

I felt the pure male heat of him even through the latex.

"You can get dressed," he said without conviction or even looking at my face.

Asswipe.

I ignored him as I yanked my pants up.

Boone was still standing there when I turned around. "I'll come find you when you're feeling better so we can talk."

I shook my head.

"You can't escape the past, Sierra. More to the point, you can't escape me. See you around, McKay." Then he flashed that killer smile—*my* smile, the one he used to bestow only on me—and backed out of the room.

After that, I fled the office.

Three days later, I fled Sundance.

I told myself I wasn't fleeing from him.

I told myself the only reason my dad let me know that Boone stopped by every day after he'd seen me at the clinic was to make sure I was over him.

I was in the clear now, with Wyoming in my rearview mirror and Arizona in my headlights.

But as the miles dragged on, I could admit that I *did* run from him.

I just didn't expect Boone West to chase after me.

1 Boone ♥

THE FIRST TIME I saw Sierra Daniels everything around me just stopped.

Time, objects and people were suspended in place as if I'd stepped into a sci-fi movie, where the hero has a moment of absolute clarity that only he experiences.

When her whiskey-hued eyes connected with mine, I knew pure joy and utter misery in equal measure.

Joy because I'd found her.

Misery because I couldn't have her.

Not then, anyway.

I still felt that *whomp* in my gut every damn time I thought of it. Of her. Even now.

A horn blared, dropping me back into reality.

Traffic in Phoenix had me missing the wide-open spaces of Wyoming. Even cruising across the desert in a transport truck beat this bumper-to-bumper bullshit.

Pain shot up my forearm. I glanced down to see my knuckles were white from my death grip on the steering wheel. I uncurled my fingers and unclenched my jaw.

Breathe, man. Stay calm.

Yeah, like that was gonna happen. It'd been seven years since I'd seen her.

Seven. Years.

Technically, that wasn't true. Sierra had shown up at the clinic in Sundance ten days ago. Our mutual shock at the unexpected run-in had been overshadowed by the fact she was so goddamned sick...

My hands tightened on the steering wheel again. It still burned my ass that she fucking *ran* away from me as if I was the dirty rat responsible for infecting her with the plague.

When I'd driven out to her dad's house the next day to check on her, Gavin Daniels refused to let me see her. While I understood his protective streak—especially given my history with his daughter—I pointed out that Sierra was an adult; he didn't have the right to make that decision for her.

That's when Daddy-O reiterated it *had* been Sierra's decision; she wanted nothing to do with me.

A reaction I'd shrugged off and blamed on her high fever.

Justification? Or cockiness on my part?

Both. But I knew in the marrow of my bones that an apathetic woman wouldn't have made such an edict because she wouldn't have cared. Sierra cared.

Being a determined bastard, I'd shown up at Sierra's house every day.

Being a stubborn McKay, she refused to see me every day.

By the third day, I recognized that even Gavin and his wife Rielle were starting to feel sorry for me. I used that to my advantage when Gavin informed me on day four that Sierra had returned to Phoenix.

My demand for her phone number garnered a "fuck no" and the door slammed in my face.

My request for the name and address of the place she worked resulted in a detailed description of the legal definition of stalking.

My promise that I would willingly let every male member of the McKay family—notoriously bad-tempered cowboys—hog-tie me to the flagpole in the middle of town and take turns beating the ever-lovin' fuck out of me if I harmed a single hair on Sierra's beautiful head had finally convinced Gavin of my sincerity.

He provided the information I wanted...after I'd signed a binding legal contract.

In blood.

Okay. Not in blood, but the pen I'd used *had* contained red ink so it was a distinct possibility. But I'd gladly sign a deal with the devil himself if it meant I had a shot at making things right with the one woman I'd never forgotten.

So here I was, trying to implement a plan of attack on the fly.

The irony of this situation? I'd had meetings scheduled in Phoenix before Sierra and I had crossed paths.

That had to be a sign.

Had to.

Maybe that was wishful thinking on my part. But no one has ever accused me of being an optimist—I'd lived with the "Brooding Boone" moniker since my third birthday.

Could Sierra see me beyond who I used to be? The borderline bad boy who'd left her after admitting I'd hidden my feelings for her from the start?

But you aren't that kid anymore.

So I'd changed. Big deal. It'd be a sad situation if I hadn't. I could thank the United States Army for the significant improvements in my life and the opportunities that joining the military had afforded me.

Way to sound like a recruitment poster, douche.

Fuck.

Where was my confidence? I was educated. I'd expanded my language skills. I'd become a team leader. I'd learned the art of compromise and negotiation. I'd effectively erased most of that punk I used to be.

But what if that's the guy she wants?

Fuck that. I could offer her things now that I couldn't before. I had a career. A pension. A nice car. A bright future.

She always had those things that you worked so hard to get. What can you give her that no one else can? What makes you special?

My mind blanked.

I heard a crack and realized I'd been grinding my teeth so hard my jaw had popped.

All of this speculation meant squat.

My male pride assured me I'd come this far and she wouldn't refuse to see me. It kept reminding me I'd had a connection with Sierra I hadn't experienced with anyone else. Unfortunately, my pride also had a sadistic streak. It suggested I'd never gotten over Sierra because she'd never really been mine in the first place.

My pride was a total dickhead most of the time.

The GPS reminded me to turn right at the next intersection and then announced my destination had been reached.

After I parked in the visitor's lot, I bent down and peered through the bottom of the windshield so I could see the Daniels Development Group office building from the ground up.

I'd always known Sierra came from money. Yet I also knew that Gavin Daniels had been responsible for that financial success after expanding the business he'd inherited from his father. Did Sierra feel pressured to make an equal—or an even bigger—mark with her role in the family business? She had the brains to do it, but did she have the drive?

Thinking back, I didn't remember that she'd been interested in carrying on the family legacy. Then again, who knows what they want out of life at age sixteen? Just because I'd known her then, didn't mean I knew anything about her goals, aspirations and responsibilities now. And I couldn't wait to find them out firsthand.

As I crossed the parking lot, I figured it was a good time to remind myself what I *did* know.

Sierra worked in Daniels Property Management on the tenth floor.

She wasn't in a relationship.

My brain hit pause. What else?

When nothing came to mind, I realized that was all I knew about her.

Sort of pathetic, really.

But Sierra had roughly the same basic knowledge about me, so we'd be on equal ground.

The thought of getting this second chance with her quickened my stride as I entered the lobby.

As I rode the elevator, various scenarios ran through my mind of how this would play out.

In the movie version of our reunion, we'd be running toward each other in slow motion, through the rain. We'd kiss like mad, pausing only to tearfully confess our eternal love for each other as the scene fades to black.

In my version, after I promised to spend the rest of my life making up for the past seven years we were apart, we'd end up on the rain-soaked ground, so hot for each other we fucked right there in the mud. Or I fucked her up against a tree. Or I bent her over a park bench. Oh hell yeah. That one was really good. Especially when I imagined my hand twisted in that gorgeous dark hair of hers, pulling just hard enough to make her gasp as I whispered dirty, dirty promises in her ear.

Jesus man, get a fucking grip. You really want to stroll in sporting wood? And is sex all you really want from her?

Well, no. But I sure as hell wouldn't pretend I wanted to be her friend either.

The elevator stopped on the tenth floor and the doors slid open.

For just a moment, I froze. Was I truly ready for this?

Don't be a pussy. You're a fucking soldier. You've dodged sniper fire and IEDs. This? This is cake.

I wiped my sweaty palms on my khakis before I strode to the receptionist's desk. I bestowed my most charming smile on her. "I'm here to see Sierra McKay."

2 Sierra

T UESDAY WAS MY busiest day of the week.

I'd been scrambling to catch up after my absence. I'd gone to Sundance to see Marin, my BFF from high school, and meet her new baby boy. And have a heart to heart with my father about my place in the company. But because I'd gotten sick I hadn't seen Marin or her sweet baby. And I hadn't had that talk with my dad, either.

Mostly because I'd chickened out. Again.

In addition to my tasks at Daniels Property Management today, I had a presentation to prep for next week for PCE—Phoenix Collegiate Entrepreneurs—a woman's business group we organized at ASU when we realized there weren't any support groups for our demographic: women starting home-based businesses or women in jobs where their colleagues were predominantly male. Ten business admin students, all female, all who'd had some level of success in starting a business, had banded together and pooled our knowledge so we could help each other. Within six months our group had fifty members and a dozen women in the community who'd volunteered as mentors.

Being a founding member of the group was one of the things I was most proud of. I still spent a considerable amount of time volunteering for PCE because creating a better business environment for women remained my passion.

I just wished I could do that here; reignite the passion I'd brought to this job. I couldn't blame my restlessness on a lousy salary. Or limited opportunities for advancement. Although I was Gavin Daniels' only heir, I'd insisted on an entry-level position at DPM. I could've gone to work for several other companies after graduating from college—I'd been heavily recruited due to my impressive resume, my work founding PCE, my GPA and the connection to my father. But since I'd indicated an interest in taking over both Daniels Development Group and Daniels Property Management when Dad retired, I figured I had at least a dozen years to learn how to run everything. Since I'd spent more time at DDG over the years, I wanted to understand DPM from the ground up.

That didn't mean I was a third-generation slacker with entitlement issues and zero work ethic. During college I'd worked as my father's virtual intern. No pay but what I'd learned had been invaluable.

There'd been resentment after I'd officially been hired at DPM. Management passed off the lowest-priority clients to me. I had bigger goals for myself than being a glorified landlord. So I convinced those clients to let me implement my ideas for total automation. Everything from direct deposit for rent collection to vetting potential service providers. Since DPM had a decent profit margin with the management fees we charged, when I cut new deals with the vendors on behalf of my clients, I passed the savings on to them.

When other DPM clients got wind of the changes…they demanded the same type of deals. Which was exactly what I'd banked on. So my first year as a glorified landlord I'd completely revamped the entire DPM payment system.

Color the CEO impressed. But he'd also been agitated that none of his long-time managers had attempted to modernize an outdated business model. So he'd rewarded me for my innovative thinking by granting me a promotion—a big promotion—from entry level to upper management.

That's when the nastiness really kicked in; the implication that I hadn't earned the promotion. My father was a brilliant businessman and the smartest guy in any room and thankfully I'd inherited some of his business acumen. But I'd risen up the ranks on my own merits. I'd put up the amount of hours I'd worked against anyone else's.

Another fun aspect of the job in addition to the assumed nepotism was the sexism and the ageism. Men I'd known for years were patronizing and condescending when they dealt with me. How could I possibly know anything about real business? The ink on my diploma was fresh. I had tits, not balls. What really rankled were the smug remarks about having Daddy fight my battles. No wonder my enthusiasm had cooled.

Two raps sounded on my office door, then Nikki poked her head in. "Your eleven thirty is here."

I frowned at my assistant. "Marty is early?"

"It's not Marty. I assumed you forgot to enter in this appointment." She sent another quick glance over her shoulder. "You want me to send him packing?"

"No. Show him in." I printed out my questions for Marty. I planned to pick his brain about what to look for when hiring a headhunting firm. PCE had reached the stage where it needed a full-time paid administrator.

From the doorway I heard, "A corner office already?"

That voice. For years it'd haunted me, a deep rasp that couldn't possibly be as sexy and compelling as I'd remembered.

I went utterly still behind my computer screen.

What the hell was *he* doing here?

A snarky inner voice said: *He told you he'd track you down.*

An equally bitchy voice retorted: *So? He told me many things and never followed through with any of them.*

"I'm impressed, McKay."

And then Boone West sauntered through my door as if he had every right to be here.

I might've ordered him out, if I hadn't been so busy drinking him in. I'd been too feverish in Sundance to mentally catalog the similarities and differences in Old Boone and this Second Edition Boone.

Old Boone had shuffled along, shoulders slumped, chin tucked down, hair obscuring his face.

Second Edition Boone had that military swagger: chin up, direct eye contact, super-sized body on full alert.

He'd filled out, becoming taller and broader. The extra height and weight looked good on him. Before, he'd worn his dark hair a little too long; it'd constantly flopped in his face. Now he sported a military cut. The shorter style accentuated the perfection of his face: the high cheekbones, the wide jaw, the broad forehead, those soulful brown eyes that sucked me in.

Boone West was still the most beautiful man I'd ever seen.

Snap out of it. You aren't a dreamy-eyed girl. You are a busy, professional woman and he does not have an appointment or the right to waste your time.

I forced my gaze to Nikki, who was openly gawking at Boone's ass.

She offered me a *sorry-not-sorry* smirk. "Buzz me if you need anything."

"You can leave the door open, Nikki. He's leaving. Immediately."

"No, *Hi, Boone, how are you today?* No, *I'm sorry I ditched your calls when I was in Wyoming because I pulled a muscle in my phone-dialing finger?* Just, *He's leaving. Immediately?*"

My mouth dropped open. "You *remember* that conversation?"

"I remember everything that happened between us, Sierra. Everything."

"Then you'll remember why I have nothing to say to you and why I'm telling you to get out of my office."

Boone shook his head at me. "I'm not leaving until I get what I came for."

Pushy bastard. "How about I give you what you deserve instead?"

"Which is what?"

"A swift kick in the balls."

He grinned. "Luckily I wore a cup. Just in case."

"Bully for you. Go away, Boone."

"Nope. We have unfinished business."

"Wrong. We were *finished* the moment you got on your bike and left me and the state of Wyoming behind. Since seven years have gone by, we're past the legally recognized statute of limitations for immoral acts and criminal behavior—not that being a selfish, lying asshat is against the law. So if it'll speed things up and send you on your way, I'll accept your apology even when it's years late."

His eyes narrowed. "I'm not here to apologize."

"Of course you're not." I pointed to the door. "Please let it hit you in the ass on your way out." I returned my focus to my monitor, dismissing him completely.

Five seconds later he slapped his big hands on my desk.

I jumped.

Boone peered over the edge of my computer screen. "Your reflexes are good. So how are you feeling? Any lingering issues from the strep virus?"

"You came all the way to Phoenix for a house call?"

"Not hardly."

"Then why are you here? I doubt the army just lets you flit around from place to place whenever the mood strikes you." *Dammit. You were supposed to act uninterested.*

He smirked because he knew he'd hooked me. "I'm glad you asked. I'm here on leave for two weeks. I intended to tell you in Wyoming that I was already scheduled to be in Phoenix directly after my stint in Sundance."

Do not react. "And this affects me...how?"

Boone's intense gaze encompassed my entire face. "Us being in the same place, at the same time isn't a coincidence, Sierra."

"Yes it is."

"No it isn't. It's fate."

My stomach cartwheeled.

"You knew it. That's why you ran from me in Wyoming."

"I didn't run. I drove."

He shrugged. "And yet, no matter how we got here, we *are* both here."

Do not get sucked into this conversation.

Awkward silence distorted the air.

Boone stepped back and sat in the chair across from my desk.

"By all means, make yourself comfortable."

"I will. Thanks."

"I was being sarcastic."

"I know. I'm ignoring it because you don't really want me to leave."

In my head I said, *Omigod, cocky much? Get out or I'm calling security.* But I would not give him the satisfaction of an emotional outburst. Instead, I said, "You are mistaken if you think I have nothing better to do than entertain you. I have another appointment—"

"I'm sure you do. You're the big executive now. Kyler was telling me about it last night."

That little traitor. And what did Kyler know about my executive status anyhow? He usually introduced me as "my cousin who's in real estate," like my job was showing residential properties.

"Surprised?" Boone prompted.

"That you've already been in touch with *my* cousin?"

"I'm staying with him and the guys a few nights."

The "guys" meaning my other cousins, Anton and Hayden.

He raised an eyebrow. "That sounded a little possessive. Ky's my cousin too, McKay."

"Like you have to remind me, West."

Boone sank back in the chair as if settling in for a good, long chat. "It's been a while since I've seen Ky, Hayden and Anton. It's weird that they're these big, grown guys and not the skinny runts I remembered. Anyway, we were talking last night and I mentioned I was coming here today. Hayden said something like 'your cousin is my cousin but that don't make us cousins' which sounded wrong coming from him because he always talked like he was reading from a textbook, even when he was annoying the hell out of us on the bus. Which reminded me about the first time *we* met on the bus. I saw you talking to Ky and thought, it figures the gorgeous new girl in town is a relative. I was so relieved to find out that *we* weren't related at all. Then Ky made a crack about kissing cousins—"

"Whatever you're trying to do, Boone...stop."

"What do you think I'm trying to do? Besides reminding you that it wasn't all bad between us?"

His agitation that I'd interrupted him allowed me to remain cool. "I think you're beating a dead horse."

Boone quirked an eyebrow at me. "That's a little folksy coming from you."

"You want it in plain terms? Fine. I have no desire to reminisce with you." I paused. "Ever."

"Bull. I know you, Sierra."

"No, you don't. Not anymore."

And that played perfectly into his hands. He bestowed that dazzling smile on me. "Then give me a chance to get to know you. Starting over would be best for us anyway."

I caught sight of Marty in the open doorway. Talk about perfect timing. "Not today. My scheduled appointment is here."

Boone banked his irritation at my brush-off and rose to his feet. After sparing Marty a quick glance, he returned that laser focus to me as I stepped around the desk.

Today I'd worn my favorite power suit: a pencil skirt the color of black cherries I'd paired with a cream-colored sleeveless shirt with a swoopy drape of fabric that allowed a hint of cleavage. My black heels were 1950s-style peep-toe pumps with white stitching and dotted with tiny cherries the same color as my skirt. I rocked this outfit and always felt a boost of confidence wearing it.

When our eyes met again, Boone didn't hide the fact I'd wowed him.

Eat your heart out, fucker. "See you around, West."

His eyes narrowed. He moved in and brushed his right cheek across mine until his lips met my ear. "You aren't shaking me off that easy."

"I can try."

Boone's soft laughter burrowed into my ear and sent vibrations throughout my entire body. "Fair warning. I'm more stubborn than you. I'm that burr you can't shake off until I get completely under your skin. I've got nothing but time to convince you we need to talk so we can fix this between us." He retreated and offered Marty a "Hey" and a chin lift before he strolled away.

I found myself watching that finely muscled ass...and wondering.

When I looked up at Marty, he lifted a brow at me. "I could've come back if I was interrupting something."

"You weren't." I snagged my suit jacket off the coat tree. "We were done."

He held the door open as we left the reception area. "Is he a friend of yours?"

"*Former* friend."

"Maybe you should tell him that."

I started to argue, but I suspected Marty was right.

3 Boone ♥

I WASN'T EXPECTING anyone to be around when I returned to McJock Central. My McKay cousins had a sweet setup, even if they had to drive several miles to get to the ASU campus.

They'd invited me to crash on their couch until my army buddy Raj got here from Fort Hood, so I'd stopped by to pick up my stuff before my meeting at the VA.

It surprised me to see Kyler sitting at the dining room table. When Ky wasn't in class he was at football practice, or at team meetings, or watching game tapes, or working out. Everyone claimed I was an intense guy, but I was a candidate for ADHD meds compared to Kyler McKay. Even now he exhibited impressive multitasking skills, performing biceps curls with free weights as he flipped through a textbook. He glanced up and flashed me a sheepish smile. It was really fucking spooky how much he looked like his dad—but a super-sized version. "Hey. Didn't think I'd see you again today."

"Did you plan on IDing me in the morgue later?"

"Nah. I figured Sierra would just maim you—that's more painful than a quick death." After his methodical inspection, he said, "You don't look worse for the wear."

"You sure I don't have icicles on my face?"

"Icicles in the desert? Dream on." Kyler laughed. "But dude. You had to expect this from her."

I ran my hand over the top of my head. "Yeah. I did. But that doesn't mean I like it."

"At least you're not bleeding. So what happened?"

"I blew it. She was prickly as a damn cactus. She acted like I'd assumed we could just pick up where we left off seven years ago."

The weight in Kyler's left hand froze midair. "You didn't tell her that?"

"No." I scowled at him. "I'm not a complete idiot."

"I didn't think so. Did you act all 'I'm in the army now, I'm a big, badass soldier and you will listen to me, woman.'"

"What the fuck? No, I didn't do that." *Did I?*

"The cold shoulder doesn't sound like Sierra." Ky frowned. "Wait, if you were at her office...I take that back. That is *exactly* how she'd react. She's got the whole Stepford thing goin' on at work."

That description fit. "Why?"

"Since she's the boss's kid, she has some whacked-out idea she has to rise above the fray. One night she got a little drunk and told me her male colleagues treat her like a bimbo who's just collecting a paycheck from Daddy until she gets married and pregnant."

"Jesus."

"Which is total bullshit. Sierra is so freakin' smart and she knows business—especially her dad's business that she's been around her whole life. I wish she'd tell those assholes to fuck off and show them bein' like everyone else and not rocking the boat won't set you apart."

"You speaking from experience?"

Kyler lowered the weight to the floor. He sighed before looking up at me. "Yep. And it's ironic I learned that from her."

"How?"

"Sierra helped me deal with family shit when it came to picking a college. Dad wanted me to go to University of Wyoming. Period. Then the football recruiters flew me'n Dad down here to talk about the program. After the meeting, while I was getting the tour of the ASU campus, Sierra took Dad aside for a 'come to Jesus' chat. Whatever she told him clicked because after that, Dad was completely onboard with me attending school here."

Now I really wanted to know what she'd said to stubborn Cord McKay to get him to change his mind. "Did she have the same chat with Cam about Anton, and with Kane about Hayden attending ASU too?"

"Those two had it easy after I broke the first barrier. Our folks decided it'd be better, if we had to go away to college, that we were together."

I wasn't a social media guy so I knew nothing of McKay family gossip until those two weeks I'd been back in Sundance. But during my time in Wyoming, I remembered my cousin Chassie telling me that ASU athletics had aggressively courted Kyler for their football program. Since Hayden had been named a National Merit Scholar, he had his pick of colleges across the country but had chosen ASU. Anton had decided on the Phoenix branch of Cochise Valley College after he'd been offered a full-ride rodeo scholarship.

"But we weren't together that much last year. Living in the dorms sucked since me'n Hayden were placed in separate buildings according to our activities and Anton lived like five miles away."

"Had to be better than living in the barracks, dude."

"Only slightly. Mase bought this place over the summer and said we could live here this year."

I raised a brow. "Rent free?"

"Hell no. Even a big hockey star has a mortgage."

Mason "Mase" Morrison, Kyler's cousin from his mom's side of the family, was a hockey phenom. He'd been signed to play professional hockey at age eighteen right after graduating from high school. I couldn't imagine the pressure the kid was under. He wasn't old enough to legally order a beer, but the future of an entire hockey franchise rested on his shoulders.

"Where is Mase, anyway?" I asked.

"Scorpions are on the road. He gets back after the game late Saturday night."

"Do you have a tough travel schedule?"

Kyler shrugged. "It's different for college teams. The profs cut us some slack for missing class, but most of us are on the five-year bachelor's program because of athletics, so we've gotta keep up our academics or face suspension."

"Does suspension happen often?"

"As of last week two freshman football players were sidelined. The idiots didn't bother going to their classes because they assumed coach was bluffing."

"I've been assigned to work with guys like that in the army. First they bend the rules, then they break them and they act surprised when they get busted for it."

"I don't understand how you're here, acting like you have a choice where you're assigned. Isn't that the deal with the military? They can force you to relocate anyplace they want, any time they want?" Kyler asked.

"Yeah. But this is a two-year experimental program involving all branches of the armed forces and the Veterans Administration. It's strictly voluntary." I grinned. "Well, voluntary meaning my CO had to put my name in for consideration."

"So you were hand-picked? Sweet. You must be a real hero with commendations and shit, huh?"

I rolled my eyes. "Hero. Right. I'm proud of my exemplary service record and all of the specialized medical training I've received. What I don't have is a BS in nursing, which would advance my rank. That's pretty much the only reason I signed on for this. The additional education."

"How does it work? How do you get to choose where you end up?"

"Since the VA system has had issues in recent years, the preliminary program is focused on active-duty medical personnel working with civilian healthcare specialists in the places with the highest number of violations. So my choices are Cheyenne or Phoenix."

Kyler's gaze turned sharp. "That's why you were in Wyoming."

I nodded. "One of the requirements is working two weeks in a hospital or clinic with a preceptor associated with that VA."

"You weren't bullshitting me—or Sierra. You'd planned to be in Phoenix for at least two weeks."

Before he could ask the question I saw in his eyes, I answered it. "I had no idea if Sierra still lived in Sundance when I showed up to work with Doc Monroe."

"But you had to expect if Sierra wasn't living in Wyoming she'd be living here," Kyler tossed out.

With the way things had ended between us years ago, I had zero expectations when it came to Sierra. But the instant I saw her…everything had changed. "When I left Wyoming, I left for good. I didn't keep in contact with anyone." It wasn't like anyone had sought contact with me either. "Besides, my dad bailed out of state. My mom moved to Montana with my sister and brother. My uncles were busy doing their own shit. And the McKays..." I shrugged. "Anyway, approval for the program happened fast, which is odd for the government. Not a lot of information has been released to us individually about specifics, but I've heard that'll change once I submit my final request."

"You did that today, didn't you?"

"Yeah." Raj was gonna flip his shit when I told him.

"You don't know where you'll be going to school?"

"I doubt it'll be a traditional campus setting like you're in. Especially since the Phoenix VA is a teaching hospital and affiliated with over a hundred colleges. I just hope the hours I spend in the classroom every week count toward my required duty hours. It'd blow if I had eighteen credit hours of instruction, plus I had to work a full forty." I shrugged. "But it's a possibility."

"Will you tell Sierra you'll probably be here for longer than two weeks?"

I shook my head and walked to the fridge for a bottle of Gatorade. "Not until I figure out what to do next."

Kyler snorted. "You know what you need to do, West."

Kiss her stupid and beg her forgiveness? Like that'd work. "What?"

"Approach her on a professional level. Show up at her office tomorrow and pile on the guilt that she'd thrown you out before you could explain you were trying to hire her. Then tell her you'd like to look at rental properties since you'll be around a while."

Ideas raced through my head—a variation on Ky's suggestion because I didn't want to tip my hand too soon. I needed to get her to spend time with me. I'd deal with any backlash of what I had to do to make that happen after the primary goal had been achieved. Wasn't it better to beg for forgiveness than to ask for permission anyway? "Quick thinking, Ky. Damn. You're good."

He grinned. "It's what I do—learn to think on my feet and adapt fast."

The doorbell rang.

Ky glanced at his phone and said, "Shit." He stood, whipped off his sweat-stained wife-beater and tossed it aside. He yanked on a *Sun Devils Football* T-shirt and looked at me. "You have all your stuff?"

"Trying to get rid of me?"

"Hell yes. The teaching assistant—I mean my tutor—is here."

I said, "Tutor? I thought I was the only one who needed extra help."

Kyler blushed. Then he disappeared around the corner.

I scanned the living room to make sure I hadn't left anything before I hoisted my duffel bag and entered the foyer.

A tall, gorgeous redhead dropped her hand from Ky's crotch when she saw me and seemed nervous that Ky would introduce us.

He didn't.

McKay, you dog. Nailing the teacher's assistant. She could teach him all sorts of new tricks.

"If for some reason Raj gets delayed tonight, you're welcome to stay here again," Ky offered.

"I appreciate it." I maintained a straight face when I said, "Study hard, but a word of advice. Staying in one position too long will cause back and neck problems. Change positions frequently."

LATE AFTERNOON I paused in the lobby of the apartment building, looking for the buzzer marked Ramos. I pushed #220 and immediately heard a static-filled, "Yo."

"It's West."

The door lock buzzed.

I took the stairs to the second floor.

Raj had left the door cracked open. The instant I stepped inside, I wished I'd left my sunglasses on. The walls and the ceiling were so goddamned pink it felt like swimming in a bottle of Kinky Pink.

"In here," Raj called out.

I stepped through a doorway into the combination living room and kitchen.

Raj grinned at me. "Welcome to the pink palace."

"How old is your sister? Don't most girls grow out of the pink phase at like thirteen?"

"Not T'Quelle. I expected she'd repaint after I mentioned it was like being inside a vagina, but she just called me a pig." Raj indicated the floral couch. "You're crashing on the sofa bed."

"Great." I dropped my duffel on the floor. "Tell me you picked up beer."

"In the fridge."

"Thank you, Jesus." I popped the top and snagged the chair across from him. The miniature dining table was covered in a frilly pink lace tablecloth. "How was the drive?"

"Long. I hate driving by myself."

"You hate doing *anything* by yourself."

"The result of having two older brothers and two younger sisters. I was always surrounded." Raj swigged his beer. "Only things surrounding a white boy like you growing up in Wyoming were fences and tumbleweeds, amirite?"

"Pretty much." I picked up a picture frame and peered at the two cute college-aged girls, one with dreadlocks and one with cornrows. "Which one of these bikini-wearing hotties is your sister?"

"They're both my sisters, asshole. Quick genetics update; when a black woman marries a Mexican man—none of their offspring look like them or each other."

Raj joked about his mixed heritage all the time. His genetics seemed evenly split. He had the height and hair from his African-American side, but he had lighter skin and hazel eyes from his Mexican side. We'd gone through basic training together. We'd attended every medical seminar, every college course, every advanced training class together. We even shared an apartment in Fort Hood. Some of our supervisors swore we shared a brain. So the army fuck-up affected us both.

"What's up, West?"

I set the picture down. "Nothing. Why?"

"I know you, man. You're brooding. What gives?"

"Woman troubles."

He laughed. "Right."

When I didn't share in his amusement, he stared at me. Hard.

"You're serious."

"Yep."

"Woman troubles," he repeated. "First time you've ever said that in all the years I've known you."

"There's a reason for that. And she lives in Phoenix."

His eyes went comically wide. Then he said, "Start talking."

Raj knew more about me than anyone in my life. But he didn't know about Sierra. "It's a long story."

"I've got time and so do you."

"It's complicated."

"You're stalling. Now you know I ain't gonna leave you alone until you tell me whatever it is that you *should've* told me a long damn time ago."

I scrubbed my hands over my face. "You know about my fucked-up childhood. So by my senior year of high school I was biding my time until graduation and I could start a real life." I swallowed a mouthful of beer. "Then she showed up."

"Who?"

"Sierra. The instant I saw her all those freakin' clichés bombarded me—a bolt of lightning, the earth moved, time stood still, my soul recognized hers, my heart stopped, I wanted to fuck her hot little body twice a day for the next hundred years…" I closed my eyes. "I've never told anyone any of that."

"Not even her?"

"*Especially* not her."

Raj sighed. "That's fucked, man, but keep goin'."

"We became friends. At first because I needed to prove my initial reaction to her was a fluke. I mean, she was beautiful, so in my experience that meant she was either a spoiled brat or a snotty bitch. But she wasn't. I found out it was worse. Way, way worse."

"What was she?"

"Perfect."

Raj said nothing.

I finished my beer and grabbed another. "I needed to stay away from her but I couldn't. So we were friends. Fuck, man. She was my *only* goddamned friend. And the entire time we were friends I knew how she felt about me."

"Please tell me you didn't take advantage of that."

I scowled at him. "I'm not that guy, asshole. I never touched her because it would've been all fucking over for me if I did. So I left Wyoming just as planned. I just didn't tell *her* that was my plan."

"Did you have any contact with her at all?"

"Not until two weeks ago." I told him everything that had happened when I'd seen her in Sundance and how things ended up with her today.

We'd each drained another beer by the time I'd finished.

Finally Raj said, "Sounds to me like you've made up your mind. She's here; this is where you need to be."

I shrugged.

"Don't give me that fake 'whatever' attitude, man. You believe it's a sign."

"Or a second chance."

"But that's up to her, isn't it? And from what you've told me, maybe she's not interested in giving you a shot. Then you're stuck here."

I glanced up at him sharply. "*I'm* stuck here. I thought you ruled out Cheyenne?"

"I'm tired after driving fifteen hours and my brain is sluggish." Raj sighed and rubbed the top of his shaved head. "But I recall that *you* weren't giving Cheyenne serious consideration." Then Raj's gaze pierced me. "Something else you wanna tell me?"

"I indicated Phoenix as my preference today after I left her office."

Raj's eyebrows went up.

"There's one other thing."

"Of course there is."

"Tomorrow I'm going back to Sierra's office and asking her to show me possible rentals." I flashed my teeth at him. "But it's not for me. It's for a *friend*."

"Ah, fuck, man. Seriously?"

"I need a place to live anyway." My gaze rolled over pink, pink, and pinker. I wasn't sure how long I could stand being here.

"Fine, do your thing with her. I don't wanna do anything except sit by the pool and work on my tan."

I choked on my beer.

Raj laughed. "Too easy."

"Asshole."

"Missed you, bro."

"Same."

4 *Sierra* ♥

B<small>Y SIX</small> P.M. I had rocked my to-do list; all twenty-seven items checked off. Which was a big *screw you* to Boone—his unexpected appearance hadn't affected my productivity at all.

Traffic wasn't horrendous. The snowbirds hadn't arrived en masse yet.

When I pulled up to my house, I grinned at my roommate Lu's dirt-caked pickup, which was parked sideways in the drive. My neighbors in this upscale and trendy housing development wrinkled their noses at her big rig as if she used it to cart pigs around—although it did smell like shit whenever she used it to haul manure. I skirted the garage and entered the backyard through the gated side of the house.

Sure enough, Lu lounged by the pool. Topless.

"Eww, put those things away! I do *not* want a face full of tits when I ask you for a hug."

Lu immediately slipped on a T-shirt and stood. At six feet two she was such a bruiser that she literally crushed me to her chest.

"What happened today that requires a momma bear hug?"

I sighed. She gave such great hugs. The type of affection I assumed other kids received from their mothers. My mom was a model-thin sack of toned flesh—not a squishy welcoming thing about her bony body.

I sighed again.

"Sierra?" Lu prompted.

"Let me change clothes and mix up a pitcher of margaritas first, okay?"

"Gotta be a doozy of a day if it calls for a pitcher." She released me and smacked my ass. "Yell before you come back out, because the girls will be soaking up the sun."

"Thanks for the tips—ha-ha."

I opened the sliding glass door and cut through the kitchen, by-passing the great room and the foyer to climb a flight of stairs. No college student needed a six-bedroom, five-bathroom house, but the fire-sale price made it a killer investment. Since I'd bought the house with cash, I didn't have a mortgage. Lu paid me a couple of hundred bucks a month that I put toward property taxes. She handled the yard work—it was a happy fact that Lu worked part-time as a landscaper. So far I'd avoided thinking about Lu graduating in May. While I wanted my BFF to seize the great opportunities she'd dreamt about since freshman year, I also hoped she'd stick around. Then we could do this adulting thing together, although I had a two-year head start in the working world.

In my bedroom, I kicked off my heels and ditched my clothes for my bikini. After twisting my hair into a messy bun, I returned downstairs to whip up a batch of margaritas. I opened the sliding glass door and yelled, "Incoming!" before I grabbed the tray.

Lu had her top on and she'd cleared a space on the table between the loungers. I handed her a glass, poured one for myself and lowered into the chaise. One long sip of cold, boozy, limey goodness and I felt the tension melting away.

"Killer margs, S."

"Thanks."

"So…your day. Were you dealing with Bridezilla again?"

I groaned. My mother's impending marriage reception resembled a circus. I had not-so-jokingly told Lu that my mom actually considered hiring Cirque de Soleil performers for the entertainment. Mom hadn't laughed when I pointed out that no one wanted to dance to the sounds of flying trapezes and limbs being contorted. I hadn't heard from her since. No surprise there. Our rocky relationship had crumbled completely after she'd returned from France and I did not miss her—or her petty, nasty bullshit. "No. Since the wedding is in a few weeks she must be on the downhill stretch and anything she changes now will cost Barnacle Bill big bucks."

Lu snorted. "You will slip up and call him Barnacle Bill to his face one of these days."

"No doubt." My mother's husband-to-be had earned his millions from the fishing boat companies he owned up and down the Gulf of Mexico. He'd retired to Arizona, away from the water. Then he started golfing as if it was his religion. He and Mom had a meet-cute when she accidentally ran over his foot on the golf course. Bill was immediately smitten by my mother's youth and beauty—and the fact she didn't care if he golfed seven days out of seven. She in turn was completely smitten with his money. A true match made in heaven.

"It's not Mommy Dearest, then… Is Dharma being a dickhead again?"

"Dharma"—the codename I'd assigned to Greg, the asshole business operations manager for Daniels Property Management—"is greasing up his pole, probably with his hair, at one of those Club Med type resorts for old single dudes. I have an entire week off from him."

Lu held her glass over to mine for a silent toast.

"My day took a bizarre turn right before lunch when Boone West waltzed into my office."

Her white-blonde pigtails bobbed when she swung her head toward me. "You're shitting me."

"I am not shitting you at all."

"What the ever-lovin' fuck? He sauntered in just out of the blue?"

I squirmed. Drained my drink and reached for more. I hadn't told Lu I'd run into Boone in Wyoming as I'd chalked it up as a fluke.

"I recognize that fidgety-ass avoidance behavior of yours, ho-bag. Spill."

"I ended up at the doctor's office in Sundance. Sergeant West was there for medical training. Total fucking shock to see him, so at first I pretended not to know him…" I told her everything.

By the time I finished she was laughing so hard she couldn't hold onto her margarita glass. "Omigod, S, that is classic. You passed out and he had to carry you? And then he gave you a shot in the ass?"

"Living life as a class act, that's me," I retorted.

"Does Boone look good?" Lu asked.

"He looks better than ever," I said automatically. The only comparison I had between Old Boone and Second Edition Boone was in my head. It'd bugged me not to have any pictures of the two of us. He'd always refused. I had one grainy shot I'd secretly snapped of him as he'd run laps around the track at the high school. But I'd lost that one in a data crash.

"What did he want?"

"No idea."

"Liar."

"Fine. He wants to…talk."

Lu refilled her glass. "About what?"

I blinked. "I don't know."

"Then maybe you ought to…*talk* to him and find out."

"Or maybe I ought to skip a conversation with him and just stab myself in the heart to save him the trouble of doing it to me again."

I felt Lu staring at me. "It still hurts that much? What happened between you two *seven years ago*?"

Yes. No. Shit. Maybe. I sighed. "When you say it like that, it sounds ridiculous."

"Then I'll toss it out there that by not talking to him, you're not allowing either of you a chance for closure. All you're doing is holding a grudge, and that's not like you."

"I don't think he wants closure, Lu."

"Well, *duh*. The man followed you from Wyoming to Arizona." She started singing Michael Jackson's "Wanna Be Startin' Something."

"Knock it off or I'll punch you in the throat."

She laughed. "Just calm your tits, girlfriend." She slurped her drink. "Besides, why would that be a bad idea?"

I tipped my head back. The sky had taken on the white film that stretched across the horizon prior to sunset. Sometimes I missed seeing the stars. Stargazing had been one of Boone's favorite things. And while he marveled at the stars, I marveled at him. My epic crush had been so embarrassingly obvious to him that I still blushed when I thought about it.

"Why are you dodging the question?" Lu prompted.

"I'm not. I'm just creating an ordered list of why that's a bad idea. First of all, he's only here for two weeks. Which means he's looking for a fling. I can't do that. Not with him."

"Why not?"

"What if I fell for him again, knowing he'll leave again? Been there, done that." I had the scars to prove it—even if they were only visible to me.

"So just hanging out and rekindling your friendship...?"

I shook my head. "He wasn't looking at me like he wanted to kick back and watch reruns of *Two Angry Beavers*." The memory hit me with a wave of happy nostalgia I hadn't allowed for a long time. We'd both laughed our asses off at that stupid cartoon. I'd never met anyone who got the offbeat humor the way he did. I'd never met any man who got me the way he did either.

"Maybe we should deal with *your* angry beaver."

I faced her. "Omigod. I cannot believe you said that!"

Lu aimed her straw at me. "Yes, you can. Your dilemma is easy to solve."

"Let me guess...your suggestion is that I fuck him."

"Yes." She held up her hand to stop my automatic protest. "Just hear me out."

Tempting to plug my ears and start singing "Never Gonna Get It" at the top of my lungs. Not that Lu would understand the reference; my eclectic taste in music baffled her as much as my penchant for watching weird cartoons.

"You've always wondered what sex would be like with him."

"And that is exactly why I *shouldn't* do it."

"You are a 'one and done' chick anyway. Why would it be different with him?"

"It just would be," I said stubbornly.

"Because you're afraid he'd be rubbish in bed?"

"Been watching reruns of *Absolutely Fabulous* again, have you, dahling?" I said in my best British accent.

"Eh, sod off, ye bloody wanker." She stirred her drink. "I'm serious, S."

"So am I. What if he's like...unbelievable in bed? Then I'd be left wanting more"—again—"and I'd worry he just fucked me because *he* always wondered what sex would be like with me." I shook my head and didn't voice my other concern; what if Boone was disappointed in my skills between the sheets? That'd be another blow I might not recover from. "It's better to wonder and leave it at that. Can we please drop it now?"

She sighed dramatically. "You are such a ballbuster when you've got a financial spreadsheet in front of you. But with personal stuff? I never would've pegged you as such a chickenshit, McKay."

I slurped my drink. "Sure you have."

"When?" Lu demanded.

"Spring break when I refused to get a Pussy Galore tattoo with you."

"Which makes zero sense since that summer you got that"—she gestured wildly—"brand thingy on your hip. Pussy Galore? Way more meaningful."

I'd succumbed to my cousin Keely's badgering and gotten inked with the official McKay cattle brand. "I told you. It's a family thing."

"Nice try at changing the subject, but back to you throwing Boone a bone."

"Awesome alliteration, Baby Spice. I thought we were dropping this."

"Not until I get my point across." She tapped her finger on the rim of her cup. "He wants the V, you want the D, so you need to do this. Fuck him one time and get him out of your system. Then you can move on. That way it'll never get to the stage that his dick isn't doing it for you anymore and there's no risk for the burn-out factor."

I stared at her, thankful for the bizarre turn in the conversation. "Burn-out factor for his…dick?"

"Yep."

"Is that even a thing?"

Lu nodded. "It's why I'm not in a relationship." She drained her margarita. "I'm a dick connoisseur. I like 'em all—fat, thin, long, short, wide, thick, cut, uncut, ruddy, smooth. There are so many colors and sizes, how can I limit myself to just one? And when I think about all the dick I've sampled, I feel a little slutty. I begin to think maybe I *should* try and settle down with the one dick that fits me above all others."

"You're comparing your va-jay-jay to a glass slipper? Find the ideal fit and you've got a dick you can commit to?"

"Exactly! But how will I find the prince of all penises if I'm not actively looking?"

I couldn't fault her logic. And if she wanted a different dick every night, who was I to judge? "Your plan to prowl for the perfect pecker is plausible."

"Now who's the alliteration queen?"

I stood, putting an end to the discussion. "I'm hitting the pool for a quick swim before I decide whether to make another pitcher of margaritas or whip up a batch of white chocolate chip macadamia nut cookies."

"Count me out for the booze. I have a quiz tomorrow and I have to study."

"I don't miss doing homework."

"I won't miss it either, but not everyone can get a bachelor's degree in three years." Lu hip-checked me as she passed by.

My reflex to correct her dried on my tongue. I'd finished my degree in three and a half years, partially from taking the basic classes at the University of Wyoming during my senior year of high school, partially because I'd grown up Gavin Daniels' daughter. I CLEPed out of a shit ton of general business classes. And Dad accused me of not paying attention to him.

Right before I submerged myself in the pool, Lu said, "We're not done dissecting this dealio with Boone, S. Because it's not going away."

Seemed to be a theme in my life today.

5 Boone

DÉJÀ VU DAY two.

Cooling my heels in the reception area, waiting for Sierra to grant me an audience.

Restless as fuck but pretending to be chill.

The magazines stacked on the glass coffee table didn't interest me.

I hadn't bothered to try and charm the snippy receptionist after she played the "do you have an appointment?" game that I couldn't win.

Yesterday I'd dressed to impress—not in a suit, but in casual clothes that broadcast my laid-back, yet professional vibe. I'd skipped that shit today. The trick to breaking down the wall Sierra had built between us was to show her that I hadn't changed. Remind her of the worn-jeans-and-T-shirt-wearing guy she used to know.

Finally, Sierra's office door opened and she sauntered toward me.

I immediately stood. Sweet Jesus. She fucking rocked business casual. The black dress sculpted the curve of her breasts and her torso, hugging her hips. The bottom flared out above her knees, drawing attention to those long, shapely legs. She hadn't worn heels and I loomed over her by a good three inches.

"You didn't used to be this much taller than me."

I shrugged. "I grew a few inches after high school."

"You showing up again today is part of your 'I'm a burr' plan to waste my valuable time?"

"You dismissed me yesterday before you let me get to the reason I'm here."

She folded her arms across her chest. "So this isn't a social call?"

"No, ma'am. I am here on business. And I'd rather discuss this in private."

Her suspicion remained when she tersely said, "Follow me."
Wheeling around, she headed back to her office.

That ass. Man. I followed her swaying hips and managed not to be
focused on her backside when she faced forward to rest her butt against
the front edge of the desk. She didn't even invite me to sit. "So you're
here on business?"

"Yes."

"What kind of business are you in the market for?"

*Dirty business, funny business, monkey business, me giving you the
business.* I told the twelve-year-old boy inside me to shut the hell up.
"I'd like you to show me apartments, condos and house rentals for an
army friend who's moving here."

She studied me. "You don't have the first fucking clue about what
my job entails at Daniels Property Management, do you?"

One minute in and I'd already screwed up. "Kyler said you were in
real estate."

"So naturally you thought I was a...real estate agent?"

Do not answer, dumbass. Do not even nod your fucking head.

"Was that why you were impressed with my corner office?"

"Clearly I screwed up in that assumption. So please enlighten me
about what you do."

Without breaking eye contact, Sierra reached behind her for a
business card and flicked it at me.

I flipped it around, hoping the text didn't swim. Big, bold black
letters on a cream background read:

Sierra McKay
Executive Vice President
Commercial and Industrial Property Expansion Specialist
Daniels Property Management

I looked at her. "Impressive. What does the title mean?"

She flashed her teeth. "That I don't drive clients around showing
them residential properties."

Ouch.

"But feel free to keep my business card in case...your *friend* needs to hire a company to oversee a full remodel or restoration of his commercial property. I specialize in coordinating all aspects of revitalizing retail spaces—any size from six hundred square feet to sixty thousand square feet."

I tucked the business card in my front pocket after making sure it listed her contact number. "To be honest, I didn't even know that was a thing."

"A very real, very complicated thing which doesn't leave me time to act as a real estate guide for you or anyone else." She pushed up from the desk. "My assistant, Nikki, will give you a list of reputable Realtors we deal with."

"So that's it?" I said tightly.

"No BS, Boone. What do you really want from me?"

"Professionally? I want a Phoenix native to help me navigate all the suburbs and figure out the best, safest and most affordable place for my friend to live. You are obviously an expert in the real estate field— which, yes, I mistakenly took to mean you could show me specific apartments, condos and houses for rent. But your skill set being way above that pay grade doesn't change the fact I still would like your help."

"Why are you pressing me on this?"

Think fast, man. "Because I trust you. If there's no commission on the line then you can be completely honest about my options."

"You mean your friend's options," she said sharply.

Fuck. I almost blew that. "Yeah. You can help me narrow down my buddy Raj's choices."

"Why does Raj trust you so much?"

"Because I'm trustworthy." *Except you're lying like a motherfucker right now, aren't you? And what is going to happen when she finds out?* I'd worry about that later; right now I had her on the hook.

Then something Kyler had mentioned clicked and I played my only trump card. "Besides, you helped Mase find the McMansion he bought last summer. Kyler wouldn't shut up about how everything went seamlessly with you involved. Even when residential rentals and sales aren't in your wheelhouse."

"That big-mouthed asshat," she muttered.

I moved in closer. "Would it really be horrible spending a few hours with me this morning?"

Sierra got that squinty-eyed stare as if she was envisioning her daily schedule.

So I quickly added, "Or I can come back this afternoon. Or even tomorrow sometime if that works better for your schedule."

"Actually, today is the only day this week that my morning schedule is flexible."

Do not *punch your fist in the air and shout* Boo-yah! "So you'll do it with me?"

Those tawny-colored eyes of hers snapped to mine. "Excuse me?"

"You'll give me an overview of Phoenix?"

She sighed. "You are such a pushy bastard, West. But yes." She eyed the file folders on her desk. "I didn't really want to deal with all of this quarterly stuff anyway."

"I'm happy to be your excuse for ditching office work for a few hours."

Sierra smiled at me and my heart damn near burst. "You tried to get me to ditch school with you once."

"I remember. Feeling flush with cash for a change, I offered to buy you a DQ chili dog. I promised to have you back in time for fifth period. You turned me down." My eyes searched hers. "Why?"

"Because I didn't want you spending your money on me," she said softly. "I knew how hard you worked for it."

Being this close to her, smelling her perfume and watching the pulse pounding in her throat...I'd wanted this, but I had no idea how to act on it because I had zero experience with starting a relationship.

My conscience snapped, *I'm pretty sure luring her in with a lie is the worst possible option.*

Sierra sidestepped me and returned to her brusque demeanor. "I'll need to speak with my assistant before we go. I'll pick you up at the main entrance in ten minutes."

"I have a call to make"—total lie and wasn't I just turning into fucking Pinocchio?—"so that'll work."

I assumed she'd loosen up once we left Stepford Central. During my twenty-three-minute stint in the reception area, I'd watched Sierra's colleagues, whose icy demeanors were identical to the one she'd perfected. I couldn't blame her for following the crowd, especially if she was trying to blend in.

But she'd never blend. She never had.

After taking the stairs to the first floor, I cut across the blacktop to a small grassy area with a stone bench. What rocket scientist decided it'd be a great idea to plant grass in the damn desert? With time to kill, I checked my cell phone and saw that my dad had called again. With only a seven-minute window before Sierra pulled up, the callback couldn't go long and I'd be done with it. I dialed and immediately began to pace.

He answered with a gruff, "Hello."

"Hey Dad."

"I started to think you wouldn't call me back. It's been a few weeks."

You don't get to lay a guilt trip on me, old man. "Life is busy and all that. What's up?"

"Chet told me you were in Wyoming."

"I spent two weeks working at the clinic in Sundance. Now I'm in Phoenix."

"Chet was pretty vague about your plans. So was Remy when I asked him." He paused. "My brothers have always looked out for you."

They wouldn't have had to if you would've stepped up and done your parental duty.

"That's always surprised me," he continued. "Growing up, they had their own little world. I never fit in. And our folks were…"

Goddamned apathetic. My grandparents had the same level of interest in me as their son had—near zero.

"Whatever. Did you really call me to talk about my uncles?"

"No. But I want to talk to you about some stuff." He coughed.

"Are you sick?" I said sharply.

"Nah. Always been a point of pride I became a workaholic, not an alcoholic. Then one day I woke up and realized that too much work has the same effect as too much booze. I'd lived twenty-eight years of my life in an absolute fog."

An uneasy feeling took root. "Did Chet and Remy put you up to this?"

"Nope. Look, this ain't a conversation to have over the phone."
He swallowed so loudly I heard it and my stomach pitched.

"If you've got any...patience with or forgiveness in your heart for
your fucked-up old man, I'd like to meet with you."

Say no. Tell him it's too little, too late.

But it wasn't. I wasn't that lonely, sad boy whose Daddy missed his
every major life event. Now I understood things weren't always what
they seemed. And hard choices were called that for a reason. Also, I'd
built a damn good bullshit meter. If his explanations sounded like
excuses offered out of delayed guilt, I'd know it.

"Boone?"

"Yeah, I'm here. Just thinking." I exhaled. "Where and when do
you want to meet?"

"I've gotta drop a load in Flagstaff sometime in the next month or
so. Could you meet me there? If not, I can drive into Phoenix."

"Flagstaff will be fine."

"Thank you."

Silence.

As I started to remind him that if his plans changed and he had to
back out—which happened more often than not—he returned to the
line, his tone gruffer than before.

"I ain't gonna cancel on you, Boone. Not this time. You've got no
reason to trust in my promises after all the times I broke them, but I
have changed. I'd like you to give me a chance to prove it."

That defensive shield I'd honed popped up automatically. I said,
"We'll see," without conscious thought.

"Looking forward to seeing you. It's been too long. Take care."

I punched the end button and checked the timer on the screen. The
conversation, at three minutes and eighteen seconds, was the longest I'd
ever had with my dad on the phone. Even when I'd lived at home, he
called to pass on the most basic information and hung up. I hadn't seen
him since my graduation from basic training. I'd invited him more out
of obligation than anything and I hadn't expected him to show up. But
he'd been there in the bleachers alongside my uncles Chet and Remy.

My mom's claim of being too broke to come was probably the
truth, but even if she'd just won the lottery she would've skipped it.

Since she and my dad hadn't married, the three of us had never been a family unit. She'd ended up pregnant two more times, so I had a half-brother and half-sister. Their dad had lit out as soon as he discovered that my mom couldn't take the kind of beatings she dished out to her kids.

Sometimes I forgot what a shitty childhood I'd had.

You haven't forgotten; you've just buried it. Addiction, abuse, neglect has no part in your life now.

How much stuff would this conversation with my dad dredge up? When he didn't have a fucking clue about some of the crap I'd gone through because he hadn't cared enough to be around?

"Boone?"

My gaze snapped up from my shoes. At some point I'd sat on the bench and Sierra stood right beside me. I'd gotten lost, which was why I rarely let myself revisit the past. "Hey. Sorry."

"Is everything all right?"

During the year Sierra and I had been friends, I'd found myself telling her things no one had ever bothered to try and pry out of me. I hadn't found that kind of acceptance again until I'd become friends with Raj. And I hadn't looked for that kind of connection with another woman.

Is that why you're so adamant about rekindling your relationship with her? To prove to her that you aren't the same bitter boy, but knowing she'd understand your past helped mold you into the guy you are now?

A warm hand touched my cheek.

I blinked and tipped my head back to look at her.

"Boone. What's going on?"

"Had a weird phone call."

"Do you want to talk about it?"

My gut tightened. That sweet concern sounded so much like my Sierra from years past.

But if I said yes…would she be a crutch? If I said no…would she pull back? And how was I supposed to decide anything when I had her tender touch on my face? When the softness in her gaze was for me?

"Don't run when I say this." I lifted my hand, trapping her hand against my face to keep it in place. "Looking at you...having you this close...makes it goddamn hard to breathe, let alone think straight." Immediately after I admitted that, I slammed my eyes shut. I could not deal with her rejection right now.

I swear to god I heard her murmur, "I know what you mean."

Then her sharp fingernails scratched my hairline. "I liked you better with long hair, West."

I smiled at her attempt to lighten the mood. "Yeah?"

"Yeah."

"Well, it's a no-go in the military. A buzz cut, the same as everyone else's, makes it impossible to wear the label of brooding bad boy when the hipsters and the rednecks look exactly like you."

She laughed.

I wanted more of that. I wanted more of this easy banter. I opened my eyes.

She tugged her hand away, but she didn't retreat. "You still want to do this today?"

More than ever. "Wow me with your expertise, college girl."

"Smartass. I'm a college *graduate*. Come on."

Sierra drove a Mercedes.

"Why are you grinning like that?" she demanded.

"You drive the same kind of car you had in Wyoming."

"Because even the new models have the highest safety ratings on the market." She smirked. "With way more drive time, I upgraded to a kick-ass stereo."

I climbed in and buckled up. "What's first?"

"Showing you the areas your friend can't afford." She paused. "Scottsdale and Arcadia."

"Where do you live?"

"Scottsdale."

I bore white knuckles as Sierra wove in and out of traffic. The music on her kick-ass stereo didn't provide enough distraction—I wouldn't have pegged her as a Taylor Swift fan.

"You okay over there, West?"

"Trying not to think about whether my life insurance info is up to date."

"Traffic is the one thing I hate about Phoenix."

"Did you always know you'd come back here?"

She weighed her response. "Dad moving us to Sundance felt like punishment, even when he did it so we could both get to know his family together. That first year was rough on so many levels. Junior and senior years of high school I became more involved with everything. The McKays expected I'd attend UWYO because I'd taken classes there my senior year, but I picked ASU."

"Why?"

"I felt like a third wheel with Dad and Rielle. That didn't mean I wasn't flipping cartwheels because they found each other. But between me and Rielle's daughter Rory, they'd never lived alone together without kids. Plus, I knew if I hated Laramie I could drive home for the weekend. Going to ASU felt more like an adult decision."

"Had your mom moved back from France? Was that part of it?"

"No. Her dipshit boy toy in Paris ditched her after he decided to settle down with a younger woman and have kids. She returned to Phoenix after my first year at ASU, a total mess. Her plan to feel young, hip and cool was to hang out with her college-aged daughter."

I groaned. "Fun for you, huh?"

"Oh, it gets better. Then she decided hooking up with a college-aged guy would prove her hotness. So, as usual, she chose the easiest option and banged *my* boyfriend."

"Fuck. Seriously?"

"Her behavior didn't shock me as much as she'd hoped. I went, 'Eh, you can have him.' In a way she did me a favor. The guy was a total 'S'up, bro?' frat-boy douchebag with a small dick and smaller ambitions."

I had no idea what the fuck to say to that. Did I laugh? She acted unaffected now, but it had to have pissed her off when it'd happened.

"Oh, so now you don't have anything to say?"

I did laugh at that. "Parents suck. At least you have one good one. Both of mine are worthless. Just say the word, baby, and I'll track down that cheating, frat-boy douchebag and beat his tiny-dick ass."

"Four years after it happened?"

"He won't suspect you waited that long to get revenge." And I'd

love to pound the shit out of a guy who'd had Sierra in his bed and
hadn't cared enough to keep her there.

Sierra laughed. "The army would approve of that response?"

"It's not like I'd wear my uniform. I'd be in total stealth mode."

"I'll take it under consideration, tough guy."

During her thorough tour of the city, I listened to her spiel without
much comment because I liked the sound of her voice and I appreciated seeing the area through her eyes. She clearly loved living here more
than she ever had in Wyoming.

After two and a half hours my stomach rumbled. "Can we stop for
lunch? It can even be fast food. I just have to eat something." I pointed
to a Cheesecake Factory. "How about there?"

"That's not fast food."

"It's close though."

"Fine." She pulled into a parking garage.

Feeling antsy, I climbed out of the car first and waited for her at the
bottom of the steps. She'd slipped her sunglasses back on, but I felt her
eyes on me. In a total junior high move, I dropped my arms behind me
and stretched. That move flexed my biceps, pecs and abdomen. I knew
she'd look.

And she did. She took such a complete look that she nearly missed
the bottom step.

I caught her with one hand on her hip and the other on her shoulder. "Careful."

Sierra peered at me over the tops of her sunglasses. "Next time you
want to remind me you're still rockin' a killer body, wait until I'm on
level ground, 'kay?"

She brushed past me so fast she didn't see my big-assed grin.

We'd been seated maybe a minute when Sierra said, "Excuse me,
I'll be right back."

I started flipping through the hundred-page menu. The text was
swimming by the time I reached page five. I closed my eyes and blanked
my mind. But when I looked again, I had the same problem. I shut the
menu and set it on the edge of the table.

Sierra slid back into the booth.

When the waitress returned, I ordered a hamburger. She looked at

Sierra. "And for you?"

"The Almond Joy cheesecake and a can of Red Bull."

After the waitress left, I said, "Just cheesecake?"

"Since it's my entire daily caloric intake...yes, just cheesecake. I'll suffer through salad for dinner." Sierra set a file folder on the table. "My assistant scrounged up a few options for rentals from one of our clients that owns both commercial and residential properties. You want to go through these?"

"Not really."

"Then what is the purpose of this lunch?"

"Besides to share a meal together you didn't have to cook for me?" I shrugged. "I wanted to sit across from you to give my neck a break from twisting around so I can see your face. Only getting a side glimpse of your glare doesn't have the same power as full-frontal."

"You want me to glare at you?"

"You *will* glare at me when I suggest we clear the air and say the shit that's been on both of our minds the last seven years. Then we could hug it out."

She smacked my forearm. "No and no. Keep it focused on *business* between us, Boone."

Dirty business popped into my head.

Sierra must've read that on my face because she smacked my other forearm. "I can leave you here if you don't behave."

Was I making any progress with her? I hated to fall back, but I didn't want to put *her* in full retreat. "So...business. You never mentioned you wanted to go into the family business."

"That's because it wasn't on my radar as a self-absorbed sixteen-year-old. But by age seventeen I realized I needed a life plan so I made one." She talked about investing her inheritance in flipping houses and her luck in getting out before the real estate market crashed. She mentioned funding her buddy Marin's home-based business. None of her triumphs were detailed in a bragging manner and she groaned about her failures.

I tried to listen without my goddamned mouth hanging open. So much for my assumption Sierra had skated through college with minimum effort. She'd even founded a college organization for women entrepreneurs. After graduating a year early, she'd started at the bottom at Daniels Property Management. Within two years she'd earned the title and responsibilities of a company vice president.

The woman was twenty-three years old.

"Say something," she demanded.

"You make everyone look like a slacker, don't you?"

She blushed. "I don't know about that. For better or for worse, I wanted to be in charge of my own destiny."

"Your dad had to be impressed with you taking the initiative."

"Maybe that was a teeny part of why I did it."

The food arrived.

After forking in a bite of cheesecake, she released a husky sigh.

I froze. Now there was a sexy sound.

"I've tried to recreate this twenty times at home and I cannot get the flavors right."

"That good, huh?"

She sliced off another chunk, closed her eyes, parted her lips and paused with the fork halfway in, balanced on her tongue.

My groan rivaled hers when she closed her mouth and slowly slid the fork out.

Fuck. Me. I didn't need a hard-on in the fucking Cheesecake Factory.

Too late.

Maybe she didn't notice my jagged breathing and discreetly adjusting my cock beneath the napkin on my lap.

Sierra's cell phone began to vibrate halfway through the meal. She answered, "Sierra McKay." Her frown deepened as she listened. "May I ask how your department ended up with that information? Not from my office. I'm positive. Because I'm the only one with access and I didn't discuss it with anyone." She rubbed the spot between her eyebrows with her thumb.

I tuned out her words and focused on the cadence of her voice. With her distracted, I seized the chance to study the face I'd only seen in memories the past seven years. The sharp angle of her cheekbones. The smattering of freckles across her nose. The line of her stubborn jaw. The tiny divot in her chin. She bit her bottom lip. A pink tinge crept up her neck.

Would she jerk away if I covered her restless hand with mine? I had this…urge to smooth the frown lines between her eyebrows with a soft kiss. I thought about all the affectionate things I'd seen couples doing without thinking, without knowing that guys like me watched with envy.

I'd never had that with any woman. Never wanted it before.

But I wanted it now with Sierra.

"No, I understand. But Greg led me to believe we'd discuss this when he returned next week. I wasn't aware you were looped in and to be honest, I do have an issue with it." She scowled. "No. I do *not* need to bring up my concerns with the CEO, who is my father, but I'll also remind you that he is *your* boss and he does have more important things to do than deal with the security breach in *your* department." Pause. "You brought it to my attention. We're dealing with it *today*. Call Mr. Avila's office and set up a meeting. I'll have my assistant follow up in thirty minutes." She ended the call and tossed the phone aside.

"Problems?"

"Greg the misogynist dick-cunt gave his fucking junior assistant a task list before he slithered off on vacation. Not only am I not *ever* under the supervision of a junior assistant, this little fuckwad thinks because Greg constantly remarks about me 'running' to my father with problems that he can too. Junior asslicker isn't supposed to have the information that he's following up on anyway. But it is a breach of protocol and now I have to speak with Greg's supervisor, who respects me even less than Greg."

"Dick-cunt?"

She glanced up with a sheepish smile. "The term covers both sexes insult-wise, so I can assure myself I'm not sexist."

I laughed.

She shoved her plate of half-eaten cheesecake aside and drained her Red Bull. "I have to return to the office."

"I figured. You don't want a to-go box for that?"

She shook her head. "I lost my appetite."

I refused to let her pay for lunch.

She was on her phone almost the entire drive back. After pulling up to the main entrance, she turned toward me. "Any questions?"

"I want to see you again."

"Any questions about *Phoenix*," she reiterated.

"I want to see you again in Phoenix someplace besides your office."

"That wasn't a question. That was a demand."

I shrugged. "We still need to have that talk."

"There's nothing to talk about, Boone."

Fuck. That. I leaned across the console. "It sucked hanging out with me today so much that you don't want to do it again?"

"This was about business. That's the only reason I agreed to help you."

"Sierra, you are so full of shit. Be honest with me, for Christsake."

Like you're being honest with her?

She opened her mouth—I braced myself for her denial, but she exhaled loudly. "Okay. Maybe it didn't suck hanging out with you. Even when you fucked around with my radio because you still have crap taste in music. But I have other things—business things—to focus on today, so can you cut me some slack, please?"

"Sure." Maybe she'd grant me a break when I told her the reason I was pushing so hard to talk was so I could tell her the truth about how long I'd be in Phoenix. "Just understand I'll jerk on that slack line and haul you in if it goes on too long." I reached for the one section of hair that always ended up stuck to the corner of her mouth. "Thanks for taking time for me today and giving me a glimpse into the world you live in now. I always knew you'd do great things, Sierra Daniels McKay." I twisted her hair around my finger and let it uncoil. "Brains and beauty and ambition. Intimidating for a lowly army grunt like me."

Sierra's gaze cut to my mouth. Her eyes heated. She parted her lips. All clear signs she wanted me to kiss her.

I had the control of a fucking saint, not yanking her forward and planting my mouth on hers.

A fucking saint.

Then she head-butted me and said, "Get out of my car, grunt. I've got names to take and asses to kick."

"See you around, McKay."

6 Sierra

AFTER TWO SPECTACULARLY shitty days at work, it was Friday night and I deserved to get my drink on.

With Greg's absence this week I thought I'd have a reprieve from the corporate crap. No such luck. I wish I could've taped the conversations as proof that men were as catty and cutting as women. Worse maybe.

At one point I had to bite my tongue to keep from demanding that Greg's junior assistant, Peterson, drop his trousers so I could affirm that he did, indeed, have balls. I'd never dealt with such a whiner. He expected management to listen raptly as he relayed how his coworkers' actions made him "feel." Evidently his emotional outbursts didn't make him feel like a whiny douchebag who needed his ass kicked. That's when I'd drifted into my *Fight Club* fantasy and imagined choking him out with my knee in the spot where his balls used to be.

The one upside to the week—besides seeing Boone twice—was using my frustration to move mountains. Literally. Lu had claimed a corner of the backyard as a place to showcase her landscaping design work. I agreed to buy the raw materials but we had to take delivery of the truckload of river rock on Wednesday. Between Lu's classes and her job, she didn't have time to fill a wheelbarrow, push it across the yard, dump it and repeat two hundred more times. Not really that many times, but it'd sure felt like it. Surprisingly, physical labor turned out to be awesome therapy for me—better than baking. Anger gone, muscles so sore I fell into a near coma after soaking in the hot tub. Plus, I had actually shocked my normally unflappable roommate. She'd expected to come home to a pile of muffins, cookies, pies, cheesecake and brownies—baking was my go-to stress reliever.

But Lu hadn't let me off the hook when I'd mentioned that spending time with Boone had been the only upside to my Wednesday.

She'd reiterated her "bone Boone and bail" stance and then she'd gone to bed. Leaving me to wrestle with figuring out what he wanted to talk about.

Why couldn't Boone just say, "Hey McKay, let's have a beer after you get off work, swap stories about what we've been doing the last seven years and I'll tell you what's on my mind?" I might've said what the hell. But the way he kept saying, "We have to talk," I heard the *dun dun dun* of ominous music in my head and wanted to run the opposite direction.

After this week's sensitivity sessions, an even worse scenario tormented me: that somehow, Brooding Boone had become "in touch" with his emotions like that fucker Peterson. That Boone might expect me to finally "vocalize" my hurt and disappointment to him about his decision to go off in pursuit of his life goals and dreams.

Screw that. Maybe we oughta discuss how much of a dickhead move it'd been when you'd given me, oh, half an hour notice *before you skipped Wyoming for good.*

Because how I felt about it now? Immaterial. How I'd felt back then? Brokenhearted and pissed off. But that wasn't news to either of us. So what purpose did talking about it now serve? None for me. Guilt was his issue; he could deal with it.

Right now I didn't want to think about anything but tracking down the keg. If I got slam-a-lammered, my cousins would let me crash with them. Apparently I amused them in that state, which was pretty rare for me.

I parked down the street from the house my cousins lived in. They'd had a rough freshman year living in the dorms. Over the summer I'd debated on asking them to live with me; I had enough room and we all got along well. Then Ky's cousin Mase Morrison had relocated to Phoenix to play hockey professionally for the Scorpions and he'd bought a McMansion with his signing bonus. So the pro hockey player, the football player, the rodeoer and the chess clubber all coexisted happily in McJock Central. And seeing the clusters of people filling up the driveway and spilling out the front door…I couldn't imagine living with this mess. I might love parties but it'd drive me batshit crazy to face the after party destruction the following day. I was about two steps away from having OCD because I couldn't function without orderliness in my personal space.

A few of the freshman chickies gave me the stink eye when I passed by. Especially when Tug Breckenridge shouted my name from across the yard and made a beeline toward me.

The brute picked me up, tossed me over his shoulder and sprinted with me hanging upside down like a chunk of meat. Tug shouted, "Lookit I found."

I smacked Tug on the ass—not that he felt it. At six foot six and three hundred odd pounds the center for the ASU Sun Devils defined massive. Tug had a thing for me, which I didn't exactly discourage. We flirted constantly but if I ever took him up on any of his outrageous suggestions, the man would blush as red as his uniform.

With my hair tangled in my face, I couldn't see, so I smacked Tug again harder. "Put me down, brute."

"Stop tickling me, Nevada."

Nevada. Since Ky lived with two other McKays and was considered "the" McKay with his teammates, the rest of us had nicknames. Hayden was "Vader", Anton "Cowboy" and I'd been saddled with "Nevada." At least a few guys on the football team knew what the Sierra Nevada Mountains were.

Kyler said, "Put her down, Tug."

"Man. Do I have to? She's warm and soft and smells good." Tug sighed and lowered me to my feet. He even brushed my hair out of my face; those gigantic mitts of his were surprisingly gentle. He grinned at me. "There's the gorgeous face I was missing. Girl, where you been?"

"Out of town, sick, and trying to catch up."

Hearing the word sick, Tug jumped back. "Whoa. Sick? Contagious kind of sick?"

"Not anymore." I slowly sauntered forward. "Unless you wanna swap spit or exchange other bodily fluids."

Just as I suspected, big, tough Tug…stammered and took off.

Behind me, a deep, sexy voice said, "I'll test the bodily fluid exchange theory any time you want...*Nevada*."

I whirled around and was face-to-face with Boone.

My heart leapt and my pulse rate quadrupled.

What was he doing at a college party?

What are you *doing here? You've been out of college for two years.*

Goddammit.

Boone had his sexy brooding face on. "Where'd your boyfriend lumber off to?"

The *he's not my boyfriend* denial died on my lips. Instead I tossed out, "Probably to get me a beer."

More of his dark-eyed stare.

"I wasn't expecting to see you here."

"Wish I could say the same." He frowned at whatever he saw happening behind me. "This reminds me of that party we were at in high school. You remember."

"I try not to think about that party, for so many reasons."

Boone's focus returned to my face. "I see it still doesn't bug you to have hair stuck to your mouth." He swept his thumb across the corner of my lips, loosening a few strands.

My lungs seized up. Boone used to do that all the time, usually while complaining that my spit had glue-like properties. That simple touch had seemed so intimate back then. It still did.

Then his questioning eyes were back on mine.

"What?"

"Why is it I get this close to you and I forget what the hell I wanted to say? Oh right, because you're usually chewing my ass about something I already said or did wrong."

I smiled. "You usually deserve it."

He smiled back and I had that cartwheeling sensation again.

"Maybe you'll get lucky and meet someone who doesn't annoy you like I do."

"You don't annoy me, Sierra. You frustrate me, but that's another conversation."

Not going there. "Have you met many people?"

"This chick asked if I was in her art history class. I said no and she still hung around."

Well yeah, have you looked in the mirror lately? "Some girls only come to these parties to bang a football player. And before you piss me off, no, that's not the reason I went to jock parties."

"Tug is the exception?"

"Tug and I are just friends. I let him go He-Man on me because he's shy around women and our back-and-forth bullshitting builds his confidence. The rest of the guys on the team are cocky. That's probably what Miss Art History recognized in you; that cockiness."

His shrug said: it is what it is.

Props to him for not denying it.

"I'm surprised they're partying tonight when they have a game tomorrow."

"None of the starters are drinking booze." I pointed out a dozen team members in our vicinity. "Water or energy drinks. Ky kicks them out early and he's in bed before midnight." When I noticed Boone looking at me oddly, I said, "What?"

"I said it before but I'll say it again. It's weird to think you're hanging out with Kyler. He used to bug the crap out of you on the bus. You'd hide from him in the back seat, remember?"

Wrong. I sat in the far back because that's where Boone always sat. "There's nothing more obnoxious than a twelve-year-old boy, so anything is an improvement."

He grinned. "Why didn't we throttle the McKay-kateers every day when we had the chance?"

"We?" I poked him in the chest. "*You* stopped riding the bus. *I* still had to deal with them."

"I would've preferred being on the bus to working two jobs."

Hayden caught my eye and started to jog over.

"Speaking of the McKay-kateers…"

Hayden draped his arm across my shoulder for a one-armed hug. "S'up?" He saw both my hands were empty. "You're not drinking tonight?"

"I've yet to reach the keg and I'm in dire need of a beer."

"I'll grab you one," Boone said, and he was gone.

Hayden caught me watching Boone walk away. I bristled. "What?"

"You two are acting awfully cozy."

"Cozy is not the word that comes to mind with Boone. He's as cozy as a grenade launcher."

"He said the same thing about you." Hayden stepped in front of me. "Just watch yourself with him, okay?"

"Sex it and exit" Hayden had the balls to issue me a warning? Asshat.

Formerly the shiest of the McKay-kateers, the lone blond of the trio had shot up and bulked out. Now a super-hottie with charisma and brains galore, he'd made a name for himself as the sweet talker who could charm any woman into his bed.

"Aw, look at you, manwhore, concerned for my virtue." I patted Hayden on the cheek. "Don't worry that pretty head of yours, brainiac. The only thing I'm making with Boone is conversation."

He laughed. "Right. I give it a week before you getcha some of that, 'cause he is as hot for you as you're pretending not to be for him. Just keep it casual, true?"

"Whatever."

"You coming to the game tomorrow?"

"Have I missed a home game yet this season?" I'd become a huge football fan over the years. Watching my talented cousin killing it on the field just kicked up my excitement level.

"No, football fanatic." He punched me in the arm. "I can't wait to see how bloodthirsty you get at Mase's hockey games this year."

Since the Scorpions were consistently at the bottom of their division, we scored great season tickets for fairly cheap. Mase had blushed when I showed him the Scorpions jersey I'd bought sporting *Morrison* on the back and asked him to sign it.

"There's an extra ticket floating around to tomorrow's game. You should invite Lu."

"Lu has to work." I returned his punch to the arm. It was our thing from our school bus days. "And dude, stop bird-dogging my roomie. She will chew you up and spit you out."

"Or she might prefer a taste of Wyoming sage in her man-meat." He smirked. "Anyway, I came over to tell you it's Meat-topia weekend."

"It is? Good thing I didn't get tickets to Sunday night's game."

"Don't bring that up with Kyler. His ticket deal fell through." Hayden frowned. "It's killing him his beloved Broncos are in town and he can't be in the stadium."

"Ky is the ASU quarterback! Why isn't he just given tickets to every damn event?" I huffed. "That is so not fair. Sun Devils stadium is his *home* stadium. He plays on that field. He deserves—"

"Simmer down, big cuz."

Boone returned with the beer before I could retort. His gaze winged between me and Hayden. "Is everything all right?"

"Sierra just gets het up when it comes to family." Hayden squeezed my shoulder in a half-hug. "That's why she needs a beer." He plucked it from Boone's hand and passed it over to me.

"That was fast," I said to Boone.

"I told Tug it was for you." He sipped his beer. "Both cups actually. Then he said he admired 'a chick who could drink like she had a dick.'"

"Tug's been influenced by Lex," Hayden complained. Then he looked at me. "Have you talked to Lex tonight?"

I shook my head. "I didn't know he was here."

"I saw him inside. He asked about you."

What was Hayden doing? Trying to piss me off and warn Boone away?

The exact opposite happened.

Boone growled, "Who the fuck is Lex? Another football player who's so freakin' *shy* with all the grid-bunnies that he needs your special help too?"

"And...I'm done here. I'll find people to talk to who aren't judgmental dickheads."

My first thought as I walked away? *Don't stop until you get to your car.*

My second thought? Even a crappy conversation with Boone at this party was better than how things transpired at the first and only party we'd ended up at in high school.

I hadn't planned on running into him that night either.

Now I was running again—away this time. I cut across the lawn, searching for a spot in the dark shadows of the house where no partiers would find me. I slumped against the stucco and sipped my beer. Warm. Yuck.

Why had Boone brought up that horrible party almost first thing? It'd been the most humiliating night of my life. Nearly eight years later, I still wanted to curl into a ball in the corner and hide my face in shame when I thought about it.

That's probably why I subconsciously hid in the shadows now—because that memory kept floating closer and closer to the surface.

Maybe letting it come won't be so bad. Things and perceptions change. You've changed.

Good freakin' thing. Because during that time of my life? I thought I was *the* shit.

I had my driver's license.

I had a car.

I had the burning desire to prove I was cool.

It was as if I followed a "How to Fuck Up Your Life" checklist for bratty sixteen-year-old girls.

Finding new friends with a "question authority" attitude? Check.

Lying to my dad? Check.

Making dumb decisions with booze? Check.

Showing bad judgment with a bad boy? Check.

I'd implemented all of those fantastically stupid choices in one night...

MY NEW PAL Kara knew where all the cool parties were. Not the "lame high school ones" but private house parties with booze and older guys.

I'd become a regular at these parties the last month. I stuck close to Kara and Angie because I was actually shy around boys and these older guys sort of terrified me. I hated that I was still hung up on Boone, even when I hadn't heard from him at all since before Christmas. So a few beers filled me with the liquid courage to approach the new guy who'd just shown up. He was seriously cute, even if he looked rough around the edges.

As soon as I smiled at him? He was by my side.

"Hey, hot stuff. What's your name?"

I smelled pot smoke on his clothes, which I ignored because...hello? Cute guy flirting with me? "Sierra. What's yours?"

"Tyler." Tyler eyed my chest first and then the cup I held.

"Whatcha drinkin'?"

"Beer."

"This is better." He waggled a bottle of Jack Daniels he'd been carrying around. "And I'm willing to share."

"What's the catch?" While there was always booze at these parties, it never was free.

Tyler grinned. "Smart girl. Do a couple shots with me and we'll figure something out."

I said, "Sure," as if I accepted shots from strange guys all the time. I drained my beer, intending to reuse the cup for the shot, but Tyler plucked it out of my hand and tossed it aside.

"No drinkin' it like a pussy. Take your shot straight from the bottle."

I snatched the bottle from him and drank. Somehow I withheld a shudder. Jesus. The stuff tasted like vomit. The Crown XR my dad drank was way better.

He laughed and grabbed the bottle back. "Eager to do what I tell you. I like that." He tipped the bottle, keeping his gaze on my chest while he guzzled. "I haven't seen you here before."

"Really? I was here last weekend."

"I wasn't. I had to work."

"That sucks. It was a great party. Been a lot of great parties lately."

"And you've been to all of them?"

I attempted a flirty smile. "Yep."

"So you don't got a job?"

"No."

"Must be nice." He knocked back another slug. "So if you ain't workin', what do you do for fun?"

"I've been stuck at home for a few months without wheels, so it's been a long time since I've had any fun. I've been making up for lost time."

"Then you're in luck, 'cause I can think of a whole lotta ways we can have fun together tonight." He passed the bottle back to me. "Drink up and drink deep."

I held my breath and managed to swallow another huge mouthful. But I didn't stop the shudder.

"Gets better by about the fifth shot. After that, you won't know *what* you're swallowing."

My warning bells went off.

Then Tyler violated my personal space and touched me without permission.

He wrapped his fingers in the necklace I wore and tugged me closer, like it was a come-along. "Heard some things about you. You've got a nice ass, pretty face too." He kept putting pressure on the necklace chain, forcing me to move closer to him.

My brain warned me to tell him that he was choking me, even as I feared he was fully aware of what he was doing.

"Now. How about we talk about payment?"

Two shots in a row on top of five beers made my head spin.

"Wanna hear your options?" Tyler said.

No. I want you to let me go. I'd barely been talking to this guy for five minutes and he acted like this? I needed to get away from him and fast. "I could just pay you."

"Nah. I'm wantin' something else. Your money is no good."

"But mine is. I figure she drank maybe five bucks worth of Jack." A hand waved a five-dollar bill between my face and Tyler's. "So consider this payment in full."

Boone.

Oh God, Boone was here. I didn't know whether to be happy or embarrassed.

Tyler released my necklace.

I sucked in a deep breath and was snapped back against Boone's chest.

Tyler glared at Boone. "What the fuck is your problem, West?"

"Don't have one, Ty. Just watching out for my girl." He tucked the folded bill in Tyler's shirt pocket. "We square?"

I remained frozen.

"You're with her? Bullshit," Tyler spat. "Kara didn't say nothin' to me about that."

"That's 'cause Kara doesn't know. No one knows." Boone dropped his arm over my shoulder. "Our families would have a shit fit if they knew we were together." Then Boone's hot mouth teased the skin below my ear. "Right, sugar bear?"

He'd said the words loud enough for Tyler to hear. But my tongue seemed to be stuck to the roof of my mouth.

"Don't pull that silent treatment crap with me," Boone warned me testily. "Tell you what. You don't get pissed off at me for bein' late and I won't get pissed off at you for drinking with another guy. 'Cause you know how jealous I get, baby."

Tyler's skeptical gaze flitted between us. He looked ready to kill Boone. And maim me.

Boone twined his fingers in my hair and pulled my head back in a move that showed his displeasure I hadn't answered him. Then he put his mouth on my ear and whispered, "For Christsake, Sierra, act like we're together or Tyler will fuck me up and then he'll fuck you."

That snapped me out of it. "Sorry, Boone. Don't be mad." I turned my head and buried my face in his neck.

Boone sighed. "Look, man, I'm sorry. She's a big fuckin' cocktease when she's been drinking." He offered Tyler his hand. "No hard feelings?"

A beat passed before Tyler shook Boone's hand. "You're lucky you got here in time. Me'n her were about to have us a private party. You'd better keep a tighter leash on her. Most guys ain't as understanding as me."

"I appreciate that." Boone curled his hand around my hip and squeezed. "Any rooms open so Sierra and I can…talk privately?"

Tyler laughed. Then he yelled, "Jimbo. Clear out my bedroom so these two can fuck and make up."

His bedroom? Omigod. This was *his* house?

"Thanks, man." Boone dropped his free hand to my ass and kept his arm around my neck, almost in a headlock as he maneuvered me through the crowd.

I felt everyone staring at us, but I kept my gaze on my feet. Even that didn't keep me from stumbling. I heard laughter and Boone's grip tightened.

He steered me into a bedroom and slammed the door behind us.

The shots hit me the same time as the reality of the situation and I felt ill.

I tripped over something on the floor and Boone caught me before I fell.

He pushed me against the door, bracing my shoulders, and got right in my face. "What the fuck were you doing?"

"I don't know."

"That is goddamn obvious, Sierra."

I closed my eyes.

"Huh-uh. Look at me. Keep those eyes open because the room will start spinning and I don't wanna deal with you being sick as well as being stupid."

Stupid. I hated being called stupid. And it stung hearing it from him. "I'm not that drunk." I put my hands on his chest and shoved him as hard as I could.

Boone wasn't expecting it and stumbled back two steps.

"Leave me alone. I don't need you to fucking babysit me, Boone."

He clenched his hands into fists at his sides and stared at me. "What the hell do you think would've happened if I'd left you alone with Tyler?"

"I would've figured something out."

"Before or after he fed you more booze, dragged you into his bedroom and raped you?"

"What?"

"Rape. Sex without consent," he snarled. "Tyler doesn't fucking care if you're conscious."

I felt sick. "And how do you know that?"

"Because he did it to a friend of mine. They were drinking and then the next thing she remembered was waking up with him on top of her."

"Oh God."

Then Boone was face-to-face with me again. "I told you to stay away from Kara. And I heard you've been here, at her brother Tyler's house, for the past two weekends."

"I didn't know it was his house." I swallowed hard. "I didn't know Tyler was her brother."

His eyes turned hard. "You just showed up at some random person's house and started drinking with strangers? Jesus. Sierra. You're smarter than that. Why would you do that?"

"Because I'm fucking sick and tired of sitting at home by myself all the time, okay? No one in this godforsaken town wants anything to do with me. So when Kara and Angie asked me to hang out, I said yes. I thought maybe I'd meet people."

"You don't want to meet the people they hang out with," he snapped. "For Christsake, Tyler is twenty-three. He's been in jail. The only people who hang around him are his loser jailbird buddies and his sister's high school friends who don't have any other place to drink."

"Then why are you here?" I demanded. "Are *you* one of his loser friends?"

"Fuck no. I showed up because I heard at school this is your new weekend hangout."

"Bull. I haven't seen you in school for weeks, so I doubt you *heard* anything."

"I only need one credit to graduate so I'm there for one class in the morning, so yeah, I heard. You're some kind of party girl now."

So?"

"So you don't need to head down this road again, Sierra. Making bad choices like you did in Arizona."

Maybe he was right. But he had no idea how alone I felt. And it wasn't like he called to check up on me like he'd said he might. I mumbled under my breath that he had no business judging me and tried to sidestep him.

He was crowding me. "What did you say?"

"Why do you care? We aren't anything to each other."

"You don't believe that because you know it's not true."

"Then what are we?" I demanded.

Boone said something under his breath.

Screw this. Screw *him* and his stupid brooding ways. I slumped against the door. "Whatever. You've done your good deed, protecting me from Tyler. Thank you. You've made it clear I'm a fucking idiot and a pain in your ass. So go away."

"I'm just supposed to what? Leave you here?"

"Yes. I've got my own car now."

Boone's hands were on my arms. "You think you're gonna drive after you've been drinking? Bullshit. What the fuck is wrong with you?"

I twisted out of his hold. "I wasn't gonna leave right now, asshole. I'll be sober enough to drive in a couple of hours. I'll just hang out until then."

"Listen to yourself. Do you really think Tyler will let you *hang out*? Especially after I convinced him that we're together? What exactly do you think the people out there think we're doing in here? Talking?" he half-sneered.

I opened my mouth to deny it, but Boone was right. "Fine. You can stay in here with me until I sober up. That oughta add to your stud reputation. That you banged me for two solid hours."

Boone blushed. Then he got pissed off. "Right. Because that's all I give a shit about. My reputation as some kind of stud. Even if we stay in here, that doesn't deal with the problem when we leave the bedroom."

"Which is what?"

"We'll have to act like we're together, so Tyler doesn't track me down and beat the fuck out of me for pulling one over on him. That's the kind of guy he is. Making him look stupid turns him psycho." He ran his hand through his hair. "Dammit. This is the last thing I wanted."

Meaning, I'm the last one you wanted to be tied to—in reality or even pretend.

"You know what, Boone? Fuck off. You don't have to act so disgusted that people will think we're together."

Boone was back in my face. "That's what you think? That being with you would be an embarrassment to me? God. You are drunk because you are not that clueless, Sierra. You know that I—"

"Shut up. We'll have a very loud and public breakup Monday morning at school. Or better yet, let's have a big fight now. Want me to scream and storm out?"

"Jesus. I'm *not* doing this with you." He gave me a once-over. "Where's your coat?"

"In the living room."

"Do you have snow boots?"

"No."

"Gloves?"

"Yes, I'm not a total idiot."

Boone scowled at me. "Did you even check the weather before you went out tonight?"

I blinked at him.

"I take that as a no. The road conditions were shitty an hour ago. They've gotta be worse by now."

"Did you ride your bike here?"

"No."

"How'd you expect to get home?"

"How'd *you* expect to get home?" he countered. "Or did you tell your dad you were spending the night someplace?"

"No. My curfew is midnight."

He glanced at his watch. "It's only nine thirty. Give me your keys."

"They're in my coat."

He blew out a frustrated breath. "When we get out there, go ahead and act like you're mad at me."

"Won't be an act." I flashed my teeth at him.

Boone jammed his hands into my hair and messed it up. He popped the button on his jeans. Then he pulled my shirt down my arm, exposing my bra strap. "There. At least it looks like we've been going at it."

My head pounded and I just wanted to leave.

He held onto me tightly as he opened the door.

A few catcalls greeted us.

Kara and Angie sidled up to me. "Omigod, Sierra. Why didn't you tell us you were with Boone West?"

Because I'm not.

"Is that why you ignored all the guys hitting on you the last month?" Kara asked. "I guess that's a better secret than what *we* thought."

"Which was what?"

"That you're a virgin working up the nerve to ask one of these guys to pop your cherry. That's why I wanted you to meet Tyler."

Boone made a growling noise that sent weird chills up my spine.

THAT MEMORY FADED and the present came sharply into focus.

I'd heard that snarl earlier.

When Boone thought I was with Tug.

When Hayden had mentioned Lex.

Now I realized Boone had made that same sound after Kara had mentioned Tyler.

Not because Boone had been mad at me that night.

Because he'd felt possessive of me.

Then.

And now.

Get the fuck out.

Maybe I did need to talk to him after all.

7 Boone

I PLAYED IT cool, not chasing after Sierra, when everything inside urged me to go after her.

"What's up with you and her?" Hayden asked.

"We're talking."

"But you'd rather be doing?"

I spared Hayden a dark look but didn't respond because it was none of his fucking business.

"Watch it with her," Hayden warned. "Sierra is family. I get that sounds stupid because you're family too."

"But?" I said without looking at him.

"But you vanished out of everyone's life, Boone. I've been around her a lot more than I have you, so…"

"If I fuck with her, you'll fuck with me."

"Count on it. Sierra isn't as much the ballbuster outside of work as she pretends to be. Guys who zero in on vulnerable shit like that piss me the hell off."

"Guys like you?"

He laughed. "Fuck you very much, cuz, but no, I was talking about *you.*"

"Me? Games ain't ever been my thing, college boy."

"From what I understand, you'll be living in Phoenix, joining the ranks as a 'college boy' soon enough, so stand down," Hayden said, the edge in his tone sharp enough to get my back up.

Who else had Kyler told? If that asshole told Sierra the truth before I—

You could've told her. You should've told her. She'll kick your balls into your brain to see if that'll shake some sense loose because you obviously ain't got any.

"Hey, soldier, are you even listening to me?"

I refocused on Hayden. "What? Did I miss another threat?"

"A suggestion. If your eye fucking turns into real fucking? Don't make promises to her that you can't keep."

Hayden walked off.

Standing there alone, holding a foamy, lukewarm beer I didn't want, I was tempted to chuck it all and head back to Raj's.

My phone buzzed with a text from my younger sister.

Oakley: *I'm bored. Tell me you're doing something fun.*

I set my beer on the ground. I sucked at texting and had to totally focus to do it.

Me: *At a party.*

Oakley: *Jealous!*

Me: *Don't be. It sucks. I want to leave. Why r u bored?*

Oakley: *I'm babysitting. The kid crashed and there's nothing to do in this house.*

Me: *Homework?*

Oakley: *Oops. I forgot to bring it ☺ but I'm not failing any classes. Yet.*

I snorted. My sister had been born with one of those brains that found anything science related fascinating and easy to understand.

Me: *U done with college apps?*

Oakley: *My counselor has been really cool, so yeah. She's making me apply everywhere.*

I had a brief moment of panic. Applying for college wasn't free. How was she paying for it?

Oakley: *STOP freaking out about where I'm getting the money to apply.*

I laughed. Brat knew me so well.

Oakley: *As much as I hate being a charity case, most admissions programs are waiving the fees, due to my "financial hardship and living in a rural area" reality.*

Me: *Did u hear my huge sigh of relief all the way in Montana?*

Oakley: *Yeah. It smelled like beer and farts.*

Me: *Brat. Later, Twig.*

Oakley: *Same to you, Coon.*

"Must've been a fascinating conversation," Sierra said.

I glanced up and said, "What?"

She pointed at the ground. "Your beer tipped over and you didn't even notice."

"It didn't tip over. I kicked it over because it tasted like shit."

"Are you a beer snob now, West?"

"When it comes to cheap, warm beer? Yep."

"Then I won't offer to get you another."

I crossed my arms over my chest. "Couldn't find anyone who wasn't a judgmental dickhead?"

"It's better to stick with the dickhead you know, so I'm back with you."

"I should be offended by that."

"And yet…you're not." Sierra sipped her beer and a foam mustache clung to her upper lip.

Jesus. I wanted to swipe my tongue over it. Lick and suck and taste her mouth for hours. When our eyes met again I swear to fucking god she was testing my control by just leaving it like that.

"What?" she asked innocently.

"So this Lex guy is a dickhead?"

"No. He's a friend of Hayden's I've been trying to hook—"

"I do not want to hear about your hookups, Sierra," I snarled.

She laughed. And kept laughing.

I leaned in and squinted at her. "Are you high?"

"What? I'd have to be high to find something you say funny? Piss off. Getting high is for squares."

"You are such a dork, McKay. Who even says *squares* anymore?"

"My dad. His vernacular is da bomb. He's totally on fleek."

I laughed. I wanted to grab her and get right in her face and tell her how goddamned much I missed this. This part had always been so easy with her. Didn't she remember?

"Anyway, growly caveman, if you would've let me finish instead of cutting me off, I could've told you that Lex has applied for an internship at DDG next semester. I've been trying to set up a meeting between him and Marty in personnel for two weeks. *Hookup* was a bad word choice." Sierra took another drink and licked her lips. "Not that it matters. Given the intense way you were texting, I figured you were making hookup plans of your own anyway."

So she wouldn't come right out and ask who I'd been texting, but she clearly wanted to know. "Sierra. I'm not interested in just a hookup while I'm in Phoenix."

The way her gorgeous eyes widened and then went soft…please let that mean she read between the lines since I was still feeling my way around this thing with her.

Still lying about it you mean.

"I was texting my sister, Oakley."

"Oh. How old is she now?"

"Sixteen." I clicked on the photos icon and scrolled until I found the one I'd taken last month. I held the phone out to her. "During my stint in Wyoming I drove up to Bozeman. I almost didn't recognize her, it'd been so long since I'd seen her in person."

"She's really pretty. She looks nothing like you." Sierra's startled gaze met mine. "That came out wrong. I meant—"

"I know what you meant." I pocketed my phone after she handed it over.

"What's your brother doing? Crockett, right?"

Speaking of high…our mother had to be smoking a big bowl when she picked our names. "He goes by Rock. He's fifteen. Plans on joining the marines. For Rock I suspect it's boot camp or jail."

Sierra shifted her stance. "Was boot camp as horrible as the movies and TV make it out to be?"

"The physical challenges weren't as bad as the written tests. I sweated bullets about my instructors finding out I'm dyslexic, since there's no special dispensation for soldiers with a handicap. I either had to keep up or they'd discharge me. It's another 'don't ask, don't tell' policy." Until they wanted to exploit you as a success story—even when they had nothing to do with your success. My only option was to spend a shit ton of money on tutors.

She blinked at me. "Whoa. Back up. I didn't know you were dyslexic. You told me you had learning issues but I thought that was when you were younger."

"The dyslexia was undiagnosed until I started high school, so that's why it took me so much longer to catch on to reading and learning when I was a kid."

"We spent weeks going over the boxes of family paperwork for my school project. Why didn't you tell me?"

I rubbed the back of my neck. "Gee, Sierra, I don't know why I didn't want to share *another* embarrassing thing about myself."

She got in my face. "I wouldn't have cared. And I wouldn't have blabbed to anyone either. It sucks that you didn't trust me. But then again, you didn't need my empathy weighing you down, did you?"

We stared at each other.

Then Sierra realized we were chest to chest and retreated.

I snagged her hand before she could get too far. "Can we just keep talking like this?"

Her eyes searched mine. "Why do you keep hinting that there's some big thing we need to talk about?"

Here was my chance. My heart rate jumped two dozen points and my hand turned clammy. Before I opened my mouth, I heard footsteps on the rocks behind us.

"Nurse West, you got a sec?" Kyler asked as he approached us.

Never failed. "What's up?"

"Some drunk chick started to fall out of her chair on the patio and Hayden tried to catch her. He ended up twisting his ankle and smacked his face into the concrete. He refuses to go to the hospital. Can you take a look at him?"

"Typical stubborn McKay," I muttered. "Where is he?"

"Upstairs." Ky threw a look over his shoulder. "Tug has already started kicking everyone out."

As soon as I started toward the patio door, Sierra fell into step beside me.

"How often are you asked to administer first aid at a party?"

"Damn near every one of them I'm at."

"I'm surprised you still go to them."

"And miss the chance to stitch up drunk guys after a fist fight or have a random chick barf on my shoes?" I said dryly. "Woman, that's what I live for."

She snickered.

"You're out of college, McKay. Why do you keep partying with the underclassman?"

"I graduated early so I still know people in school. So far this year I've just been to parties here. It's weird. Maybe I have outgrown them."

People still milled around in the house. As I started up the turn in the stairs, I saw we had rubber-neckers trailing behind us.

I found Hayden stretched out on the floor in the hallway in front of his room with a bag of frozen tater tots pressed to his face. "So chivalry ain't dead after all, huh?"

"Fuck off."

"I'll take a look at your face first." I stepped over Hayden and lowered to my knees to get closer. "Where'd you hit?"

"The ground."

"No, what part of your face hit?"

Hayden lifted the bag of frozen potatoes.

I hissed in a breath. An angry-looking cement burn scraped his cheek but hadn't started weeping fluid yet. A bruise had already welled up on his cheekbone beneath the scrape. I didn't see that any part of his face had been split open, so there wasn't any blood. "Does your head hurt?"

"Sudden, massive headache."

"Over-the-counter pain meds will help. You can take eight hundred milligrams of Tylenol or Advil every six hours. Keep icing it. But if the swelling increases? Go to a clinic."

"Fine."

I slid over and picked up his foot. "Let me know if it hurts when I start poking around."

"You just want to see if I scream like a girl," he retorted.

"Dude. I already know that you scream like a girl."

His lips twitched. "Asshole."

I slipped my hand beneath his calf. The area around his ankle was swollen. "Did you hop or hobble into the house?"

"Hopped up the stairs, tried to hobble down the hallway and when that hurt, I crawled."

"Did you feel anything pop?"

"No."

"When you put weight on it, did you feel anything grinding?"

"No."

"Ooh, are you a doctor?"

I glanced up to see a brunette with an enormous rack dropping to her knees across from me.

"No, I'm not," Hayden drawled, "but if you wanna play doctor, hot stuff, I'm game."

"Not you," she said, wrinkling her pert nose. "Him." She batted her eyelashes at me. "I just love doctors."

I'll bet you do.

"And you're hot. Like really hot. And young too," she said in whispered wonder, leaning over Hayden's head.

"You'll have to move back," I said to her. "You're blocking the light."

"No problem, Doctor."

Curling my fingers over Hayden's toes, I gently pushed until his foot was at a right angle. "Any pain with that movement?"

"Some. Not bad though."

When I pushed the foot up more, Hayden hissed in a breath. Same reaction when I shifted his foot side to side.

"What's wrong with him?" Perky Tits asked. "Does he need an operation?"

"He just needs to rest and let the swelling go down."

"Maybe your helpful assistant oughta check the swelling in my groin," Hayden suggested.

Jesus, Hayden, really?

Perky Tits looked confused.

"What's the diagnosis?" Hayden demanded.

"It's sprained. Elevate it and ice it fifteen minutes every hour is about all you can do. If the swelling isn't down by Monday, go in for X-rays to make sure it's nothing more serious."

I stood and so did the brunette. I saw Sierra leaning against the wall, her lips curled into a smirk.

"Is there anything I can help you with, Doctor? Like shouldn't we be in bed?"

"We?"

"Oops." She giggled. "I meant *he*. Shouldn't we get him in bed?"

"He crawled this far, he can crawl the rest of the way."

"Oh. Okay." Then she beamed a smile at me. "Where's your office? I'm between doctors right now."

No, you'd like to be underneath a doctor right now. "Look, I'm not a doctor. I'm a nurse."

Another confused look. Then she tittered. "Oh, you are a funny one."

"What's funny about that?"

"Everyone knows that men can't be nurses. That's a woman's job."

Be a waste of breath to try and set this bimbo straight, but I'd try. "I am a nurse. An army nurse, actually."

Her lips formed a pout. "If you weren't taking new patients, you could've just said so," she said with a girlish pout.

Sierra sidled up to her. "Okay, Donna Reed. The 1950s are calling. Why don't you toddle on back there?"

Perky Tits spun around to face her. "My name is not Donna." She stomped off in a huff.

"Dammit, Boone. Why didn't you tell her the best way to help you would be to take care of me? Letting me rest my weary, injured face in the soft pillows of her chest?" Hayden said with a whine.

"For shame, Hayden McKay," Sierra said on a mock gasp of outrage. "You'd take advantage of her giving nature?"

"I would've given her back plenty, trust me. Now I'll be dreaming about those tits, crying in my pillow that they're forever lost to me."

"Poor baby."

Hayden crawled the last ten feet to his room.

The hallway had cleared out, leaving Sierra on one side and me on the other.

"You had quite the little fan group there, *Doctor.*"

I scowled. "You mean Perky Tits?"

"I mean the half a dozen other women hovering while you examined numb nuts."

"I didn't notice."

"Don't bullshit me, West. You didn't feel the lovesick looks they shot your way?"

I locked my gaze to hers. "No. I didn't notice. Know why?" I started toward her, prepared to tackle her ass to the carpet if she attempted to run. "When I'm around you, Sierra, you're the only woman I see. And before you toss out a smartass retort, I want you to really think about what I just said. Because you know damn well it's true. How many hot little coeds were flitting around here tonight?"

"I don't know."

"Neither do I." I paused to let that sink in. "I didn't come here for them. I came here for you."

Her breathing had gone choppy. Her face and neck were flushed.

I pressed closer. "How long you plan on playing this game of cat and mouse with me?"

"That's what you don't understand; this isn't a game to me. You blow into my life and act like you have every right to be here."

"I do have every right."

"Wrong. You don't know me anymore. Not like you think you do."

"I am trying like hell to change that. You shut me down at every turn. Every. Turn." The way I'd gritted that out sounded as if I'd swallowed gravel.

But my gruff tone put fire back in her eyes. She slapped her hands on my chest hard enough I felt the sting as if I was shirtless.

"*Every* turn? Really? We've seen each other *three* times. That's it. Just two days ago you swore that you came to see me in a professional capacity. So you don't get to act all growly and frustrated with me, fucker, because I haven't thrown myself at you."

"Is everything all right?" Ky asked from the middle of the hallway.

"It's fine, we're fine," Sierra answered. "We're discussing what came first, the chicken or the egg. It's always been a hotly contested debate between us."

Her unique way of deflecting things hadn't changed—totally smartass. Still made me smile.

"So what's the definitive answer?" Ky asked.

I said "chicken" the same time Sierra said "egg."

"You two are so full of shit," Ky said.

"Some of us more than others," she retorted.

"Boone, before I kick you out, I forgot to ask if you need a ticket to the game tomorrow? I have an extra one."

"Wish I could go, but I'm working the day shift tomorrow and Sunday."

"Working," Sierra repeated with a frown. "Why are you working when you're on leave?"

Fuck. Me.

In my peripheral vision, I saw Kyler backing away, shaking his head at me, and Sierra saw it too.

"Answer the question, Boone."

"Because I'm not on leave anymore."

"Then why did you tell me you were?"

"Tuesday when I saw you I *was* on leave. Wednesday when I saw you I'd made some changes so I wasn't on leave."

"*You* can change your military duty status just like that?" she snapped. "Bull."

"It's complicated."

Her eyes turned hard. "Are you even in the army?"

"Yes, I'm in the army."

"Where do you live?"

"I'm based out of Fort Hood. But as of this week I'll be living in Phoenix." I took a step toward her. "This is what I wanted to talk to you about."

"Because it's some big secret?" Realization dawned on her face. "Did everyone know about this but me?"

Jesus. This was spiraling. "No, just Kyler."

"So, you managed to tell *him* the truth, but you fucking *lied* to me?"

"Look, it's not what you think—"

"I think nothing changes with you." Her bitter laugh sliced through me. "You manipulative bastard. The tour of Phoenix was to check out housing areas for you, wasn't it? Not for a *friend*."

"My army buddy Raj and I will be sharing a place, so technically..."

Don't offer excuses; offer her an apology. "Sierra, I'm sorry. I didn't want you to find out this way. I told you we needed to talk—"

"Omigod! You are *not* blaming this on *me*."

The hurt in her eyes was more than I could take. "I'm not blaming you. Let's go someplace private where we can hash this out."

"No. I can't do this with you, Boone. Not again." She started to back up. "I have to go."

"Now? In the middle of our goddamn conversation?"

"It's not a conversation. It's you trying to justify your dishonesty."

"You're right. I—"

Sierra silenced me with *talk to the hand* as she brushed past me and disappeared down the stairs.

I waited, half-hoping she'd storm back up after remembering something else she wanted to knock me down a peg for.

But I heard the distinctive sound of a door slamming hard enough to rattle the rafters.

Then I heard nothing but the silence of my own stupidity.

I slid down the wall until my butt hit the carpet. I rested my forearms on my knees, tempted to hang my head between my knees too.

From down the hallway, Anton yelled out, "Way to go, Romeo."

I held up my middle finger.

Hayden crawled out of his room and sat across from me. "Dude. You suck at this. You need some serious advice on how to deal with women."

Before I could tell him to fuck off, because Christ, he was *nineteen*, and I hated that he was right, Anton said, "No, he needs a damn reality check. Boone. Buddy. Why are you doin' dumb shit to screw this up with Sierra?"

"I'm not doing it on purpose."

"Really? So it was an *accident* that you lied to her about finding a place to live for your *friend*? An *accident* you lied to her about how long you'll be in Phoenix?" Hayden said skeptically.

My head fell against the wall. "When you put it that way..."

"There is no other way. You lied."

"Twice," Anton inserted helpfully. "What were you thinking?"

"Within five seconds of walking into her office the first day, I fucking knew that even if it took me two goddamned years to convince Sierra we're meant to be together, it'd be worth any lie in the short term for a chance at the long term with her."

Silence.

I glanced up.

Hayden pretended to knuckle away a tear.

Asshole.

"Why didn't you tell her that just now?" Kyler said.

"What was I supposed to do? Tackle her, sit on her and make her listen to me?" I snorted. "Right. Like you guys would've let that happen." I pointed at Hayden. "Dickhead there already warned me tonight that I'd better watch my step around the precious. And it's not like I don't already have another contract out with you psycho McKay motherfuckers for maintaining good behavior with her."

"Explain that, West."

I relayed my deal with Gavin, which in hindsight meant I provided them with a legit reason to make fun of me for the rest of my fucking life *and* to beat the fuck out of me.

After they finished laughing, Kyler crossed his arms over his chest. "Now that this is in perspective for us... When she stomped off? That's when you should've taken her in hand and put it in perspective for *her*."

"*Taken her in hand*?" I repeated.

Kyler shrugged. "Taken her someplace private, explained what you needed to and dealt with her attitude."

"You've had experience with that?"

"A time or two." He smirked. "A woman like Sierra? She'll see how far she can push you. She expects you to push back."

"That's why you need to keep her guessing where that push back line is," Hayden added.

"If that doesn't work, buy her something," Anton suggested. "Just not a puppy."

"Or jewelry. That's like saying 'please wrap this necklace around my dick and assume you now own it,'" Hayden said with a shudder.

I looked from Hayden to Anton to Kyler. "You guys don't have a fucking clue about women, do you?"

Hayden cheerily said, "Nope."

Anton said, "Does anyone, really?"

"Awesome. Thanks for nothing."

"*Ah ah ah.* But we are gonna give you something," Hayden said.

"What?"

"Another chance with Sierra, cynical fucker," Anton said.

"Come over Sunday night after you get off work for food and football," Ky said. "Be ready to explain everything to her. Sierra gets mad fast, but she's not unreasonable."

"Except for some reason we cannot understand, she seems to like you," Anton said.

"Fuck off, McKay."

"That's the thanks we get for playing the love doctors between you two?" Hayden made obnoxious kissing noises.

I ignored him and stood. "Seriously, guys, I appreciate it. This thing between me and Sierra...it's important. See you Sunday."

8 Sierra

MY FAVORITE THING about fall wasn't the break from the brutal summer temperatures.

It was that fall meant football season.

I loved football—a love my dad passed down to me. Since he had custody of me on the weekends growing up, he'd usually tape the games so it wouldn't interfere in our limited time together. So when I became a cheerleader in high school and knew little about the gridiron, Dad insisted watching games would be the best way for me to learn. I fell in love with the sport. From that moment on, we plunked ourselves on the couch for college games on Saturday. Pro games on Sunday, Monday and Thursday nights. We were both Cardinals fans and over the years we've attended as many live games together as we could fit into our schedules. Sometimes we even talked on the phone during the games.

With tonight being Meat-topia and a family Sunday Night Football event, I'd spent the day watching other games in between bouts of baking. Since Lu wasn't around and I didn't need to gorge on cookies and cupcakes, I froze all the goodies to take to the PCE meeting Tuesday night.

Bull. You're hiding the evidence of your manic baking spree because Lu would know something was up with you.

So what? Putting all thoughts of Mr. Liar Liar out of my head had required lots of egg cracking, butter whipping and dough punching.

I rang the doorbell to my cousins' house with my elbow since my hands were full.

Ky opened the door and grabbed the top two containers. "Sorry. I would've helped you carry this from the car."

"I thought I had it under control." Story of my life. I followed Ky into the kitchen.

After I set the containers on the counter Ky hugged me. "Thanks for coming over." Then he scowled at my Cardinals T-shirt. "Good thing I know your taste in brownies is better than in football teams."

"Hilarious." I eyed his Broncos jersey. "We could cut up your shirt and use it for extra napkins if we run out," I suggested sweetly. "Or better yet, toilet paper."

"Ooh, I felt the burn of that one all the way over here, Kyler," Hayden said from the stool at the end of the counter. He held out his arms, expecting his hug. "Gimme some sugar and no lip about my wearing of the orange."

That's one of the things I loved about my family; the open affection. I noticed Hayden had his leg propped up. "How's the ankle?"

"The swelling is down, but it's still sore."

"You probably shouldn't have gone to the game yesterday. We were on our feet for the entire thing," I pointed out.

Hayden grinned. "It was worth it to see Ky kicking ass."

"True dat." ASU had lost the game after the defense had fucked up, but Ky had great stats. I lowered my voice. "QB is okay today?"

"I'm fine," Kyler said. "It sucked to lose but that means we're more focused on preparing for this week's game against OSU."

I scanned the dining and living room. "Where's Anton?"

"Out manning the grill, obsessing about the smoke to sweetness ratio of his ribs," Hayden said.

"Just as long as he doesn't obsess to the point we don't get to eat the damn ribs. I am starving." Mase lumbered in. At least *he* was wearing a Cardinals jersey. At six foot five, with shoulders as wide as the doorframe, his big body threw a shadow across the kitchen counter. He had shaggy reddish-brown hair and a baby face—a face that sported a black eye and a swollen lip from last night's hockey game. According to my cousins, Mase's baby face disappeared the second he laced up his hockey skates. I didn't see that side of him, just the shy guy who let his housemates do most of the talking.

"Thanks for letting me hang out, Mase. This is the second time this weekend."

"Love having you here, Nevada. And is that what I think it is?" He leaned over the foil-covered glass baking dish.

"Yep. I figured you all burned extra calories so you deserved a treat."

"You are the best woman on the planet," Hayden declared. "Why can't I find someone like you?"

"Because you're not looking?"

"Got me there."

"He's auditioning," Ky said with a snort. "Very few of them get a call back."

"Damn straight." Mase and Hayden bumped fists.

I glanced out the patio and saw Anton headed in with a huge foil-covered pan. I rushed to open the door.

"Thanks, darlin'. Happy to see your pretty face, because you always add class to our meals."

Cowboy to the core. Charmer to the core. Deadly combination for a lot of women. For me, it was just fun to sit back and watch these boys come into their own as men.

"Knock knock," sounded from the foyer.

Speaking of men…of course Boone was here.

You'd better get used to seeing him at family events since he's, oh…fucking living in Phoenix now.

No matter. I was an adult. I'd deal. I'd just ignore him.

But somehow I started humming pretty loudly as I aligned the dishes buffet style. In addition to the potato salad and cornbread muffins I'd brought, someone had cracked open a can of baked beans.

Anton pulled back the tin foil to reveal the biggest pile of ribs I'd seen outside the Crook County Fair cook-off. Next to the ribs were ears of corn.

"That looks like heaven," Mase said on a reverent whisper.

"It is. Dig in while it's hot. The game starts in thirty."

Bottles rattled and I glanced over to see Boone setting a case of O'Doul's on the counter. He stepped back and I noticed he was wearing scrubs. Scrubs were not sexy.

But scrubs were sexy as sin on Boone West, RN.

The jerk.

He offered me a tentative smile and said, "Hey, McKay."

Immediately three other people said, "What?"

"Now I see the need for nicknames," Boone said. He handed a bottle to Hayden.

Mase snagged an O'Doul's. "You've gotta have beer with ribs. Got to. And this stuff ain't half bad."

I grabbed a bottle. I twisted the top off and took a big drink. I said, "You weren't *lying* about this near-beer being good," to Mase while I looked directly at Boone.

His jaw tightened. Then he leaned in and said, "Did I hear you humming 'Lyin' Eyes' right after I walked in?"

"Yes. I love the Eagles."

"Bull. You always hated it when I played Eagles tunes."

"But the song fits, doesn't it?" I said sweetly. "Are you a Miranda Lambert fan?"

His eyes narrowed. "Gonna bust out into a chorus of 'White Liar' next?"

"Probably. And I'll follow it up with 'Would I Lie to You' by Eurythmics. I considered tossing in 'Little Lies' by Fleetwood Mac, but Motorhead's 'Don't Lie to Me' is in line with my angry mood about the whole situation."

"Christ. I'm sorry, okay?"

"Heartfelt apology there, scooter." I poked him in the chest. "Not okay. Not even fucking *close* to okay."

He struggled to respond.

I let him.

Finally he said, "Please give me an opportunity to offer you a sincere apology and a chance to explain everything after we eat."

Say no and walk away.

"Why should I care?"

"Because you've wanted to see me grovel for a long damn time."

"Not. Good. Enough."

"Since you like tossing song titles at me. Here's one that fits—"

"'She Hates Me' by Puddle of Mudd," I snapped. "Good call on that one."

"Wrong." Then Boone invaded my space, the expression in his

dark eyes was somewhere between haunted and frustrated. "Let me finish. Every time I've heard 'I Won't Give Up' by Jason Mraz I've thought of you. Of us. Every time, Sierra. Tell me you didn't think of us when you heard it."

I didn't retort or back away. My stomach pitched. My chest felt tight, as if I couldn't get any air. Music has always played a big part in my life. It played a big part in my friendship with Boone because our musical tastes were so diverse. But the fact he'd mentioned *that* song? The one tune guaranteed to make me think of him and what could've been? That spoke to me on a level no amount of groveling or "I'm sorry" ever could have. Maybe it was against my better judgment, but I found my anger toward him softening somewhat. I could be civil long enough to hear his apology.

"You have *one* shot at offering me a fucking stellar and believable request for my forgiveness, West."

He didn't offer a cocky smile. He just quietly said, "Thank you."

I turned back toward the food and saw our cousins pretending that they hadn't been watching us whisper fight.

Mase piled his food on a platter; evidently a regular-sized plate wasn't big enough. "Seriously dude, these ribs are fucking awesome. I'm so glad you guys moved in." He paused and looked at Anton. "Not to seem ungrateful for this spread, but what are we having next month?"

Anton wiped his hands on a towel. "Brisket and sausage."

Mase actually whimpered.

Boone cocked an eyebrow at Kyler.

"Anton is the meat master and Mase is a self-professed 'meat-atarian' after his mom turned vegan his last year of high school. Once a month we have Meat-topia. The rule initially was no chicks, because we'd never get laid again if they saw us eat like this."

"But then Nevada showed up with brownies, so she's totally in."

I raised my bottle to Mase.

"Ky, can I borrow some clothes? I don't need barbecue sauce on my scrubs."

"There's a basket of my stuff on top of the dryer. Pick anything but the Broncos jerseys."

"No self-respecting Cowboys fan would be caught dead wearing one anyway," Boone shot back.

"At least you're consistent," I said to Boone.

"Meaning what?" he said warily.

I smirked. "Your taste in football teams is as crappy as your taste in music."

His gaze lingered a bit too long on the Cardinals team logo stretched across my chest before his eyes met mine. "Back atcha, babe."

Mase and Ky were sitting at the dining room table when I noticed Hayden hadn't moved. "Hey, sweetie. Would you like me to fix you a plate? And if you promise not to spill, maybe next time you can sit at the grownups table with the rest of us."

Ky and Mase laughed. Anton said something about a sippy cup.

"Piss off, all of you."

"Seriously, hop-along; what do you want?"

"Some of all of it."

After I loaded his plate, I took it into the dining room.

Back in the kitchen, I stood next to Boone watching him play Jenga with a pile of ribs. He looked over his shoulder at me. "Promise you won't watch me eat, McKay."

"I've seen you eat."

"Not like this you haven't."

Just like that, I was thrown back to the times I'd ended up cooking for him, when I'd figured out he'd probably never had enough to eat. His appetite had gone beyond typical teenage boy eat-everything-in-sight hunger to real hunger. "This ain't my first Meat-topia, soldier boy. See if you can keep up."

Boone bypassed my potato salad, so I said, "Hold on," and spooned some on his plate.

"What is this?"

"German potato salad. Try it."

He squinted at the pile. "Isn't potato salad supposed to be...yellow? And have...potatoes in it?"

"Not all potato salad is yellow. It looks a little brown because I didn't have red onions or Yukon gold potatoes, but it tastes awesome."

"What else is in it?" he said suspiciously, like I'd attempted to sneak in zucchini.

"Bacon, caramelized onion, mint and sauerkraut."

"You always did mix some weird shit together but it ended up tasting good." Boone came to a full stop when he saw the pan of brownies. "What is that?"

"My all-access pass to Meat-topia. Salted caramel brownies baked on top of chocolate chip cookie bars and finished with marshmallows, coconut, M&Ms, mini peanut butter cups and raspberry buttercream frosting."

"Hearing that description, my blood sugar just shot up fifty points."

"You have to try the brownies," Mase said. "You've never tasted anything so good."

Boone's gaze hooked mine. "You want me to taste your goodies, Sierra? Lick up some of that cream like a man starved for such sweetness?"

Heat shot down my center straight between my legs.

A devilish smile curled his lips.

Anton had outdone himself with the ribs. The guys were stuffed to the point I thought I might have to roll them into the den for the football game. They rallied long enough to help tidy the kitchen and direct me on where to put the tiny amount of leftovers.

Kyler grabbed the dishrag out of my hand. "I didn't invite you over to eat with us and expect you to do the dishes as payment."

"I know that. I just ate too much and if I sit in front of the TV I'll fall into a food coma. So you go watch the game and I'll be in when I'm done out here."

"You sure? You've been looking forward to this game all week."

I hip-checked him. "Oh, I'll be in to put you Denver Donkey lovers in your places when the jeers about the Cards stomping them gets too annoying."

"You wish." He held out his hand. "Standard bet, no points spared?"

"None needed," I said and shook it.

"I'll put twenty on the Cardinals," Boone said from behind me.

"Sweet. Easy money. You coming in to watch the game?" Ky asked him.

"I'll help Sierra finish the dishes." After Kyler left, Boone said,

"Wash or dry?"

"I'll wash."

"They do have a dishwasher."

"Which is already full of dirty dishes." I paused to stack the plates. "I checked."

Boone waited until I was elbow-deep in soapy water before he said, "I am sorry. I should've been honest with you about how long I'll be in Phoenix. I should've told you I needed a place to live. Totally fucking stupid on my part to skate around all that stuff."

I waited for him to tack on a "but"...but he didn't. I set a soapy plate in the empty side of the sink and said, "Why did you lie?"

He rinsed it. Dried it. "Fear, maybe? I don't fucking know."

I reached for the next plate.

"Maybe I worried you'd think I was a creeper if I said, 'Guess what? I'm part of a pilot program between the armed forces and the Veterans Administrations medical personnel. I'll be living in Phoenix and attending school here the next two years. Is housing available in your neighborhood?'" His laugh resembled a groan. "Which could actually be considered a death wish since your dad warned me against stalking you."

I whipped my head toward him. "You talked to my dad? When?"

He draped the dishtowel around his neck and rested his butt against the counter. "You refused to see me when you were sick. Then after he happily informed me that you'd gone back to Phoenix, I...was a little pissed you'd left. So I demanded he hand over your address and phone number, and well, you can imagine how *that* went over."

"What did he do?"

Boone's cheeks turned pink. He brought his clasped hands on top of his head like a suspect under arrest. That movement caused his T-shirt to ride up.

My gaze zoomed to the hard ridges of his abdomen and a tease of dark hair that disappeared into his waistband. His silence had me peering over at him, half-afraid he'd seen me checking out the map to his treasure trail.

But his eyes were closed. "He gave me the address to your office and told me what floor you worked on."

"I can't believe my dad just handed it over."

Boone looked at me. "Not until he passed on three articles of what constitutes stalking behavior. And not until I..." He emitted an embarrassed laugh. "Not until I told him I'd let all the bad-tempered McKays beat my ass in public if I ever did anything to hurt you."

"What?"

"Yeah, that was my brilliant idea to prove my sincerity or whatever. I just didn't expect him to take me up on it and actually make me sign a fucking contract."

I had to have misheard him. "You signed a contract. With my dad. Allowing my family to beat you up...?"

"If I ever harmed a hair on your beautiful head."

"Boone. Why would you do that?"

Then those soulful brown eyes were close enough I could discern flecks of gold. "Because I want a chance to get to know you and for you to get to know me, so we can see where this goes."

"And if it doesn't go anywhere?"

His expression said he didn't buy that at all.

Neither do you.

Boone touched my face, so sweetly, so tenderly I couldn't breathe. "Please. Think about it."

After what he'd told me? About how he'd talked to my dad *before* all this happened? How could I not? I managed to choke out, "I will."

Relief passed over his face. "Thank you."

"You're really here, in Phoenix, for two years?"

"Yeah. I'm working at the VA and I'll be taking classes. Some of the details are still vague—and that's not *me* being vague, that's just how the government works. So, see? I have no idea why I wouldn't just tell you that." He tugged at the strands of hair that stuck to the corner of my mouth and tucked the hair behind my ear. "Does knowing I'll be here longer than two weeks change anything?"

I managed to keep from blurting out "Yes!" and said, "We'll see."

He continued to caress my cheek as he locked his eyes to mine. "I've had your face in my head for so long...imagining what I'd say if I had the chance. And now that I'm right here in front of you, I can't come up with anything more original than you're just so damn beautiful, Sierra."

"It's safest to stick with a classic."

He laughed. "I am happy to see that smart mouth hasn't gone all PC."

"Oh, it has. But that's a business thing. When I'm not in a suit and heels representing DPM? All filters are off, baby."

Boone was close enough I felt the press of his lower body into mine. Close enough I saw the rapid pulse in his throat. Close enough if I stood on my tiptoes, I could taste those full lips. Close enough if he lowered his head just a little, he could taste mine.

Step back! Step back, step back, step back. You are supposed to be thinking about this. Not tossing caution aside because he paid you a compliment. Step back and retain some dignity.

I cleared my throat. "Boone?"

"Yeah?"

"Can you dial it down some?"

He frowned. "What?"

"Lower the wattage of the intensity that is Boone West."

He took a big step back. And another. Then he turned away to rest his hands on the top of his head again. He blew out a breath. Now his T-shirt rode up in the back, giving me a peek at the curve of his spine above his hips. Nice. *Very* fucking nice.

Stop ogling him.

When he turned around I had to pretend I hadn't been checking out his ass. And damn near drooling at seeing his T-shirt pulled against the muscles in his back. How had he achieved such ropy forearms? That was some serious sexy right there.

"Let's finish the dishes."

It didn't take us long. We didn't fill the air with chatter but it wasn't uncomfortable either. More contemplative.

The guys whooped and hollered in the den and Boone and I looked at each other.

"I'm too damn restless to sit still."

"Me too."

"Come on, I have an idea." He clasped my hand in his and we exited the patio door and entered the garage. He flipped on the lights and headed toward the rack of sports equipment.

"What are you doing?"

"There's a basketball hoop out back. Let's shoot baskets."

"I love doing that almost as much as I love Greg's junior assistant calling me during lunch."

He stopped in front of me. "When was the last time you played?"

"Like fifth grade. Why?"

"Bet you thought boys were gross in fifth grade. Bet you thought you'd never kiss a boy and never ever ever kiss with tongues."

"And your point is?"

Boone grinned at me. "Everything changes. If you haven't actually tried messing around with a basketball, how do you know you won't love it?"

I narrowed my eyes at him. Did he intend for that to have a double meaning?

"Try it. If it sucks we'll stop. Then you can watch me draining three pointers and dunking in an effort to impress you."

"I don't have the right shoes."

He glanced at my flip-flops and shrugged. "We're not playing one-on-one. It's stand and shoot. You'll be fine."

"Boone, I don't—"

He loomed over me. "Work with me here. There has to be something that'd get you out on that court."

My hormones launched a mutiny and seized control of my mouth. "You could take off your shirt."

He blinked at me in utter surprise. Then he said, "Done. Let's go."

On the court, he grabbed the edges of his shirt and slowly lifted up, exposing his flat abdomen, then that fan-fucking-tastic chest. As he faced me, he granted me a look that ignited a slow curl of heat in my chest and the flames licked lower...and lower.

"Sierra." He drew my name out in a honey-coated rasp. "Dial it back."

Shit. I closed my eyes. I shouldn't have asked him to take off his shirt.

Gee. Do you think?

"Pay attention to how I'm shooting."

"Fine. Whatever."

Thud thud thud echoed off the cement as Boone dribbled. Then he pivoted and launched the ball at the hoop.

Swish. He made it.

Afterward, he sauntered over to me. "Your turn. Do exactly what I did."

"Including the weird pivot?"

"Including that."

I didn't dribble the ball. I carried it to the place where he'd stood.

"Gotta dribble."

Mine was a double dribble for sure. Then I pivoted and threw the ball over my head at the basket.

It hit the side of the house.

Boone raised both eyebrows. "Interesting technique."

"Thank you. Where'd you learn yours?" He didn't play sports in high school. But that didn't mean he didn't have the skills to play. Working two jobs had left him little time for normal teenage pursuits.

"Army. Ends up being a bunch of downtime and there's always a basketball court. The black guys loved showing us up. Except…they didn't all of the time." He pointed at me. "You missed so you have an H. My turn."

"I think those rules suck."

"What do you suggest?"

"Uh, that we don't play basketball?"

He laughed. "Nice try." He hustled to center court. "Watch closely."

How could I not? He had his damn shirt off. I could spend all day drooling over his chest. All day, and night, and part of the next day.

Dribble, dribble, dribble. Jump.

Swish.

Dammit.

I stormed to the middle. "Gimme the ball."

"Hey, not so fast." He dropped the ball between his feet, then he crouched down. "This is supposed to be fun. We used to have fun together, remember?"

"Because that wasn't organized fun."

"Really. The McKay/West project we worked on for three fucking months wasn't…organized?"

I couldn't help but smile at him. Then I poked him in the chest. "Stop ruining my example with logic."

"Do you really want to quit playing?"

"What else would we do?"

His gaze slid over me. "I have a suggestion, but I guarantee it'll peg the intensity meter."

"I might choose that over this."

"Jesus. Don't get my hopes up, McKay." He moved to stand behind me. "Maybe you just need a few pointers."

Then his arms came around me, but he held the ball out in front of me. "Watch my hand position. Up and out."

"Always? For the best result?"

"I don't get what you mean."

"Variables. Isn't that a thing?"

"You mean, like a field condition?"

God. Stop with that sexy rasp in my ear.

"How about we just concentrate on you making this one shot?"

My breathing turned choppy. He had to feel the increased movement of my chest rising and falling with the way my back was pressed against him.

"Power comes from here." He squeezed my arms with his. "Tighten your core, that'll keep you stable."

Stable. I was starting to come unhinged. And the core part of me that tightened wasn't my damn abs.

"Hold the ball. Dribble a couple of times and then shoot."

Boone stepped back and I almost crumpled into a pile. The man was such a powerful force. Once again the universe proved the joke was on me. I'd asked him to tone down the intensity. But this playful, helpful, goddamn sweet side? A hundred times worse. As I stood there, clutching a ball, I understood that I had no defense against this man. None. A good offense wasn't even a good defense.

"Concentrate, Sierra. You can do this," he said in a "yay team!" pep rally kind of voice that I never in a million years imagined I'd hear from Brooding Boone West.

That was the last straw.

I whirled around and whipped the ball at him. "Who are you?"

When he peered over his shoulder with a smirk, all cute-like, I wanted to punch him. Seriously. How was I supposed to resist this?

You can't. More to the point: You don't want to.

"What is going on with you?" he demanded.

"I don't know!"

"Well, who am I supposed to ask?"

I might've snarled at him before I stomped into the yard where it was dark and I couldn't see his chest dripping with sweat, or hear that rough voice in my ear, or feel his hard body pressed behind mine or wonder why I was even fighting this.

He shuffled across the grass and stopped behind me, so close his exhalations drifted across my hair. He said one word. "Talk."

"I don't know what—"

"Look at *me*, Sierra. Talk to *me*. Not into the damn air."

I faced him. "Fine. I want to talk about new rules."

"New rules. When did we have old rules?"

"Before. Unspoken ones."

Boone studied me. "What the fuck are unspoken rules?"

"You know. Before. When we were friends. We hung out. We ripped on each other's choice of music. We argued about TV shows. We heckled each other's favorite movies from the 80s—"

"Again with all the negativity, McKay," he said with annoyance. "We had some of the same favorite movies like *Top Gun*, *The Princess Bride* and *The Terminator*. But I'll never understand what you saw in *Dirty Dancing* because that one is just plain stupid."

"You want to talk stupid? How about *Blade Runner*?" I shot back. "This is what I'm talking about! You complained when it was my turn to pick a movie and I acted like you were a grumpy pain in the ass. You pretended not to notice that I had a massive crush on you." I took a breath. "Those rules."

"Those weren't rules," he scoffed. "But whatever. New rule." He bestowed that dangerously devilish grin. "No rules."

I put my hand on his chest to push him back. "Stop being cute!"

Just like that, he did.

Boone flattened his palm over my hand on his chest. He dropped his other hand to my hip, spreading his fingers out and squeezing my flesh; the erotic intimacy nearly liquefied my bones. Then he upped the ante and pressed his warm, firm lips to the base of my jaw. "Truth between us, Sierra. I'm not the cute couple guy. I'll always be intense. Especially when it comes to this. Especially when it comes to *you*. I've wanted you for too fucking long to pretend it'll be anything less between us."

I slid my hand across his chest to feel the increased pounding of his heart and felt my pulse race in response. "It's always been like this. I didn't imagine it, did I?"

"No, baby. You didn't."

The interruption from Kyler calling out our names was probably for the best.

Boone stepped back. He brought my palm to his mouth for a soft kiss. "We'll pick this up later."

Later tonight? Later this week? When?

By the smirk on his face, he knew exactly how much he'd flustered me.

Not with the admission of the need between us, but that he hadn't indicated a time when we'd have another chance to act on it.

9 Boone

KY HAD DONE me a solid, interrupting at that moment.

I didn't have much willpower when it came to Sierra, probably because I'd had titanium-coated resolve during our friendship before and things were different now.

Very different. *She's the one who's holding back, not me.*

I sent her a sideways glance. She'd wrapped her arms around herself as if she was cold. Thankfully I'd slipped my shirt back on before I'd followed her across the yard, or this might look more like an interrupted hookup.

"What have you two been doing?" Kyler demanded. "It's almost halftime and you haven't watched any of the game."

"Gimme a break. I was cooped up inside all day. We've been out here shooting hoops." I pointed to the basketball by the goalpost. "Why?"

"I saw the basketball. I just didn't know where you guys had disappeared to."

"Sierra thought she saw a kitten run across the yard and we went to check it out."

She snorted beside me.

"Are you coming in to watch the second half?"

"Who's ahead?"

"Denver. Seven to zip."

I looked at Sierra. "You sticking around?"

"I think I'll head home to call my dad so he and I can commiserate about the game in real time. See what my roommate has going on this week." She raised an eyebrow at Ky. "Want me to leave the food?"

"You have to ask?"

"I will have to take a brownie to Lu."

"I hope Mase didn't eat them all," Ky grumbled.

Back in the kitchen, Sierra said to me, "No bullshit about your housing situation. Do you need me to refer you to a Realtor?" as she sliced two brownies.

"You ditching me as a client, McKay?"

"You weren't ever my client, West."

She had that same piece of hair stuck to her mouth. I loosened it and tucked it behind her ear. "If you'd pass along a name, that'd be great, but it's pretty much impossible for me to look at anything this week."

"Why?"

"I'm in training. Once they've worked with me a few times, they'll have a better idea where to utilize me. I do have some...limitations."

"Such as?"

"Such as, I choose not to be a charge nurse. There's more paper-work. I don't do med carts for the same reason. I'm great at the heavy lifting. I end up being the go-to guy for IVs since I've done so many. I'd rather be on the floor taking care of my patients than dealing with staffing issues so I'll skip the management track."

Sierra smiled at me and fuck if I didn't just eat it up.

"What?"

"I love to hear you say 'my patients.' It is obvious you love what you do, Boone. Any hospital is lucky to have you."

I felt my neck heat. "Thanks."

"Although, you did jam that needle in my ass a little harder than you needed to."

"Bull. You were feverish. Everything is more amplified, including pain."

"No." She tapped her chin as if deep in thought. "I clearly remember you offering to kiss it and make it better."

"Now I know you were delusional. I'd never even joke about that. It'd be highly unprofessional."

"Maybe you're right. Maybe that'd been wishful thinking on my part...me telling you to kiss my ass."

I hooked my arm around her neck and ruffled her hair until she squealed. Christ. When had I reverted to a twelve-year-old boy?

But she didn't look like she'd minded. In fact, she wore the cutest smile. One I'd seen a lot during our "friend" days.

I smoothed her hair back in place as an excuse to touch her. "In all seriousness, can we find some time to see each other?" I traced the edge of her jawline with the backs of my fingers. "Maybe toward the end of the week?"

"I liked our one-on-one time tonight." She wrinkled her nose. "Except for the actual basketball-playing part."

"So a sports date is out?"

"Sports date. Like we go to a sporting event?"

"No. Like we play racquetball or golf. Maybe go rock climbing or to a batting cage to hit baseballs."

"Boone. Those are *horrible* ideas for dates."

I laughed.

She grabbed the plate of brownies. "You have my number, West."

That was better than I'd hoped for. "See you around, McKay."

After she left I sliced off a chunk of brownie—a huge chunk, Mase could suck it since Sierra spoiled him with this all the damn time—and poured myself a glass of milk.

My thoughts wandered to Sierra's earlier comments about rules. Specifically the "unspoken" rules that had existed between us. Rules I'd set, but she'd abided by without question.

Total dick move.

Yet we'd ended up better friends for it. Sierra was the first girl I'd had a real friendship with. I'd loved every minute of how she'd been able to give me shit and take it without getting all weepy and girly. Or throwing herself at me.

I remembered too, the last day things had been easy like that between us; the week of prom. A prom that I hadn't asked her to, for a number of reasons, so I'd been avoiding her. But I'd seen her across the football field after school, her hair shining in the sun almost as brightly as her smile, that goddamn laugh of hers drifting to me on the spring breeze and once again, I couldn't resist the pull of her...

I WAITED, OH, three minutes after her good buddy Marin took off before I strolled over to where Sierra sat in the grass. My heart sped up like it did every time I saw her.

Sierra gave me a droll stare.

I flopped beside her, stretching out on my back and groaning, "Man, I'm so fucking whupped."

"No, *Hi, Sierra, how are you today?* No, *I've been ditching your calls because I pulled a muscle in my phone-dialing finger?* Just *I'm so fucking whupped?*"

"Touchy today, aren't we?" I filled both hands with grass and showered her with it.

"Hey! That's it. I'm leaving."

She looked so damn cute when she pretended to be mad at me.

Then Sierra started to stand, so I grabbed her around the waist, tackled her to the ground and rolled her in the grass, ignoring her yelps.

I kept my hand on her stomach, holding her in place, and I leaned over her. "Hey. If it isn't sexy Sierra McKay. You're looking damn fine today. Is that a new shirt? It does amazing things for your...eyes." I aimed a quick grin at her. "Did you do something different with your hair? The chocolate-colored tresses are so silky and shiny in this sunlight."

"You're a dickhead. And I'm still mad at you."

"No, you're not." *You're as crazy about me as I am about you and that sucks.*

"Yes, I am."

"Then how come you're still here?"

Sierra pointedly glared at my hand pressing into her stomach, my fingers spread out like a starfish so I could touch as much of her skin as possible. But the heat created some kind of suction with my palm and I felt her belly ripple from my touch. No freakin' way was I moving my hand now.

Those striking whiskey-colored eyes met mine.

I wanted to know what she was thinking as she gazed up at me. Did she see the same longing in my eyes that I saw in hers?

Then she looked at me with regret and forced herself to sit up, dislodging my hand. "You suck at returning text messages, West."

"I've been studying for finals and covering Alan's shift since he's on vacation. Or I've been working out."

"I can tell. You've got some beefy biceps going on."

I lifted my arms and flexed. "Check 'em out. Go on."

She bumped me with her shoulder. "No. It might compromise your virtue if people saw me feeling you up."

"Might be worth it." I let my gaze take in every nuance of her pretty face. I wanted so badly to trace the curve of her stubborn jaw. Once with my fingers. Once with my mouth. A breeze wafted over us, ruffling her hair, which still had green chunks twisted in it. "Sorry for throwing grass at you." I started to lean in and noticed Sierra's focus was on my throat. Could she see how being this close to her sent my pulse pounding? I plucked two pieces of grass out and let them spiral to the ground.

"Boone—"

"Relax," I said gruffly. "I'll get 'em out."

She remained motionless as I began at her scalp and worked my way down the silken strands of her hair. She had to know I was deliberately dragging this out. But I had this chance—it might be the last one to touch her casually—so I took it.

"Why didn't you return my texts?" she asked.

"I suck at texting. What did you need to talk to me about?"

Once again, Sierra's gaze roved over my face. She saw too much, the intensity in my eyes, the change in my breathing, my lips parted to release shallow breaths, the hard set to my jaw as I fought the urge to press my lips to that sexy, sassy mouth of hers.

When she continued studying me, I murmured, "Sierra?"

"Oh. Right. I wanted to see if you were coming to the branding next Saturday. You don't have to help with the actual work part, just come to the after-party."

"Why the invite? The McKays need a West whipping boy? Or are your dad, psycho uncles and cousins gonna castrate me?"

She turned her head and sank her teeth into my wrist. Hard.

"Jesus, McKay! Let go."

She slid her mouth free and licked her lips. "Yep. As salty as I expected."

"What'd you do that for?" And why had I liked that bite of pain? I imagined her dragging her lips across the red marks as she looked up at me with those big, questioning eyes.

"Because you're being a dick."

"Remind me not to really piss you off," I muttered.

"Too late. I'm already mad at you. Anyway, I'm filling in the blanks on the McKay/West feud for the entire McKay family. I wondered if you wanted to be there since you helped with the research."

I pulled a section of her hair from the corner of her mouth and tucked it behind her ear. "I can't. I'm working a twelve that day."

Disappointment flooded her face.

"But I heard there's a pre-graduation party at Phil Nickels' parents' cabin at the lake that night."

She said, "Are you going?"

"I wouldn't have told you about it if I wasn't."

"Cool. Then I'll show up. Think Angie, Kara and Tyler will be there?"

"I'll flatten that fucker Tyler if he comes anywhere near you." I didn't bother to hide the menace in my tone.

"So we'll have to pretend we're together again?"

God, I hope so. "Maybe."

"You have to be tired of that."

"Never." I needed to get things back on the friendship track so I lightly butted her forehead with mine. "I gotta finish my workout. See you around, McKay."

"DUDE. TELL ME you did *not* eat the last fuckin' brownie!"

I blinked at Mase and the memory disappeared. "No. There's a couple left. Brownie hoarder much?"

"So? I never get home-baked stuff. Ain't no one said I gotta share."

"He'd rather have a plate of homemade cookies than a blowjob," Hayden said, hobbling to the counter.

Mase nodded. "True dat. Any chick can learn to give a great blow-job, but learning to make killer desserts is a fucking art form."

Kyler followed Anton into the kitchen. He smirked at me. "Sierra looked a little mussed up when she walked by. Were you making time in the kitchen? Or did you go back outside and get distracted looking for that poor lost pussy?"

"Jesus, Kyler."

He laughed. "Don't even fucking start with me, West. I owe you."

"But when you two do finally find the balls to get balling, don't do it here, okay?" Hayden said. "I don't need to hear you doing my cousin, cuz."

"I find this whole cousin stuff...disconcerting," Mase said.

"Wow, Mase, big word," Anton said, clicking away on his phone. "I'm proud."

"Gotta keep up with you college guys. But you hafta admit it *is* weird. Sierra is your cousin"—he pointed to Kyler, Anton and Hayden—"but she's not yours." He pointed to me. "And yet they're all *your* cousins, but she isn't."

I shrugged. "No different than you being cousin to Ky and no one else."

Hayden leaned forward and slapped Mase on the arm. "You totally dropped the puck. You aren't related to Sierra, so you could've made a play for her and her tasty baked goods."

"Sierra is smokin' hot, don't get me wrong; she's too bossy for me. I want a sweet, docile woman who bakes like Betty fuckin' Crocker and looks like Selena Gomez." Mase sent Anton a look. "Hey, cowboy. Your sister Liesl bakes, right? How old is she?"

Without looking up from his phone, Anton said, "I will shove a hockey stick up your ass and turn you into a human Popsicle if I *ever* see you eyeballin' my sister, puckhead."

That was my cue to go. "Good luck at the game on Saturday, Ky."

"Win or lose, there's a party here Saturday night. Swing by if you have a chance."

10 *Sierra*

L U HAD BEEN complaining all week that she was bored.
Every night she dared me to mix up my routine and go out with her.

Monday night I passed on heading to the strip club—despite her cajoling that her favorite "strip and go naked" drinks were two for the price of one.

Tuesday night I was so keyed up after my PCE meeting that I would've accepted her invite to play craps at the Talking Stick Casino if I hadn't gotten cornered by a new member.

Wednesday night I worked late and came home to find Lu splashing in the pool naked with a dick-that-fits contender.

So Thursday night when my phone rang and my hands were wrist-deep in dishwater, she said, "Hot damn!" and answered the call on speakerphone.

"Sierra's phone, Lu speaking. Whatcha need?"

"Hey Lu. Uh, you're Sierra's roommate?"

"Roommate, groundskeeper, pool boy when my wild girl wants to role play." Lu added a loud *rowr*.

"Jesus, Lu, knock it the hell off. Just ignore her, Boone."

"Is this a bad time?"

"No, it's the perfect time because I'm bored out of my mind," Lu answered. "Please say you called to offer us entertainment options, Mr. Sexy Voice."

"Actually, that's why I called. Wanna meet at Blue Smoke? Shoot some pool and have a drink with us?" Boone asked.

"Who's us?"

"Me and my roommate."

I started to say, "That sounds—"

"Like a snooze fest," Lu said with a yawn. "It's Thursday night—Ladies' Night! I wanna dance and drink two-for-ones on your dime."

"So get your rowdy selves to Diego's." another voice in the background said.

Evidently Boone had us on speakerphone too.

"Do you know where that is?"

Lu snorted. "I haven't always lived in Scottsdale. We'll be there in forty-five."

I rolled my eyes. Of course Lu knew where Diego's was; she prided herself on finding places to party outside of the normal college zone.

"Halleluiah!" Lu grabbed the dishtowel, wound it up and popped me in the ass. "Get moving, we have to leave here in fifteen."

"Ouch! God, Lu. That mark is gonna swell up."

"Better have Boone look at it. He's a professional." She waggled her eyebrows. "You want to turn the other cheek—ha-ha—and have me put one there too? It'll give you a valid reason to drop your pants when you first see him."

"You are literally a pain in my ass."

She yelled, "You're welcome!" as I booked it up the stairs.

When I entered the kitchen fourteen minutes later Lu made a sizzling sound. "Looking hot tonight, S. Man, I wish we were the same size. I'd love to wear those leather pants."

I adjusted the bottom of the bronze and black peasant blouse. "It's not too over the top for a weeknight?"

"Nope. It's so you, Sierra. Classy club wear."

"Thanks. And check you out in the snakeskin dress." Lu was all muscles and curves. And pigtails. I swore before she graduated I'd drag her to the salon and force her to ditch the Baby Spice look.

"You driving?" She shoved her cell phone in her small purse. "Maybe I should drive too. That way if you and Boone hook up..."

"Not happening tonight."

"I noticed you didn't say 'not ever happening' which means it *could* happen tonight."

The more I argued the more she'd keep at me and probably relay our entire conversation to Boone just to see my reaction. "So are we both driving or what?"

"Yes. You'll have to follow me since I know a shortcut."

I cranked the music in my car, singing along, so my head was full of lyrics, not possibilities about tonight.

Diego's sat on the outskirts of Glendale in a strip mall, surrounded by other bars and restaurants. There seemed to be everything from a honky-tonk, to a karaoke bar, to sports pubs.

I parked next to Lu in the jam-packed lot. We fell in step as we headed to Diego's, which didn't have a line to get in like many of the clubs, especially on ladies' night.

"You've been here?" I asked.

"A few times. It's even busier on the weekends. Sometimes they have great bands, but during the week it's just a DJ."

The bouncer checked our IDs, stamped the backs of our hands and waived the cover fee.

Once we were inside, Lu said, "Let's walk through." A mere ten steps later a trio of guys intercepted us.

"Looking good for ladies' night," the cute guy in the middle drawled. "There's room at our table."

"Aren't you just sweet," Lu said with a huge smile. "Right now we're looking for our friends."

"If they're as hot as you, invite them too."

Lu steered us away. We'd reached the end of the first row when two burly guys invited us to join them.

Again, Lu dealt with letting them down with a wink, a flirty pat on the arm and a cooing *bye-bye*. I attributed her unparalleled man-handling technique to her near-professional dating status. While I enjoyed college parties, in clubs I felt like I was on display—guys gauged you as a potential hookup; women eyed you as competition.

"Do you see him yet?"

Then there he was.

A bottle of beer in his hand, the lights from the bar providing backlight that outlined his smoking body. He wore a tight, black, short-sleeved T-shirt that hugged the muscles in his shoulders, biceps and chest as if the material had been specifically designed for him. His angular face had a hint of scruff and my belly fluttered because it made him that much more gorgeous. Although half a dozen women surrounded him—no surprise there—he never focused on any one in particular. He kept scanning the area.

For me.

That was some heady stuff.

He'd always had this way of finding me in a crowd. When those dark eyes locked with mine, I felt the power of this connection between us down to the marrow of my bones.

Boone smiled—god, that smile was a freakin' beacon—and I started toward him like I was being pulled in by a tractor beam.

His eyes heated, his nostrils flared and he set his beer aside, muttering apologies as he cut through his throng of admirers and moved with one purpose: getting to me.

Maybe I'd been too hasty denying I'd end up in bed with him tonight, because right now, stripping this man naked and seeing his hot look of utter possession as he fucked me was the best idea in the history of the world.

We met in the middle...and that's when it became awkward.

Boone tempered the lust in his eyes. Yet, he slowly slid his rough-skinned palm up the outside of my arm in a caress so erotic I felt it sizzle across my entire body. He dipped his head and brushed his cheek against mine. "You look stunning as always, McKay."

"So you were checking out my kickin' clubbing outfit?"

"You're not stunning because of what you wear."

An African-American guy with a shaved head and amazing bone structure sidled up beside Boone. But before he said anything, his focus locked on someone behind me.

It was a natural instinct to turn around and look, even when I knew exactly who had grabbed his attention.

Lu.

I turned back around quickly and caught Boone eyeing my ass.

He flashed me that panty-melting grin. "You and leather? Stuff fantasies are made from, sexy."

The guy next to Boone dropped to his knees in front of Lu. "Marry me."

She laughed. "Aren't you a charmer?"

"If I say yes, can I prove it by peeling away the snakeskin that's covering your spectacular body?"

"Only if you use your teeth." She cocked her head. "Blindfolded."

He clasped his hands together in front of her. "I think I love you."

"Knock it off, Raj," Boone said.

Raj rolled to his feet and demanded, "Woman, what is your name?"

"Lu."

"Lu? Huh-uh. That's the name of a car mechanic. An old, balding white guy with a stogie in one hand and dirty magazine in the other. Your mama did *not* birth an angel and name her Lu. Baby, what is your real name?"

I held my breath. Lu hated her name. Her nickname growing up had been Lug—a double whammy, a dig at her name and her size. She'd christened herself Lu the first day of college.

She offered her hand. "Lucinda Grace."

What the hell? She'd told him her middle name without making him work for it?

Raj ran his mouth across her knuckles and nuzzled the inside of her wrist. "I'm Raj. The man who's gonna ruin you for all other men."

"Raj," she cooed. "Let me try that out. See how it sounds rolling off my tongue." She let her head fall back. "Yes, Raj. Right there. Oh, baby, oh Raj, you know I need it harder." Then she said, "Raaaaaj," on a throaty moan, dragging his name out to six syllables.

I didn't dare look at Boone. Or Raj for that matter.

"Your lips were made to say my name, Lucinda Grace."

"My lips were made for a lot of things. Buy me a drink and let's discuss some of my favorites in detail."

He yelled, "One glass of champagne for finding the woman who'll bear my children," at the bartender and slipped his arm around her waist, directing her toward the bar.

Lu sent me a wicked look over her shoulder. "Black snake moan is gonna have a whole new meaning tonight, girlfriend."

And they vanished into the crowd.

"So now you've met Raj," Boone said dryly.

"It *is* a pity that our roommates don't get along." I looked at him.

"Is that his play? Propose, flatter and fuck? Because Lu has her own playbook."

"They oughta be well-matched then." His eyebrows drew together. "But that's a first for Raj."

"For *Lucinda Grace* too."

He chuckled and took my hand. "Now I'm glad we drove two cars." Boone stepped up to the bar. The man was so rugged and masculine I couldn't look away from him. "What do you usually drink?"

I'd like to drink you down. In one greedy gulp.

"Sierra?"

"A…margarita."

He ordered a margarita for me and a Corona for himself.

I rested my forearms on the bar next to him. "So…soldier. Come here often?"

He gave me that "you're a dork" smile I remembered. "First time. You?"

"First time. Lately I've been too busy to hit the clubs. Parties are more laidback. Or they're a drunken free-for-all which is also fun."

"Sounds like the first weekend furlough during basic."

"Do you have much time to go out to the bars now?"

Boone shrugged. "There's a group of us that hang out on base. But it's pool tables, darts, music on the jukebox. I prefer laidback too. You have a bunch of friends around here? People you used to hang out with before you moved?"

"No. I started at ASU with a clean slate. Random roommate assignment, which ended up being Lu. I keep a professional relationship with the people at DPM that I manage directly. Wouldn't be a good career move to knock back Irish car bombs with my assistant. Or ask my accounts receivable manager to hold my legs during a keg stand."

"Smart."

"This year I've spent more time with the McKay-kateers. It's easy with them, and their parties are fun. Lu drags me out on the weekends if our schedules mesh."

When Boone's eyes bored into mine, I braced myself for his next question. "So do you…date?"

"I'm team 'hit it and quit it.' In, out, done. There's no mixed signals. What about you?"

"Same."

Why I decided to push him...no fucking idea, but I did it anyway. "So no sexy army nurses have rocked your world? You thought, damn, I could do this again. Then you're hanging out, not just for the sex, but because you like her. Then she starts leaving her shampoo in your shower and both sets of your friends stop trying to fix you up because you're considered a couple?"

Boone studied me. By the hard set of his jaw I knew I'd struck a nerve. Would he answer or deflect it back to me?

Do you really want to know how many women have had their hands on him? Because no matter what he says, you'll only focus on all those women who wanted to keep him, but couldn't. And you know how that feels.

"You know what? Don't answer that."

The bartender delivered the drinks and Boone fished out his wallet to pay.

That made this feel like a date.

Is that what you want?

Boone slid my drink over.

I said, "Thank you," and stepped aside, assuming we'd find a table.

But he set his hand on my shoulder, stopping me. When I looked up, he was right there.

"From the day I left Wyoming, I've been one hundred percent focused on getting as much medical training as I could handle. I live, eat and breathe army life. I've never had such a sense of purpose. I've never been a cog that makes the wheel run smoother. Now I am. I'm proud of what I've done and there's still so much more that I want to do. I chose this life because I have a future and the past doesn't matter. So yeah, I've been content with one-offs. I'm up-front about that. Never had a woman's shampoo bottle in my shower. I don't do couple dates because I've never been part of a couple. I haven't been looking for a woman. Haven't needed one. Haven't wanted one. Then I saw you in Sundance. Now I'm here and I know I'll never be content with a one-off with you."

Shit. Was it hot in here?

I gulped down three mouthfuls of margarita and chanced a look at him.

Brooding Boone? Bye-bye. Beautiful Boone smiled. "Did that answer your question?"

"Yes-sirree, it sure did. Wow. A very thorough answer. You get an A-plus-plus for detail."

He laughed. "So fair is fair, McKay. You ever had a guy...leave his tools in your shed?"

I choked on my drink.

Of course, Boone thought that was the height of hilarity.

But it didn't get me off the hook from answering him. "Nope. No guy's tools. I don't need them. I have my own and can take care of things myself."

"That can be taken a couple of different ways."

"Let your imagination run wild."

The wild look in his eye indicated the man had a very vivid imagination.

"I think the DJ is about to start playing music." I faced that direction, standing on my toes for a better view. When I spun back around, Boone was glaring at the guy lounging at the bar next to me.

He leaned over and gritted out, "Keep your eyes off her ass."

I froze. No need to check to see if Boone's threat had scared the guy away. Heck, it'd almost scared *me* away. I sent Boone a sideways glance. He wore that bad-tempered look again. The scruff on his face made him ten times scarier looking, but it also made him ten times hotter.

Then his voice was in my ear. "You mad?"

"No. It *is* bad behavior to stare at someone's ass."

"Can I tell you a secret that might piss you off?"

"With a lead-in like that? You'd better."

"The guy saw me staring at something in a stupor and checked to see what had my attention. When he saw your ass...well, McKay, it *is* fucking mesmerizing in those leather pants so I don't blame him even when it pissed me the fuck off."

"Omigod." I blushed. "I'm never wearing these pants again."

"Maybe not in public, but feel free to wear them around me in private anytime."

I had no doubt that Boone could peel these pants off me in ten seconds if I gave him the chance. "Where do you think Lu and Raj are?"

"Skipped off to the karaoke bar. That's not my thing."

"Mine either. Besides, I don't want to witness Lu and Raj one-upping each other with dirty sexy songs as foreplay."

Boone gave me a considering look. "Give me an example of a dirty sexy song."

"'Gett Off.' Prince."

"Nice."

"Your turn."

"'Closer.' Nine Inch Nails."

"Oh. Yeah. I love that song. Very dirty sexy. Okay, you win."

Boone smirked at me. "And for my winner's prize, you're dancing with me."

11 Boone

SIERRA COCKED HER head, those shrewd eyes searched mine. "Not a good idea, Boone."

"Why?"

"Because we've never danced together."

"Exactly why we need to do it now."

"How do I know that you're not a shitty dancer who'll tromp on my toes or embarrass me with disco moves?"

I braced my forearm on the bar and leaned in, losing my train of thought when I caught a whiff of her sweet perfume and beneath that sweetness, the earthier musk of her skin. Brushing my lips across her ear, I murmured, "Only one way to find out if I've got the moves like Jagger, McKay."

She laughed. "Okay."

I clasped her left hand in my right, towing her behind me until we reached the farthest edge of the dance floor.

Sierra brought our clasped hands up and rested her left hand on my right shoulder, keeping our bodies a proper distance apart like we were in fifth grade gym class.

"Nice try, but you belong here." I circled her arms around my neck. Then I placed my hands in the small of her back with my forearms resting on her hips. "Much better."

"Says you. But if your hands migrate toward my ass, you'll get a knee to your nuts, West."

I chuckled. "Tough talk."

"Try me."

"If you want to touch my nuts all you've gotta do is ask, no need to get violent about it."

She had no response for that.

Conversation was the dead last thing on my mind as I finally held this woman in my arms. She matched her rhythm to mine. Even our breath synchronized as I felt the rising and falling of her chest and her exhale across my neck.

I bit back a groan. I'd always known we'd move together like this—which was why I'd never allowed our bodies to touch during those months we first got to know each other. I'd even lied about why I planned to skip prom, claiming I didn't have the money or the right transportation. But the truth was if I'd seen Sierra dressed to the nines and then spent the entire night body to body like this? I would've had her stripped bare as soon as we were alone and I never would've left Wyoming.

"What are you thinking about?" she demanded. "Because you're making some Neanderthal noises."

"I'm thinking about the real reason I didn't ask you to prom."

"Is this the 'I wouldn't have been able to keep my hands off you' excuse?"

"Not an excuse, Sierra, and you damn well know it."

Her disbelieving snort vibrated against my neck. "I'm so glad you were able to keep your virtue and my hymen intact when you took off a month later."

I wasn't falling for her attempt to rile me, which in turn would rile her and give her an excuse to stomp away mad. "That's the only time in my life I've come close to being virtuous."

"I think you had 'virtue' confused with 'self-interest,'" she retorted.

Sliding my left hand up past the nape of her neck, I sifted my fingers through her hair until I had a good grip. "You're going there? Good. We need to get this shit out in the open, so we can move on from it." I felt the ferocity flicker in my eyes, knew she saw it and didn't bother to try and hide it. "I secretly ate it up that a girl like you had a thing for me. That you saw me beyond the bullshit of my life. But goddammit, don't pretend you didn't know how I felt about *you* that whole time."

"I *didn't* know," she said hotly.

"Bull. You were the *only* person I spent my nonworking hours with. I didn't hang with the guys. I didn't have any friends at school besides you, Sierra."

"Because you were too busy working toward getting the hell out of Wyoming to bother with any of that normal teen life stuff."

"So why did I go out of my way to make time for *you*? Only you? Because you were the most important person in my life." In pressing my point I ended up increasing my grip on her hair. "What we were to each other was always deeper than just friends."

"I didn't want to just be your friend, Boone."

"You'd have less resentment toward me now if I'd turned our friendship into something more and then left?"

"You didn't give me a choice." She twisted out of my hold and broke eye contact. "I hated you for that."

The knot in my gut tightened. "Hated?"

"With the power of a thousand fiery suns kind of hatred that a sixteen-year-old girl excels at. After you left, I spent most of the summer in Paris with my mom. I got rid of that pesky virginity as soon as possible to a sophisticated—and experienced—French college senior named Jean-Michel."

I ground my teeth together.

"The worst part wasn't you not taking me to prom. The worst part was finding out, literally at the last minute, that you *had* cared about me the way I'd dreamed you would." Her gaze sought mine. "Then you kissed me and satisfied your curiosity so you could move on."

"No. No," I repeated, more vehemently, "that goddamn kiss wrecked me, Sierra."

She went utterly still.

"*Wrecked me*," I repeated. Curling my hand beneath her jaw, I feathered my thumb over her bottom lip. "I didn't kiss another woman for a goddamned year because I couldn't get *this* mouth out of my mind. I kept flashing back to that smile, the one that dazzled me the first time we met. Or the sneering one that pissed me off, because it managed to be cute and a little mean. I remembered how badly I wanted to bite this pouting bottom lip when you were being a brat. But mostly I remembered how your lips softened beneath mine from that first touch."

"Then you remember the taste of my tears, too."

Those words hit me as hard as a punch to the gut. But I soldiered on, continuing to gently stroke her lower lip, while inching closer. "And you know the taste of mine," I said softly.

That startled her. Then she whispered, "You're right. God. I'd...forgotten."

"You think it was easy for me? That I just climbed on my bike and never looked back? Never thought about you, never wished my life circumstances had been different so I didn't have to make that choice?"

She shook her head. "But it did get easier to block it out, didn't it?"

No malice distorted her words. She'd been speaking for herself as much as asking me. "It did. And then there were times when I imagined what it'd be like when I finally saw you again."

"It's not exactly been us holding hands, having heart-to-hearts and hugging it out, has it?"

"No. But you haven't kicked me in the balls either, so I'm still ahead of the curve."

That earned me a smile.

And I shamelessly caressed the bow of her upper lip with my thumb, as if I could make the touch erotic enough that she'd let me use my tongue next time. When her breath caught, I groaned.

"Boone. What are we doing?"

"I'm pretty sure I'm about to kiss you." I shifted the position of my hand, lightly resting it on her throat. "Are you gonna run?"

Sierra's eyes were affixed to my mouth. "Not right this second. But I reserve the right to freak out afterward. So you'd better make this good."

Of course she'd throw down a challenge. Such a fucking temptation to smash my lips to hers and devour her. Give her a preview of how explosive it'd be when we finally sated this hunger with more than just hot, grinding kisses.

And yet...that's what she'd expect. I didn't have to prove there was heat and passion between us. It'd been there when neither of us really knew what to do with it. Sierra needed a reminder of the other side of me, the tender side I'd only ever shown to her.

I pushed her hair back before I framed her beautiful face in my hands. I nuzzled her cheeks, letting the scruff on the edge of my jaw brush the corners of her lips.

Her soft, surprised moan flowed into my ear like a smooth shot of whiskey.

That. Right *there.* I craved more of that.

I took my time aligning our mouths. Kissing the divot in her chin before I began to lightly tease my lips across hers. Each pass a little longer until the pressure of my mouth on hers was constant. No tongue, just languid dedication to relearning the shape of her mouth beneath mine. Even as my head spun with the incredible intimacy of this—the tightening of her fists in my shirt, her soft sigh gusting across my lips, the tiny squeak when I used my teeth—I committed every reaction to memory just in case this was all I ever had from her. I'd keep it with all the other memories I had of her, of us. She had no idea of the power those memories held for me.

We swayed together, the pace set by our bodies' rhythms, not the music.

So addictive, this druggingly sweet exploration. The whisper-soft glide of my lips, taking in little sips of her breath from hers as she exhaled.

My tongue followed the seam of her lips. On the second pass, I pushed in deeper, my tongue connecting with her teeth. On the third pass, she opened her mouth fully and it was ON.

Lust told sweetness to take a fucking hike and poof—it was gone.

Desire ruled—until passion overtook common sense and then all barriers between us fell away as if they'd never existed.

Twisting my hands in her hair, I held on, feeling her fingernails digging into my shoulder blades as she clung to me because we were spiraling, spinning. Locked together and completely consumed by the hot, wet, greedy, balls-to-the-wall kiss. Kissing like we were already naked and about to hit the fucking sheets.

Soon. Fuck. Me. Please let it be soon. Because this is perfection.

Anything that intense can't last. It shouldn't last or it loses the impact.

Sierra sensed it at the same time.

The kiss ended.

But I felt like we'd finally begun.

"Boone," she panted against my throat.

"I know, baby," I whispered in her hair. "Me too."

"Then you know I have to go."

Jesus Christ on a jumbo jet. She had to...*go*? After that?

Dude. It's not like she didn't warn you.

I counted to ten. Then I managed, "You're freaking out?"

"Yeah."

"Why?"

"I thought I was ready. For you. For this."

"You're not?"

"I need some time to think."

"Sierra. Christ, woman, you're scaring me. Are you having second thoughts?"

That's when she looked at me. "The truth?"

"Always."

"You walked back into my life less than two weeks ago. We've been together half a dozen times. This is the first time we've had any intimate contact. And that? That was life changing. I'm pretty sure if I was already on fire and you asked me if I wanted more gasoline I'd say 'yes please' just to get me some more of that."

"That's the most flattering thing you've ever said to me."

She poked me in the chest. "It wasn't meant to be, jackass. I'm getting caught up in the whirlwind of you and when it stops and spits me out, I won't know where—or who—I am."

"I am not going anywhere this time." I kissed her forehead. Her cheeks. Her mouth. "Don't run. Please."

"I'm not running, but this...reminded me of the last time we kissed. It reminded me that you have the power to break me."

"Listen to me." I trapped her face in my hands. "The only reason I came to Phoenix is because you're here. There. I fucking said it. You. Are. It. For. Me. You always have been. So that power to fucking crush a heart to dust? Runs both ways." I dropped my hands before I used them to shake some damn sense into her. I forced myself to step back. I forced myself to start walking away.

"That little confession isn't helping clear my head, West," she yelled at me.

I turned and smiled at her—not a nice smile. "It wasn't supposed to. See you around, McKay."

12 Sierra

TOSSED AND turned for hours after I'd left the bar.

I'd known that Boone would kiss me. I'd wanted it. So when it finally happened tonight...I thought I'd prepared myself.

What a joke.

Reliving the sheer perfection of how thoroughly he'd kissed me was making my breath catch even now.

It was just a kiss.

No matter how many times I told myself that...I didn't believe it.

It hadn't felt like *just a kiss.*

Looking into Boone's eyes, I knew it hadn't felt that way for him either.

And then he'd told me the truth.

The only reason I came to Phoenix is because you're here. There. I fucking said it. You. Are. It. For. Me.

So his kiss hadn't been to remind me of the past; it'd been a promise for the future.

A future I never thought we'd have.

Because the first time he kissed me was also the last time I saw him. For seven years.

God. I didn't want that to happen again.

I shut my eyes.

Every sight, sound, scent and feeling I'd had that night crashed over me. Sleep wouldn't come but the memories did...

THE BRIGHT MOON glow that night had sent silvery light across the clearing.

Seemed a little strange, Boone calling me out of the blue and asking me to meet him. I hoped it meant something more than he was bored.

I ignored the snarky voice in my head, asking why I went running every time Boone West crooked his little finger at me. But I hadn't seen him since his graduation. He'd slipped back into the not-returning-texts zone. School had ended two days ago and my summer plans were still up in the air.

I put my car in park and killed the ignition. Butterflies danced in my belly. Where had this nervousness come from? I was out here with Boone. Mr. Trustworthy. Mr. Oblivious.

His butt rested against his motorcycle seat. His booted feet crossed at the ankle. His arms folded over his chest. He wore a super tight T-shirt which displayed the ripped muscles in his arms and the ridges in his lower abdomen. I'd seen that shirt on him a dozen times and every time I whispered a little *thank you* to the T-shirt gods.

Stop gawking at him.

Nothing wrong with being attracted to my best guy buddy.

Was there?

No. Especially when he didn't have a clue how I felt.

I walked up to him, my hands jammed into the back pockets of my jeans. "You summoned me?"

Boone frowned at my attire. "Wasn't tonight the dance?"

"No. It was last night."

"Oh. Was it fun?"

"I don't know. I skipped it."

"But…you said that night at the lake you wanted to go."

I shrugged. "Marin is at her grandma's for a week so she wasn't going. Besides, they probably only played country music."

"You should've gone."

But I knew you wouldn't be there.

"You asked me here to chew my ass about a dance I didn't go to?"

"No."

"What are you doing out here, anyway? Did your bike break down again?"

"Funny. It was a great night for a ride. I lost track of time. When I pulled over, I realized I wasn't far from your place."

"So you called me." Instead of just showing up at my house. That made no sense. Especially if Boone thought I was at the dance. What was going on with him? He acted...jumpy.

"You got any decent tunes in that piece of crap car you're driving these days?" he asked.

The Mercedes was hardly a piece of crap and he knew it. Boone also knew that the only reason my dad had bought it was for the safety features, including an excess of air bags after the air bag in my first car failed to deploy during my car accident. "I'll play music as long as you don't bitch about what it is."

"Deal."

After I rolled down the windows, I plugged my iPod into the stereo system. I mimicked his pose against the car, standing opposite him.

Boone grinned when the music started. "Foo Fighters. Cool."

"Don't get used to it. The next song might be by Flogging Molly."

"I don't even know what the hell that is, McKay. You're more *urbane* than me."

"Right. Seriously, West, what's up? It's not like you to text me, demanding I meet you out in the middle of nowhere. Especially this late."

He lifted an eyebrow. "Since when is ten late?"

"Since my dad grills me about where I'm going at ten at night and who I'm going with."

"Did you tell him you were meeting me?"

"Yeah." I smirked. "He said not to let you drive my car."

"Smartass." Boone paused and tipped his head toward the sky. "As much as I love how bright the moon is, I miss seeing the stars on nights like this."

"Me too."

Neither of us said anything for several minutes.

"But this moon-gazing shit is killing my neck." He moved to lean next to me and my pulse skipped a beat. "Much better. So, what are your plans for this summer?"

"I've thought about becoming a carny."

"Yeah? What's the appeal? Getting hooked on meth? Hooked on pot? Hooked on fried food? Or is it getting to rip off little kids every day? Maybe you'll grow a mustache and get a bad tattoo."

I laughed. "You've weighed the pros and cons way more than I have. I was just in it for the unlimited cotton candy."

"What's option two for your summer?"

He was more persistent than usual, so I hedged, in case he had a specific reason for asking my plans—like he wanted to spend the summer with me. "I don't know. It depends."

"On?"

"How much my mom and dad argue over me and where I should be. My mom's boyfriend bought a place in Paris with an extra bedroom, so she wants me to stay at least half the summer with her." I shot him a sideways warning glance. "I haven't mentioned this to my dad yet."

"Why not?"

"I just found out yesterday. He'll ask me what I want to do, and like I said, I'm not sure."

"But he gives you a vote in your options?"

"Yes. What about you? Now that you've graduated, what are your plans?"

"Well, that's the reason I asked you to meet me."

My stomach performed a hopeful summersault.

But as usual, he didn't elaborate. He just kept looking skyward.

"Boone? I'm lousy at guessing games, remember? So just tell me."

"I won't be here this summer because I joined the army."

I gave him a ten-second pause and hip-checked him. "You have a bizarre sense of humor sometimes."

He faced me. "I'm not joking. I joined the army."

A sick feeling took root as I realized he was serious. Then I...exploded. "Why would you just up and do that?"

"It wasn't an impulsive decision. I've been thinking about it for a while."

"How long?"

"Almost three years. Since my youth forestry counselor suggested it when I was sixteen."

And this was the first time he'd mentioned it? After all the time we'd spent together? "But we're at war! The military sends the newest recruits over there." Another horrible thought occurred. "You've got medical training, which means they'll put you on the first cargo plane and drop you right in the middle of a combat zone."

"Sierra. That's what I want."

"To get yourself killed?" I demanded.

"No, to help keep others from dying."

"But you do that every day as an EMT."

"It's not the same. I can't make a living as an EMT in rural Wyoming. I'm tired of being broke and there are a lot of things I'd like to do with my life that I can't do if I'm stuck here."

"Then go to college like normal people do."

Boone scowled at me. "If I don't have money for a car do you really think I've got money to go to college? Or that anyone will lend me the money?"

"Then we'll ask my dad. He'll float you a loan. Heck, he'd probably just give you the money since you saved my life."

He pushed off the car. "I don't want your money or your charity."

"What? I'm only trying to help. You took that the wrong way."

"Did I? What part of making it on my own is confusing to you? I have to do this. I *want* to do this."

"So there's no talking you out of it."

Boone shook his head. "It's a done deal."

I wanted to scream at him, throw myself at his feet and beg him not to go, but that was the epitome of childish. Instead, I tossed off a breezy, "Fine. Whatever. Go be a hero. Get yourself killed. Later." I sidestepped him and ducked around the front of the car, hoping to make it inside before my tears were obvious.

But he latched onto my upper arms and forced me to look at him. "You don't mean that."

"Yes, I do."

His gaze roamed over my face. "Then why are you crying?" he demanded softly.

"Because I hate that you're doing this stupid thing. And I hate you." The last word came out as a sob.

"No, baby, you don't."

"Don't call me that!"

"Sierra. Come here."

"No! Don't touch me."

"You don't mean that either." Boone crushed me to his chest.

I fought him for a few seconds, swinging punches that didn't land, yelling and thrashing, but he just held on. I gave up fighting the pull of him and clung to him as I cried.

How many times had I imagined Boone holding me, stroking my hair and murmuring sweet things to me? Hundreds.

But never like this.

My voice was muffled against his chest when I finally spoke. "When do you go?"

"Tomorrow morning."

I squirmed away from him. "You're just telling me *now*? When did you sign up?"

Boone looked away.

"Tell me."

"Three days after your accident."

All the air left my lungs. I forced my lips to form the word *why*.

"Because that night at Tyler's party when I told him we were together? I wanted it to be real."

"You think I would've shot you down?"

"No." His eyes were locked on mine. "I know you would've said yes."

My cheeks burned with mortification; he'd known how I felt all along.

"You understand my history. Since I was twelve years old I've been counting off the damn days until I can get the hell out of Wyoming. Last fall, the start of my senior year, I was taking the prep classes I needed and I was getting a year of practical experience as an EMT and moving on was finally within my grasp. And then you showed up.

"From the moment we met on the bus, you sucked me in. You were so gorgeous, feisty, funny and sweet—and so easy to talk to. I tried to stay away from you, but something about you, Sierra, just kept pulling me back."

I stared at him, absolutely speechless.

"That night at the party I wanted to kill Tyler for thinking he had the right to put his hands on you. After the accident, I about lost my fucking mind because you were hurt... That's when I knew you could keep me here. If I got involved with you, like I wanted to, I wouldn't leave. And I *have* to leave. I had to have a solid plan to go so I enlisted."

"No." I found my voice and said it louder. "No." Then I was screaming at him. "No, no, no, no, no! You don't get to do this to me, Boone. You don't get to treat me like a friend, and then tell me you've always felt more for me...the night before you *fucking* leave! You don't get to make me feel guilty for you joining the army because I have some kind of magical hold over you. That's total bullshit and it's not fair!" God. This could not be happening.

"Not fair? You think this has been easy for me? Especially the last four months? When we've been together all the damn time because I couldn't stay the hell away from you? And I had to act like it's not fucking *killing* me when you look at me like your world would be perfect if I just kissed you."

Infuriated, I slapped my hands on his chest and shoved him. "The only thing you can kiss, Boone West, is my ass." I spun around and considered kicking over his stupid bike as I skirted the back end of my car. Jerk. Asshole. Jerkoff. Asshat. He wanted to leave me? Fine. He could just go. I'd be better off.

Such a fucking liar you are, Sierra.

"So that's it?" Boone shouted. "That's how you're gonna say good-bye to me?"

I whipped a U-turn and marched back up to him. "How did you expect I'd say goodbye? Strip my clothes off and let you take my virginity in a field of wildflowers under a full moon? Screw that. I'm saving my virginity for someone who deserves it. And. That. Is. Not. You." I punctuated each word with a poke on his hard chest.

Boone said, "You do that," in a throaty rasp I'd never heard from him. "In the meantime, I'm taking this." He wrapped one hand around the back of my neck and clamped the other on my butt, pulling me in for a kiss.

I should've shoved him away. But his kiss was like a drug. Intense, determined, amazingly seductive, as if he was trying to convince me that his passion for me was—and always had been—real. That he'd been imagining this kiss for as long as I had. That he'd wanted it as much. Our mouths and tongues clashed and I slipped my arms around his waist, my hands clutching his shirt as if that could keep him here.

The kiss was beyond anything I'd ever experienced. Rough and sexy, bringing alive things inside me that I'd heard about but had never felt.

Then Boone slowed it down. The kiss became soft. An unhurried tease, as if we had all the time in the world to explore. To learn each other.

But we didn't. By this time tomorrow, he'd be gone.

I kept kissing him even as my tears fell.

Then Boone's hands were on my face, trying to wipe away the moisture.

He moved his mouth back; I felt his lips against mine and his breath in my mouth as he whispered, "Sierra. Baby, please don't cry." He planted tender smooches on my trembling lips. His mouth wandered down my neck and my entire body erupted in goose flesh. He nuzzled the sweep of my shoulder and stopped, breathing against my skin.

I had to bite my lip to keep from sobbing when he strung soft kisses along my collarbone, right where the injury from the car accident had hurt the most. But that pain was nothing compared to the pain I felt now.

Boone entwined his fingers in my hair and tipped my head back. His beautiful eyes were dark with remorse and something else, something that made my pulse quicken. "I knew it'd be like this between us."

"But it's still not enough."

He didn't answer. He just consumed my mouth again.

While kissing him was better than I'd dreamed, it still felt like someone was stabbing me in the gut with a rusty knife as Boone took the kiss deeper, until I feared I'd never get out.

I broke away first, resting my forehead to his.

"Sierra—"

"Don't say anything."

We stayed like that for a long time. Not looking at each other, clinging to each other, so close but so far apart.

I whispered, "I have to go."

"Not like this."

"There's no other way. This was your choice."

He placed one last soft kiss on my lips.

I pulled away from him. "Goodbye, Boone."

"See you around, McKay."

I hadn't looked back. Not once. Not even in the rearview mirror when I bumped over the cattle guard.

I just drove away.

AND FOR THE first time, in a long time, when I thought of that night? It wasn't as painful.

Maybe being older helped.

Maybe the passage of time helped.

Or maybe the fact Boone was back in my life again made all the difference.

With that surprising, comforting thought in mind, I finally fell asleep.

13 Sierra

TWO OBNOXIOUSLY LOUD knocks sounded on my bedroom door Saturday night.

I didn't have time to dive into my closet before Lu burst in and said, "Sierra! What the hell? Get ready for the party."

"I'm not feeling it tonight, Lu."

"Bull. You'll feel it if you get your ass outta bed and into something slutty like this."

My BFF had gone all out for the party. She'd tied the billowing ends of her low-cut poet's shirt below her breasts, showcasing the flame tattoo around her navel above the plaid skirt. The rest of her outfit, fishnets and patent leather over-the-knee dominatrix boots, brought to mind Bavarian bar wenches. Despite the contrasting styles, I'd be damned if the outfit didn't work. "You are da bomb, Lu."

"I know, right? So get up and slip on the mermaid dress."

I wore the mermaid dress—nicknamed such because the metallic material resembled shimmering fish scales and the skintight fabric fit to my every curve—whenever I needed a pick-me-up. "I already told you I'm not going."

"You are killing me here. This isn't like you. Lying in bed navel-gazing."

"It's been a rough week. I'm taking time to regroup and reassess."

"Reassess tomorrow. Hit the party for one hour. If it sucks you can go." Her pause lasted like fifteen seconds. "Kyler is your family. Today was a huge game for him. You know he wants you there helping him celebrate."

"I was *at* the game, which is the important part. Besides, I doubt he'd even notice if I didn't show up—and that is not a statement of pity."

"It's a statement of fear. You're skipping the party because you're afraid Boone will be there."

"Afraid?" I snorted. "Uh, no."

Lu flopped on the edge of my bed. "You're giving Boone way too much power. You were happy living your life before he showed up. And you'll be happy living your life after he's gone. A blip in the radar. That's all he is."

Boone wasn't a blip on the radar. That was the problem. He was the whole fucking map.

"You need a mood enhancer. What's the shot your sister Rory always makes?"

"A 'bang me from behind'?"

Lu snapped her fingers. "Let's pregame with those. I'll line up the shot glasses, you find that inner slut and let her come out and play."

It was impossible to resist Lu in a party mood. I loved her for that. "Fine. I'll get ready. But I'm not wearing the mermaid dress."

LU KNOCKED BACK three shots to my one. Mine was more like a half shot, which turned me into the DD.

Parking was a bitch. Why did the neighbors in this upscale neighborhood put up with this? It wasn't like the house was just down the street from frat row.

I'd never seen so many people. Lu spied her senior design project partner and they strolled away, arm in arm, singing the school fight song.

As I wove through the throng, I didn't recognize a single person. Maybe I oughta take it as a sign I'd outgrown these parties, because a few kids looked like high schoolers. What was Mase's personal liability if the cops showed up? Maybe he wasn't home. That would upset me more, to think Kyler was throwing parties because he thought he deserved it.

Stop being Debbie Downer and have some fun.

A bunch of jocks were standing on the steps, obstructing the entrance to the house, assigning a number to every female that walked by.

"Four."

"Six."

"Jesus, are you guys drunk? She's a two at best."

Laughter.

Tempting to kick every one of these douchebags in the nuts. As I tried to slide in behind them, I accidentally bumped one of them.

He whirled around with, "Watch it."

"Then quit standing in front of the door."

That had him blocking it even more. "Aw, hey baby, don't be like that. You're hot. Hang out with us. We'll show you a good time."

"Pass. I'm meeting someone. Now let me through."

Surprisingly, he moved. I'd just made it inside when I heard, "Face and body a solid eight."

"Yeah. Too bad she opened her mouth 'cause it dropped her to a three."

Bite me, fuckers.

Music blasted. The air temp inside was stifling. I scanned the clusters of people, hoping to spy Lu's pigtails, when I caught a glimpse of the action in the living room. A guy sat in the center of the couch, two topless blondes straddling him, one chick riding each thigh. They were making out like crazy. They took a break to focus on the man whose eyes were closed and he wore a stupid, happy grin.

Yeah, Mase was completely down with this party.

I was jostled. I was groped. I was cajoled into taking pictures.

I was so over all of this.

Thirty minutes had passed when I finally gave up looking for Lu. I cut through the dining room, hoping to find Ky.

He wasn't at his usual station in the kitchen. I fought the crowd and ended up outside.

It was a zoo out here too.

Anton and his group from rodeo club were in the backyard, leaning against the fence in that sexy casual way cowboys were so good at. Anton smiled at me, tipped his hat and returned his attention to whatever tall tale his buddy Diaz was spinning.

Tug and the other players wearing *Sun Devils Football* jerseys were gathered around the keg. Ky had to be close.

I found him out by the grill, each arm around a girl, a cup of beer in his hand.

When Ky noticed me, he forgot the women and barreled over, an enormous grin on his face. "Sierra! You came!"

That damn smile. I couldn't help but grin back. "Sweet game today."

"You were there?"

"Don't be a dumbass. I never miss any of your games."

"Man, it just...gelled. The last quarter we were in the motherfucking zone! It was beautiful."

"I know. I'm so proud of you, QB."

"Thanks for coming tonight. It's kinda crazy and I'm a little drunk but it means a lot that even now that you're a company bigwig, you're not too cool to hang out."

"Never, cuz. I'm a McKay-kateer for life."

"Damn straight." Laughing, he picked me up and tried to spin me around, but forgot he was holding a beer and spilled the entire thing down the front of my shirt.

I leapt back. The empty cup hit the ground.

"Shit! Sorry, sorry, sorry."

"Don't worry about it. Nothing says I had a rip-roaring Saturday night more than reeking of sour beer."

The girl to my left snickered.

When I looked at Ky again, he was blushing. "What?"

"Uh, your shirt is transparent when it's wet, and you can tell, I mean, it's not like I'm staring at your...but, uh, it's kinda obvious you're not wearin' a bra."

I glanced down. Sure enough, the wet shirt was as clingy as plastic wrap.

Fucking fantastic. I crossed my arms over my chest. "Thanks, Ky."

"I said I was sorry." Kyler shoved his hand into his pocket, pulled out a key and thrust it at me. "Here. Grab a T-shirt from my room."

Confused, I said, "You keep your bedroom door locked?"

"During parties? Yeah. Don't need people fucking or puking in my damn bed."

Smart. "Thanks." I snatched the key and pressed my forearm across my chest again. "I'll be right back with this."

"No rush."

The chick on Kyler's left said, "Why does *she* get a key to your bedroom and I don't?"

"Because I said so." He smacked her ass. "Run along now. I'll come find you later."

Lovely, Ky.

As I walked away, I heard him say to his other female companion, "Can I get you to do me a favor, sweetness?"

"Anything," she said eagerly.

That man had women lined up around the damn block.

I saw a flash of pigtails and flattened myself against the wall; I couldn't deal with Lu right now. When the coast was clear, I wove through the drunken people clogging the stairs.

Few revelers had breached the second floor besides a couple sucking face on the bench seat and another couple playing strip poker as they waited to use the bathroom.

I headed down the hallway to Ky's room. But first I stopped at Hayden's door and turned the handle. Locked. Interesting. Next I tried Anton's door. Also locked. So there was a difference between this place and a frat house.

I'd just unlocked Kyler's door when I heard, "Sierra?"

I froze.

Boone.

My flight instinct kicked in. I pushed the door open just far enough to sneak inside and then I slammed it shut and locked it.

That was the height of maturity.

Heart hammering, I pressed my shoulders against the door and tried to calm down after that spike of adrenaline.

Three soft raps vibrated by my head. "Funny, McKay. Let me in. I want to talk to you."

"So talk."

"I'm not saying this through the goddamned door," he snarled.

"Let. Me. In." Pause. "Or I'm coming in."

"Empty threat since I'm the one with the key."

Boone could just wait a damn minute until I didn't look like I'd entered a wet T-shirt contest.

I crossed the room, eyeing the stack of T-shirts neatly folded on the dresser. I had a split second to wonder if Ky did his own laundry or if one of sideline bunnies did, when I heard the locking mechanism click.

I wheeled around, watching in shock as the handle turned, the door opened and Boone stepped inside.

His focus stayed entirely on me as he shut and locked the door behind him.

"What are you doing in here?"

"I told you I was coming in."

"You're so determined to corner me that you picked the fucking lock?"

"No. Ky gave me a key."

"Bull. Ky gave me *the* key."

"Evidently he has more than one key." He started toward me—a smooth predator that'd spied his prey. His gaze moved down the column of my throat to where the shirt gapped and then homed in on the transparent material clinging to my breasts.

I fought a shiver at the hungry way he studied my chest. His gaze darted from one stiff nipple to the other. I felt the need to blurt out, "Ky spilled his beer all over me."

"Remind me to thank him," he murmured.

Then he invaded my space completely.

My dizziness wasn't from lack of oxygen to my brain. That twisting, turning, yearning sensation was all because of him. His scent, the heat from his body, the way his breath buffeted my exposed flesh in choppy, staccato bursts.

No man ever looked at me the way he looked at me right now.

I was tired of fighting this.

Why was I fighting this?

No. More.

I trembled when his index finger followed the edge of my shirt from my collarbone down to the first button. On the painstakingly slow journey up the other side, he used two fingers; the rough edges of his knuckles made a whispering sound across my skin.

He stroked the center of my chest, opening his fist like a flower and flattening his palm beneath the hollow of my throat. We weren't looking at each other, our mutual attention focused on him touching me.

When he inched his hand beneath the edge of my shirt and encountered the upper swell of my breast, his patience vanished.

Almost blindly Boone curled his hand around the nape of my neck and brought his mouth down on mine.

He wasn't asking.

He was taking.

And I let him.

Boone tasted like whiskey and need.

When that falling sensation hit me again, I realized just one taste of him and I was drunk on him.

Tonight I needed to do more than I'd done the other night—clutching him tightly while he made a mockery of every man who'd ever kissed me. I'd waited a lifetime to experience his primal need and raw hunger.

Boone ripped his mouth free to trail kisses down my throat. Then his hot, wet mouth engulfed my nipple. Sharp teeth, teasing tongue, suctioning kisses on the stiff peak. Boone savored me as if he had all night.

I wanted him frantic. I wanted grunting, growling, rasping vocal evidence of him losing his cool. I wanted to crack the lid on the passion he bottled up.

"Boone." My nipple slipped from his mouth and he nuzzled the valley between my breasts. "My turn. Don't move."

As I smoothed my fingertips over the deep cut of his triceps and the muscled grooves of his forearms, I rubbed my lips across his left pec. When the hard nub of his nipple rose up to greet me, I opened my mouth over it, blowing a hot puff of air out through the cotton fabric.

A deep groan rumbled and then he pulled away.

Looked like my turn lasted about thirty seconds.

Next time? I wouldn't ask.

He curled his hand around the front of my throat and reconnected our mouths. His tongue fucked along mine, thrust and retreat, again and again until my head spun.

My brain functioned enough to keep touching him. I inched my hand down the center of his body until my fingers connected with the waistband of his athletic shorts. The elastic stretched as I pulled it down. The stubborn material caught on his hipbone, but another tug and his athletic shorts hit the carpet.

Handy that Boone wasn't wearing underwear.

I formed my fist around his hardness covered in warm, satiny skin.

Somehow we'd ended up against the edge of the bed. Using both hands, I pushed his ass to the mattress. Then I was on my knees, my hair teasing the insides of his thighs when I bent my head and enclosed the tip of his cock between my lips. His musky scent, his salty taste...I opened wider to take more of him, when his strong hands—and even stronger will, apparently—tilted my head back, dislodging his cock from my mouth.

"Jesus, Sierra," he hissed. "Stop."

"No." My eyes issued a challenge as I pushed the head of his cock just past my lips, letting it rest on my bottom teeth as I flicked my tongue over that sweet, sweet spot beneath.

The way his eyes and nostrils flared...yeah, he hadn't really meant stop.

But he choked out a soft, "Why?"

"Because I want you. I want you like fucking crazy. But that's not obvious with the hot and cold way I've acted. So let me show you how hot it can be."

I nuzzled his shaft where it had bounced back up against his outstanding abs, taking a moment to worship those hard ridges with my tongue. As I slowly jacked his cock, I rubbed my face across the lower half of his abdomen. High on the scent of his skin, drunk on this taste of power, I brought the rigid flesh into my mouth bit by bit.

His hips jerked.

When the very tip of his cock kissed the back of my throat, I swallowed.

"Fuck."

I sucked hard and was rewarded with a grunt. I bobbed my head, eager to push past my comfort zone and see how far I could take him.

"I need my hands on you."

I didn't remind him this was my show, because it was his dick, after all.

His eyes held a wild look I'd never seen as he placed his hands on my head, his thumbs resting on the corners of my mouth. I started to make a fist around the base of his shaft when he grated out, "No hands. Just this mouth."

Okay. Boone telling me what he wanted? Really hot. Keeping my eyes on his face, I set my hands on his thighs and rubbed my lips back and forth across the smooth curve at the top of the head.

"Lick it."

My tongue darted out and licked a drop of precome before dipping into the slit searching for more.

"Lick lower."

I swirled my tongue around the rim, watching his eyes avidly follow every movement.

So Boone liked to watch. I could definitely work with that.

"More," he said in a gravelly tone.

"More what," I breathed against his damp flesh.

He shivered. "Of everything."

I smiled. Since he held my head, I had to lean forward to get his cock in more than halfway. Then I clamped down and sucked.

"Motherfuck. Do it again."

That's when he set the rhythm and the speed.

I couldn't tear my gaze from his face, flushed with passion. His eyes glittered with lust as he watched his cock tunneling in and out of my mouth.

It wasn't long before Boone hit the boiling point.

His quads went rigid beneath my stroking fingers. "Sierra," he warned.

I increased the suction and he went still a moment before that deep rasping groan left his mouth as warm thick spurts of his release coated the inside of my cheek and the back of my tongue.

When I closed my eyes and swallowed, he slid his hand to the base of my throat so he could feel me drinking him down.

That was the hottest act of possession I'd ever experienced.

I'd barely let his dick slip out of my mouth when someone started pounding on the door.

Immediately I jumped up.

"Whoa. Where are you going?"

"Someone is beating on the door."

"Ignore it. We're not—"

Louder pounding. "Let me in, dammit. It's Ky."

Boone swore behind me.

I grabbed the T-shirt that had fallen to the floor when Boone first barged in and I pulled it over my head. I flipped the lock the same time Boone said, "Don't you unlock that fucking door, Sierra."

"I'm dressed. I'll see what he wants."

"Goddammit—"

I slipped out and slammed the door behind me.

Ky was at the bottom of the stairs when I caught him. "Kyler. What's going on?"

"The cops are here."

"Shit."

"They're being pretty cool because things *did* get out of hand." Ky set his hands on my shoulders and practically shoved me out the side door. "I need your help."

"What's going on?"

"Ana, one of the girls I was with tonight, got a minor last weekend. She wasn't drinking tonight, but if she gets caught here...they could kick her out of school since it'd be her third offense."

I almost said, *Third one for this school year? It's only the end of October!*

But Ky kept talking. "I don't need this on my conscience and she knows she better not show her face here again after this. But for now, can I get you to drop her off at her dorm?"

"This is why you...?" *Interrupted my sexy time with Boone? And isn't he gonna be thrilled that I bailed a-fucking-gain after things got heated between us?*

Fuck. The man would be on a rampage.

Or maybe he'd be really mellow after that blowjob.

Either way, it appeared I wouldn't be around to find out.

"Aren't the cops checking IDs of everyone leaving the party? They'll catch her that way."

"Yeah, but, ah, she's already under a blanket in your backseat."

"What! Are you serious?"

"Look, we were, ah, talking over by the hedge when the cops showed up. She panicked, jumped the hedge and then...fuck, I had to talk to her through the damn hedge before the cops caught her. I told her to look for your Mercedes because you never lock it."

"Aren't you just Mr. Prepared when it comes to damsels in distress. Helped a lot of underage drinkers hide in the bushes, have you?"

Ky's sheepish smile was there and gone. "No comment. Anyway, everyone has to take a breathalyzer before the cops will let them leave."

Fucking awesome. This just kept getting better.

"But since you're over twenty-one there's a different line for you."

"There's a *line*?"

"Yeah." He smirked. "It was a hoppin' party before it got busted."

"Where's Mase? Will he get in trouble?"

"Since the cops were asking for his autograph? Not likely."

"Direct me to the shorter blow-and-go line. You owe me big time for this, Kyler McKay."

"Thanks, Sierra. You're the best. Did you and Boone have a good...talk?"

"No, but he was getting a pretty spectacular blowjob when you interrupted us, so yeah, I'll let you deal with him because he oughta be in a great mood."

14 Boone ♥

I RANG THE doorbell.

I paced as I waited for-fucking-*ever* for her to come to the damn door. Did she have to stop for a snack on the way? Because the house was freaking gigantic.

The lock clicked. From behind the door as it swung open, Sierra said, "Did you forget your key again?"

"Didn't we already have a discussion about keys tonight?"

She froze inside the doorframe.

So did I when I saw the tiny red bikini she had on.

Jesus. It was like she'd waved a red flag in front of a bull.

"Boone. What are you doing here?"

I lifted a brow. "You're surprised? After you blew me and ran off?"

She blushed. "I didn't run off. Didn't Kyler tell you what happened?"

"No. I'm not exactly happy with *Kyler* tonight."

She swallowed hard.

All that did was remind me how fantastic it'd felt when she'd done that with my dick in her mouth. I took a step toward her. "You and I are done with parties, Sierra. *Done*. For good. From that first one seven years ago to the one tonight. Done. It never ends well for us."

"True."

"If Kyler wouldn't have had the worst timing on the planet earlier, would you have still run off afterward?"

Sierra started to back up. "I don't know."

Fuck. Not what I wanted to hear from her. "Tell me you meant it when you said you were so far gone with wanting me that you had to have me right then. Tell me you didn't suck my cock like a fucking dream because you had some twisted revenge fantasy going on."

"No! God, no, Boone. I did want you—I *do* want you. You needed to know how much. You needed to know right then."

I unclenched my jaw. "You undid me. That sassy little way you flicked your tongue. The smirking curl to your lips before you took me deep. How you just swallowed me down. Then…"

Sierra moved forward. "Then what?"

"Then you bailed so fast I thought maybe it didn't mean—"

"Anything? Seriously?" Her voice escalated and she whapped me on the chest. "You thought it was just another fucking blowjob for me?"

"Don't yell at me. You left without a word, without a text, without a call, without anything."

"I was a little busy getting breathalyzed, having my ID checked, sneaking an underage girl out from underneath the cops' noses, driving her back to campus, all while I still had the taste of you on my tongue and every time I took a breath all I could smell was the scent of your skin and that intoxicating cologne you wear." Her chest was heaving when she paused. "Besides, the phone line runs both ways, asshat."

"Asshat. Really? After *you* fled the room, leaving me naked with my damn dick flapping in the wind, by the time I got dressed and downstairs, you were gone. However, *Lucinda Grace* was in fine form, drunk as hell, back-talking a cop, so I interrupted knowing Raj would kick my ass if I let his woman get hauled off to jail. Luckily the cop handed her over to me, so I ended up half-carrying, half-dragging her to my car, which was about a mile from party central. Then after I dropped her off at Raj's, I realized my damn phone was dead and I drove around for half an hour in cookie-cutter suburbia, searching for your house, not knowing how you'd react to me tracking you down."

Now my chest was heaving.

We stared at each other.

Sierra said, "So yeah, no more parties for us."

Then she took a step back and another. "As far as how I feel about you tracking me down, Boone?" Dropping her arms like a gunslinger reaching for her weapons, she yanked both strings on her bikinis bottoms at the same time and the two red triangles floated to the white tile floor, landing like arrows pointing toward her. Then she reached behind her back, unhooked the bottom strap of her top, pulled it over her head and flung it aside.

Sierra was beautifully, gloriously naked.

Beautifully, gloriously naked and trembling in front of me.

Fuck. Me.

I couldn't remember my cock ever being as hard as it was right now.

Without looking away from her, I kicked the door shut hard enough the house shook.

Her eyes roved over my chest with such hunger that my nipples tightened. "Lose your shirt."

In one fluid movement I removed it and chucked it on the floor.

As I sauntered over to where she'd pressed herself against the wall, I dragged the heel of my hand down the front of my athletic shorts to adjust my cock.

"Look at you. Christ. You're fucking perfect. Everywhere." Those sweet tits. The long expanse of her torso. The sexy swell of her hips and the tempting dark strip of hair between her soft thighs. Muscled calves and be-ringed toes. All mine for the taking.

I curled my hand around her hip, scraping the edge of my thumb over the tattoo just below her hipbone. Angling my head, I skimmed her collarbone with an openmouthed kiss. "I could eat you alive. Every inch. Top to bottom." I planted kisses up the side of her throat to her ear. "But I'm gonna start in the middle."

She exhaled a breathy, "Yes."

Immediately I dropped to my knees. I glanced up at her, to see her staring down at me. "Sierra, keep your hair back so I can see your face."

"Why?"

"I want to watch your eyes when you come."

She trembled and nodded. Then she slid her left foot out, widening her stance.

Oh sexy girl, you want this bad and I'm gonna give it to you so, so good.

With the palm of my hand, I lightly stroked her leg from her knee to her hip. I leaned in, nuzzling the sensitive inner flesh, and caught the scent of her. My mouth homed in on it, landing on the soft strip of hair. I allowed a moment to bury my face right here and fill my lungs with her musky sweet perfume.

My fingers followed the rise of her mound and then spread her open, baring all that glistening pink flesh to my gaze and to my mouth. I pressed my lips to the hot skin, intending on gifting her clit a butterfly kiss. But as soon as my lips connected with the slick proof of her arousal, all plans for sweet kisses vanished.

The woman was so fucking wet my mouth was sliding around.

So wet for me. For what I could do to her.

Closing my eyes, I flattened my tongue, gathering as much of her essence in one short lick as I could. I groaned. "God, you taste fucking amazing."

I lapped up one side of her fleshy folds and down the other, stopping to tease her clit until she wiggled and squirmed. But I still couldn't get close enough. Deep enough. I needed more of the tang of her coating my throat, more of Sierra's essence filling me, more of it covering me.

With *more more more* on a continual chant inside my head, I used my right hand to hold her against the wall when I gripped the back of her right thigh and brought it over my left shoulder.

"Boone!"

Better. Fuck. That was *so* much better. Now I had all of her. Right. *There.*

I dragged my thumb down that pretty pink split in her sex and pushed it inside her.

Almost instantly her body rewarded me with a new sheen of wetness.

Her hand gripped my hair so hard it hurt.

I gorged on her. No tongue technique, just raw fucking hunger as I ate at her.

"Boone. Please."

I paused to breathe, but I kept rubbing my mouth over this beautiful part of her that had become my new obsession. "Sierra...I just...need..."

"What?"

"I need it fucking *all*. Give it to me." I dove back in, my mouth all over the place.

She went crazy when I used my teeth.

I went crazy when her fingernails dug into my forearm.

I settled over her clit, relentless in getting her to come.

And then she did. Her belly clenched beneath my hand, her thigh tightened around the back of my neck and all that smooth skin around her clit seized up and pulsed beneath my mouth like fucking applause.

A husky moan drifted down to me as she rode out her orgasm on my face.

Yeah. That's it. Take it.

When the pulses faded, I growled against that tender flesh because I wanted more. More of the tart taste of her glazing my face. More of her soft thigh pressed against my cheek. I blew a stream of air across the wet tissues, holding fast when she gasped and tried to retreat. "No. Don't move."

Her hand shook when she pushed her hair out of her face.

"Sierra. Look at me."

Her eyes were still heavy-lidded with lust.

"Never get enough of this. I could fucking *live* here. Just survive on the fucking taste of you…" I dragged my mouth up the inside of her thigh and met her gaze. "Again. I need that again. Right now."

"*You* need it?"

"Yeah, baby, I do. This pussy is goddamn addictive."

Sierra said, "I don't think I… Omigod! What are you…?" Her head fell back against the wall and she moaned. "Whatever *that* is? Don't you dare stop."

I found the finesse I'd lacked earlier and built her up more slowly, despite my cock protesting that it was time for a turn. I glanced up at her to see her peering down at me.

That's when she came. So hard and fast she didn't make a sound as my tongue drew lazy circles on her quivering clit.

It was hot as fucking fire.

I backed off and brushed my wet mouth across her belly, lowering her leg, even when her standing leg was decidedly wobbly.

Standing, I reached for the condom in my pocket before shoving my athletic shorts to the floor.

Sierra watched me with those big hazel eyes as I ripped the package open and rolled the condom on.

Less than a foot separated us. I braced my left hand on the wall by her head. Then my right. I lowered my head, she parted her lips and our mouths collided.

Every atom in my body fired with need as all that soft bare skin rubbed against mine.

Sierra's touch had turned frantic, her hands were in my hair, following the cords straining in my neck, then trailing down my chest and belly until her fingers connected with my cock. No delicate touch this time; she closed a fist around it and squeezed.

I tore my mouth free from hers and panted against her neck, "Wait."

"We've waited long enough." She turned and nuzzled the side of my head. "Please."

And I was done.

Dropping my hands to her ass—god, I loved that squeak she made—I said, "Wrap your legs around me."

I reclaimed her mouth as I centered her left leg above my hip, then pressed her back against the wall to lift and position her right thigh.

She wiggled, pushing down to where my cock was trapped between us.

"Sierra," I said, against her lips. "Keep your eyes on mine."

I snaked a hand between us and circled my cock at the base, then slid her up so the head rested at her slick opening.

With both hands free I pressed my palm over her left breast and curled my left hand around the right side of her face.

I pushed inside her, trying not to grit my teeth because she was so fucking tight.

When her eyes started to flutter closed, I squeezed her breast. "Look at me."

"Boone."

"Feel me. All of me. I want to know that you're right here in this moment with me."

"I am."

My fingers traced her cheekbone and the hollow beneath. Then I outlined the swell of her bottom lip and the upper bow, mapping her face while I stared into her eyes.

I'd paused with my dick halfway in. Not only was Sierra's tight, wet heat and the promise of more killing me, my legs were bolstering us both, and my core was picking up the slack. My entire body shook and I needed relief. I couldn't stop the snarl when I canted my hips and slammed home those last few inches.

"Oh god. Boone."

I rested my forehead to hers, panting like I'd been hammering into her for hours, and it'd been one stroke. "Fuck." Her nipple stabbed into my palm and I pressed my fingers into the soft flesh of her breast, which was completely covered in goose bumps. "You feel perfect. I knew you would." I kept an eye lock on her as I withdrew and thrust again.

"Yes. More." She swallowed a groan when I rocked up, deep, hard and fast.

I fit my mouth to hers; the kiss was wet and messy. An open-mouthed clash of primal sex noises as I started to fuck her without pause.

Sierra's fingernails gouged my ass and she started pumping her hips for faster friction so I knew she was close.

I clamped my hands on the insides of her legs and pushed her thighs open so they were almost parallel to the wall. Then with my groin in constant, grinding contact with her clit…KABOOM.

And I didn't have a fucking prayer of holding back when she clawed at me, moaning my name with throaty reverence as she came. Her pussy walls clamped around my dick with rhythmic pulls so intense my legs bobbled as her body proved it owned me, just as much as her heart and soul had already laid claim to me.

I let go with a harsh grunt, my release made sweeter and more perfect with Sierra whispering, "That's it, Boone. Give me all of it. Don't ever hold back with me."

"Fuck." I shuddered through every pulse with my face buried in her neck. I kept thrusting—for how long, I had no idea, time had no place here—just small pumps of my hips, even after the last hot spurt, unwilling to lose this connection with her.

Her grip tightened on my hair. "Don't stop."

I opened my mouth over the spot on her neck that caused her to squirm and gasp. When I used my teeth, she whimpered. When I teased with butterfly flicks of my tongue, she begged. And when I sank my teeth in and sucked hard on that sweet sensitive flesh? She emitted a little scream and bucked against me as she came again.

Hottest. Fucking. Thing. Ever.

The bonus? My dick was an iron rod again by the time she finished. I nipped her throat one last time before I took those lips.

Although I'd tried, sort of, to keep it slow and sweet this time...it wasn't. It would be fast though because I couldn't get enough of how amazing her body felt wrapped around mine, how quickly she clamped down those tight inner muscles to keep me deep inside every time I bottomed out.

I plowed into her, my head spinning, my body primed once again to detonate. I ended the kiss, letting my head fall back as my balls lifted and I started to come, closing my eyes to fucking savor every hard jerk of release. My last conscious memory before the orgasm engulfed me was of her sassy little tongue licking sweat trickling down my neck.

After my vision cleared and the blood stopped roaring in my head, Sierra's mouth brushed my ear. "You, Boone West, are a sexy beast when you come."

I groaned against her throat. My legs were cramping. So was my ass. We needed to take a break—a small one, at any rate. "So where's your bed, McKay?"

15 Sierra ♥

BOONE CARRIED ME to bed.

It was one of those passionate, romantic, swoon-worthy scenes like in the movies. My legs were secured around his waist. My elbows rested on his shoulders as my hands gripped his hair. My neck was arched and he dragged openmouthed kisses down the side, sending shivers flowing over every inch of my naked skin. How could he see where we were going? I chalked that up to some kind of super soldier skill.

And Boone's hands. God, those big, rough, amazing hands had such a tight grip on my ass I could feel every individual finger digging into my flesh. He'd leave bruises, because I bruised like a peach, but I wanted them. I welcomed them. I couldn't wait to turn around and look over my shoulder and see proof of Boone's passion embedded in my skin.

He lifted his mouth long enough to say, "Christ, is your bedroom in Mexico?"

I snickered. "Last room on the right. It's kind of a big house."

He gently deposited me on the bed. Then after he shut and locked the door, he tossed the condom in the trash, rewarding me with a full view of his magnificent ass. All hard and round and just…yum.

Boone spun around and stopped with his hands on his hips. "Did you just say yum?"

"Uh-huh. I was looking at your ass."

"Really."

My gaze zeroed in on his cock, which was hard again. "Is your dick feeling bad because I said your ass is yummy?"

He grinned. "You showed my dick earlier just how yummy you think it is."

"So you've gotten over your pissiness about the surprise blowjob during a college football victory party?"

Boone fisted his cock in his hand. Keeping his eyes on my chest, he slowly stroked up and down.

My body just went...done. Hot, wet and ready for that bad boy again? *Yes. Please.*

"This is a total dick question."

"And you're addressing it to me?" I looked pointedly at his crotch. "Shouldn't you be talking to...?"

"Jesus, you're a smartass even in bed."

"Lucky you, huh, baby?" I cooed.

Boone closed his eyes and muttered something before he looked at me again. "I'll rephrase. The question I'm about to ask might be taken as rude, but I'm asking anyway. Are you on the pill?"

"Yes. Why?" I knew why and my girl parts quivered with excitement at the thought of no condom between them and that badass dick Boone had going on.

He pounced on me, shaking the bed. Then he settled his body on top of mine so we were face-to-face. The fire in his eyes caused my belly to flip. With deliberate slowness, he brushed his lips over mine. "I want to fuck you bare. Nothing between us. I'm clean. The health report is three months old but I haven't been with anyone in that time." Another teasing pass of that succulent mouth across mine. "I have access to the document on my phone."

"Okay. Equally dick-ish question back to you." I paused. "Do you have the document on your phone so you can say, 'Let's skip the condoms, I'm clean, I'll prove it?' And then most women don't ask to actually look at it?"

The anger I expected didn't appear. Instead he smiled at me. "McKay, I'm so fucking proud of you right now I could clap."

"Why?" The weight of him, the heat of him, the scent of him, god, the reality of him was turning everything hazy.

Then he increased that level of heat another fifty degrees with more drugging kisses. "Because you didn't just assume I'm telling you the truth about being clean. You questioned it."

"Oh. Well, *go me!* for passing the 'truth in medical intentions' pop quiz from my very favorite medical professional."

Those hot brown eyes just watched me.

"What?"

"You're nervous."

"Of course I'm nervous."

"Why?"

I cupped his jaw and my thumbs met in the middle of his lips. I outlined that damp flesh, bottom and top. "Because this is *you*. I've wondered what this would be like with you since the first time you looked at me on the bus."

"And what just happened in the foyer? My mouth between your legs until you came on my face twice and then my cock slamming into you so hard neither of us could fucking breathe? What was that?"

"Some pent-up aggression on your part. Some desperation on my part. I wanted that. Trust me. We both knew the first time it'd be about intensity. But this is different. We've dealt with the lust. Twice. So much lust, Boone," I murmured against his mouth, "that there wasn't time for nerves. So I'm anxious because I don't know what to expect now. Not that I have a fear of disappointment."

"But you do have fear of something."

"Yeah."

He kissed me. "Tell me."

"Now that we're lovers…that's not all I want us to be to each other."

"Sierra. Baby, the last two weeks haven't been some calculated buildup. Now that we've banged each other's brains out, I won't be scouting for a new conquest."

"I know that. It's just…"

Warm, firm lips glided over mine. Then he kissed my cheeks, the corners of my eyes. His mouth migrated to my ear with more of his barely-there kisses. An unfamiliar dizzying rush of need swamped me.

Boone whispered, "You think too much."

He rolled and I was on top of him. But with the way he'd crossed his arms over my back, he retained the upper hand from below. He nudged my jaw with the top of his head, his prompt for me to bare my neck to him.

Which I did without hesitation.

His nuzzles were surprisingly sweet. Achingly tender. Completely unhurried. The heat of his breath in my ear elicited a head-to-toe shiver and a soft moan.

"I'll never lie to you." More heated breath and the pass of his soft lips on my ear. "I'll want you naked. A lot. A whole, whole lot. I can't think of any better way to show you how I feel about you than when we're like this. Just us here in this place that is ours alone because we can make it whatever we want it to be. We can be...smug in the knowledge that it's never been like this, for either of us, ever, with anyone else."

In that moment I felt Boone West reach inside my chest and wrap his big hands around my heart. It didn't scare me, this hold he had on me. It felt right.

I sighed.

He chuckled against my throat. "Freak-out done?"

"Mostly."

"Can we get back to being freaky now?"

He was such a guy. "By all means, West, bring it on."

Once again I found myself flipped onto my back.

Boone was right in my face. "Condoms. What did you decide?"

"Oh, this is up to me? I'm thinking maybe you'd better double bag this bad boy." I wrapped my fingers around his shaft at the base and he hissed. "He seems a little ornery."

"Si-er-ra. Focus. Condoms. Yes. No."

"You told me you're clean—I will be checking that medical report as soon as your phone is charged up—and I'm on the pill, but you didn't ask if I'm clean."

"I know you are. You had blood work done in Sundance. An STD screen was part of it to rule out all factors for infection and fever. I was worried about you so I checked your labs when they came back to make sure nothing was missed."

"I appreciate you looking out for me." I touched my lips to his. "Sounds like we can skip condoms."

Boone smashed his mouth to mine.

Damn but the man could kiss.

This kiss was pure seduction. Soft, melting, teasing. Licking his way into my mouth, easing back to brush the scruff on his cheek across my lips, sending a spike of heat straight between my legs. He circled my right wrist with his left hand and slid my arm up above my head. Then he threaded his fingers through mine, squeezing slightly. The callused edge of his thumb made lazy circles around the bone in my wrist. If I closed my eyes and concentrated, the movement mimicked the way he'd traced his tongue around my clit.

My clit throbbed hard once in remembrance and I moaned.

Boone trailed biting kisses down my neck to the ball of my shoulder. His right hand skimmed my side from my hip up to the outer curve of my breast.

I held my breath each time his teasing fingers almost reached my areola. I'd been so focused on that, I'd lost track of his mouth.

Then wet heat engulfed my nipple, followed by a hard suck.

My back bowed off the mattress.

He shifted, pressing his hip over mine to keep me still as he continued to torment my breast with lazy flicks of his tongue and cool puffs of breath.

Through it all, he kept my hand clasped above my head, his heavy arm stretched out over mine so I felt every flex of his powerful biceps.

Boone's silence as he showed me the pleasure he took in my body served as a reminder of his intensity. Every touch was so electric that when I glanced down, I expected to see flares of blue lightning dancing across my skin. Then he fed me languorous soul kisses that rocked me to the marrow of my bones.

He moved with sensuous intent as he switched sides, teasing the wrist bone of my left hand and pinning it above my head. His left hand traveled down the center of my body until his fingers breached the curls between my legs. He followed the seam of my sex to where I was wet. Really wet.

His rumble of satisfaction vibrated in my lips and tongue as he kissed me, sending a reverberation down my throat and exploding in a wave of tingles throughout the rest of my body. He stroked my slit, stopping at the top to tease the bundle of nerves nearly hidden in the folds of my swollen sex. Then another long, slow sweep down and he pushed two fingers inside me.

With his mouth controlling mine, I couldn't arch up. Every swirl across my clit and two-fingered plunge proved that he set the pace. I couldn't force this orgasm to happen on my own. It was his to give me.

When my thighs started to shake and I dug my nails into his forearm, he didn't pause in his rhythm, but he pulled back so our lips were barely touching and gritted out, "Give it to me. I want to feel you coming around my fingers."

"Boone."

"You're close. I can feel it. Let it go."

I sucked in a breath of air on a gasp when Boone fastened his mouth to the side of my throat, in the one place guaranteed to set me off again.

And it did.

I shattered. My pussy pulsing around those thick fingers, my clit throbbing against the hard press of his thumb.

By the time that bonus O faded, Boone had levered himself over me.

A whisper-soft kiss crossed my brow. "Sierra."

"Mmm?"

"Look at me."

I managed to unroll my eyes from the back of my head and opened them slowly.

That tight feeling in my chest expanded when I gazed into that gorgeous face. We were really here. Together. Like this. The way we'd always wanted.

His gaze never left mine as his hands moved to the insides of my thighs, spreading them wider as he started to work his cock into me. "You are so fucking tight."

"That's because you're packing a cannon."

Once he filled me completely, he brushed his lips over mine. "Feeling this hot, wet pussy bare around my cock? This might be rocket fast. Put your hands on my ass and hang on."

I murmured, "You're so bossy," but my fingers were already digging into that smooth, hard muscle.

"You can complain when I don't get the job done."

When he slammed back in twice in rapid succession, I might've screamed.

Cocky man just chuckled against my neck. Then he pushed up so he could watch his cock tunneling in and out of me. "You're so wet. Fuck. It makes me crazy to see that. Makes me want to bury my face in you again."

"Anytime you want to do that, feel free. You don't even have to ask."

That got his focus back on my face. He angled his head and bit my bottom lip, holding it between his teeth like he'd held my clit. Flicking his tongue over it like he'd teased my clit.

My clit pulsed hard.

Then he let my lip go, only to kiss me in that fleeting manner, so he could watch my eyes as he fucked me.

The man was an animal in bed. His instincts were unparalleled. He knew when I needed more pressure on my clit but not harder thrusts. He knew I needed the stroke of his hand—on my leg, my side, my chest, my neck—to hit that next level right before I unraveled. So the soft scrape of his nails up and down the outside of my thigh pushed me that much closer.

Boone's tongue swirled just inside my ear. "You ready to come?"

"I can't come on command," I panted. "But I'm close."

Then he was back to kissing me. Hard. Fucking me. Hard. He eased back to say, "Come now. Let me see it."

He did some flex and grind motion with his hips.

Sensations hit me from all sides: Boone's breath on my lips, the throbbing in my clit, the rocking of his pelvis, the tight clamp of my pussy muscles around his cock, which was pulsing hard as he groaned above me.

Whoo-yeah. He could be as bossy in bed as he wanted after that.

My skin was sticky, my nipples ached, my throat was dry.

I'd never felt so...spectacular. And not just spectacularly fucked either.

BOONE KEPT ME spooned against him as we caught our breath. He trailed his fingers up and down my arm.

I rolled over and faced him. Or rather, I faced his bare chest. His muscled bare chest. Now that we were lovers, would he let me touch him and kiss him any time I wanted? Would he let me lick and suck and taste? I bent forward and placed my lips on the upper curve of his left pec.

God. He smelled so good. I parted my lips, gliding them back and forth across his damp skin. He tasted good too. I flattened my palm on the right side of his chest to hold him in place as my mouth wandered to explore the left side. Was that thick slab of muscle always hard? Or was he flexing? I rubbed the side of my face across the top of his chest, loving how the firm flesh felt against mine. I buried my face above his sternum, letting his chest hair tickle my lips as I breathed him in. I liked that he had some chest hair. I didn't like furry, but super smooth was kind of weird. The delineated line of his lower pecs grabbed my attention and my tongue darted out to follow the deep cut. How often did he have to lift weights to stay so amazingly ripped?

My fingers had been caressing the right side of his chest and my thumb connected with his nipple. I pressed kisses back up his torso until I reached the flat disk, circling it with just the tip of my tongue. Then I lapped at it, tasting the salt and musk of him. I used my teeth, watching how fast the disk pebbled when I blew a stream of air across it. I played around doing what I wanted until I realized Boone hadn't said anything for quite some time. And I could feel his heart beating much harder.

I peered up at him.

"Having fun?" he asked in that sexy, growling tone.

I forgot about after-sex talk and everything else when faced with the glory of his chest. "Sorry."

"Don't be. I loved it."

"You did? But I wasn't doing anything specific like trying to turn you on."

Boone curled his hand around the side of my face. "That's why I loved it. But it did turn me the fuck on. Watching how much you liked touching me."

"So I really can touch you any time I want?"

He laughed.

"Why is that funny?"

"Because of the look on your face. Like I've just given you a present."

"Being here with you in the present is the best present I've ever gotten."

Then I found myself flat on my back with Boone on top of me.

He hadn't been kidding about being turned on.

16 Boone 💜

I COULDN'T SLEEP.

I should've had the best sleep of my life in Sierra's bed, with her wrapped around me.

But I was panicked. I needed to move. So I could think. So I could breathe.

When Sierra shifted her position, I escaped.

I found my athletic shorts in the foyer where I'd left them and slipped them on before I made a beeline for the sliding glass door in the kitchen and stepped into the night.

The patio tiles were still warm, as was the air. The light from the pool cast shimmery shadows across the water. I paused by the edge. Since I hadn't seen exercise equipment, I couldn't burn the feeling off. Maybe a quick dip would loosen me up. Cool me off. Keep these thoughts from churning and becoming murky.

I eased down the steps into the water that was colder than expected. I wished I could turn off the pool lights. Darkness and water would be my own sensory deprivation tank. To get that effect, I closed my eyes when I submerged myself, holding my breath until my lungs ached. I popped up like a cork and bobbed around for a bit before I sank below the surface again. I repeated this process a dozen times until the jittery feeling was gone.

After I climbed out of the water, I stretched out on the cement and stared at the sky. No clouds. No stars. Just the continual orange glow of urban light pollution. I closed my eyes. That panicked thought jumped out first thing.

She'll think you're a freak.

How can I tell her the truth?

How can you not tell her? She will know. It's not like it won't be obvious.

It hasn't been so far.

Haven't you lied to her enough? A lie of omission is still a lie.

Fuck.

I'd always resented my parents. But until that moment, I hadn't really understood how much they'd fucked me up. I'd always told myself I didn't care. And I hadn't—not until now. Not until it mattered. Not until this ignorance in yet another part of me that had nothing to do with my dyslexia might cost me the one thing I couldn't bear to lose—Sierra. Either by seeing her pity if I nutted up and told her the truth, or by sensing her frustration if I didn't and she witnessed my inadequacies firsthand.

How fair was it that I could be so spectacularly fucked...after the most fucking spectacular night of my life?

I don't know how long I lay there, mired in dark thoughts.

I heard the whisper of feet crossing the pavement.

Sierra.

She probably thought I'd run out on her.

Maybe I should have. Maybe she would've been better off.

No, you fuckhead. You are here. You will goddamn deal with this. If she kicks your ass to the curb it won't be because you weren't honest with her.

A beach towel landed on my belly and I jumped.

A puff of air flowed over me as she spread a towel out beside me. Softer scraping as she settled next to me on the cement.

I tucked my towel under my head as a pillow.

She broke the silence first. "You're freaked out."

"Yep." I didn't elaborate—yet—and she didn't ask.

But she reached for my hand.

My heart raced.

One little thing. One thoughtful gesture that reminded me that I wasn't alone. One small sign of solidarity with me.

But that was all it took.

I was all fucking in with this woman. No holding back anything.

I said, "I didn't mean to wake you."

"You probably wouldn't have since you're so stealthy, Mr. Army Soldier, but the alarm for the patio door went off."

In my haste to escape I hadn't noticed the alarm—so much for my special training. "It did?"

"It's funny how many times I've been woken up by a door alarm. Lu actually keeps track of how many of her hookups sneak out in the middle of the night."

"Do they know that she knows exactly when they bail?"

"No. Which is why it's so funny." She paused. "Until it happened to me."

My gut twisted. "You thought you'd get up and find me gone?"

"I wasn't sure. I figured it was your turn for a freak-out moment since I've had several and hit the road at every major turning point so far."

"The thought had crossed my mind to just…go."

"Even if I would have found you gone, Boone, I would've come after you. Like you always come after me." She squeezed my hand.

I squeezed hers back.

It didn't seem odd that we were lying side by side on her patio, in the middle of the night, staring at the starless, cloudless sky.

"You want to talk about *why* you freaked out?" she asked gently.

"Yeah." I paused. "And fuck no."

Sierra laughed softly.

She didn't push. She didn't say anything. She didn't have to. I knew even if it took me a fucking hour to find my balls and spit this out, she'd still be right there beside me, waiting.

I compiled an ordered list in my head. High points. Low points. Problem was, they were all low points.

Quit stalling and man up.

It took two tries before I forced the words out. "I freaked out because I've never spent the entire night in bed with another person."

"Never?"

"Never."

"Not even as a kid?" she asked.

"Nope. Even with the shitty places we lived with my mom, I never shared a bed with my brother or sister."

"You shared a bedroom with them?"

"Yeah. I spent plenty of nights in a sleeping bag on the floor."

"What about during sleepovers with friends?"

I released a bitter laugh. "I didn't have friends. On purpose, so no one knew how fucked up my home life was with my drugged-out mother. The closest I came to a sleepover was on the rare occasion I stayed with Aunt Carolyn or my uncles Chet and Remy."

Sierra didn't say anything. That's when I noticed she'd started sweeping her thumb across the back of my hand, down to the bone in my wrist and back up. Maybe she wasn't conscious of the constant movement. Maybe it was a way of calming herself. But that tender touch soothed me. Or maybe she knew I needed a connection to her, however small.

Back to supposing. Back to stalling. You started this, finish it.

I inhaled and exhaled, trying to stop my heart from racing like a trapped rabbit's.

"Then I moved in with my dad and had my own room and a double bed. Man. I loved having all that space to stretch out in. The last thing I wanted was to share that with anyone. Even temporarily."

"So your high school hookups?"

"Didn't happen there."

"I drove past your house once." She paused. "Okay, more than once, but less than a hundred times. I always hoped you might be outside working on your motorcycle when I passed by and I could act all innocent. 'Oh, Boone, you live here? I didn't know that. But since I'm in the neighborhood…'"

I allowed a small smile at that image because that was exactly how the Sierra I'd known would've played it. "What happened after the 'Since I'm in the neighborhood' scenario?"

"In my sixteen-year-old fantasy world? We made out like crazy. I think I let you touch my boobs."

I groaned. "Goddamn you had a nice rack. I tried so fucking hard not to stare at it." I brought our joined hands to my mouth and kissed her knuckles. "You still have an outstanding rack, baby."

"And now you can touch it any time you want."

Silence settled between us again.

When I didn't speak, Sierra prompted me. "So you had your own bed at your dad's. After that?"

"In the army I had a cot. Or occasionally a bunk bed. Never had to share. Actually, we weren't allowed to share."

"I'll just ask this straight up. You are fucking hot as hell, Boone West. You didn't lack female attention when you were in high school and I doubt a healthy, sexy, young, buff, gorgeous soldier chose celibacy."

"I chose hookups. Which I told you. Always at her place so I could leave after. Yeah, I was that fucking douchebag 'one and done' guy."

"There's no judgment, so don't get testy."

I blew out a breath. "Sorry. It's just hard to admit, to you of all people, that I've never done the whole cuddle, snuggle thing except while waiting for my dick to get hard. I fucked, then I went back to my place. Alone. Every time."

"Hence the 'no shampoo bottles in the shower' reality," she said.

"Yeah."

"So you don't do the whole cuddle, snuggle thing longer than necessary to get laid...because you don't like it?"

"Being with you the last couple of hours? That's the longest it's ever been for me." I held myself rigid, intending to pull away the instant I detected any pity.

Sierra just groaned. "You probably felt smothered because I am a very friendly sleeper. Sorry about that."

She'd apologized to me because I'd bailed? As easy as it'd be to let that stand, I wasn't one to blame others for my shortcomings. "Christ, Sierra. Don't apologize. You need to know these weird things about me so you don't think any of it has to do with you. That I'm fucked up."

When she didn't immediately respond, my leg started to bounce with nerves.

Sierra placed her hand around the top of my quad and squeezed— harder than I expected. It wasn't harsh, but it did remind me to stay focused. "As long as you've opened this door, Boone, you need to take me through it all the way. Because I'll be honest with you, I like the whole cuddle, snuggle thing. I want that with you. Not just after you fuck me, but when we're watching TV, or like this if we're just lounging by the pool. Earlier you said you can show me how you feel about me when we're naked and our body parts are connected."

I couldn't help but grin at her vague reference to body parts.

"But shoving your dick in me is not the only way to show me that you care. I'm affectionate, so you'll just have to deal with that."

And here was the moment of truth. "And if I don't know how?"

"How what? How to deal with me being affectionate?"

"Yeah. I've never had that."

"You've never had what? Affection?"

"Drop the confetti and sound the alarm—we have a winner. Just don't expect a hug as the prize for guessing correctly." That didn't make me sound like an emotionally stunted asshole at all. Jesus.

"I'm confused. So cut the sarcasm and talk to me."

My Sierra. Patient and understanding...until my flip response forced her not to be.

She deserves better.

No kidding. Why the fuck had I even started talking about this? Did I want to chase her away?

"Boone," she said sharply.

"It's another fucked-up thing in my life to add to the others."

"Tell me."

"Junkie mom. Aloof dad. They both resented me and neither of them liked me much. So they didn't bother faking affection. They yelled at me, or in my mom's case, she beat on me, but did either one of them ever give me a hug? Nope."

She let that sink in before she murmured, "Never?"

"Never. Not once. And this isn't something I'd exaggerate, because who the fuck wants to admit that to anyone?" Before Sierra asked if I'd ever confessed this to anyone else, I kept talking. "My mother was 'drugs not hugs.' Bad thing about her being high was she didn't give a damn about eating so I went hungry. The good thing about her being high was she didn't take out her bad mood for *not* being high by beating the crap out of me."

"And your dad?"

"He wasn't around until he had no choice but to take me in. So he's too fucking macho for that hugging shit. He couldn't even give me a half-assed bro hug when I graduated from basic. It was the norm with him and I didn't realize it was...abnormal until I had this weird fever dream during a visit to the ER. In my dream all these dads and sons were on this big baseball diamond, slapping each other on the back. High fiving. Hugging. And me and Dad were in the bleachers watching, not looking at each other. That's when I noticed Dad didn't have any arms."

"Whoa. Heavy shit, Boone."

"It wasn't a drug-induced hallucination, just a fucked-up glimpse into my psyche. The total lack of emotion or affection would make me a textbook example of why Freddy sets fires or why Billy is a bully, except I didn't let it become a thing. I didn't let it define me or use it as an excuse. But from an early age I was adept at slipping lies into conversation so my shitty life was explainable instead of pitiable. In grade school, when kids complained about getting dumped off at their grandparents' house for the weekend, I chimed in I was tired of it too...when I never spent a single night at my grandparents' house. In middle school I'd call the cafeteria food crappy and refuse to eat it when the truth was I didn't have enough money for lunch. In high school I'd tell people I didn't have a car because my dad insisted we work on the classic he'd bought for me together. You already know I lied about having a girlfriend who lived out of town." I groaned out of pure embarrassment. "Sounds like a bad made-for-TV movie, doesn't it?"

"Sounds...rough."

I couldn't look at her. And I closed my own eyes as if it'd keep me from looking inside myself.

After a few moments passed, Sierra said, "While I'm grateful you told me all of this, I want to know what it means for us."

"It means I don't know how to be the normal kind of guy...boy-friend...whatever. The hand-holding, cuddling-up, sleeping-together-all-night, Netflix-and-chill type. That's part of why I freaked out. I'd started to feel that I don't have anything more to offer you now than I did seven years ago."

My breath left my belly when Sierra climbed on top of me. I could feel us chest to chest. Her face was so close to mine her breath drifted across my lips.

"Boone West, you look at me right now."

My heart hammered when I peeled my eyes open.

I expected to see pity on her face; instead I saw ferocity that brought my heart into my throat. "The only difference between us is I've had my family show me love and let me love them back. You haven't. That is not your fault."

This understanding about the things that formed me, without judgment, without pity…this was my definition of love.

I studied her. This woman who fucking owned me. "Sierra. I don't know how to do this."

"What?"

"Love." My hand and my voice shook when I touched her face. "The other reason I freaked out? What if what I want from you is too much? Everything you are, everything I am when I'm around you…that's the life I want with you. It's always been you."

Shock flashed in her eyes, followed by recognition. She whispered, "You knew. That's what you meant the night you kissed me. You told me if we'd been together the way you wanted, you wouldn't have been able to walk away from me."

"It wasn't a bullshit line. You scared the hell out of me, Sierra. Without thought, without knowing what it meant to me, you gave me a small taste of your affection—and we were just friends. I'd never had that and I almost couldn't wrap my head around the fact it could be better." I traced the arc of her cheekbone with my thumb. "Tonight proved that wrong. Jesus, woman. I…" I paused. Breathed. "I'm at a loss to even find words for how everything shifted in my world tonight."

"Mine too."

"Neither of us would've been ready for that seven years ago. Everything in my life was a struggle. You deserved more than a broke, broken kid. You probably deserve more than me now, but I've thrown it all down for you tonight. Everything I've never told another soul."

"I'll be honest…you have utterly wrecked me tonight."

I waited for her to explain or act very Sierra-like and offer me reassurance. But she didn't. I'd had years to process this; she'd need more than five minutes, so I forced myself to let it go. For now.

Finally she said, "We have a history and like you mentioned that first day in my office, it wasn't all bad. I just never understood how deeply the good parts affected you. *This* is the start over point for us, Boone." She swallowed hard.

Point for my girl for keeping it together. Because if she started to cry, Christ, I would too. I cradled her face in my hands and locked my gaze to hers. "I'm all in with you, Sierra. All. Fucking. In."

She turned her head and kissed my wrist, nuzzling her cheek into it with a sigh. "That right there, Boone. The way you reached for me without thinking? That is affection. You do things like that around me all the time—you always have."

I did? Get the fuck out. Maybe I wasn't entirely hopeless.

"And you're always messing with my hair, which hits all the sweet, sexy and possessive buttons. You watch me closely." She smirked. "I'm not talking about the way you leer at my ass. But how you study my face, my eyes, my body language. As if you want to provide me with whatever I need—before I even know I need it. I'll be honest…you were right to challenge me that I'd always known you'd felt more for me than friendship. Sometimes I used to catch you looking at me like…"

"Like you were a work of art that I wanted to lock away because no one would ever appreciate your rare beauty like I would?"

"Sweet talk and dirty talk coming from this sexy mouth… Not sure which one I like better." She brushed her lips across mine with deliberate seduction. "And speaking of sexy…tonight when you were on your knees with your mouth on me, the hungry sounds you made, the words you said, the way you used that wicked tongue…knocked my entire world off its axis." Her body trembled. "Sex wasn't just a game changer for us, but a life changer. It opened all of this up, things you wouldn't have told me before. Seven years ago I wasn't ready for you— for this—and neither were you."

My eyes searched hers. "But now?"

"Now? We go forward and learn how to be *all fucking in* together."

I brought her mouth to mine and kissed her from the depths of my soul.

When our bodies started arching and moving together, searching for that ultimate connection, I said, "Bed, now," against her lips.

Sierra slid down my body, planting kisses on my chin, on my throat, on my collarbone and finally placing a warm, soft, lingering kiss on the left side of my chest that I felt through the skin and muscle, straight to my heart.

We were in a dream-like state weaving through the dark house, hand in hand. Landing on the twisted sheets in a tangle of arms and legs, kissing and touching. Eager, yet still patient enough not to push the pace.

So when I finally levered myself over her, our skin damp and marked with love bites, our mouths swollen, her hair tangled and spread out on the pillow in a swath of dark silk as she writhed in eagerness, all I could think was *mine*.

Her eyes were closed as I teased the head of my cock between her legs.

"Sierra."

"Mmm?"

"Look at me."

"But I want to stay in this slow and dreamy state. In this cocoon." She turned her head to the side, offering me her throat.

"I want your eyes on mine."

Sierra did look at me then. "Why?"

"Because I get off watching them when I do this." I plowed into her with one fast snap of my hips.

Her back bowed up and she gasped. And came right away.

Hard not to feel cocky about that.

I continued to watch her as I fucked her slowly. Every time she looked away, I said, "Eyes on me."

Her face softened. "Boone." She touched my throat. "This is real."

My arms shook. My gut rippled. My ass cheeks ached.

"I promise if you close your eyes and reopen them I'll still be here."

How had she known that was my fear? That this was all just a dream?

"Let go. Take what you need."

"I have what I need. You." But fuck if my balls weren't boiling with the need to come.

Sierra put both hands on my chest. "Stop. Back up."

Pushing to my knees, breath heaving in and out of my lungs, I watched as she scooted to the side of the bed.

Wearing that sassy smile, she beckoned me over. "New position. But after this, we've gotta give it a rest because I'm getting chafed."

I glanced down at my dick and my knees. Both a little red. I'd put up with a lot of soreness if I could stay buried in that tight pussy all night, but her being chafed was a different story. Leaning over, I kissed her, a slow tangling of tongues and sweet licks and nibbles. "If you're too sore, I can stop."

"No. I just want to try this." Her cold feet landed on my belly and she inched her toes up my torso. "With my legs on your shoulders."

My inner beast roared a "fuck yeah" snarl and I pulled her up higher. My cock homed in on her pussy almost without my assistance and I slid back inside.

Sierra reached for my hands and pulled me down. "Rest your weight on me."

Damn. That felt good.

I kept a slow pace until Little Miss Position Changer said, "Stop," again.

"What?"

"We're taking a break after this, so maybe you'd better make this one count."

She was seriously telling me how to fuck her?

Of course she was.

I loved that—even when it sort of annoyed me.

So I lowered her heels to the mattress and dropped to my knees.

"What are you doing?"

"Making this one count. Any objections? You have another position in mind?"

No surprise that she didn't offer suggestions.

Only after I made her come with my mouth did I return to making love to her.

Her soft sighs were as satisfying as her gasps and groans. Her gentle touches and melting kisses were what I needed.

After I poured myself into her again and my mouth was tasting the sweet flavor of passion on her skin, she whispered, "I want you in my bed all night, Boone. But if you need…space. There's a blanket on the couch in the living room."

"Thanks. But I'll be fine right here."

17 Sierra

BOONE SLEPT IN my bed all night. Not entwined with me but I'd just been happy to wake up and find him still there.

Although it'd been a late night, I wasn't one for sleeping in.

Before I tiptoed out of my bedroom, I tucked the covers around Boone's shoulders. I wanted to smooth my hand over the nape of his neck and kiss his forehead, but I wouldn't chance waking him.

I grabbed my exercise clothes. I used a corner of the extra family room for a workout space—I'd never be a toned gym-rat, but I did feel healthier if I worked up a sweat. After setting the program on the elliptical for forty-five minutes, I hit shuffle on my iPod and did my time in hell.

Most people I knew could multi-task while churning away on an exercise machine. Not me. Music was the only thing that distracted me enough not to say *fuck this* and hop off the machine to do something productive that I actually enjoyed.

After I finished, I poked my head into my bedroom and saw Boone still sprawled in the same position. I smirked at seeing the scratch on his shoulder blade, knowing he bore my marks in other places, as I bore his. I left the door cracked open and headed to the kitchen. Without the music from my iPod blasting in my ears, the events from the past twelve hours raced through my mind.

Last night had been a revelation.

Okay, a night filled with a bunch of revelations.

We'd hit that explosive physical stage, where sex is everything; a drug, a tonic, a crutch, a relief, a necessity, more vital than food or sleep. I'd never experienced that combustion or that type of obsession.

Neither had Boone. It hadn't surprised either of us we experienced it together.

While the physical connection had been astounding, the emotional upheaval it'd brought with it...that'd been a total shocker. To both of us. To Boone, because he actually spoke of things he'd kept shoved down deep. To me, because I had no idea how much those things had affected him.

No fucking idea and it cut me to the quick.

I paused in front of the refrigerator and pressed my forehead against the cool metal door, needing a moment to let the truths about his childhood slowly wash over me before my distress swamped me entirely.

The indifference to his existence.

The complete lack of any affection.

My heart ached for him.

Ached.

From the moment I'd met Boone and we'd become friends, I'd wished for more from him. Until last night I hadn't realized how much of himself he had given me. Just me. He'd let down his guard during the times we'd spent together. He'd gotten to be a cocky, sweet eighteen-year-old-boy, flirting with a girl he liked, talking about everything and nothing. I loved those times with him.

But he treasured them because they were the only ones he'd had.

God.

To think that back then, and all this time, he'd held me up as his ideal? He wanted what no one before me had bothered to give him? I almost told him he was mistaken to put that much value in me. But he felt the way he felt and I'd never discount that. Never.

It seemed everyone in his life had discounted him.

Except me.

The tears I'd held back since last night fell in silence.

When the alarm for the patio door had gone off, I'd experienced fear and a feeling of loss. I'd sent the universe a silent plea. *Don't let this be the end. Don't let him have regrets.* After I mustered the guts to crawl out of the bed that smelled like him—like us—to reset the alarm, that's when I'd noticed him in the pool.

I'd watched him from the shadows, submerging himself and surfacing as if he'd been practicing drowning. But that had been Boone's way of reasserting control…and reminding himself to breathe.

So after I'd gained control, warning myself not to fucking cry because it'd send him running, I'd strolled out, alerting him to my presence. Hoping he'd open up to me, even if that meant dealing with his regrets about cramming as much sex as we could into as short a time as possible and his need to walk away or even cool it.

That's the conversation I'd expected.

Not Boone telling me he didn't know how to love.

I clapped my hand over my mouth to stop my anguish from spilling out. My anguish and heartbreak and horror and fury that he didn't know how to love someone because he'd never had love. Or affection. Or any of the normal exasperation and elation that came with loving someone and them loving you back.

So he'd focused on having a purpose. Did he think only then would he be worthy of affection and love?

No, no goddammit, he'd been worthy all along. How strong his will had to be to withstand a life without casual touches, without spontaneous hugs, without that comfort in knowing you were loved.

Right then I resolved to give him that every day. He would know my touch, even just in passing. He would know his value to me in every possible way so he'd never have to wonder again.

I crossed to the sink to wash away the evidence of my tears. I'd never want Boone to think I pitied him—I didn't, but I knew that's what he'd think if he saw me bawling. The last thing I wanted was for him to retreat. I wanted him here, where I could be what he needed.

After I made a pot of coffee, I tossed all the ingredients for banana bread into a bowl. While the oven heated, I mixed the batter, greased the pans and shoved them in the oven, all while slurping down my first cup of coffee. When I turned around from putting the dishes by the sink, I noticed Boone leaning against the doorjamb watching me, looking adorable with his hair sticking up and dark scruff on his face. "Hey."

I didn't wait for him to come to me. I nearly had a skip in my step as I skirted the center island and circled my arms around his waist, pressing my cheek against his chest above his heart. "Morning, sleepyhead."

Immediately Boone's arms closed around me.

His heart pounded beneath my ear. And the hand running up and down my arm felt clammy—almost like he was nervous.

Of course he's nervous. He told you things last night that he's never told anyone else. Things often look different in the light of day.

But for me everything was much clearer.

We held onto each other for a long time.

When Boone tipped my head back and smiled into my face, I puckered my lips for a good morning peck. But he devoured me. He didn't caress my cheek or my throat or my breast. His entire focus was my mouth, my lips, my tongue, my breath. After ending the kiss, he smiled into my face again. "Good morning, gorgeous."

I had to reach back for the counter because my legs were as mushy as banana skins.

"Thanks for letting me sleep in. That bed of yours is awesome."

"It's even more awesome when you're in it." I snagged a cup off the shelf. "Coffee?"

"Sure. What are you making that smells so good?"

"Banana bread."

"The same kind you used to make?"

I slid the coffee in front of him. "I made banana bread for you before?"

"Once." He wrapped his hands around his cup. "It had pineapple and chocolate chips in it."

"I don't remember that."

"You made a lot of good stuff for me. And you used me as a guinea pig, so maybe that's why you don't remember."

"All of that?" I waved dismissively. "An attempt to impress the hot, brooding senior I had a major, major crush on."

"It worked. The sandwich you made me that first day?" He sipped his coffee. "Still the best one I've ever had."

"I don't remember what it was. I do remember thinking, 'Boone West is in my house. I'm having lunch with Boone West. Do not be a dork.'"

He smiled. "But you were a dork and that's why I liked you."

I liked we could look back. "So do you have to work today?"

"No. Do you?"

"I have a few things to do later, but I can do them from here. I don't have to go in to the office."

Boone set down his cup and began to stalk me. "So we have the whole day to do whatever we want?"

"Mmm-hmmm. Got any ideas?"

Then he was right there. He hoisted me onto the counter. "I'll need to fuck you at least twice more."

"Our parts were getting chafed last night and we decided to give it a rest, remember?"

He scooted in until we were groin to groin. "My part is ready to say good morning to your part."

I kissed him. "Let's have breakfast first."

"Then what?"

"Are you antsy?" *Are you hinting around that you want to leave?*

Of course he read the anxiety in my eyes. "Hey. Not trying to bail on you. It's just…" His quick smile was just short of sheepish. "Now that I'm your man, am I supposed to clean out your gutters or some other 'honey do' list stuff?"

"Dude. I don't know any more about this weekend couple stuff than you do. I thought we'd probably just…hang out by the pool, or watch football, or spend the afternoon in bed, then eat something."

He curled his hands around my face. "This *all fucking in* stuff is awesome."

I almost laughed it off, but his intensity…holy shit.

Boone got closer yet, peering even more deeply into my eyes. "That wasn't a flip response because you suggested sports, sex and food."

"I get that."

"Does it scare you?" He stroked my cheekbones with his thumbs.

"It doesn't scare me." I flattened my hand over his heart. "It excites me. It humbles me."

"Humbles you? Why?" The intensity in those dark brown eyes didn't lessen. "Even after everything I told you last night?"

"*Especially* after everything you told me. And here you are, owning up to how you feel first thing this morning. No backtracking. No excuses."

"You thought I might say, 'Sorry, babe. I said some stuff last night that I didn't mean'?"

"I don't want to piss you off by saying I didn't know how you would react. Or what would happen this morning."

Boone rested his forehead to mine.

Although he held me gently, his entire body vibrated with tension. "But I know what I wanted to happen," I said softly.

"What?"

"This."

"Can you be more specific?"

I tipped my head back to look at him. "That there is an 'us' and it's a new beginning, not just closure from our past. That we're both *all fucking in.*"

He breathed a sigh of relief. "You're my past and my future. We *are* gonna figure this couple communication shit out, Sierra."

"I know. So let's get the big stuff out of the way first."

"Big stuff...like?"

"Like I want you to move in with me." I laughed at his utter look of shock. "Not expecting that one, were you?"

"No, ma'am. But you've got my attention."

I busied myself refilling our coffee before I laid out my plan. I looked at him. "You want logical or emotional first?"

"Logical."

"You've been looking for a place to live. I have a six-bedroom house."

"So I'd rent from you."

I sighed. "Okay, it doesn't appear that we can separate logic and emotion. You're probably going to be over all the time because we're *all fucking in.* I have a kick-ass house with a pool and a big garage. You need a place to live. Logically you should live here."

"Lu pays rent?" he asks.

"Yes. She does yard maintenance and I pay the utilities."

"Even if we share a bedroom I'll pay to live here."

I hated talking about money. "You could pay for part of the utilities."

Boone crossed his arms over his chest. "What's that run a month?"

"In the summer months when it's brutally hot it's about twelve hundred bucks. The rest of the year, half that."

"So you're happy getting the short end of the stick and paying more than your fair share? In your own damn house?"

I slapped my hands on the counter. "Keep that in mind, West. It *is* my house. If I want to give Lu a break on rent because I trust her and like having her live with me? I can. Same with you. I'm not going to take extra money from you that I don't want or need to run this house because you feel you owe me. I don't think you're a charity case, either. I own this house. No mortgage payment. I knew when I bought it I didn't need this much space. But it was one of those real estate deals I couldn't pass up. The price was ridiculously low and I had capital gains I had to invest in something. So the only payments I have on it are utilities, insurance and property taxes. You don't want to live here without paying something? Fine. But I don't expect you and Lu to foot the bill so *I* can live here free and clear."

He walked around the center island and stopped behind me, bracing his palms on the edge of the counter, caging me in. "Jesus, you're stubborn." He rubbed his lips across the top of my ear. "I'll pay the utilities. We'll talk about the grocery bill later. For right now..." He dragged an openmouthed kiss from the hollow below my ear, down the side of my neck, making sure to hit every blasted hot spot he'd discovered last night. "I'm ready for my breakfast."

My body was a mass of goose bumps even when my skin went hot and tight. My vision turned hazy. My brain veered offline when he peeled my yoga pants down my legs. Next he stripped off my T-shirt. He licked up my spine, starting at the small of my back. By the time his tongue reached the band of my bra, his hands had it undone and he tossed it aside.

"Boone—"

"Turn around."

I did and his mouth was on mine as his hands cupped my breasts, then followed the outline of my body, stopping at my hips.

He eased up on the kiss to say, "Hop up on the counter."

But he needn't have bothered telling me as he lifted me up without any effort.

The hunger in his eyes sent another shiver through me.

As did the possessive growl when he put his hands on the inside of my thighs and pressed them open, baring me to him completely.

Boone didn't say another word. He just lowered his head and feasted on me.

My initial worry about being naked in my kitchen with the morning sun streaming through the windows and highlighting my private parts...vanished with each flick of his tongue, with every long lick, with every sucking kiss.

He was relentless.

I was unprepared for how fast he could get me off.

The orgasm sideswiped me in a throbbing, pulsing, hair-pulling, toe-curling burst of sensation.

I didn't even mind his cocky little chuckle.

He'd earned it.

Boy, had he ever earned it.

My ears were still ringing and my head was filled with the white fluffy clouds of post-orgasmic bliss when Boone tugged me upright.

He said, "Hang on," and pulled me off the counter, keeping his hands on my ass as I locked my shaking legs around his waist and circled my arms around his neck.

The man could multitask like no one's business; he carried me, almost blindly since his mouth was busy on my throat. He growled, "Need inside you now," and laid me on my back on the kitchen table.

Boone didn't take his eyes off mine as he shoved his athletic shorts down. He fisted his cock and jacked himself. "You're wet enough to take me."

Not a question.

That confidence, that passion, that raspy voice...all of it, sexy as fuck.

Then those rough-skinned palms were on my knees, pushing them apart.

Seeing the way his eyes glittered and the determined set of his jaw, I felt the need rising in me again. Tingles, chills, anticipation.

He slammed his cock into me to the hilt in a near-punishing stroke. I gasped and locked my ankles above his ass.

He grinned and did it again. He angled forward to take a nipple in his mouth, not wavering in the pounding rhythm he set.

I couldn't look away from him. So beautiful and fierce lost in passion and answering his body's demands. When I began to slide up the table from his powerful thrusts, I latched onto his biceps to anchor me.

That caused him to slow down.

Boone layered his chest over mine and planted the palms of his hands beside my head. He gave me that dirty grin and began to do a circle and grind thing with his hips.

I managed to choke out, "What the hell is that?"

His lips teased mine with whisper-soft kisses. "Like that, do you?" He pressed down on the upstroke, giving my clit extra friction.

"Yes."

"Come like this for me." Another feather-light, seductive kiss. "I fucking love to watch you come."

"Might be too soon," I panted.

He shook his head. "You're almost there." His mouth migrated across my jaw. He proved my readiness with the steady rocking of his pelvis until I unraveled again.

After I floated back to earth, he whispered, "You're beautiful."

"Boone."

He picked up the pace. His hard fucking with table-thumping ferocity lasted half a dozen strokes. Then he threw back his head and let go.

Before he fully recovered, the timer on the oven started to ding.

I scrambled upright. I'd totally forgotten about the banana bread.

Then Boone was in my face. "Not letting you go without this." He kissed me with the mix of surety and sweetness that I needed. How he'd picked up on that in less than twelve hours...

Don't dissect it; accept it as your good fortune.

Against my lips, he murmured, "You deal with the banana bread. I'll wipe down the counters."

"We are such a great team already."

He laughed. "All fucking in, baby."

My body was still humming with pleasure when the front door opened and Lu's voice boomed from the foyer. "Me'n Raj are here, so put some clothes on."

Boone sent me a cocky grin before he called out, "We are dressed and in the kitchen."

Lu came around the corner with Raj directly behind her. "I thought I smelled banana bread. But I figured you two wouldn't surface from the bedroom for at least three more hours."

"In a house this size? Why would we limit ourselves to one room?" Boone replied, keeping his eyes on mine. "Lucky thing you weren't here half an hour ago."

I tried to hide my blush behind my mug of coffee.

"It looks like you had time to wipe the butt prints off the refrigerator, Miss Neat Freak," Lu said.

"We didn't do it against the fridge," I retorted.

Raj muttered something to Boone. Whatever Boone said had Raj giving him a huge grin and a fist bump.

And they said women were bad, gossiping about sex.

I squinted at Lu as she shook out four Excedrin tablets. "You don't look too hung over."

"Oh, I am." Lu popped the pills and took a big drink of water. Then she looked over at Boone. "Thanks for keeping me from getting arrested last night and for dragging my drunken ass to Raj."

"No worries."

"I'm glad it didn't mess up your plans with Sierra."

"Nothing would've kept me from her last night." He repeated, "Nothing."

That swoopy sensation started in my belly and spread lower. Boone's gaze hooked mine and I was powerless to look away.

"Knock off the eye-fucking," Raj said with a sigh. "We gotta talk about some stuff and then you two can go back to rockin' the rafters."

Lu stopped beside me and rested her head on my shoulder. "I'm gonna punch your cousin Hayden in the junk next time I see him for making me drink shots last night."

I petted her hair. "Poor baby. I warned you not to fall prey to his Fireball challenge."

"True. Now I can add that to my 'never ever' list of booze."

"So what did you need to talk about?" I asked.

"Living arrangements," Raj said.

Boone and I exchanged a look. Good thing we'd already discussed this. Well, not this part specifically. "Since you're as crazy about Lu as I am, and you're used to living with Boone, you're welcome to move your stuff here, Raj."

He grinned. "While that is downright sweet and thoughtful, for now, I think my woman wants to move in with me. At least until my sister gets back and kicks us out." He dipped his chin toward Boone. "West is staying with you?"

"Yes." Imagining waking up with Boone every morning and sharing the same space the rest of the time...hello belly flip. But I'd never had a roommate besides Lu. What if Boone and I weren't compatible with the day-to-day roommate stuff?

"Then it's settled. Lucinda Grace, baby, get your things."

"You're ditching me?" I said to her.

"Temporarily." She lifted her head. Something in my face had her turning toward Raj and Boone. "Can you guys give us a moment?"

"Sure." Raj said, "I'ma make you get your stuff outta my car anyway, West. Come on."

As soon as they were gone, Lu slumped against the counter and snagged her water bottle. "You were baking first thing this morning, S."

"Just making breakfast for my man."

She rolled her eyes. "How freaked out *are* you about Boone moving in?"

"It was my idea. It's just surreal. Yesterday we weren't together and now we're living together."

"I might've been slam-a-lammered last night, but Boone was frantic to get to you, Sierra. Frantic."

I smirked. "That's because I blew him and ran off before he'd put his pants back on."

Lu choked on her water. "No way. At the party?"

"Yep. Classy, huh? I didn't plan to blow and bail, trust me."

"No wonder he tossed me onto the sidewalk and peeled out as soon as he saw Raj's pearly whites." She laughed. "That is fucking hysterical, S. Another classic Sierra moment to add to the others."

"Promise you won't tell Raj."

"I'm sure he already knows and Boone asked him not to tell me." Her smile faded. "I don't want to lose the ability to talk to you, or you to me, because we're juggling keeping lovers' confidences now too."

"Me either."

"And if me'n Raj call it quits, and Boone is living here with you..." She snorted. "I can't even voice that possibility because it's so ridiculous."

"What? You and Raj breaking up?"

She nodded. "Won't happen. With him...all the pieces just clicked. For both of us."

"I'm happy that you found the one true dick that fits." I dodged her arm punch and laughed.

"So I'll just ask you straight out; is this thing with Boone about sex and making up for lost time?"

My kneejerk reaction was *I don't know.*

But you do know.

"The man is a fucking machine. Sex with him? Ah-may-zing. Physically we're in synch. But we spent a lot of time talking last night and things are different for us. More solid." I groaned. "Jesus, Lu. Please tell me I'm not letting my body make this decision and I'm ignoring common sense."

"If that were true, it'd be the first time since I've known you."

"Thank you for that."

"You're welcome." Lu drained her water. "Come on. Help me pack some stuff."

I waved her off. "Go on. I don't need to see your sex toy collection again."

She stretched and her shirt rode up, giving me a glimpse of the hickeys in a heart shape around her tattoos.

"Cute love bites," I said.

Lu glanced down. "Oh. Those. They're starting to fade. You should see the ones on my ass."

I blushed and said, "Pass."

"You're so cute, pretending you don't have marks like this all over yourself." Before she walked out of the kitchen, she said, "While I'm sorting through my sex toy collection, you sure you don't want me to leave the big, black dildo? Since I don't need it anymore?"

Do not blush. "No! It's not like I can repurpose it."

"Maybe you can't, but I can." Lu smirked. "Come on. Maybe I can give you a few tips."

18 Boone ♥

COULD NOT keep my hands off Sierra.

Not that I'd tried.

Not that she acted like she wanted me to back off.

She couldn't stop touching me either.

I'd never been high, but if it felt anything like this? I could understand it.

Because Sierra had become my addiction.

In less than twenty-four hours I couldn't imagine my life without her.

I'd said as much to Raj when he'd swung by to drop off my stuff a few hours ago.

He'd opened the back end of his SUV and unloaded my few belongings. I didn't own much besides clothes and the college medical textbooks I'd kept. I'd never stayed in any place long enough to accumulate more than a few basic household items—most of which were in storage in Fort Hood.

"This is all your stuff?" Raj asked.

"I've got a few boxes in my car, but this is all I brought to your sister's place. Why?"

Raj shot a look at Sierra's house. "Only people I've ever known our age that lived in a place like this were drug dealers."

I laughed. "Sierra is a dealer of sorts—a wheeler dealer in the real estate market. Don't worry. Everything is on the up and up with her."

"That ain't what concerns me, B."

"Then what?"

"You have a chip on your shoulder about paying your own way in all things. You've never let me buy you a beer without repaying me in kind. So how's it gonna work with her? No matter how crazy you are about her, I don't see you agreeing to livin' in her house without—"

"A detailed spreadsheet of who pays for what?" I supplied.

"Something like that. I'm betting you haven't discussed it at all."

"Actually we have. Not as detailed a discussion as we need to. Sierra already knows about my pride, or the chip on my shoulder, or whatever you wanna call it. She understands since she knows where I—where it—came from. Dividing up the grocery and utility bills isn't a concern compared to my fear that my honesty about how I feel about her is too much for her to handle."

"Since you're basically a relationship virgin, I'ma give you some advice. Women love that honesty shit."

"So I didn't fuck up by telling Sierra I loved her after our first night together?"

Raj's jaw dropped. "You're kidding me."

I laughed. "Yeah, man. I'm messing with you. I didn't say the 'L' word, but I did tell her that she's it for me." Since I'd kept my true feelings from her before, this time she deserved to know from the start that I wasn't fucking around with her heart.

He sighed. "Just…cool it down from here on out. Give it more than a damn day before you get into the serious stuff."

"Like you gave it more than a day with Lucinda? You barely gave it more than a *minute*."

Raj appeared ready to argue. He wanted to tell me his situation was different. Instead he just sighed. "We'll check this convo for now."

"Fair enough." I carried both duffel bags and my suitcase into the house and dumped them outside Sierra's bedroom.

Where they remained three hours later.

A soft hand landed on my belly and I jumped.

"Sorry. I didn't mean to wake you," Sierra said.

"What'd you think I was asleep?"

"You were frowning. I thought you might've been having a bad dream."

I covered her hand with mine. "Not possible when I'm living the dream with you."

She laughed. "You do realize that not every day will be like this."

"Like what?"

"Lazing in the sun by the pool after a night of hot sex."

"Seriously? Good thing I didn't fall for your trickery and unpack all my stuff." I pushed up out of the chaise as if I intended to leave.

"Boone."

I leaned over her, shoving my shades on top of my head. Then my hungry gaze tracked every delicious inch of her. "I love the way you say my name." I bent to place a kiss between her tits, which were all but popping out of her red bikini top. "Hang on." I slipped one arm beneath her knees and the other arm beneath her shoulders and lifted her from her chair.

Sierra wreathed her arms around my neck. "What are you doing?"

"Making you wet again." I nuzzled her ear. "I'm annoyed that you only mentioned the hot sex from last night and not the hot pre-breakfast round. When I had my face between your thighs and then I fucked you on the kitchen table." I sucked on her earlobe and bit down, tightening my hold when she squirmed. "Or did you forget?"

"God no."

"Good answer." I started down the steps into the pool.

She sighed when I submerged us a little deeper than hip level. "You meant this kind of wet."

"Disappointed?"

"If I say yes…you'll go all sexy, growly He-Man and make me wet that way too, won't you?"

I placed a kiss below her ear just to watch her shiver. "Probably."

Sierra shifted her body, facing me, wrapping her legs around my waist and crossing her ankles behind my back. "This is good too."

"Agreed." I squeezed her ass cheeks in my hands and took her mouth in a teasing kiss. I only ended the kiss so I could plant kisses down her throat to the edge of her bikini top.

"You *are* going to unpack your bags tonight, right?"

"Uh-huh." Almost. If she'd just arch a little I could nose aside the fabric and get my mouth on her nipple.

"Do you want your stuff in my room or would you rather have one of the empty bedrooms?"

I lifted my head and looked at her. "It's your house, Sierra. Tell me what you want. Tell me where you want me and my stuff."

"I want you in my bed, Boone." She ran her wet hand across my cheek and the side of my head. "My closet is a little full. I can clean a few dresser drawers out for you, but I'm thinking until you're more...settled, it might be easiest to keep your stuff in the small bedroom across the hall."

"But you only want my things across the hall, not me."

"Yes." Sierra kissed me. "I don't want you to feel trapped. So maybe you'd feel less panicked if you had your own space to retreat to if need be. Then you could gradually move into my room, or maybe you'll decide you prefer to have a dressing room of your own."

I studied her eyes, hating to see wariness. "I don't have a ton of stuff. Moving a lot guarantees I travel light. That said, I'm not gonna cram more into your overstuffed closet. I'll keep my clothes in the spare room. But I would like one of the nightstands and a couple of dresser drawers. It'd be a pain to have to get my bondage equipment out of the guest room whenever I wanted to use it on you."

She laughed. "In that case you can sleep in the guest room."

"Not a chance." Keeping our eyes locked, I brushed my mouth across hers. "I want everything I've never had. I want to know what it's like to fall asleep with you in my arms." I nibbled on her bottom lip. "I want to wake up in the middle of the night and do wicked things to you until you're awake, wet and frantic." I licked the inside of her upper lip. "I want your face to be the first thing I see in the morning."

"I want that too."

"So this isn't going too fast?"

"It's going as fast as we let it, Boone." She pressed her mouth to mine. "If it careens out of control we can always pull back."

"Such a smart woman."

"But I do have to ask you a favor." She played with my chest hair. "I told you my mom is getting remarried. Would you come to the wedding with me?"

"When is it? So I can ask for that day off."

"It's on a Saturday afternoon... Three weeks from yesterday, actually."

Fucking figures.

"Excuse me?"

I glanced up at her after I realized I'd said that out loud. "I said it fucking figures because that's the day I'm supposed to be meeting my dad in Flagstaff."

"Oh. After what you told me last night…I'm surprised you keep in touch with your dad."

"That's the thing. I don't. But he called me out of the blue…that day I tricked you into showing me around Phoenix."

Sierra head-butted me. "You mean the day you *lied* about your friend moving to Phoenix."

"You're always gonna lord that over me, aren't you?"

"Yep. Keep talking."

"He asked if I could meet him because he had some things to talk to me about face-to-face. I said sure, never believing he'd follow through with it." I paused. "But he did follow through. He called me this week and said he scheduled the load he has to drop off with a firm date and everything. But I can cancel it."

"No. If you haven't seen him in almost a decade, that's more important." Her eyes roamed over my face. "Do you have any idea what he wants to talk about?"

"Not a clue. But I'm not going to waste time thinking about it."

Sierra squeezed my shoulder. "I'm here anytime you want to talk to me, Boone, about anything."

"Thanks." I kissed her and realized I already felt less anxious about the meeting. No matter what Dax West said, for the first time in my life I'd have someone waiting at home for me to talk about it.

LATER, WE WERE curled up on the couch, watching football highlights before the Sunday night game started, when the doorbell rang.

Sierra looked at me. "Did you order pizza and forget to mention it?"

"No. Maybe it's Lu and Raj?"

"Lu would've used her key."

"True. You weren't expecting anyone?"

"No." She groaned and stood. "God, I hope it's not my mother."

"Did you tell her about us?"

"Omigod, no! If I tell her I have a live-in boyfriend, she'll accuse me of trying to steal the spotlight from her wedding. I haven't texted my dad the news either." She pushed her hair out of her eyes. "I'm selfish. This is our time. We've waited long enough for it."

The doorbell rang three more times.

"Impatient, whoever it is." I followed her to the entryway.

Sierra opened the door.

Kyler, Hayden and Anton were on the steps with four pizza boxes and a twelve-pack of soda. Kyler studied us both, head to toe. Then he grinned. "Doesn't look like we're interrupting anything important."

"Not that we'd leave even if you'd answered the door in your robes," Hayden added. "But we figured there'd be a chance of finding Boone strung up by his balls and who wants to miss that kind of entertainment?"

"Jesus, Hayden," Anton said.

"Why are you here?" I asked.

"To watch football," Ky said. "We brought food."

"I see that. But what's wrong with your TV?" Sierra asked.

"Nothin'. We just wanted to make sure you were okay."

On one hand, fuck them for implying I'd ever hurt Sierra. On the other hand, thank fuck for them for looking out for her.

"Come in. There's room on the coffee table for the food." Sierra kissed Ky's cheek as he walked past—and then socked him in the stomach.

"Hey! What was that for?"

"The kiss was for giving Boone a key to your room last night. The punch was for making me smuggle Miss Underage out from under the cops' noses." She propped her hands on her hips. "I can't believe Mase is okay with all the parties you've had lately."

"He's not okay with it, especially not after last night and the cops showing up and busting people," Ky said. "I never expected it'd get out of control so fast."

"That's what happens when you're a football star," Anton said. "Everyone wants to bask in the glory of your presence."

Ky flipped him off.

"Where is Mase?" I asked.

"Watching game tapes before he leaves in the morning. He asked for peace and quiet so we're giving it to him," Hayden said.

"We figured you'd have the game on tonight," Ky said to Sierra. He tipped his chin toward her Cardinals jersey. "Ugly shirt, by the way."

His Broncos T-shirt earned him a sneering once-over. "Back atcha. Past time to retire the Manning T-shirt. Oh right, that's the *only* reminder of the Donkeys' former glory years, since they suck donkey dick this year."

"Knock it off, you two," Hayden said. "Focus on the common goal of jeering at the Panthers and the Vikings the next few hours."

Hours? So much for my plans to keep her occupied on that couch, not thinking about any balls besides mine.

You are such a romantic, classy motherfucker, West.

Anton drawled, "Interesting addition to the entryway, Sierra."

"What?"

He pointed behind her. "That."

Everyone turned and looked. Uncomfortable silence followed.

Very uncomfortable silence. Because there was a ten-inch black rubber dick stuck to the center of the catchall table with a heavy-duty suction cup.

Where the hell had *that* come from?

"Looks like someone forgot to put their toys away," Hayden said. "But if there's another explanation, I'd love to hear it."

All eyes swung to Sierra.

"It's not mine!"

Then I felt those same curious eyes on me.

Fucking awesome.

"Dude. Is it wearing a cock ring?" Anton asked me.

"How the fuck would I know? It's not mine!"

Hayden shook his head. "This is TMI—but denying it? Come on, cuz. 'Fess up."

"It's Lu's," Sierra blurted out. Then she hastily added, "Lu's idea of a joke. She mentioned repurposing it." She lifted the key ring from the base of the dildo. "See? Just a harmless key ring. Not a cock ring that'll make your dicks pull a turtle."

More silence.

"There's always that *one* person who takes it too far," Kyler dead-panned.

"Go." She shoved him. Then she shoved Anton and lastly Hayden, who looked like he had another question. "We'll meet you in there."

I grabbed her as soon as we cleared the corner in the kitchen. "You okay with them being here?"

"As my man would you escort them out if I asked?"

"Hell yeah."

"I'm fine with it. They're nosy about us and they have shown up other Sunday nights to catch a game with me." She wound her arms around my neck. "Why? Are you not okay with them hanging out?"

"Just as long as they're gone as soon as the fourth quarter is over."

"Got plans for me, soldier?"

"Beyond you on top of me, with my hands on your ass as you ride me hard?" I followed the contour of her body, from her hips to her tits, which were mashed tightly against my chest. "Not really." I fused my mouth to hers, kissing her because I could.

"This *all fucking in* thing really is awesome," she whispered against my lips between soft smooches.

Someone cleared their throat. "Where are the paper plates?"

Sierra stepped back. "I'll get them."

No one said much as we polished off the pizzas. The McKay-kateers were more subdued than usual. I suspected hangovers all around.

At first Sierra sat beside me on the couch. It surprised her when I pulled her onto my lap. I didn't want to take baby steps with her affection; I wanted to fucking run with it.

I trailed my fingers up and down her arm. I twisted her ponytail around my finger. I caressed the top of her thigh. All normal things most guys had probably done a hundred times by the time they reached my age. But this was a first for me. Watching football with my family and having my girlfriend snuggled into me. A strange sense of contentment rolled over me.

Sierra went to scrounge up ice cream at the start of the fourth quarter. She'd stayed on my lap long enough my legs had fallen asleep. As soon as the pins and needles feeling vanished, I got up and used the bathroom. I stopped to take a picture of the black dick and sent Raj a text:

Me: *Forget your dick since Lu has u by the balls?*

He responded immediately

RJ: *Not my D – my D has another 4 inches on that puny wannabe.*
RJ: *PS – FUCK OFF*

I started around the corner when I heard my name and stopped.

"...Boone seems good with all of this." Hayden said.

"Why does that surprise you?"

"Whoa. You don't have to get defensive," Hayden said.

"I'm not defensive. I'm protective, which is entirely different."

"Protective of Boone? Why?"

I held my breath. Surely she wouldn't tell him or their other cousins about our private conversation last night.

"Because of what he and I are to each other now. I'm protective of that, so that makes me protective of him. Maybe I'll even be secretive about all of this." She paused. "How you think that'll go over in the gossipy McKay family?"

Hayden laughed. "Well, darlin', you'll probably find out soon enough."

"Omigod, seriously? Who fucking blabbed already? You?"

"Who do you think blabbed?" Hayden volleyed back to her.

"Kyler."

"Yep. He already told his folks that you and Boone...reconnected."

"Why?"

"I'd like to say it's only because he's happy for you two, but I'm pretty sure he used the news to deflect their interest from him because he doesn't want his family knowing all the stuff he's been up to outside of football."

"That little fuckface. I should've gut-punched him a lot harder."

My tough-talking woman.

"Look, Kyler, Anton and I...it sounds weird but we're all invested in this thing with you and West."

"Please tell me you jackasses haven't been taking bets on when Boone and I would finally do the deed."

"We're not douchebags who'd do that to our own family, Sierra."

"Sorry. I'm just..." She paused. "Paranoid that something or somebody will try and ruin this for us."

I promise you that won't happen.

"Boone almost ruined it when he fucked up with you that first party. After you took off, we all told him to stop bein' a lying dumbass, man the fuck up and tell you the truth. We even gave him a place to do that when we invited him to Meat-topia last weekend. You needed that push. Last night he needed a push. I called and invited him last night only after you showed up."

Don't you take all the credit for this, asswipe.

"You're lucky I'm so forgiving." Sierra laughed. "But you're all a bunch of romantic idiots."

Hayden laughed too. "Guilty."

"I suppose I need to talk to my dad before the McKay gossip reaches him."

"Gavin doesn't know about you and Boone?"

"Of course he knows Boone is back in my life. Boone made that clear to him before he left Sundance and relocated to Phoenix like a crazy man."

I fucking loved the mix of awe, sweetness and resignation in her tone.

"But I haven't called him today and shared the news that Boone is living here after all that went down last night." She paused. "I probably wouldn't use those exact words to describe it."

"It must've been some night. I've never seen you blush that hard, cuz."

Sierra dropped her voice and I couldn't hear her response but it caused Hayden to laugh.

I walked into the kitchen and stopped, my gaze moving between

Hayden and Sierra. "Am I interrupting something?"

"Nope. Just giving Sierra a hard time about her lousy taste in men," Hayden said with a smirk.

I looked at her and cocked an eyebrow.

She skirted the kitchen island and wrapped herself around me. "I believe my McKay cousins are taking credit for us getting together."

"I'll admit they gave me opportunities, but the credit belongs solely to you, gorgeous." I kissed the top of her head. "Six minutes left of the fourth quarter."

"Even I can take a hint that broad. Me'n Anton would've cleared out at halftime. But you know how Ky is. Football and pussy are the two main focuses of his life." Hayden stilled. "Shit, Sierra, that was crude. Sorry."

"Doesn't make it less true. And it's not like I didn't know that."

Anton walked in from the living room side and swiped a soda. "That ain't entirely true. Ky cares about his grades." He popped the top and took a long drink. "As evidenced by the fact he's banging both his literature tutor *and* his statistics tutor."

Hayden's eyes narrowed. "Why the fuck would Ky need tutoring in statistics? He's like a statistics savant."

"Apparently he gets more pu"—Anton amended—"personal attention if he perpetuates the dumb jock stereotype and then miraculously gets an A in the class. So I can't fault him for his strategy. Besides, did you see his math tutor?" He whistled. "Smokin' hot."

"Is she a curvy redhead?" I asked. "Because I could see why he asked for extra help."

"How would you know what she looks like?" Sierra demanded.

I kissed her pouting mouth. "She showed up as I was leaving McJock Central. It was hard not to notice her, with her sucking Ky's face off and shoving her hand down his pants."

"Maybe she was just looking for his calculator," Hayden said, attempting innocence.

Anton snickered. "Dude. You couldn't even say that with a straight face."

"True. Which is why when we go out Wednesday night, he's not invited." Hayden looked at me. "You coming this week?"

"We'll see. Sierra and I haven't talked about our schedules."

The knowing look Anton and Hayden exchanged had Sierra blushing again.

"Maybe if you fuckers hadn't dropped by unannounced we—"

"Would've left the bedroom to work on a *schedule*? Bullshit." Hayden stood and clapped me on the shoulder. "Just text me this week and let me know what's up." He pulled Sierra away from me and hugged her. "Don't be a stranger."

Then Anton hugged her. "You should come Wednesday night."

"So I can sneak you shots."

"That's not the only reason we want you there."

"Yeah. You can sneak us beers too."

Sierra shoved Anton. "Go."

"Hey QB!" Hayden shouted. "Two minute warning."

Kyler came around the corner. "I know. Game's not over yet."

"Dude. The score is twenty-seven to fourteen. The game is over."

"But, what if—"

Hayden actually grabbed Ky by the shirt and pulled him. "We've worn out our welcome with the love birds. Time to fly."

Kyler scowled at him. "Fine. But if the Vikings catch up—"

"It'll be a miracle on the turf that you'll be able to watch over and over on ESPN highlights," Anton said, herding him out the door.

I locked the door behind them before I faced Sierra.

"Is it just me, or were the last few hours a little bizarre?"

I stalked her. "Bizarre. Kyler was the only one who gave a damn about the game. Anton was on his phone the entire time. And Hayden...did he follow you into the kitchen to get a play-by-play of our activities last night?"

"Maybe. But I think he was more interested from an academic standpoint."

"Academic?"

She headed into the great room and shut off the TV. "He's super analytical. I think he wanted to know if the naked scenarios we'd each created in our minds over the years lived up to the hype."

I stopped short of reaching for her. "Did Hayden ask you that outright?"

"No. But I got the feeling if he could've cornered us individually and asked us, he would have."

"For academic reasons," I said.

"Indubitably."

I chuckled. She cracked my ass up.

"So do you want to talk about this week's schedule?"

"We should."

She sauntered closer. "But do you want to?"

"Not really."

"I have an idea for something else you could do." She walked her fingers up my chest. "It involves clothes removal."

I circled my fingers around her wrist and brought her hand to my mouth, nipping the base of her thumb. "Show me."

Sierra twisted her hand to thread our fingers together, then she towed me past the foyer.

Immediately my head filled with images of her naked. Her tits bouncing, her ass shaking, her lips parted in ecstasy as I thrust into her again and again.

She stopped so abruptly I ran into the back of her.

"Sorry…" Then I saw why she'd stopped. My duffel bags and suit-case were still in the middle of the hallway.

She opened the door across from her bedroom and flipped on the light. "Here you go. Your own dressing room. Come find me when you're done."

"Done? What? I thought we were…" I angled my head toward her bedroom door. "Clothes removal? Remember?"

Her snicker had my gaze sharpening.

"Oh, you thought I meant something else?" She poked me in the chest. "Not until you remove these clothes from the hallway and put your stuff away, soldier."

"Sneaky." My dick actually pouted. "Where will you be?"

"In the bedroom. Naked. Working on next week's schedule."

That was the fastest I'd ever unpacked.

19 Sierra

"**F**ANTASTIC MEETING TONIGHT."

I faced Dr. Phyllis Mackerley, the head of the business outreach program at ASU, who was also the first mentor who'd agreed to help us get PCE organized and running. She'd gone above and beyond for PCE and for the six of us who'd started the organization. "Thanks, Phyllis. The enthusiasm is contagious. It's like we've hit another level of engagement."

She patted me on the shoulder. "You've shown them that anything is possible, Sierra. And you've accomplished that in a way that doesn't only use your experiences as examples. PCE has become something of a think tank, and you, my dear, are why so many members are eager to work outside of the proverbial box."

I blushed. Praise from her meant more than I could ever express. "I love being a part of something that has the potential to help women pursue their dreams. And everyone's dream is diverse enough that it's a constant challenge finding the resources to make PCE worthwhile to them."

"Exactly." She glanced at her watch. "For all the excitement, we adjourned early. Do you have time to grab a cup of coffee or a drink?"

I still found it hard to fathom that Dr. Mackerley now considered me her colleague, not her student. "I would love a margarita."

"I'm leaning more toward wine. Shall we meet at Emmaline's? In fifteen? I have a quick call to make."

"Sounds great. See you there."

Tamarin offered to close up after she and Karene finished their workshop proposal guidelines. I waved goodbye and gathered my things, dumping all but my planner in the back of my SUV. Emmaline's, an upscale wine and craft-cocktail bar, was only a five-minute drive, but I had a few thoughts I wanted to jot down while they were still fresh.

Emmaline's had the New York edgy vibe, with brightly colored walls, small clusters of lounge areas, low-slung chairs upholstered in obnoxious patterns that didn't match each other or anything else, all centered around a coffee table crafted from pallets. The lighting imbued the space with a bluish glow that managed to be relaxing and flattering. So I noticed couples cozied up everywhere.

That made me think of Boone. Shoot. I wasn't sure when it came to this whole couple thing...was I supposed to let him know I'd be home late? I'd checked my messages right after the meeting and I hadn't heard from him, so I probably didn't need to worry.

The waitress seated me in a cozy corner. Two sides of the lounging area were floor-to-ceiling bookcases. Dinged up, scarred, the finish wearing thin, but it added warmth to the space. I was an interior design junkie; interior design had been my second career choice after business.

I ordered a margarita and flipped open my planner. In the notes section, I listed the comments from the members during and after the presentation. Their reactions and questions showed me where I needed to tweak certain aspects or expand on topics.

"I'd think the diligence was for my benefit," Phyllis said as she slid into the seat opposite mine, "but since you're no longer my student and don't need to impress me with your work ethic...the notes must be for your benefit alone?"

I grinned at her. "I hope for the members' benefits. If I don't write this down right away, I forget."

"I'm happy to see that is not just an age thing," she said dryly.

She ordered a glass of pinot and I set my planner aside.

The drinks came and we toasted. I sipped and sighed. "That might be the best margarita I've ever tasted."

"'Handcrafted cocktails' is not just an advertising slogan here. I'm afraid tequila in any form is off my drink menu. Which I blame on a week in Mexico and extremely poor judgment."

I laughed. "Someday I'd like to have stories like that, that I'll never tell."

"You're young. You have time."

Unlike my male colleagues, Phyllis never made my age sound like a drawback.

"You said you spoke to the personnel manager at your day job about weeding through the application process for a fulltime director?"

"Yes. I didn't lead the conversation, I hit on some of the points you and I discussed to gauge his first response. When I brought up hiring a headhunter, he strongly discouraged it."

"Why?"

"Since PCE is nonprofit, we'd be better off hiring a firm that specializes in that. The downside is the employee pool we'd be recruiting from is used to extra incentives during the recruitment process."

Phyllis rolled her eyes. "Potential employees want extra perks for even considering a position?"

"Yep. It's the norm and not the exception. As is the list of requirements some recruits demand before starting negotiations. I don't see that kind of...entitled attitude being a good fit for PCE. We definitely don't want to bring in someone that has a vastly different vision."

"I was afraid of that."

I blinked at her. "You were?"

"Yes. That's why it's best to do an informal poll with industry professionals before taking the next step." She swirled the wine around in her glass. "What was his advice?"

"Hire from within."

"Precisely."

"Which is great in theory...?"

"It's great in reality too. I can think of half a dozen qualified candidates right now. Can't you?"

I swallowed a mouthful of margarita, allowing a moment to appreciate the blend of orange and lemon with the smoky flavor of tequila. What had they put in this to get those ratios so perfect?

"Sierra?"

"Sorry. Having a margarita-utopia moment." I shot her a quick grin. "To answer your question...I can think of two people that might be contenders. Tamarin and Jessica."

"They're both on my list too." Phyllis studied me over her wine-glass. "Who do you think is on the top of my list?"

"Alexis?" I guessed.

"No." She paused. "You are on the top."

"Me? Seriously? But I already have a fulltime job. I didn't give you the impression—"

"No, dear, you haven't." She patted my arm. "And that's the real shame. You are everything PCE needs in a director, Sierra."

I didn't bother to hide my shock. *Me? Really?* kept pinging in my head.

"You've poured your heart and soul into PCE from the start. I've always believed you're the driving force behind why it started out successful and continues to grow every year. No one is more invested in taking it to the next level. You told me tonight that you love it. That's why you need to seriously consider taking the position."

"Phyllis. Is this an offer?"

"Yes. I'll have the details drawn up and send you an official offer this week."

"I…shit. I don't know what to say."

"I'm hoping you'll say yes." She held up her hand to forestall my argument. "Please hear me out. I'm so proud of everything you've accomplished. I'm proud to have played a small role in your growth as a businesswoman. I'm delighted you still come to me for career advice, though for the life of me I'll never understand why you insisted on starting entry-level at Daniels Property Management."

I laughed. She'd said *entry-level* like it was VD.

"I suspect you're struggling more in your position than you let on. I can't claim to be surprised. We've come a long way in the business world. But there are those…men, usually, who keep putting their wing-tips on our foreheads and kicking us back down the ladder because we've dared to climb it."

"I'm still sporting tassel marks on my behind from one manager's diatribe this week." Fucking Greg.

Phyllis leaned in. "I've met your father. I know he is a hard-working and fair man. While I understand your reluctance to bring company issues to his attention, I have to ask…if he wasn't your father, would you have the same reaction?"

"If my father didn't own the company, chances are as a senior-level VP, in a subdivision of the main corporation, that I wouldn't have the ear of the CEO. So in some ways, the accusations that I get special consideration and privileges because I'm the daughter of the CEO are true."

"Damn tight spot you're in."

"What keeps me going is the belief that change comes from within. If I say screw it, this isn't worth it…the status quo wins, and I've let down the women in the company who are hoping that I'm the one who can set things right."

She blinked at me.

Crap. Had I pissed her off?

"Sierra McKay, I am so fucking proud of you."

The F-bomb? From Dr. M? Get the fuck out. "Uh…why?"

"You're actually practicing what I preach. Few students do that out in the real world. Your tenacity is admirable. And yet, I really believe you'd be happier if you spent your working hours in an environment where you're needed and where your true passion lies. So please read over the offer for PCE this next week. Take some time to think it over. Call me if you have any questions."

"I will. Thank you. For everything."

"Thank you. You are my shining star student, Sierra. I want to make sure you get the chance to show the world what you can do." She pushed back and stood.

I stood too and gave her a hug. "Drive safe."

"Hope to hear from you soon."

After Phyllis left, I settled in and tried to process everything that'd just happened.

But my mind was swimming with too many possibilities, too many variables, too many questions. This type of decision was out of the realm of my experience. And the people I'd normally talk to about it…well, one just offered me a job and the other owned the company I worked for.

I did have one more option.

After I got in my car, I activated the hands-free option for my cell phone and said, "Call Rory." I didn't worry that I was calling too late; night owl Rory would rather do anything than sleep.

She answered the call by saying, "Please tell me you're using Bluetooth so I don't have to worry about you wrecking your car when you're talking to me."

"Hands-free, all the way, baby. And I'm not *that* bad of a driver."

She snorted. "It's the big city. Everyone is in a hurry and you don't have to be the bad driver to end up in a car crash."

"Let's start over. Heya, sis. How's life in the woods with your very own flannel-and-jeans-wearing lumbersexual?"

"Fantastic. But I prefer Dalton to wear no shirt."

"I don't blame you. Is it creepy to say I'd ogle him without shame if I saw him demolishing big logs with just an ax and his rippling muscles?"

"Kinda creepy, but I'm sure it'd put a swagger in his step, despite the fact he's your business partner as well as your brother-in-law."

"Blow him a kiss for me, because I know he's close."

"Hang on."

I heard background noises and then a sigh.

"I'm back. Damn distracting man. What's up?"

"I miss you. I need to talk to you and I wish I could just drive over to your house right now."

"Me too. I hate that we live so far apart. Why'd you have to move all the way to Arizona?"

"Why'd you have to move to the middle of nowhere, Montana?" I countered.

Rory laughed. "I ask myself that same question sometimes. But you didn't call to talk about me." She paused. "So your dad and my mom told me Boone West is back around, specifically in Phoenix."

Rory's mom had married my dad when I was sixteen and Rory was twenty-two. Since we both had been only children, we'd immediately latched onto each other. I believed we were closer than blood siblings because we were both so grateful to finally have a sister.

"Sierra?" she prompted.

"Sorry. Yes, Boone is in Phoenix."

"Is he out of the military?"

"He's still in the army. It's this big complex political program that's allowed him to be on educational leave while on active duty."

"But he's in Phoenix because you're there?"

"I'm not the only reason he's here, but I'm the biggest reason."

"How deep are you in with him?"

"He's living with me."

She went quiet for a moment.

"It's good, Rory. Better than I ever imagined."

"I still feel the need to punch something. Like his face."

I grinned. She was such a tough talker. "You're loyal and I love you for that. But I didn't call to talk about my relationship with Boone."

That surprised her. "You didn't?"

"No. I need some career advice." I passed the turnoff to my house and decided to keep driving. "This stays in the sister vault." We created the sister vault as a place where we shared things we didn't want her mom or my dad to know about.

"Got it. So what's going on?"

"I was offered another job today."

"Since when were you looking for another job?"

"I wasn't." Rory knew about my involvement with PCE so I didn't have to waste time laying that part out. I could delve right into the pros and cons list I'd already started to compile. I talked for a good five minutes without interruption, but I wondered if we'd lost the connection because Rory rarely let me ramble on. "You still there?"

"Yes. Just trying to process it all. First off... Damn, girl, I am so freakin' proud of you! What positive forward motion in your career just to be offered the position."

I grinned. I knew she'd understand. "Thanks."

"Second, it has to feel empowering that you're the most qualified person to expand the company beyond the start-up phase."

"It is. PCE has always been more than just a service organization I belonged to in college."

"Which is why your former advisor knows you're the best person to take PCE to the next level," Rory pointed out. "And I have to ask this, so don't be coy or downplay your abilities. But didn't you consider applying for that top spot?"

I chose my words carefully. "Yes. And no. Yes, because ego aside, I've been involved in every aspect of PCE since its inception. No one is as familiar with the ins and outs as I am. That might be because I'm a bit of a control freak."

Rory gasped. "You?"

"Takes one to know one."

A moment of silence followed. I sensed Rory gearing up to get nosy.

"Look, I know you *said* you didn't call to talk about Boone, but I have to ask—"

"If the reality of being naked with him lives up to the romantic fantasy I've held onto for seven years? Especially since I was a virgin the one and only time he kissed me?" I paused. "Well, I asked him to move in with me within a few hours of us hitting the sheets the first time."

Rory laughed.

"Right now...it's intense and glorious and necessary. Sex could be all-consuming if that was all there is between us. But there's so much more than that."

"When you're past that fuck-your-brains-out-twenty-four-seven stage, call me and I'll share my tips on how to train and tame your man."

I heard my brother-in-law Dalton repeat "Tame?" in the background and I knew Rory was in for it.

Then Dalton's voice came on the line. "Sorry, Sierra. It's past Rory's bed...*tame*. Later."

Click.

I WASN'T EXPECTING Boone to be home since his shift went from noon to midnight. But his vehicle was in the garage. I found him in the kitchen, books, notebooks and papers spread out across the breakfast bar. I tossed my laptop bag and purse on the table just as Boone spun around on his barstool.

"When did you get off?" I asked him.

"I was waiting for you to come home so we could both get off."

The possessive way he growled that as his hot eyes ate up every inch of me sent tingles zipping down my spine. "Boone."

Then he gritted out, "Fuck. Me."

"What?"

Boone stood and started toward me. "Look at you. All professional and put-together in your sexy-assed business suit."

"Sexy-assed?" I repeated.

"Uh-huh. Oh, that skirt is perfectly acceptable in a business environment. Not too short. Not too tight." His eyes roved up my body. "So's the blouse. Not too see-through. Not too low-cut. On any other woman this outfit might actually look boring."

He finally let his gaze connect with mine.

The primal lust in his eyes sent fire licking along my skin. I was shocked my clothing hadn't spontaneously combusted from the heat between us.

"But on you? It's way hotter than if you were wearing nothing but a garter belt and pasties."

I managed to eke out a soft, "Why?"

"Because it issues a challenge. It screams power. It demands, 'Are you man enough to peel back the armor?' It reminds me that I'm the luckiest motherfucker on the planet that you're *mine.*"

He snarled the last word.

Then he was on me. Hands in my hair. Mouth owning mine. Body to body as he drove me backward until my ass met the sliding glass door.

Boone's need swamped me. He wanted me like this. As the woman I was now, not the girl I'd been. I didn't have to prove I was smart and strong and feminine. He knew it. Celebrated it. Embraced it.

I surrendered completely; to the moment and to him.

But when my grabby hands reached for him, Boone broke the kiss.

Circling my wrists, he pinned my hands above my head on the sliding glass door. "Leave them there." Then he nosed aside the collar of my blouse so he could make me squirm, make me wet with that wicked mouth on my skin.

"I'm gonna fuck you like this," he panted against my neck. "Wearing this suit and those bang-me-baby high heeled shoes."

"Yes. Please."

Boone rocked his hips into mine and reconnected our mouths in a hot, wet kiss.

I couldn't get enough of the slow stroke of his tongue, how he teased and took. His fingers slipped the buttons on my blouse free with such deliberate care that the sound of his fingertips scraping the fragile fabric made me arch closer. I wanted the calluses stroking my skin.

He trailed biting kisses from my lips to my ear. "Hold still."

I could only moan. The fuzziness in my head, the tightness of my skin, the wetness between my thighs made my thoughts incoherent beyond the word *more.*

Sudden freedom around my ribcage meant he'd popped the front clasp of my bra. Immediately he pushed the lace cups aside as well as the edges of my blouse. He flattened his palms above my breasts and smoothed his big hands down my torso slowly, making sure every inch of my soft skin felt the rough touch of his.

When he reached my hips, his grip tightened. He ended the panty-drenching, body-shaking-soul kiss, but kept his lips on mine when he said, "Turn around."

I gasped when my bare chest connected with the cool glass. My nipples hardened when Boone's strong grip on my wrists forced my arms up higher.

"Brace yourself," he murmured in my ear.

He shimmied my skirt up until the fabric bunched around my waist.

I groaned when my butt cheeks met the hard bones of his hips and his thick cock pressed against the crack of my ass.

Two fingers traced the cleft and he pulled the thin fabric of my thong aside.

Boone brushed my hair over my shoulder and placed a surprisingly soft kiss on the sweep of my shoulder. "Spread your legs."

As soon as I did that, he started to stroke me with one long finger, from the wetness pouring from my opening to my clit.

"You like this."

"I like everything you do to me."

He scraped his teeth down the back of my neck with the same rhythm he stroked my clit. "Tell me what'll make you come."

"Shoving your cock into me would do it."

"Mmm."

That small *mmm* reverberated from the back of my neck all the way down to my tailbone.

I thought Boone would torture me with the mad skills of his fingers until I came, but he held me open and impaled me in one hard, fast, thorough thrust with that magnificent cock. "Yes. God. More. Please."

"Give me your neck," he demanded.

From our first intimate encounter he'd discovered that hot spot and exploited it shamelessly with his hungry, sucking mouth.

Thrashing beneath him, my mind hazy from pleasure, my body teetered on the brink of orgasm. He rested his hand between my hipbones to hold me in place as he fucked me, but that hand position also allowed his thumb to apply constant friction on my clit.

"Come for me and I'll give it to you harder," he murmured, his deep voice a rumble against the sensitive skin of my neck.

I was so wet his thumb slid around in the slipperiness, forcing him to adjust his hand and use his fingers to pinch that swollen bundle of nerves.

Pinch.

Teeth on my neck.

Cock driving into me.

I only lasted about three rounds before that coiled tension unspooled. I gasped with each hard throb; my fingers squeaked against the glass as I tried to hold on to some reality before bliss sucked me under.

My pussy spasmed around the thick intrusion of his cock and Boone hissed in my ear, "Jesus, Sierra. Fuck, fuck, fuck. So good."

He hammered into me. Grunting, growling deliciously dirty words I only half-heard through the veil of pleasure still surrounding me.

When Boone started to come, I shook myself out of my sexual stupor to watch him in the glass, such fierce masculine beauty undone...by me.

I almost came again just from that.

In the aftermath, he buried his face in my hair. He wrapped his arms around me, giving my arms a rest. His chest heaved against my back. His body shook.

When his breathing leveled out, I turned my head and brushed my hand down the side of his face. "Hi."

He groaned. "Fuck. I'm such an animal when it comes to you. I didn't even say 'Hello, baby, how was your day?' I just—"

"Made me wet, made me ache, made me come like a banshee and made me feel like the most powerful woman in the world? Yep. That about covers it. And you'll never ever hear me complain about that, West." I wrapped my arms around his arms wrapped around me. "Don't apologize. This explosion of need is part of who we are to each other and what we are together. It's hot, it's sexy, it's overwhelming. It's also new and fresh and just so tempting that we can fuck each other stupid, or hard, or sweetly anytime we want."

"Thank you." Boone planted an openmouthed kiss behind my ear. "It's your own fault for being sex in a business suit and heels."

I laughed softly.

He straightened my clothing before he fixed his own. Then he hugged me and smooched my lips with a chaste kiss. "So, baby, how was your day?"

20 Boone

"**I**'M OLD."

Raj looked at me like *WTF dude?*

"I'd rather turn a Taser on myself than go out tonight. I just want—"

"To go home and cuddle up with your pookie-bear?"

"Fuck you. Just because you call Lucinda pookie-bear doesn't mean I have a stupid pet name for Sierra."

"I'm way more creative than pookie-bear as a pet name for my sweet Lucinda."

"Which means your pet name for her is something worse than pookie-bear."

"My pet name for her is fucking awesome."

"Then share it."

"This name doesn't leave this car, or I will put you in fucking traction, feel me?"

My buddy—such a damn drama queen. "I feel ya. Hit me with it."

Raj smirked. "I call her sugar snatch."

"She lets you call her that?"

"Better than my first attempt…honey dripper. Don't need to crack the K-Y with her, if you know what I'm saying."

"Jesus."

He laughed. "So why you wanna be a pussy and skip the fun shit?"

I scrubbed my hands over my face. "Because I'd rather shower and veg in a quiet place for a few hours. It's been a loud day. A college pool hall ain't gonna let my mind rest and reset." I stared out the window at the city lights. It'd been a crap day and I'd be happy to see the ass end of it.

UNBREAK MY HEART   207

"Hey. You weren't the only one who failed. Both Jenkins and Abele did too. So climb off the pity train, man. New place, new rules. We've been in this position before. Several times."

"I get that. I appreciate the Raj *rah-rahs*. It just felt different."

"Jenkins and Abele don't have dyslexia as an excuse. They just flat-out fucked up. Way worse than you did."

Dyslexia as an excuse.

Fuck that. I never used it to explain away something dumb that I'd done. I hated that my fucked-up way of learning was a disability. A fucking handicap.

It's a flaw—an unfixable one at that.

Closing my eyes, I dropped my right hand between the seat and the door, making a fist, squeezing it so tight my forearm started to ache. "Drinking in a college dive bar...I can't believe I let my cousins talk me into this."

"Ah, that's part of where this 'I'm old' crap is coming from. We're not that much older than them."

"I feel years older."

"Well, dude, you're acting like a grumpy old man, so knock that shit off. Sierra's coming, right?"

"After she gets done at work." Maybe she'd change into those skinny jeans that made me wanna bite that ass of hers. Then again it'd be pure fucking torture to watch her bent over a pool table all goddamned night. Not to mention, if other guys were eyeballing her ass? I'd start blackening those eyes.

"What the hell, West? You're growling like a junkyard dog over there."

I loosened my fists—because both of them were clenched. "You ever known me to get into a bar fight just for kicks?"

"No. Why?"

"I've never been a 'back off, asshole' type when some random dude looks at or flirts with a chick I'm with."

Raj squinted at me. "I don't remember the last chick you were with at a bar."

"That's what I'm saying. I never cared before. But it'll be a whole different story with Sierra. I won't handle it well. College bars? Worse than military bars for being a fucking meat market."

"I've seen you leave with hookups, but this 'my girlfriend' shit is new. No wonder you're freaked out. Lemme think on it."

Raj tapped his thumbs on the steering wheel, which was his only annoying characteristic, so I ignored it.

"We'll use the FPCON security alert scale. Normal level—guys looking at her. She's hot, West, they're gonna look. Let them. You do not engage. Got it?"

"Can I give them an 'I'll rip out your fucking eyes and shove them up your ass' glare?"

"Negative. That's engaging. Level Alpha—a dude talks to and flirts with her? Issue a verbal warning. If he still attempts to get her attention knowing she's with you? You can move up to Bravo level and engage."

"Just thinking about this is pushing me to level Charlie." I inhaled. "I'm full-on Delta level if any guy touches her."

The pool hall was a dive and interchangeable with a dozen others I'd been in over the years. The McKay-kateers had scored two tables in the back. Raj and I went to the bar and ordered a pitcher and five glasses. We weren't carded, which explained why my cousins already had a pitcher on the table.

"Hey," Hayden said.

I introduced Raj and then poured us two cups of beer.

"So how long have you guys been hanging out at this place?" I asked.

"Just since the start of the year." Anton lifted his glass. "After we discovered the cheap beer."

"A skill all college students require," Hayden said.

"What did you find out about classes?" Kyler asked me.

"Nothing new. We started clinicals today, so we're working with our preceptor."

Anton asked Raj, "How often do you have to go back to base?"

"Right now? Every four weeks for three days of active duty. We can stretch that out to every six weeks when we're in school."

"Then again, they could call us back tomorrow and demand a week's duty," I said.

"We'll be racking up those frequent flyer miles the next two years,"

Raj said. "Or racking up highway miles. It sucks ass bein' stuck on base without a vehicle."

"You're both career military?" Anton asked.

Raj nodded. "Didn't plan on it when I enlisted. But now I can't imagine another way of life."

"My dad was career military until he lost his leg after a combat mission," Anton said. "He's a cop now. But he told me he'd still be in if he had all of his parts." He gulped a mouthful of beer. "I'm considering ROTC. Been thinking about it since the end of last year."

Kyler and Hayden were both too dumbfounded to speak. Which I figured was a blessing because they'd probably say some dumb shit to Anton.

"If you're serious," Raj said to him, "come talk to me. I've got a buddy who's not a recruiter around here so he doesn't have a quota to meet. He catches heat for his honesty, 'cause he knows military life ain't for everyone, but he's a good guy to talk to."

"I appreciate that, Raj." Anton pointed at his cousins. "Not a fucking word outta either of you. I'm trusting that this stays right here, between us."

"Jesus, Anton, you don't even have to ask us," Kyler grumbled.

"Or exact a pinkie promise," Hayden said.

Anton said, "You're a jackass," to Hayden, but he said it with a smile.

Then all eyes zoomed to me. "What?"

"Sierra can't know either."

I raised an eyebrow. "I'm on year seven of my military service. I know how to keep my mouth shut."

Kyler eyed the pitcher with regret. "I'm wishing I could get shit-faced right about now."

"Let's play pool," Hayden suggested.

I followed them and leaned against the wall to watch.

Ky dropped in two solids and scratched on his third shot.

"You seem on edge. What's up?"

"Sick of all the bullshit that goes along with bein' a football player."

"Anton is tired of the drama with the rodeo team," Hayden said. "And my peer groups are already making schedules and assigning study groups for fucking midterms. I'm taking twenty credit hours. I don't need the extra pressure."

Bad attitudes all around. I questioned why I was here. I wasn't imagining Ky and Hayden sending Raj dark looks as if he'd become the enemy. I pulled out my phone and texted Sierra.

Me: *This sucks. Don't plan to stay long.*

SM: *I've had a 💩 day and just want to go home* ☹

I smiled that she used the shit emoji rather than the word.

Me: *U done?*

SM: *In the car. Be there in ten.*

I could deal with this for ten more minutes.

MY PHONE RANG with my sister's name on the caller ID. Never good news when she called me. "Oakley? What's up?"

"Mom is high again and she's drunk. She forgot to pay the electric bill so the power company cut the power sometime after I went to school. Now it's dark out here, like really dark, and I'm hungry and with no power I can't cook anything. Plus, I have a calc test tomorrow. Am I supposed to study by candlelight?"

"Take a deep breath, sweetheart, and calm down."

"I hate this, Boone. I hate *her*."

My stomach bottomed out. "I know. Where's Mom now?"

"Passed out in her bedroom."

"Take a picture of her and send it to me."

Silence. "You don't believe me! You think I'm just like her, lying to manipulate you and—"

"No, I don't. Just listen to me." I turned toward the wall, keeping Kyler and Hayden at my back. "We need proof of her fuck-up. Take pictures of anything drug related. And the booze. Take pictures of her passed out. Can you do that?"

She sniffled. "I don't know what good it'd do unless you're calling social services. And you know how I feel about that."

"Fine." Oakley lost her shit last time I'd brought it up. Not because she had a fucked-up dependency on Mom, but because she and Rock had spent a year in the foster system. It killed me I hadn't known about it. "Can you get to town?"

"I've got my motorcycle."

"Pack enough clothes for a few days and anything else you'll need."

"Boone. I don't have any place to go."

Frustrated by the way her voice broke, I almost punched the wall, but I managed a calm tone. "I'm calling the motel I stayed at last time and I'll get you a room for a week. But you have to promise me you won't let Mom know you're there or let her stay with you."

"I promise. But what if she calls and asks me where I am when she sobers up? What do I tell her?"

"That you're staying with a friend. After that, don't take her calls until you hear it's okay from me. Promise me."

"I promise. Thank you, Boone. I know this isn't your problem—"

"You're my sister, Oakley. If I can help you, I will."

She was crying so hard when she hung up I couldn't understand her.

I did an internet search, found the motel and called. "This is Sergeant Boone West. I stayed there a few weeks ago with my sister? You remember me? Great. Look, I'm in a bind. I'm coming to visit my sister again and I'm not sure what day I'll be there, it all depends on the army clearing the paperwork." I forced a laugh when the desk clerk commented about too much red tape. "That's the government for you. Anyway, I'll reserve a room starting tonight. My sister will be there shortly so go ahead and give her the key. I'll pick mine up when I get there." I hated to lie, but they wouldn't rent a room to a minor. "You ready for my credit card?" I pulled my Visa out of my wallet. The numbers swam and I blinked twice but they remained a jumbled mess.

Fuck. Fuck. Stress made the dyslexia worse. And I'd had a stressful day before this. I'd have to swallow my pride and ask Raj to read me the numbers so I could repeat them to the motel clerk.

I turned around.

Sierra had just walked in. Her scowl morphed into concern when our eyes met. Then she was right there, close enough to touch. "What's wrong?"

I said, "Can you please hang on a second?" to the motel clerk and hit the mute button. "Same old crap with my mom. I'm reserving Oakley a motel room, but I'm so...pissed off I can't even read the numbers on my goddamned credit card." My face flamed when I said, "Could you read them to me and I'll repeat them to the clerk?"

"Of course."

On automatic, I turned back around, away from my McKay cousins' questioning eyes. I pushed the mute button again. "Sorry about that. I'm ready to give you the number now."

Sierra spoke the numbers directly into my ear and I relayed them to the clerk.

After a little more small talk, I hung up, relieved Oakley would have a clean, safe place to stay for a few days. I returned my credit card to my wallet and my wallet to my back pocket.

Sierra kissed me, bringing my attention back where it belonged: on her beautiful face.

"Thank you."

"Let's get out of here. This place has a bad vibe."

We approached the table and Raj said, "What's up?"

"Family stuff with my sister so I've gotta go deal with that."

"Okay. Call if you need something. If not, I'll see you at oh eight hundred."

"Later."

The McKay-kateers were strangely subdued as we walked away.

Once we were alone in Sierra's car, I leaned over the console and kissed her, desperate for her taste to wash away the bitterness. Needing a reminder that my life and my future were with her. It was easy to get sucked into a dark place when a reminder of my ugly past literally came calling.

Her fingers were cool against my cheeks. "Sit back and close your eyes. Get your head together. We'll talk after we get home."

WHAT DID I do once we got there?

Stalled.

I showered. A long, hot shower that wasted resources and time.

My phone rang with a call from Oakley as I entered my room, towel wrapped around my hips. "You all right?"

Oakley expelled a shaky sigh. "It's surreal being in this hotel room alone. I'm better now. I promised I wouldn't cry, but thank you so, so, so much, Boone."

"I'm just glad I could do something. Heads up; the only reason they're letting you stay there as an unattended minor is because I told them I was coming to visit. So if they ask you when I'll be there...tell them you don't know."

"I hate how good I've gotten at lying."

"Me too, Twig. I can't believe I forgot to ask before...where's Rock?"

"In juvie. This time it wasn't his fault. But they locked him up for two weeks anyway. I think that's why Mom got high; she felt guilty."

"Mom got him shipped off?"

"Yeah. He took the car without permission according to Mom, but *she* gave him the keys. She didn't remember that and she called the cops and turned him in. They found drug stuff in the car—which was hers. He passed the drug test or he'd be locked up longer. He's better off there than here this week."

She had a point. "It's getting late. Get some rest. Let me know how you're doing tomorrow. If you need anything just call me. No matter what time."

After I hung up, I sat on the folding chair, hunched over with my forearms on my knees. My head pounded like fifty people were yelling inside my skull in fifty different languages.

Welcome back to dyslexia dysfunction, Boone! We missed you.

Turn it off.

Shut it down.

Drown it out.

I dressed in my running clothes and sent Sierra a text:

Went 4 run

Phone attached to my waistband, earbuds in, I slipped out the front door.

The housing developments were a clusterfuck so I pounded the pavement on the main thoroughfare. It'd be just my luck to get hopelessly lost tonight. With my music cranked I could barely hear the traffic.

So overriding the voices with louder noise worked.

Or maybe running myself ragged worked.

An hour and a half later I returned to the house. I'd erased all traces of Brooding Boone but I wasn't in the mood to talk. Would Sierra understand that? Or would she push?

Inside the entryway I kicked off my shoes and set my phone and earbuds on the catchall table next to BBD—the big black dildo.

The scents of vanilla and chocolate drifted from the kitchen.

I stood there debating what to do next, when Sierra appeared.

She sauntered across the tile, stopping in front of me close enough our thighs almost touched. Wordlessly she slid her hands beneath my T-shirt and pressed an openmouthed kiss in the hollow below my ear.

I closed my eyes.

Her cool fingertips traced the ridges of my abs. Stroking. Slowly exploring. I wanted to let my head fall back and beg her to put her hands all over me like this. With no agenda. No race to get naked so we could start fucking.

Whatever sound of pleasure I made pleased her because I felt her smile against my neck.

My arms hung by my sides like clubs. Needing something solid to hold onto, I latched onto her hips. Despite the temptation of her warm curves beneath my hands, I didn't pull her closer.

She sighed over the damp spot she'd left on the curve where my neck met my shoulder. Goose bumps cascaded down my arms, my back and my chest and I shuddered.

So she did it again.

And again.

And again.

Sierra kept her face buried in the crook of my neck, breathing heavily, her fingers digging into my sides even as her thumbs lazily swept across the line of dark hair below my belly button.

As much as I wanted to ditch my shirt so no barriers existed between her stroking hands and my skin, I didn't want to break the spell she was weaving around me, around us.

She inched her fingers up higher, stopping to caress the middle of my torso. First with the tips of her fingers, now warm from my skin, then she used her whole hand, flattening her palm and spreading out all ten fingers like a starfish. Finally she dragged the rougher skin of her knuckles across that same area, as if she needed to know all the different ways my flesh felt against hers.

While she touched me, her mouth sought the tender spots on my neck. Changing it up from a whisper-light brush of her lips, to a more aggressive suck, to a teasing lick.

I was utterly fucking lost to her. To this arousing tenderness.

She traced each individual rib. Her questing hands reached my chest and she mapped every cut of muscle. She ruffled the hair on my chest. A reverent finger followed my collarbone back and forth. She touched my nipples but didn't pinch or pull, she just kept up the same maddening stroking until they pulled into hard, tight points.

I wanted her wet mouth there. Sucking. Using her teeth. Flicking her tongue over the tips. Blowing a cool breath across the friction-warmed skin. I growled with hunger, the image of her dark head bent to my chest, just like that first night, when she played with my chest in fascination.

"Boone."

"Uh." She'd rendered me monosyllabic.

"Go to bed. I'll lock up and be right there."

"Hurry." My breath drifted across her ear and she shivered.

Her hands slowly moved down my torso and from beneath my shirt.

My eyes were still closed when Sierra stepped away.

I could barely put one foot in front of the other as I stumbled in a daze down the hall to her—*our*—bedroom. I stripped in the darkness and crawled naked between the cool sheets.

She kept the lights off and closed the door behind her.

The bed barely jiggled when she crawled across it. She tapped my hip to get me to roll to my belly.

That's when I expected she'd end the night by massaging my back until I relaxed enough to talk—that seemed a very Sierra-like move.

But she continued with the loving touches. The soft kisses. The tender caresses. I hadn't been aware of all the places on my back that were pleasure triggers. The zigzag of her fingernails down my spine. The pattering of her fingertips on the nape of my neck. Random swirls and circle eights across my lower back. Love bites as she outlined my shoulder blades with her mouth.

The erotic way she touched me...my cock should've been painfully hard, aching for relief. I should've been grinding it against the mattress seeking additional friction.

But the other parts of my body—flesh and muscle and bone, long denied this type of thorough, reverent contact, told my dick to stand down.

My last coherent thought was that I should roll to my back, so I could wrap Sierra in my arms like I did every night before we fell asleep. But I was so blissed out I couldn't even manage a one-word answer when she whispered, "I'm *all fucking in* with you, Boone. Don't forget that I'm here for whatever you need. Get some sleep."

I HAD A nightmare.

My mom locked Oakley in her room, screaming, "You want light? I'll give you light!" as she set fire to the house and burned my sister alive.

Talk about a rude wakeup.

I attempted to level my breathing. I glanced across the gulf between us; Sierra curled up on her side of the bed facing away from me.

She'd been nothing but thoughtful and supportive, giving me the connection I hadn't known I'd needed.

And how had I repaid her? By shutting her out.

Yeah, I was some great boyfriend.

Fuck. I needed air.

I managed not to wake her as I dressed and then snuck out of the bedroom.

As I wandered through the dark house, my thoughts moved faster than my feet.

I worried about Oakley.

I worried about Rock.

I hated feeling helpless at my mother's hands again.

I hated not knowing what my dad needed to talk to me about.

I hated feeling I'd let Sierra down.

I hated getting scheduled for a midnight to noon shift the next two days.

I pretty much hated fucking everything.

Booze wasn't the smartest choice, but I needed to calm down. I'd already tried exercise and that had failed. I couldn't swim because the door alarm would wake Sierra. Mindless TV wouldn't do anything but piss me off even more.

Booze it is.

The liquor cabinet in the kitchen had tequila, rum, a bottle of high-end Crown and Jack Daniels.

While I preferred the Crown—Sierra's taste was wearing off on me—doing shots of it would be a waste. I grabbed the bottle of Jack.

I twisted the cap off and drank deeply. Classy, not to bother with a glass.

I took a breath and swallowed another mouthful.

And another.

And another.

And another.

Then I forced myself to inflate my lungs fully with a slow breath and exhale. I did that four more times, one for every shot of booze. I'd learned the trick from Corky, an older medic who'd served in the Gulf War. But he'd cautioned me to only use it when I'd exhausted other options.

It was only the third time I'd resorted to it in seven years.

The first time had been after I'd lost a patient.

The second time after I'd failed three tests, three days in a row because of dyslexia stress.

And tonight.

I had a water chaser and I put the bottle away.

The whiskey hit me. Not like a freight train—more like a VW bus.

I made it to the couch in the great room. The room didn't spin when I closed my eyes and the tight feeling beneath my skin had loosened. The constant bombardment of worst-case scenarios faded too.

I pulled the afghan over me and drifted off.

The whirring grind of the coffee maker woke me up. I rubbed the sleep from my eyes and glanced at my watch. Seven a.m. Sierra was right on schedule this morning.

I fucking loved that she was so consistent.

I got up and headed for the shower.

Sierra was standing in front of her laptop when I joined her in the kitchen ten minutes later.

The first thing I did was kiss her. An in-her-face, balls-to-the-wall, full-body kiss.

I loved the dazed look that put in her eyes. "Morning, gorgeous. You look fantastic and you smell like a million bucks." I brushed my mouth across hers again. "You even taste great."

She poked me in the belly. "You are so cocky."

"What?"

"Don't 'what' me, Boone West. You started the morning mouth fuck so I'd stop wearing lipstick."

"I crave the taste of your lips and your mouth, baby. Not that waxy chemical shit." I grinned against her lips. "Morning mouth fuck, huh? I like that."

"I like it too." She smirked back. "I just put on lipstick in the car now."

I grabbed a mug from the cupboard and filled it with coffee, crossing over to refill Sierra's cup. When I turned back around she wore a quizzical look. "What?"

"Why'd you sleep on the couch last night?"

I started to play it off as insomnia.

Sierra shook her head. "You are about to tell me a little white lie, or change the subject. I didn't push last night about what happened with your sister. I'm pushing you now."

"Yeah? You sure you wanna hear about my nightmare where I watched my psychotic mother torch the house and my sister?"

She bobbled her cup. Then she drew in a slow sip of coffee. "I'm sorry. I knew you were restless last night. Did sleeping on the couch help?"

"The five shots of Jack Daniels helped."

"I imagine so."

I don't know why the hell I'd expected her to pass judgment on me; she never did. "Thanks for trying to take the edge off last night."

Her lips quirked which meant she was thinking dirty thoughts.

"With the *massage* thing," I stressed, "but I wouldn't have turned down a blowjob."

"Really? You like blowjobs? Huh. I wasn't sure."

"Smartass. So you gonna bust my balls or do you wanna hear about Oakley?"

"Bust your balls," she muttered. "Sometimes I think you forget I'm not Raj."

I lifted a brow. "I promise you I never discuss my balls with Raj."

"Point taken. Go on."

I gave her the short version of the Oakley situation.

Sierra said, "She's lucky to have you, Boone. You didn't have anyone."

"I haven't heard from her yet this morning so I'll call her after you go to work."

"Yay, I can hardly fucking wait for this day to start after the spectacular shit show I dealt with yesterday."

Guilt punched me in the gut. I was a self-centered prick last night. "What happened?"

"Finger-pointing at DPM. Greg neglected to update the paperwork for a lease renewal with a fairly big client and we lost the account. He tried to blame it on his assistant, Melissa, claiming he finished the project and she misfiled it. He fired her. Melissa had expected that, so she'd come to me earlier in the day with documentation of all the things he's fucked up over the last year. So I think I finally have enough evidence of his misconduct to take to the big boss." She looked at me over the rim of her coffee cup. "Unfortunately, the big boss in this case is not my dad. After I assured Melissa I'd find her another position at DPM, she said it'd be worse for her if she stayed. Which sucks ass because she was a great employee."

"Will any of this backfire on you?"

She shrugged. "We'll see. Then, to make my day even better, I dealt with mama drama when I received an email from my mother."

I frowned at her. "An email?"

"Yes. Evidently that's how today's busy socialite corresponds with her daughter. And because I was curious about what warranted a fucking email, I opened it and then I wished I wouldn't have."

"Why? Did she ask you to fill in as a bridesmaid?"

"That's not even funny to joke about." She rinsed her cup and put it in the dishwasher. "Apparently someone is hosting a bridal luncheon for her. Since I hadn't RSVP'd she wondered if I planned to attend. She was so condescending about being 'understanding' if I couldn't go on such short notice."

"When is the luncheon?"

"Saturday."

"*This* Saturday?"

"Yep. She claimed my invitation must've gotten lost in cyberspace. But I know that she didn't even bother to invite me in the first place."

I couldn't tell if Sierra was hurt by this or just pissed off. I turned her around and tugged her against me. "That's shitty. I'm sorry. I'm betting you RSVP'd with a big 'fuck you' in all caps."

"Hell no. That's what Ellen wants. So you can bet your ass I *will* be at that luncheon." She pecked me on the mouth. "I have to go. Will I see you tonight?"

"I work midnight to noon the next two nights."

"I'll be late, but not that late."

"See you later, McKay." I clamped my hands on her face and gave her a morning mouth fuck goodbye...just because I could.

21 Sierra

LATE SATURDAY MORNING I'd arrived on time for the bridal luncheon at the new "club" my mother had joined upon her engagement to Barnacle Bill.

After I assured her I'd be in attendance for what she called her *big, special day*, she'd sent me a link to her bridal gift registry—which I ignored. Then she'd tacked on a "reminder" of the appropriate attire for a fall-themed soiree at a prestigious country club.

Rebellious Sierra dreamed of showing up high as a kite, wearing a black leather halter and disco-era gold lamé pants. But practical Sierra with the business degree chose the high road and a nondescript dress that allowed me to fade into the background. I hadn't bothered with jewelry. My mother's friends' accessory of choice was a glass of white wine or a pumpkin spice martini, so I secretly lamented that I'd left my flask of Crown at home.

I wandered around, not making polite chitchat as much as listening to conversations.

Which I soon discovered were boring as hell.

Charity this, charity that. Caterers, florists, scheduled luncheons.

Yawn.

Bored women with nothing better to do than decide how to spend hubby's money on pet causes while indulging in a three-martini lunch with their other bored society friends.

Cynical?

Yep.

I vaguely remembered my Grandma Daniels encouraging my mother to become involved with service organizations. Early in my parents' marriage my mother had embraced the idea of being the wife of Gavin Daniels, heir to a real estate company. She'd spent time at my grandparents' country club. She'd tried to look the part of the corporate wife. Problem was, she hadn't acted like a corporate wife. Her infidelities embarrassed my father—personally and professionally—and he'd cut his losses with her early on.

Luckily my relationship with him hadn't been a casualty of the demise of their marriage. At least I'd grown up with one stable parent who proved that unconditional love exists. I was very proud of the fact that I *am* my father's daughter.

That's why I was wrestling with my decision on whether to leave DPM.

Phyllis wasn't pressuring me. I'd had a text from Rory asking if I'd made a decision. I still hadn't mentioned anything to Boone about the offer to run PCE. It wasn't that I didn't trust him. I'd just never been in a relationship where I could discuss issues in my professional life. I saw myself as captain of my own ship. Asking for advice almost seemed like asking permission and that was something I wouldn't do.

Break out into a chorus of "I Am Woman" why don't you?

That thought made me smile.

My smile faded when I remembered the whole debacle with Greg's assistant Melissa this week and her refusal to stay on at DPM. It'd hit me... How could I, in good conscience, take a position at PCE advocating for *all* women in business when I couldn't help even one woman in my own business?

I couldn't.

I needed to fix things at DPM first. Figure out a way to effect change from within and earn the respect of the guys I worked with. That would be the best use of the skills I'd learned at PCE and there was no better proving ground for leadership.

Made up your mind, just like that? Would you stay in that position if it wasn't a family business? If you weren't worried about disappointing your father?

No, I wouldn't stay at DPM. I would've taken the job at PCE the moment Phyllis offered it to me.

This wishy-washy back-and-forth stuff...no wonder I hadn't talked to Boone. I changed my mind every five minutes.

Armed with the knowledge that nothing would get resolved today, I focused on the party, hanging back to watch my beautiful, blonde mother. She'd already claimed the spotlight. She looked stunning in a dark teal pantsuit that hit the mark between classy and trendy. For once she wasn't trying to appear younger and hipper than anyone else in the room. But she'd always been a chameleon, changing her appearance and her personality to fit the social situation or the man she was with. Being Barnacle Bill's babe motivated her to ditch the hair extensions, the skinny jeans, the bohemian jewelry and embrace the upper crust's idea of respectability and act her age.

I couldn't help but wonder how much she hated that. Or how long *this* phase would last.

I'd gone through phases of my own with her. In my childhood she'd used me as a pawn or a wedge against my dad—not that I'd known it at the time. Then in my preteen and early teen years, she'd morphed into being my friend more than a parent. We shopped. We did all the girlfriend things she should've been doing with her own friends and not her fourteen-year-old daughter. She attempted to turn me against my father with outright lies and manipulation. It still caused me a pang of shame to admit she had succeeded on a few occasions, convincing me to think the worst of my dad.

By the time I'd grown into my body and my looks—her words, not mine—she encouraged open defiance of my father's rules. She'd let me skip school when she had custody of me. She'd let me throw parties on the weekends and provide booze for us. My friends were in awe of her; she was the coolest mom ever. So it was a blow to my fifteen-year-old pride that they preferred to hang out with her more than with me. She'd complain if I attempted to do homework, reminding me that men prized beauty and physical desirability over brains. Another shameful thing I'd actually believed for a time.

During those formative middle teen years when she claimed a girl "needed her mother" she took my dad to court, demanding full custody of me. I'd bought into her false flattery and her promise to always be there for me. Yet, when I'd ended up in jail for shoplifting, she hadn't been around at all. My need for her approval had turned me into her mini-clone; an entitled brat with no thought to the future beyond next season's fashion trends.

My father had put an end to it by pulling up roots and relocating us to Wyoming while my mom had flitted off to Paris with her man *du jour*.

To this day I wasn't sure if living a totally different lifestyle in Wyoming was the best thing that'd ever happened to me or if my mother's relocation to Paris and her having no influence on my decisions provided the catalyst I needed to change. The Sierra McKay who returned to Arizona to start college in no way resembled the Sierra Daniels who'd left Phoenix three years prior.

Thank god.

I'd come into my own during that time. I hadn't done it alone; I could thank my dad, my new stepmom Rielle, my new sister Rory, the close connections I'd found with my new family and friends in Sundance, Wyoming. Even the heartbreak Boone West had brought about by leaving had helped transform me.

A transformation my mother hadn't liked at all.

I'd grown self-confident enough in my years away from her that I'd hoped we could find common ground to reestablish a new, different mother-daughter relationship.

Then she'd fucked my boyfriend and thereby fucked any chance of being part of my life.

Four years later I was still good with that decision.

Which made me wonder why I was even here, waiting in *line* for the woman who'd given birth to me to acknowledge me.

She waited until she finished her conversation before signaling me to approach her.

"Mother. You look amazing."

For that compliment I earned a somewhat sincere smile and the kiss-kiss cheek brush.

"Thank you, dear." Before I could say anything else, she addressed the person in line behind me, with an effusive, "Joan! Darling, how are you?" dismissing me completely.

No surprise I practically skipped toward the bar.

I ordered Crown, but the snooty bartender informed me their top shelf whiskey was Jameson, so this event wasn't starting out very promising.

"So kiddo, how long you think this phase will last?"

I faced Char, my mom's best friend, the only other person who'd also suffered through years of the foibles of Ellen Bertrand Daniels. "I think she's found the love of her life and her true identity."

Char scowled. "With Bill?"

"No, with all of Bill's *bills*."

She snorted. "I think we're both sitting in the back table. The crude friend and the daughter ain't welcome in the prime seating areas."

"It's just as well. We're closer to the bar."

"Amen, sister." She touched her bottle of Miller Lite to my lowball glass. "Did you tell Ellen not to invite you to this?"

"No. Why?"

"When I saw the guest list the first part of the week and you weren't on it, I chewed her ass. Then I warned her if she didn't invite you, I'd tell these snooty new friends of hers about the time she pissed in the birdbath at the Wrigley estate." She flashed a mean grin. "I still may do that. But the point is, you're her only kid. She oughta treat you better."

I shrugged. "It is what it is, Char."

"Well, she's jealous of you, that's what it is."

"Right."

Char leaned closer. "I'm serious, Sierra. She failed to turn you into a replica of her. She knows while she seeks validation and approval from all men, you only seek it from one man." She swigged her beer. "Your father."

Her insight didn't surprise me as much as the fact she was still friends with a woman as insipid as my mother.

"Ellen and I have been through a lot over the years," she started, which meant I'd voiced that comment out loud. "We're friends more out of habit than anything. My invite to this shindig surprised the hell out of me. But Ellen needs to rub it in that she's stepped up to a higher social standing. Sort of sad, when you think about it, because I've never given a shit about any of that."

"You're the only friend she hasn't fucked over."

"Oh, she's fucked me over plenty of times. I forgave her mostly because I know I'm the only real friend she has left and I felt sorry for her. But I'm done." She bumped my shoulder with hers. "I say we leave with a bang, kiddo."

And so it began.

Clarissa somebody, who adored Ellen to the ends of the earth, was so, *so* thrilled that her dear, *dear* friend would once again join the ranks of those in matrimonial bliss.

Polite applause.

Patricia somebody relayed the cute story about how Bill and Ellen had met and how she'd snagged his heart.

Char came up behind me and whispered, "More like she snagged his wallet," and handed me my second whiskey.

Irene somebody delivered a heartfelt toast about welcoming Ellen into the club, and jokingly added she was now eligible to be a golf widow like the rest of them.

That's when it occurred to me why my mother hadn't belonged to this kind of club before she'd met Bill. Single women, who looked like her, could probably cherry pick her next husband—from any of theirs.

Clarissa settled Ellen behind a beautifully decorated table to open her gifts.

Apparently I shouldn't have ignored the bridal registry link since all of her gifts were some sort of Swarovski crystal. So my "His and Hers" hand towels—his with a golf motif and hers with a shopping theme—were a little weird and a lot out of place.

Just like you.

I snuck away and snagged my third glass of whiskey. The stuff didn't taste half bad after the third glass.

At least we didn't have to play stupid party games and we were dismissed for the luncheon portion. Sadly, Char and I weren't assigned seats at the same table in the back after all. The finger foods were interesting, if a little bland, and there weren't nearly enough of them.

I listened to the table conversation as I nibbled on my itty bitty square of lemon poppyseed cake.

"June is just heartsick over the whole thing," the woman across from me confided to the entire table. "Can you imagine?"

"Marybeth told her not to book that venue," the silver-haired woman next to her retorted. "But June just followed her own agenda, like always."

"Does the postponement of this fundraiser mean June is being reassigned to something else? Because I *will* take issue with that if Clarissa foists her off on me," a woman my mother's age groused.

They were still talking about fundraisers.

And me with no little cocktail forks to jab in my ears. I snickered...which brought their attention to me.

Seven pairs of judgy eyes homed in, scrutinizing my face, hair, clothing and beverage choice.

"I'm sorry, we're being horribly rude," the gossiper said. "It's so lovely that you could join us."

I said, "Quite," with a straight face.

"Of course, many of us were surprised that Ellen had a daughter...um, your age."

That was a polite save.

"Yes, Ellen looks far too young," a pearl-wearing woman added.

"I'm sure she's attributed her youthful look to clean living and good genes. I'm just lucky to take after her."

Just then, a lowball glass filled with amber liquid appeared above my cake plate.

Char, that instigator, had bribed the waiter to deliver another whiskey to me.

With all eyes on me, I tried my damnedest to be classy by keeping my pinkie off the glass as I lifted it and sipped as if I was on the set of *Downton Abbey*.

"And you live in the Phoenix area?" the don't-foist-June-on-me woman asked.

"Yes, in Scottsdale."

Pleased looks all around.

At least my address passed their approval.

But old-sour-puss-pearl-wearer #2 wasn't done grilling me. "You own? Or rent?"

"I've owned my home there for two years."

"But you're so young."

I leaned forward as if I intended to dish the dirt. "I don't mean to sound like I'm bragging, but I've been told that I could pass for a twenty-year-old."

"But Ellen told us you *were* twenty."

I laughed. "Honey, please. I'll be thirty-*one* next month."

"Well, I'll be." The ladies exchanged a smug look and tongues would be wagging later.

That's what you get for putting me in the B section, Mom.

But my glee quickly vanished. I didn't know why she'd invited me if she didn't want me here.

That's when I missed my Dad. He liked me. He wanted me around. In fact he'd texted me yesterday just to tell me that he loved me and missed me. I was such a crappy daughter for not responding right away, with a million kissy face emojis and sparkly pink hearts.

No time like the present to rectify that.

I didn't even pretend to be discreet; I pulled out my phone and sent him the emoji-filled text I should've sent yesterday.

Dad: *That's a lot of hearts. You okay?*

Me: *I'm at Mom's sucky bridal luncheon and I miss you.*

Dad: *Sorry. Is she being…?*

Me: *The same old Ellen? Yes. Except she wears pearls when she ignores me now.*

Dad: *I love that you have a sense of humor about this, sweetheart.*

Me: *Only because I know I have you in my corner no matter what.*

Dad: *That's sweet. I appreciate it. So how much have you been drinking? LOL*

Me: *Eyeing drinky-poo #5. This lousy country club doesn't even have Crown.*

Dad: *The horror. Get out of there right now. Clearly it's totally sketch.*

I laughed out loud. Literally. My dad was such a dork sometimes. I glanced up to see if anyone had noticed.

The entire table was watching me. And hooray, my mother chose that moment to look over. She glared at me, then she glared at my phone. Defiantly I held it up higher and sent another text.

Me: *Uh-oh. Busted texting at the table by the bride-to-be. Gotta go.*

Love you.

Dad: *Love you too. You have a DD Miss Drinky-poo #5 at 2:00 on a Saturday afternoon?*

Shit. No I didn't. But I would.

Me: *I'll figure something out. Seriously, I've gotta go. Her deadly glare is heating up the plastic on my phone and it's melting to my hand.*

Dad: *HAH! Text me later so I know you got home safely. XO*

I looked up and yep, Mom's eyes fired daggers at me. I made a show of pocketing my phone and excusing myself before I headed to the bar.

Drink number five went down smoothly. Probably not good to drink on an empty stomach. I wandered over to the cake table. If I put four mini-squares together it might actually make a normal-sized piece of cake. I did that and carried my spoils back to the table.

Damn. No fork. Well, they called it finger food for a reason, right?

My tablemates appeared uncomfortable with the fact I was, oh, *eating*. Their discomfort turned to judgy silence when Char dropped off drink number six.

I was feeling pretty mellow and wanted to leave on a high note, but driving was a no-go. Boone hated texting but I couldn't exactly call him and say, "Hey, babe, I've knocked back six drinks just to make it through this stupid party and now I'm tipsy, so can you please haul that hot ass of yours over here and pick me up?"

I snickered. That's exactly what I texted him.

B-Dub: *OMW*

Me: *Cool. Oh, and can you pick up a bucket of fried chicken on the way? The food here SUCKS*

B-Dub: *No*

Me: *Dammit, I can't find the emoji sticking its tongue out, so imagine that, k?*

B-Dub: *Stop dirnkign*

I squinted at his text. Stupid autocorrect.

But that's when I realized autocorrect hadn't fixed it. I was seeing what Boone struggled with every day. That configuration of letters probably looked right to him.

No wonder he didn't like to text.

No wonder I was falling in love with him, the man who trusted me enough to share his vulnerability.

Great. Now the "I love you, man" phase had kicked in.

Another text popped up from my assistant Nikki:

NZ: *The quarterly reports for the Prestwood expansion are not where they're supposed to be.*

Me: *There's nothing on the checkout sheet about who might have them?*

NZ: *No. I didn't misplace or misfile them.*

Damn you, Greg, for not owning up to your fuck-ups and putting every assistant in the company on edge.

Me: *I'd never accuse you. If you can't find them they're gone.*

NZ: *I hate to bring this up, but I think someone in the office is trying to sabotage you. You need that data to compile your report. No data, no report and you look incompetent.*

I briefly closed my eyes. Dammit, the words were blurring.

Me: *Whoever took it is an idiot to think I wouldn't make backup copies. I scanned everything and sent a copy to the secure server as well as my personal cloud for this type of situation.*

NZ: *I figured you did, because you're on top of things, but I thought I'd ask. Do you need me to do anything else?*

Me: *You know the next two projects on tap, so see if the files containing that data are missing. Make a list and we'll discuss on Monday.*

NZ: *Will do. Thanks boss* ☺

When I glanced up from my phone and saw the distasteful looks, I offered a benign smile. "I'm sorry, you probably think I'm being horribly rude, but I'm not. See, I wasn't initially invited to this event and being the boss, I do work on Saturdays so being out of touch isn't an option."

They blinked as if *work* was a foreign word.

"Do any of you have jobs outside the home?" When no one answered, the whiskey started talking. "None of you wanted a career outside of…whatever it is you do all day? You're content to boss the servants around? Have lunch at the club and brainstorm ways to help the less fortunate? No offense, but that kind of life would drive me batshit crazy. I didn't graduate from college and gain all this knowledge so I could support my husband behind the scenes and run a household. I run a *company*. A multi-million-dollar corporation. I have employees who rely on me. I have bosses who rely on me. And since I've reached this level of responsibility, I can't just politely pocket my cell phone in my twin-set and ignore my business just because it's the weekend. I'll bet none of your husbands left their cell phones in their lockers this morning before they strutted onto the golf course."

Two of the woman looked surprised, two looked defiant, two looked embarrassed and one woman looked annoyed.

My drinky-poos caught up with me. I excused myself from the table to search for a bathroom.

Upon exiting the ladies' room, I saw my mother across the narrow hallway, pretending to study the photos on the wall, but I knew she'd been waiting to pounce.

She faced me. Her eyes had the nasty glint that promised this ass chewing would be a doozy. "Are you happy now that you've humiliated me in front of my friends on what's supposed to be my big, special day?"

"How exactly have I humiliated you?"

"Where would you like me to start? By getting drunk? By shoving cake in your mouth as if you were food deprived?"

"I *am* food deprived. You can't have an open bar at noon and then skimp on appetizers."

She adopted a patronizing expression. "I wasn't aware an open bar was an open invitation to get drunk. No one else seems to have taken advantage of free booze or taken issue with the food."

"I'm sure none of your friends noticed as they were too busy gossiping."

"You certainly presented something for them to focus on with that embarrassing and tacky gift you passed off to me."

My cheeks heated, more from anger than embarrassment.

"I specifically told you what to buy me and as usual you ignored me."

"Newsflash; it's called a gift for a reason. You don't get to dictate what gift I buy you."

"If you had, you wouldn't have disgraced yourself and shamed me."

"Shamed you," I repeated. "No. That's what you're doing to me right now. Barely acknowledging my existence. Putting me at a table with a bunch of pearl-clutching do-gooders whose only purpose are their pet charities? Yeah, no wonder I was drinking. But I suppose it was too much to hope that I might've had a seat at your table, for your 'big special day.' After all, I'm only your daughter."

Her lips curled into a sneer. "Grow up, Sierra. You've always been such a brat if you're not the center of attention."

Same old shit, different day. I didn't know why I bothered with her.

"Not to mention your complete and utter disrespect for me when you had your cell phone out and were texting during the entire event. How does that make me look? Like I raised a rude child with zero manners."

If I pointed out Dad raised me, then she could pass the blame onto him, so I said nothing.

"Now I have to worry that you'll employ that same 'humiliate my mother' tactic at my wedding."

"Wrong. It won't be an issue because I'm not coming to your wedding."

She rolled her eyes. "Again with the bratty, threatening behavior."

"So with that…I'm done." I turned away.

Boone was striding toward me. With each step he got closer, that hollow space inside me shrunk.

Then his strong arms were around me. He kissed me squarely on the mouth—not a sweet lover's peck but a quick reminder of his possession and his passion for me. He peered into my eyes and whatever he saw there had him concerned. "What happened?"

"Nothing I wasn't expecting. Can we—"

"Who, exactly, are you?" my mother demanded.

Boone held his hand in front of my mom's face, but he never looked away from me when he said to her, "Hush. I was talking to her."

"Can we just go? I parked—"

"You don't get to hush me—"

"Don't interrupt Sierra again," he warned in a low, menacing tone.

Out of the corner of my eye I saw her jaw drop. No one ever spoke to her that way.

But my man did. "How did you get here so fast?"

"Raj drove me. We left right after your dad called. He wanted to make sure I knew—"

"*Gavin* called you?" my mom interrupted.

Boone stood straight. Shoulders back, his big body facing the threat. Every inch of him a soldier. He flicked a dismissive glance at her. "Don't interrupt me again. I don't give a damn who you are. You're just being rude."

"Now you know where Sierra gets it," she shot back.

Oh no she didn't.

And Mom just kept poking his buttons. "How do *you* know Gavin?"

"I've known him for years. But you don't have a clue who *I* am, do you? So what does that say about you?" He glared at her. "Oh, so now you're *not* going to interrupt me when I ask you a direct question?"

I choked back a laugh.

"It says that what's going on in your daughter's life doesn't matter to you. Guess what? It matters to Gavin. And it matters to me. So I won't bother introducing myself."

He threaded his fingers through mine and led me away.

22 Boone

"**Y**OU'RE MY HERO, Boone. Seriously."

Gavin Daniels was *my* hero for putting up with Sierra's bitch of a mother and managing to raise such a beautiful, caring, smart, kind daughter.

Christ, that woman was a nasty piece of work.

"The only thing that would've made it better? If you'd marched in wearing your army uniform."

Sierra actually swooned against me.

Or maybe the whiskey had kicked in.

"But then she would've known your name, right? Because you're labeled with it on the front."

"Yes, there's a name patch on the right side of my uniform. My rank is on the left side and both sleeves." I stopped for a moment and scanned the area. It seemed every other car in this parking lot was a Mercedes. I pressed the horn alarm on her key fob to save time.

She'd parked in the back row as far from the building as possible.

That was telling.

I let the horn blare and didn't care if it was a dick move. The golfers teeing off at the first hole could deal with it for another minute. Although I could admit disappointment a *Quiet, please* sign didn't pop up over the perfectly manicured hedge.

Sierra laughed. "I have to use the horn button thingy all the time. I never remember where I park, especially in parking garages. I mean, who pays attention to that stuff?"

"You should always be aware of your surroundings."

"Says army soldier guy who always checks the perimeter. Amirite?"

She bumped her hip into mine and stumbled.

I caught her around the waist. "Careful."

She twined her arms around my neck. "You are ridiculously hot. I could stare at your beautiful face forever."

Good to know my girl was a sweet drunk. I kissed her smiling lips. "I hope so."

"Can I tell you a secret?"

"Sure."

"My feet hurt and I think I have blisters. I hate these stupid, ugly shoes. My mom bought them for me as a peace offering and she didn't even notice I was wearing them today. So I'm in pain for nothing."

"Hang on." I leaned down far enough to hook my right arm behind her knees. I lifted her up, cradling her to my chest. "This'll save you a few steps."

Sierra buried her face in my neck. "You really are my hero, Boone West."

I set her on her feet beside the car to open the passenger door.

"Just a sec." She clutched my arm while she removed her shoes. Then she pulled back and let one shoe fly, quickly followed by the other. They landed on the blacktop with a muffled thump.

Except she was drunk and had lousy aim so the shoes didn't go far.

She dusted her hands together. "There. Now I feel better."

I was trying really hard not to laugh. Not only was my girl a sweet drunk, she was a funny drunk.

She stepped around me and hopped into the seat. "Oh. And make sure you run over them when we leave. At least twice."

I did laugh at that. I climbed in the driver's side and had to move the seat back first thing. How could Sierra drive crammed up under the steering wheel?

And then Sierra was crammed against the steering wheel and me because she'd crawled onto my lap. "Hi."

"Uh. Hi. What are you doing?"

"Seducing you." She hit the lever that lowered the back of the seat to the horizontal position.

Fuck. She'd hiked her dress to her hips, exposing those smooth thighs I loved to be between. My hands immediately sought contact with her skin.

Warm lips landed on mine. I could detect the flavor of whiskey. I got the full taste of it when Sierra shoved her tongue past my teeth.

Stop this. Pull back.

Easier said than done when the woman was pulling out all the stops. Her hands gripping my hair. That hungry mouth feeding me hot, wet, deep kisses. Her lithe body writhing on mine. Then she started that teasing pelvis roll that drove me crazy.

She backed up to get a better angle and her ass bumped into the horn. She broke the kiss with a laugh. "Oops."

But that allowed me to regain my senses. "We can't do this."

"Yes we can. I've wanted to do it in a car with you since I was sixteen. Just give in to the moment. I'm on top. I'll do all the work."

"Another time, in a less public place." I didn't tack on *when you're not drunk.*

"Boone—"

"Stop." I clamped my hands on the backs of her legs. "I don't want these creepy country club dudes seeing this hot ass bouncing up and down, okay?"

That caught her attention. She sighed and kissed the hollow of my throat. "Okay. But promise me we'll do it in a car. In a kinky role-playing game, where you're wearing your uniform and you pull me over. I tell you if I have another traffic violation I'll lose my license so I'll do *anything* not to get that ticket…"

I groaned. "Have you been watching porn?"

She giggled. "They're full of really great ideas."

I slapped her ass. "Get back in your seat and behave."

"Yes, sir, officer."

Smartass.

Once we were both buckled up, I peeled out of the parking spot and ran over her shoes. Then I put it in reverse and backed over them.

Sierra laughed hysterically.

Then she asked me where I'd hidden the fried chicken because she was starved.

Next time I glanced over at her—like two minutes later—she'd conked out.

She didn't stir when I lifted her out of the car or when I carried her into the house.

I settled her on the couch instead of the bedroom so I could keep an eye on her. After I tucked an afghan around her and kissed her forehead, I noticed Lu standing between the great room and kitchen.

"Didn't mean to startle you." She dipped her chin at Sierra. "Rough time at the bridal luncheon?"

"A seven-whiskey luncheon, apparently."

"Yikes. Poor thing." She returned to the kitchen.

I followed her, wondering what she was doing here.

She's Sierra's roommate. She lives here.

"Raj fell into bed after he came back from dropping you off. I'm letting him sleep." She scanned me, head to toe. "You're wiped, dude."

"Midnight to noon shifts suck, which is why I mainline caffeine." I gestured to the groceries strewn across the counters. "What're you up to?"

"Cooking. Living in this house with Sierra and this dream kitchen has spoiled me. So I'm making Raj dinner. Shish-kebobs, mushroom risotto, arugula salad and angel food cake."

I whistled. "Lucky man. But I know it's not his birthday."

"I wanted to do something nice for him."

"He'll appreciate it. Neither one of us is a great cook."

She started chopping something green.

"So I'll let you get to it."

"Stay, if I'm not keeping you from something. I promise I'll clean up my mess when I'm done and Sierra won't know I destroyed her kitchen."

Weird thing to say. "Cool. I'm grabbing a bottle of water. You want one?"

"I'm good. I'll have a glass of wine when I open the bottle to make the salad dressing."

I took a seat at the breakfast bar.

Lu lowered her knife and studied me. "It'd probably be good for us to get to know each other better, since Raj is your BFF and Sierra is mine."

"Agreed. So should I call you Lu or Lucinda Grace?"

"Lu." She scraped the greens off the cutting board into a small bowl. "Sierra called you to rescue her from luncheon hell?"

"Her dad called me first. Apparently they'd been texting during the event and she told him how much she'd been drinking."

"Gavin has your phone number?"

"He insisted on having it when I was in Wyoming."

She smirked. "Of course he did. He usually calls me because he frets about Sierra being around her mom—with good reason." She paused. "If you know Gavin, then do you know Ellen too?"

I shook my head. "Sierra didn't talk about her that much when we were in high school. Today was the first time we crossed paths."

"And your first impression?"

"Nasty bitch who doesn't deserve to have a daughter as awesome as Sierra."

"Amen."

"Have you spent much time around Ellen?" I asked her.

"Enough to know you're dead on the mark with your opinion of her. I'm sure Sierra told you about Ellen MILF-ing Sierra's boyfriend. I was around for that fun situation. As well as Ellen groveling for a few weeks, followed by her extreme nastiness when Sierra wouldn't have anything to do with her." She shuddered. "The ugly things she said to her own daughter? Shocked the hell out of me."

"You get along with your parents?"

"Of course. They are awesome. How about yours?"

I doubted Raj had shared my story. "My mother makes Ellen look like a dream. My dad was around as little as possible. Which is why it sucks that I agreed to meet him in Flagstaff the day Ellen gets married." I fiddled with the cap on my water. "Did Sierra ask you to go to the wedding with her since I can't?"

"Nope. Ellen is not my biggest fan. She disappeared for a while, maybe…nine months to a year. She didn't come to Sierra's college graduation. Then she popped back up with her new boyfriend, Barnacle Bill."

I raised an eyebrow. "Barnacle Bill?"

Lu laughed. "Now Sierra has me calling him that. She is gonna totally fuck up and call him that to his face one of these days."

"Where'd the name come from?"

"Sierra came up with it when she was drunk after Ellen bragged about Bill's big...fishing boat business."

"Sierra was funny as hell today after I picked her up. Is she always that way when she's been drinking?"

"Just when she's drunk. Not after like two drinks. There's a difference. She doesn't do it very often, but yeah. She's funny when she's around the right people. So you've never seen her slam-a-lammered before?"

I swigged my water. "Once, at a party in high school, and it was far from a funny situation."

"Huh."

"What?"

"I forget that you've known her that long."

A timer dinged. Lu used oven mitts to pull a pan from the oven.

A curl of sweet scented steam teased me as she set the pan on a wire rack. "That smells great. It's not surprising you've been roommates for so long since you both like to bake."

Lu rolled her eyes. "I bake because I like it. Sierra bakes when she has something on her mind or if she's upset."

I went still. But my brain sifted back through the times I'd sampled her baked goods.

I'd noticed she had cookies on her desk the day I'd shown up at her office for my Phoenix tour. A result of seeing me the day before?

She'd brought the elaborate brownie coma dessert to McJock Central. Because she found out I'd lied about how long I planned to be in Phoenix?

The morning after our first night together she'd whipped up a loaf of banana bread. In response to everything I'd told her about how fucked up I was?

The night we were at the bar and I'd dealt with Oakley, she'd made cupcakes after we returned home. Due to her crappy day and work and dealing with her mother?

Christ. Why hadn't I seen the pattern?

I wondered what she'd whip up after her mother's luncheon from hell.

"She talked about you sometimes," Lu said, interrupting my thoughts.

My gut tightened. "She did?"

"The first time she mentioned you was after the Ellen MILF-ing incident. She said she was glad Ellen had picked a douche she didn't really care about and not you because she would've committed murder." Lu smirked. "But to be fair, she didn't clarify whether she meant she'd kill her mother...or kill you."

I forced a laugh. "I deserve to be sliced and diced if I ever hurt Sierra like that. *I'd* hand her the fucking knife."

"So what happened in your past that had her swearing she'd never get involved with you again? Then two weeks later you're living with her? And now Mr. Overprotective Daniels calls *you* to rescue her instead of me?"

"No offense, Lu, but if Sierra hasn't told you? I won't either."

"Jerk. So infidelity wasn't an issue between you two. A fuck-and-run encounter wasn't it either."

"I'll point out while you're pointing that knife at me that infidelity will *never* be an issue between Sierra and me." I paused. "I spent years hoping for another chance with her. The last thing I'd ever do is fuck her over."

"That's a relief. Because Raj would miss you if I was forced to kill you." She thwacked a clove of garlic on the cutting board and I jumped.

Jesus.

"Keep in mind...that as a landscaper I know where to bury the bodies and how deep."

"Good talk." I patted the counter and said, "I'll just...go run in traffic where it's safer."

Her maniacal laughter followed me out of the kitchen.

Seeing Sierra curled up on the couch...I just wanted to pull the covers over us and hide away in our cocoon for a while. I scooped her up and carried her to the bedroom.

I stripped to my underwear, closed the blinds, locked the door and slipped between the cool sheets. Sierra still wore her dress. I'd left it on, not wanting to wake her up even when I craved feeling her bare skin against mine. Wednesday night when I'd been in a piss poor mood, prowling around the house, I'd hated the hollow feeling of falling asleep alone on the couch.

I brushed my lips across the back of her head and breathed in the sweet perfume of her skin, a scent that calmed and aroused me.

She shifted, rolling over and finding "her" spot on my chest. I automatically adjusted until we were positioned how we fell asleep every night.

Closing my eyes, I kissed the top of her head.

She said, "Mmm. My hero. I love you. Being in love with you is better than just being *all fucking in.*"

I didn't move.

Drunk talk, my subconscious scoffed, *she won't remember when she wakes up.*

But I would. Holy shit would I *ever.* I doubted I'd think about anything else all day.

White spots danced behind my eyelids. I forced myself to breathe.

I love you. Being in love with you is better than just being all fucking in.

Those words repeated on a loop in my head at least a dozen times.

What did I say to her when she woke up?

I couldn't ignore that she'd put herself out there. We hadn't hit the three-little-word stage—not that I knew what the fuck that meant. I'd heard them talk about it on TV and in the movies like it was some magical higher "level" in a relationship.

I loved Sierra. I'd probably always loved her, even back when I didn't know what love felt like.

And you know that now? After two weeks with her?

Yes.

I'd been ready to blurt out my feelings for her in the kitchen the morning after we'd spent the night together the first time. But I figured she'd be skeptical and confused if I said, *I don't know how to love, but I'm in love with you.*

Or else she'd believe the best sex of my life had spurred the confession.

Why are you wrestling with this? If you're sure you love her, act sure. Man the fuck up and tell her.

My heart raced like a motherfucker when I said, "I love you too."

I held my breath as I waited for her to react.

She didn't.

That's because she's passed out and she won't remember this, dumbass.

That negative thought...could piss off.

I'd said it once; I'd say it again now that I *knew* I could say it.

I fell asleep with a smile on my face.

A WARM, WET mouth surrounded my cock.

Nails scored the tops of my thighs, followed by the swish of silky hair across the sensitized flesh.

Soft sucking and swirling licks.

Fuck that felt good. Talk about a realistic dream.

Fingers rolled my balls as that suctioning mouth glided up and down my shaft, now fully erect and hard as steel.

I groaned. "God yes."

"Boone."

I blinked and lifted my head off the pillow. "Sierra?"

She pushed herself upright and glared at me. "You were expecting someone else, fuckface?"

"No! I thought I was dreaming about a blowjob." I scrambled up so we were almost face-to-face. How long had I been out? I noticed she'd ditched the luncheon dress, leaving her naked. And I could feel the sheet rubbing on my bare ass. "You stripped off my boxer briefs."

"Duh." She rolled her entire body forward, teasing my lips with hers. "I needed full access to your dick." After licking my lower lip she sank her teeth into it. "You awake now?"

"Uh, yeah."

"You do know that I'm the one sucking your big, hard love rod and not some random chick in a dream."

"Uh, yeah."

"Good." Sierra angled her head and nibbled along my jaw. "I love this part of you. So strong and sharply defined. Gives you such a killer profile." She flicked her tongue across the stubble on my chin. "I love how this feels on my tongue. So rough."

My pulse sped up as she dragged an openmouthed kiss down my throat, straight to the patch of hair in the middle of my chest.

"You know how obsessed I am with how your scent lingers here." She moved her head back and forth, rubbing my chest hair on her cheeks and her lips, then pressing her nose into the center and inhaling.

I didn't arch into her when she imprisoned my nipple between her teeth. I loved how she knew how far to push me in nipple play. Mine were so goddamned sensitive—she'd figured that out the first night. She'd joined me in the shower before I'd gone to work yesterday, biting, licking and sucking my left nipple as she'd jacked me off. I'd seen fucking stars after that one.

"I love your body, Boone. All the ridges and dips and hollows that are perfect for my lips and tongue." She chuckled as she slid her mouth along the edge of my ribcage.

The vibration tickled—as she knew it would. Damn intuitive woman had memorized all of my ticklish spots. Some I wasn't aware I had since I hadn't let previous lovers explore me like this.

She nibbled on my hipbone until I squirmed. Then she dipped her tongue into the grooves of my abdomen, taking her own sweet time to follow every line until my stomach quivered.

Before she pressed a wide, flat-tongued lick down my flexor muscle, her hair slid across my torso in a tantalizing arc, from my collarbones to the tip of my cock. "Sierra."

"No."

"No...what? You don't even know what I was gonna say."

"I know what you were gonna *do*. Lure me back up there with that sexy, dirty smile and those heated eyes with the promise of melt-my-brain kisses. Then you'd flip me onto my back and fuck me." She licked a circle around the rim of my cock, causing it to jump off my stomach, closer to her mouth. "Sorry. Maybe after."

"After what?"

"After I blow your mind with a killer blowjob."

I curled my hand under her jaw, forcing her to hold still and look at me. "I wasn't gonna do anything. I wanted to tell you something."

"What?"

My heart sped up. "That I love you."

Her jaw would've dropped if I hadn't held onto it.

"After I tucked us in, you told me you loved me. You said that being in love with me was better than being all fucking in." I swept my thumb over the sensitive skin beneath her jawline. The way her eyes darkened gave me the answer I needed. "That wasn't drunk talk. You meant it, didn't you?"

"Yes."

"Why tell me then?"

"If you would've bailed after you heard me say it then I would've blamed it on drunk talk. But I heard you say it back to me. I didn't dream that, right?"

"You didn't dream it. And I didn't say it back to you as if we were just exchanging compliments. I said it back to you because I fucking *mean* it, Sierra. I love you."

Her eyes shone with tears and that was so not like her. "Boone."

I dropped my hand from her face and growled, "Come here."

Then her mouth was on mine.

We kissed slowly. Steadily. Softly. In between the drugging kisses, we whispered lover's confessions and promises of devotion.

It ranked right up there as one of the best moments of my life.

I eventually rolled Sierra onto her back. I rested my forehead to hers. "I need you like this. Looking in your eyes as I tell you how much I love you."

She murmured, "Yes."

Things started out with tender intentions—at least on my part. I loved having her hands mapping my shoulders and chest and hips as I drove in and out of her. I loved the sensual glide of her lips and her tongue in my mouth and on my throat. I loved that a leisurely roll of my pelvis as I thrust into her wet heat caused her to arch into me, mashing her soft breasts against my chest. I loved the sting of her nails digging into my ass, sent chills up my spine, down my legs and across my arms. I loved how the sound of my voice in her ear made her moan. I loved when she told me the time for sweet lovin' was over and demanded that I fuck her until she screamed.

Our bodies were damp with sweat from the friction of hot skin on hot skin. We were breathing hard, kissing messily, pushing to reach that pinnacle where the intensity became throbbing, pulsing release.

Sierra hit that peak first. She didn't scream, but it was damn close.

I watched her as she came. Seeing her get off did it for me every fucking time. Especially when her spasming sex clenched around my cock as I rocked against her to prolong her orgasm. I didn't have a fucking prayer of not coming like a damn geyser.

I didn't stay lost in the post-orgasm white noise for long. Sierra slapped my ass hard and said, "I love you, but you're heavy, we're sticky, and I'm hungry."

I pressed a lingering kiss to her mouth before I eased out of her and pushed back onto my knees. Sitting on the edge of the bed, I tried to catch my breath and my balance.

It didn't surprise me that Sierra already knew how to work *I love you* into casual conversation. Would it stop feeling so important if *I love you* became a toss-away phrase?

Right now it seemed monumental because I'd never said that to anyone before. Not even in jest.

Where was the line between being stingy with saying the words so they didn't lose impact and overusing them?

Overthinking this much?

Sierra straddled my lap. "No brooding allowed or I will tickle you. Because I know all of your ticklish spots now, West."

I laughed. "You do?"

She ran her fingers down the front of my throat as if she wanted to feel my joy. "You laugh so much more than you used to. You smile more too."

"I have a lot more things to be happy about in my life now, Sierra."

"That makes me happy." She outlined my lips with the tip of her tongue. "But I still think I oughta prove I know where all your ticklish spots are."

23 Sierra

AFTER LUNCH ON Monday afternoon I bit the bullet and started a pros and cons list of taking the PCE job, because I would see Phyllis at the weekly meeting the following night, when Nikki knocked.

"You have a drop-in guest. No, it's not Sergeant West."

The man loved his military title. I did too. "He or she?"

"She. Her name is Mrs. Nash. That's all the info she'd give me."

"Send her back, please."

I'd cleaned my hands with antibacterial gel and downed four aspirin, suspecting I'd have a screaming headache by the end of the day.

A woman who looked to be in her seventies entered my office.

I said, "Come in and have a seat." She perched on the front edge of the chair, reminding me of how regally Mia's grandmother positioned herself in *The Princess Diaries*. "I feel like we've met."

"We have. At your mother's luncheon. I'm Mrs. Nash."

"Well, Mrs. Nash, what can I do for you?"

"You can listen, for starters." She kept her hands folded in her lap, but her eyes nearly shot flames from beneath her glasses. "I overheard your conversation at the end of the luncheon. And I have to say, it angered me. Very much. The more I thought about it, the more I realized that you are every bit as snobby and judgmental as you accused the luncheon attendees of being."

I bristled and my polite veneer started chipping off. "What exactly did I say that was so offensive?"

Her mouth tightened. "You all but said that a country club was the last place you'd ever look for the type of women you needed as business mentors. Then you went on to point out that most of the women considered marrying well their greatest accomplishment. And these pearl clutchers had nothing useful to offer young women your age. That we were dinosaurs holding onto a one-dimensional and superficial way of life. But if you ever needed advice on the proper way to pour tea, or tableware arrangement, or a list of caterers, florists and dog walkers, you'd keep the group in mind."

Stupid whiskey. I didn't recall saying...all of that. Yet I couldn't defend myself because it did sound like something I'd say.

"Given that you're so proud of the time you spend volunteering at Phoenix Collegiate Entrepreneurs, I expected better."

How had she heard of PCE? "What is it you want from me, Mrs. Nash? An apology?"

She sniffed. "It wouldn't be sincere. The point of me coming here is to educate you."

I hadn't been expecting that. "You're going to educate me."

"Yes. You call yourself a feminist but do you truly know what that means? And I'm not looking for a definition in the historical context. You're proud to be a feminist, Ms. McKay. It'll surprise you to hear that I'm a proud feminist too."

She'd piqued my interest. "I'm listening."

"Your generation is so determined to slap labels on everything. To declare 'this' is definitively wrong and 'that' is absolutely right. You all claim to be so open-minded, but the mind is only open to those women who are exactly like you. Anyone who isn't on the same path is...antiqued."

"Are you talking in generalities? Or specifically about the work I've done at PCE?"

"Both. But as far as PCE specifically? Would you ask me to volunteer as a mentor?"

I didn't quite mask my reaction fast enough.

She shook her finger at me. "I couldn't possibly offer any useable skills because I'm helpless myself, right? As 'just' the wife of the CEO of a multi-million-dollar brokerage I have no skills to offer. I'm only in his shadow. I lunch at the club. I futz around in my garden. I walk my poodles. I have an old-fashioned poured and waiting for my husband when he arrives at the house cleaned by my staff. Is that an accurate assessment of what you imagine my life to be?"

"So tell me I'm wrong."

"You're wrong. Not entirely, I'll admit. I do futz around in my garden and walk my dog. I also organized a food drive for the no kill animal shelter. I secured funding—over a luncheon—for a transitional home for women leaving prison. I sponsored a botany class for underprivileged children." She paused. "That was what I accomplished last week."

Holy crap.

"But what we—women like me who volunteer—do isn't seen on the same level as what you do because I don't earn a paycheck. We're not *workers*. We don't belong to the workforce."

I suspected any argument I offered would be countered with a better one.

Oh Sierra, you rattled the wrong cage this time.

"Giving back isn't just accomplished by writing a check. Out of our husband's checking account, of course, because we're not savvy enough to handle our own finances." She cocked her head. "I'm the interim treasurer for a charitable organization that provides scholarships to women in need. I am proud of the fact that I can write checks for tens of thousands of dollars each month—money we earned. While working our tails off. Yet...my tax return shows zero income. So is that my worth?"

My mouth had gone dry. Probably from my face flaming hot out of embarrassment.

"This has been an argument among women for several generations—what constitutes real work and value. It's not us against you, or you against us. All women should get to choose whatever path in life makes them happy and fulfilled. If that's donning a power suit or a police uniform and leaving their home, then they should be compensated on the same level as men doing that same job in the workplace. Women in the workplace don't have the right to look down on women who choose to stay home with their children or who choose to volunteer their time rather than charge for it."

I cleared my throat. "Would you care for coffee? Or water? I'll need something to wash down all the crow I'm about to eat."

She laughed and I was completely charmed. "Got my point across, did I?"

"And then some. Look…I'm sorry for the snap judgments and assumptions I made and erroneously pontificated about on Saturday. Your indignation is justified. And while I'm embarrassed, I'm also grateful that you had the guts to call me to task. Please. Accept my sincerest apologies for offending you."

She blinked at me. "You are not reacting at all as I expected."

"I'm nothing like my mother," I said sharply.

"You don't have to tell me that, dear."

"Sorry. That—she—is a touchy subject with me."

"I imagine. I'll phrase this as…delicately as I can. But are Ellen's tendencies part of the reason you were so adamantly against anyone who might have surface similarities?"

I laughed. "God no. My opinion was based on ignorance and assumptions. No one can shoulder the blame for that except me."

"Ms. McKay. I am delighted to hear that. No excuses, no qualifications. Just the admission that you messed up. I appreciate the apology."

Would she leave now? I hoped not, because I wanted to pick that shrewd brain.

"I knew your grandmother Daniels." Mrs. Nash studied me.

"You did?"

"Yes, actually I served on several boards with Grace for many years."

"I knew she volunteered a lot." I paused. "And I'll phrase *this* as delicately as I can…but I gathered that her volunteerism stemmed from her unhappy marriage."

"You're not wrong. But neither did Grace fit the mold of the bored socialite."

"Is your friendship with my grandmother why you decided to come here today?"

"Partially. I wouldn't have pulled the 'your grandmother would be so ashamed' card. I might've used her name to remind you that the things you were prejudiced against were in your own family history." She smiled. "I'm so very glad it didn't come to that."

"Me too. Do you have time to get into this a little deeper with me?"

I held up my hand. "Not to argue. But I'd love to hear more about the executive side of your volunteerism."

"I'd like that."

I buzzed Nikki and asked her to bring in coffee. Then I directed Mrs. Nash to the seating area—a less formal environment to continue our discussion.

We spent the next hour talking. Or rather, she talked; I listened and took pages of notes. She seemed very interested in PCE's philosophy of providing capital to women starting home-based businesses. She seemed shocked when I inadvertently let it slip that that concept had come from me.

As she rose to leave, I tossed out, "If you're free tomorrow night, I'd love to take you to the PCE mixer."

"I'll make time. But I do need to know if it'd be clichéd if I wore pearls?"

I laughed. That was proof there's a little smartass in all of us.

BUT AFTER MRS. Nash left, I felt completely unmoored.

So much of what I thought I'd known had been flipped on its fucking head.

I looked out the window in my office to the world beyond the glass, almost as if I was seeing it for the first time.

The recriminations came immediately. What the hell did I know about anything? God. I was a baby in the world of business. Why had I believed I was qualified to run an organization like PCE? Moreover, why had Phyllis asked me?

Because she knows you'll work yourself into the ground to make it successful. For other applicants it'd just be a job. For you...it's so much more.

Would I be better served to focus on my role at DPM? Stop listening to excuses about why things never changed and become proactive?

Even if that meant losing long-time employees?

Yes. If I fucked it up, at least I tried to fix it—which was more than anyone else around here had attempted.

I heard the office door open and close, then the tiniest whisper of footsteps across the carpet. Only one person in my life existed in stealth mode.

Strong arms circled me completely. He pulled me against his chest as if he wanted to pull me inside him.

Yes, please.

Boone's mouth journeyed down the side of my throat until he found *his* spot on my neck. Every time his warm lips landed there, I felt like he marked me, reminded me that I was wholly his.

He murmured, "I missed you."

At one time I would've pointed out it'd been less than eight hours since we'd seen each other; he couldn't possibly have had time to miss me. But this was what I gave to him. Someone who missed him too. "Back atcha, babe. What are you doing here?"

"I wanted to surprise you with a nooner. I planned to yank your skirt up and fuck you over your desk." He sank his teeth into the side of my throat and I squirmed. "But I got a late start so I'm filing that idea for another day."

"I've never had sex in this office."

He groaned. "Don't *tell* me that."

"I assumed you knew."

"I assumed that every fucking man in this office building had the fantasy of doing you in your ivory tower. I just didn't realize none of them had the balls to give it a try. Not that I'm unhappy I'll be the first and only dude you'll bend over for in here."

I laughed. "Such a way with words, West." I turned around so we were chest to chest and wreathed my arms around his neck. My gaze roamed over his face.

"What?"

"Sometimes when I look at this gorgeous face I've only seen in my dreams the past few years, I can't believe you're really here."

His sexy growl sent a curl of heat through me.

He framed my face in his hands, giving me tender kisses. "Can you play hooky the rest of the day?"

"What would we do? Spend it in bed?"

"Yes. After I fucked you in the living room. Maybe the kitchen. Definitely the pool. And the shower. *Then* we'd hit the bed." His slumberous gaze rolled over me. "I kinda like having sex with you, McKay."

I forced my eyes wide. "Really? Because I was starting to worry you didn't. I mean you only had your wicked way with me twice yesterday and once this morning."

His eyes clouded.

"Boone. I was joking."

"Promise me it'll always be like this between us."

"Hot and sexy and all the damn time?"

"No." He paused and whispered, "Real."

My heart and my lungs and my ovaries pretty much exploded right then.

That's when I noticed he wasn't in civilian clothes. I eyed his scrubs, wondering if he had them custom-made to allow for those bulging biceps. "Where's your stethoscope?"

"I leave it in my locker."

Beneath his name on his nametag was a bunch of letters. I ran my fingertip across his chest below the white rectangle. "What do these mean?"

"They're the medical areas I'm certified in."

"That's a lot."

"They're army courses. The designation doesn't mean anything to anyone but me."

"If they weren't important they wouldn't be listed, would they?"

"Probably not."

I glanced up at him. All traces of teasing Boone were gone. "Something else going on? Did you hear from Oakley? Or your dad?" I knew he worried his dad would flake on him.

"I talked to Oakley earlier. She says the electricity is back on, Rock is home and Mom has been...decent."

"That's all good to hear, but something has put a wrinkle in your brow."

Boone retreated and rubbed his hand across the top of his head.

"Me'n Raj were called into the hospital early today and were told all of our shifts this week had been cancelled. No explanation. Our preceptor doesn't know what's going on either. And our liaison on base is out of the office for two weeks."

"Has this happened before?"

"No." Boone started to pace. "But it's not like I can poke around and ask questions of anyone else in that department. We're in a tight spot. Me'n Raj working with a civilian medical program while we're still on active duty...it's so far out of the norm that there is no precedent."

"I'm confused."

He muttered, "Welcome to the club. There's some funky stuff going on with our transfer papers or whatever they're calling it today. Christ. Red tape is no joke."

My stomach plunged. "Something funky like...they might demand you return to Fort Hood?"

I appreciated that he looked me in the eye when he said, "I'm not sure."

I wanted to yell, *I just got you back! You can't leave again.* But he could be yanked away from me at any moment.

Clearly that was a real possibility if he was worried enough to mention it to me.

I wandered over to the window. I'd intended to talk to him about the PCE offer tonight. After my discussion with Mrs. Nash, I realized that perceptions were always skewed. Everyone had a different way of looking at things, so maybe I needed Boone's take on this opportunity. But he had more than enough on his mind with the military stuff that was his career. So it appeared I'd continue to wrestle with the biggest decision of my adult life on my own.

Boone moved in behind me. "You okay?"

"I've been better, to be honest."

"What can I do?"

"This. Keep me wrapped up in you."

Several long moments passed. We stayed like that, me resting against him as we both gazed out the window.

Finally I said, "My mom called today."

"Did she apologize?"

"Sort of. My dad and I call it an 'Ellen apology'—along the lines of 'I'm sorry you made me yell at you.' She asked if I was still mad or if I planned to attend the wedding. And if I had a 'plus one' she needed to know your name so the wedding coordinator could add you to the seating chart."

"Jesus. What'd you say?"

"I hadn't decided if I was coming. I'd have my assistant call her wedding coordinator when I solidified my plan. The bratty kid in me wanted to say, *Neener neener! Suck on that!*"

He chuckled.

I turned my head and kissed his jaw before I stepped aside. "You have an entire week off?"

"Looks like. I won't know what to do with myself. Since Raj is in the same boat we'll figure something out."

"Just make sure you don't—"

Before I finished, the door banged open.

Greg stormed in, Nikki hot on his heels, silently apologizing with her eyes.

"You want to explain this memo from personnel? Which is total bullshit. But I expected no less from you." Greg's sneer became a leer when he saw Boone. "I see your secretary covers for you when you want to play grab-ass—"

"Watch it," Boone said in that don't-fuck-with-me tone.

Of course Greg cowered. He also shut his mouth, which was the real bonus.

"Nikki is my assistant, not my secretary. In the future, if my door is closed? Do not barge in. That's a violation of privacy, which is spelled out in the employee handbook. Since we have a meeting in ten minutes to discuss that memo, I'll ask Frannie from personnel to bring a handbook for you so you can brush up on protocol."

Greg acted like he wanted to argue, but for once, he did the smart thing and left.

"That's the little fucking weasel giving you grief?"

"Yes."

"Want me to beat him up for you?"

I laughed. "I'd love that. But I have to fight my own battles."

"My money is on you. And you are smoking hot when you go all 'I'm in charge, get the fuck out' badass businesswoman." He kissed me. "See you at home, McKay."

24 Sierra

WEDNESDAY NIGHT I arrived home from work, hoping for the peace and quiet that used to exist in my house.

But rap music booming from the stereo system greeted me as I passed through the laundry room into the kitchen. I paused in the doorway.

Raj sat on the counter, his upper body bouncing to the beat. Boone stood at the stove with his back to me as if he was cooking.

I snickered at that crazy thought.

Beer bottles were scattered here and there. As were bags of groceries. Dishes remained piled in the sink—dishes that had been there since Monday. The door to the dishwasher was open, the full rack of clean dishes pulled out. I knew they were clean because I'd done a load Sunday night and apparently I was the only one who knew how to run such a complicated machine.

Snarky much, McKay?

Now Boone's voice was chastising me inside my own head.

For the past four days I'd tried to roll with it, chill out, be cool, adopt the "it's all good" mindset, but it was becoming increasingly harder to do. Logically I understood by inviting Boone to live with me that I'd essentially told him my house was his house. We'd both expected adjustments to sharing the same space. We'd even joked about it. But I guess my man thought I'd been joking when I told him to pick up after himself and return whatever space he'd used to the way he'd found it. Meaning…clean and clutter free.

I'm a neat freak. I wasn't always this way, especially as a teen. But by age seventeen, I'd tired of living in constant chaos and had a Mr.

Clean epiphany. Lu accepted my need for neatness as a house rule—and didn't pass it off as one of my personality quirks. She kept the common areas in the house up to my standards. I didn't give a damn if her bedroom, bathroom and the extra room she used as a study were a mess. Those were her personal spaces. Plus she could just shut the doors; out of sight meant I didn't mind.

But Boone...totally a dude. Used to living with another dude. Evidently Raj was as messy as Boone. No wonder they were such compatible roommates. I shuddered thinking about all the empty pizza boxes, carryout containers, wadded up paper products, bottles and cans that cluttered available horizontal space in their apartment. I had no problem imagining it because my house had started to look like a bachelor soldier's flophouse.

And this was one area. I hadn't even been in the great room since I'd cleaned up Sunday night. Boone had invited the McKay-kateers, Mase and Raj to watch the football game. It seemed Sunday nights were becoming a family night. I was cool with that; Boone needed a connection in Phoenix besides with me and Raj. Him having family and friends over? Not the issue. The issue was his "let's deal with this mess later" attitude. Because as soon as we were alone, he had us both naked, sweaty and fucking—like my pussy had an expiration date.

Not that I was complaining. The newness of being red-hot lovers hadn't worn off. In fact, he'd ramped it up even more the past four days. As much as I loved his single-minded focus, as if I were the sun and he needed to bask in me, as if I were an adrenaline rush he craved, as if giving me multiple orgasms was his sole purpose in life...I had the teeniest suspicion the extra body-pounding encounters were because he didn't have anything better to do.

You'd rather Boone had done the dishes this morning instead of doing you?

Well, no, but that wasn't the point.

I shifted backward and my heel caught on a mountain of laundry. An avalanche of Boone's clothes nearly covered the laundry room floor.

That was the point.

What the hell had he been doing all day that he couldn't toss in a few loads of clothes during the nine hours since I'd seen him last? It wasn't like he was trying to juggle his job, his schoolwork, his training and his soldier stuff. His worries about the schedule change earlier in the week ended up being unfounded. It'd just been normal civilian personnel issues. So he had a week off. Basically a vacation! He should've been doing what needs done.

Reminder: Boone is not your employee. He's a grown man who does not need you micromanaging his daily schedule or his life.

Right then, Boone turned around. The way those beautiful brown eyes lit up and the enormous grin that bloomed across his face when he saw me? Total fucking swoon moment.

He strode toward me. Before he uttered a word, he snaked his arm around my lower back, yanking my body against his. A tiny growl escaped and then his mouth landed on mine. His kiss was soft and searching. Sweet. Not the macho mouth fucking I expected.

I sighed and swayed into him fully.

Boone, being Boone, immediately made adjustments to better accommodate me.

Maybe you should try that.

I barked at the snark generator in my head to shut it and lost myself in my man's welcome home kiss.

Against my lips, Boone murmured, "I fucking love you, McKay."

I smiled. "I fucking love you too, West."

"Come on." He took my hand. "I gotta show you this."

I said, "Hi, Raj," as Boone towed me past the breakfast bar.

We stopped in front of the island.

Don't look at the mess on the counters.

"I made dinner!" Boone announced with pride.

It appeared that he'd used every pan I owned. "What did you make?"

"Hot turkey sandwiches with mashed potatoes, gravy and stuffing. It's ready to dish up anytime you are."

"Boone. That is awesome." I pressed my lips to his in a lingering smooch. "Thank you."

"I want to learn how to cook so you don't end up doing it all. That's not fair to you."

I felt a little weepy…and sort of like an asshole for my previous bitchy thoughts.

Then Boone smacked my ass. "Go shed the skin of the corporate exec. We'll eat when you're done."

"Sounds good." I looked at Raj. "Are you staying for dinner?"

"Yes ma'am. Lucinda Grace is studying at the library tonight. I'm not used to bein' alone. So here I am, hanging with B."

"Me'n Raj finally hooked up the PS4. We're testing it out tonight."

"Cool," I said offhandedly. "I'll change, clear my head and be back in ten."

I kicked off my heels and sighed when my toes sank into the plush carpeting. The door to my bedroom—our bedroom—was shut. I pushed it open and flipped on the light.

So much for my few moments of serenity. I'd made the bed before I left. I didn't care it looked rumpled, but I did care about the gym bag and the huge duffel. I eyed the stuff spilling over the middle to my side of the bed. My first thought? His shit wasn't supposed to be in here for this very reason.

Then the hamper caught my notice. What the fuck? Why had he dumped all of my clothes all over? And mixed them up? I had a dual-sided hamper for a reason—so I could separate what went to the drycleaners from the regular wash.

"Sierra—" Boone said, barreling into the room. He latched onto my upper arms to keep from knocking me over. "Shit. I forgot to put that stuff away. I got busy…"

Busy doing what? You weren't busy doing the damn dishes.

He gently turned me around and curled his hands around my face. "Grab your lounge clothes and hole up in the bathroom. I promise when you come out this'll all be gone, okay?"

His eyes held remorse. Not a look I'd seen very often so I knew he was sincere. "Okay."

He kissed my mouth, the tip of my nose, between my eyebrows and the top of my forehead.

"Before I go, I need to point out that your explosion of stuff is why I gave you another place to keep it."

"I know. I'll be contained over there from now on. I promise."

I kissed him hard and swatted his ass as I headed to the bathroom.

Ten minutes later I'd scrubbed off the day's stress, donned my lounge clothes, put my hair up and was ready to eat.

Boone gave me a head-to-toe inspection and when our eyes met, I knew he'd take great pleasure in tearing the workout tank top and yoga pants off my body. "Let's eat."

The food was pretty good for a first attempt. There was a lot of it, which seemed to be Boone and Raj's main criteria. And there wouldn't be leftovers, much to Boone's dismay.

After the meal, Raj helped me do the dishes. Someone had at least emptied the dishwasher while I'd been decompressing, so that was a plus. By the time I'd cleaned the kitchen to my specs, an hour had passed.

When I heard the video game start—the sheer volume sent me outside to the patio.

I'd brought work home I could've done in the office, but I wanted to backtrack records and I was always getting interrupted and I'd lose my spot or my train of thought. I had ten years' worth of data to crosscheck. Data I should've gone through the proper channels to get, but I'd asked my dad for six months ago. Since this was a pet project of sorts, I worked on it when I had time.

When my eyes started to burn and my mouth was dry, I realized in my effort to escape, I hadn't brought anything to drink. The second I opened the sliding glass door, the noise assaulted me, louder than ever.

Enough.

They weren't chasing me out of my own house with this. I marched into the living room and focused on the noise, not the huge fucking mess.

"Guys," I yelled. "Turn it down."

"Hang on a sec," Boone said, hand busy on the game controller, eyes rapt on the screen.

"Take that, motherfucker!" Raj taunted.

"You cocksucker. That was a total dick move."

"All's fair in *Doom*, baby."

And they were ignoring me. Awesome.

"Hit pause. Right. Fucking. Now." I might've shrieked that.

The noise ceased.

"What?" Boone asked, a little testily.

Sorry I had to yell at you to get your attention away from a video game, asshole.

"Turn it down. You guys aren't the only ones in the house."

They exchanged a "what's her problem, it ain't that loud" look.

"It's echoing down the hallway."

"Fine." Boone turned the game back on and pointed the remote control at the AV equipment. The volume dropped.

"Wait! Fuck, I wasn't ready," Raj said.

Boone hit pause again. "Quiet enough for you now?"

"Peachy, dude."

My sarcasm was lost on him—or lost in the loud fucking noises still pouring from the speakers.

I poured myself two fingers of Crown and retired to my room. So I couldn't even watch TV to wind down. My eyes still burned from looking at computer screens all day so I had zero interest in reading. I pulled out my phone and checked Facebook. Boring. Where did these people get the time to post so much stuff?

Then I opened Snapchat. I clicked a shot of me holding the lowball glass of Crown over my head and pinged Lu.

She responded immediately with an image of her face pressed into a textbook.

My phone buzzed with a text message.

Lu: *Wazzup?*

Me: *I might need hearing aids. Or a machete.*

Lu: *Why?*

Me: *R&B are playing a LOUD video game.*

Lu: *I wondered how you'd like that. You're right. It is loud.*

Me: *Is that why you aren't studying here?*

Lu: ☺

Me: *You suck. I miss you* ☹

Lu: *Miss you too.*

Me: *Why are you at the library?*

Lu: *In the BFF vault?*

Me: *Of course.*

Lu: *Needed break from Raj tonite.*

Me: *Why? The dick don't fit anymore?*

Lu: *LOL. No! Just too much togetherness. He's in my face all the freakin' time or n my pants. I have school & a job.*

Me: *I hear ya. I'm feeling very stabby w/B*

Lu: *Why?*

Me: *He's messy*

Lu: *How messy?*

Me: *Like an F5 tornado messy.*

Lu: *HAHAHAHAHA*

Me: *Not funny! Third nite I've come home to dishes in the sink, stuff from Sunday is still in the great room. His dirty clothes all over laundry room & bedroom. He even dumped out my hamper. As far as the kitchen…he cooked dinner. Yeah yeah yeah he's trying. But then he left the fucking mess for me to clean up. Took an HOUR. That 'if you cook you don't have to clean up' rule doesn't apply since I've cleaned up EVERY FUCKING TIME.*

Lu: *Ooh all caps = mad Sierra!*

Me: *Fuck yeah. Now loud video game and HE acted annoyed when I asked them to turn it down. Fuckface asswipe. I can still hear it.*

Lu: *Come to the library. It's quiet here.*

Me: *Thanx. But I'll drink my Crown and go to bed.*

Lu: *Wish I could sleep. Big tests tomorrow and Fri. Be a late one for me.*

Me: *Sorry, hon. Miss you* ☹

Lu: *Let's hang this weekend. Just us. No messy boys* ☺

Me: *Deal. XOXOXO*

I didn't feel like texting anyone else. Or scrolling through social media. I didn't even feel like popping in my earbuds to drown out the constant sounds of gunfire and explosions.

Maybe you just want to be mad.

No. I had legit complaints about the state of my house.

Then talk to him about it instead of stomping around griping about it under your breath.

That last helpful advice sounded like my dad's wife Rielle. I adored that woman. Not just because she loved my dad like he needed after the shit-show he'd suffered through with my mom. Rielle taught me real life skills. She never treated me like her husband's bratty kid—although I'd certainly acted the part a few times during the years I'd lived with them.

After downing the whiskey, I cut the lights and crawled between the sheets. I'd tuned out the game enough to drift off. Then I heard the sound of breaking glass and that shot me straight out of bed.

Shit. Was someone trying to get into the house?

I cracked open the door and listened. I heard that shattering glass sound again. It echoed from the great room.

Stupid video game.

I grabbed my favorite blanket and my cell phone. Boone could play his obnoxious video games at a million decibels. I'd just sleep on the patio.

"SIERRA."

The voice startled me out of a deep sleep.

"I'm picking you up. Hang on."

I pushed his arms away. "Don't." I blinked and pulled the blanket around me. "Why'd you wake me up?"

Boone loomed over me. "Because I'm not letting you sleep in a fucking lawn chair the rest of the night. Jesus. It's bad enough that you've been out here this long."

I yawned. "What time is it?"

"Three something. Raj and I lost track of time. I went to bed and you weren't there. I searched the whole house and couldn't find you."

"Did you look under the gigantic pile of your dirty clothes in the laundry room?"

"What?"

"Never mind. I would've been fine out here. You should've let me sleep, since it took me so long to *get* to sleep."

"Fuck that. I can tell you're cold. Let's go inside and warm you up."

It wasn't until we were in bed and he'd wrapped me in his warm body that I understood what he meant by *warm you up*. He'd drawn out his caresses and kept kissing my shoulder, each kiss a little closer to my neck.

"Let me make your body burn," he rasped in my ear.

I pushed away from him. "Just because you're wide awake at three a.m. doesn't mean I wanna be your post-video-game booty call."

He stiffened. "Booty call? What the hell?"

"Yes, booty call. Wanting sex when you've got nothing better to do. It's bad enough I have to be up in four hours to go to work. You don't get to use me—sex—as a sedative to help *you* sleep. Especially when you didn't give a damn that your video game was loud enough to chase me out of the fucking house."

"Whoa. You're pissed off about this."

"I'm tired. I don't want to talk. I don't want to fuck. I just want to sleep. So goodnight." I rolled away from him to my side of the bed, giving him my back.

Or the cold shoulder.

I DIDN'T WAKE him up the next morning before I went to work.

I could claim I did it out of thoughtfulness, letting him sleep in.

But the truth was, I didn't feel like rehashing our middle-of-the-night argument and he'd insist on it. He'd insist on makeup sex and well, I didn't feel like that either.

Hormonal much?

Boone wasn't around when I got home from work. As I searched for a note in the kitchen, I saw the space hadn't gotten trashed since I'd scrubbed it last night. His laundry remained in a pile in front of the washer and dryer but the family room had been tidied. I checked outside. Boone had cleaned off the patio...or maybe it'd been the pool maintenance guy.

So I followed my usual after-work routine. I changed into exercise clothes and hit the elliptical machine for forty-five minutes.

No sign of Boone after I finished.

I showered.

No sign of him after that either.

It wasn't like him to be out of communication.

Maybe he was called in to cover a shift at the hospital.

Or maybe he's pissed off.

I spread my notes across the coffee table and my research materials on the couch for an article I was working on for a trade magazine. They'd contacted me to write it, which was cool, if a little unusual, especially when the submission time frame was so short. I had to email it by Monday morning. I'd just compiled an ordered list of my sources when Boone barreled in.

And I do mean barreled.

He saw me and said, "There's the woman who rocks my fucking world." Then he flashed that dirty-sweet smile and he was on me. Literally. His knees bracketing my thighs, his hands in my hair, his mouth plastered to mine in a morning mouth fuck. Pressing me into the couch cushion with such force I panicked that he'd break the frame—or my back.

But the man didn't release any part of me until he was damn good and ready. After he placed a soft kiss over my heart, he murmured, "I missed you today." Then he muttered that he needed a shower. He hopped off the couch and strode away, leaving everything in disarray; my notes, my papers…me.

Those I-wanna-eat-you-alive kisses made me think Boone wasn't pissed at me.

Good. Now I could give the article my full concentration.

I closed my eyes. Where had I gotten to before the interruption? The main theme was the importance of…what?

Dammit. Think.

The importance of organization.

I snorted. That was simplistic. It needed more punch right off the bat.

Wait. Where'd I put that magazine with the kickass bullet points?

I shuffled through the papers that'd tumbled together when Boone had jumped on the couch. I found the information and jotted down notes, moving between hard copies and my laptop.

When Boone returned with a beer, he picked up the papers I'd stacked in order and set them on the coffee table so he could sit next to me. Right next to me. Thigh to thigh. With his arm draped along the back edge of the couch, allowing him to drag those clever fingers across the ball of my shoulder and down the outside of my arm.

He turned the TV on but couldn't stand the commercials so he constantly flipped through channels. It drove me crazy, which was why I rarely watched TV with him.

"Did you eat dinner?" he asked.

I just realized I hadn't. "I had other things on my mind and I forgot."

"How can you forget to eat?"

"It happens to me all the time."

"Raj and I spent the last three hours playing basketball with some of the guys from the hospital. I haven't played a pick-up game that intense for a long time. So I'm starved."

"I would've thought you'd stop for food on your way home."

"I was hoping there'd be food here."

I did cook frequently, but not every night. "I'm not sure what's in the fridge."

"Pretty much bare," he said, reaching for his beer. That he'd set on the coffee table. Above my paperwork.

"You went to the store yesterday."

"Just for the hot turkey sandwich stuff." He kissed my temple with his beer-cooled lips. "Are you hungry now?"

Meaning...do you feel like cooking us something?

Not so fast. Maybe he asked so he can go get you both food.

"No. I'm good. I want to get this done."

"What are you working on?"

"An article for a trade magazine."

"What's it about?"

I looked at him. "What's the article about or what's the magazine about?"

He shrugged.

"Accepting your limitations and learning the true value of organization."

"Huh. Cool." *Flip, flip, flip.* "What is the true value?"

I almost snapped, *It's a hardware store on Baymont Street, why don't you go check it out now?* Snapping at him wouldn't solve the problem. "That's what I'm trying to figure out. And I can't do that with the constant channel flipping. It's distracting."

So much for not sniping at him.

Immediately he pulled away from me. "Maybe you should work in your office and not in the only room in the house with a TV."

"Or maybe you should go find something to eat since you're starved and I can finish what I started, where I set up to work first."

"Fine." Boone pushed to his feet and disappeared again.

I heard cupboard doors banging. Water running. Pans clanking.

Did he expect me to follow him and take over preparing his meal? *Dream on, buddy.*

He annoyed me beyond words today.

Now I was mad and distracted so I needed to find a different location to work.

I closed the lid on my laptop. I picked up my papers, stacking them crossways to keep them separated. Hugging it all to my chest, I hoofed it upstairs to the family room at the opposite end of the house from the great room.

I'd done nothing with this big space except create a corner to stash my elliptical machine and other workout gear. I gave the ugly-ass floral couch the stink eye. It was a castoff from my mom; she insisted I could "repurpose" it but there was no freakin' hope for it. It sucked it was the only furniture in here.

I dragged the weight bench over to use as a table.

A cloud of dust puffed up when I plopped down on the couch.

I sneezed four times.

Awesome.

Somehow I managed to focus—the absolute silence helped—and I finished the rough draft for the article in three hours.

I gathered everything for the third time and returned to the kitchen to load up my laptop bag.

Boone had left the pan, his bowl and spoon, a sandwich plate and a wadded-up plastic sleeve from a box of crackers…right where he'd finished with them.

Just pick it up and put it away. It's not that big of a deal.

But it was. If I picked up after him from the start, he'd expect I'd always do it. It was setting precedence. I did the same thing with my clients; made a point to be upfront from the start about their responsibilities and mine.

Boone is not your client.

I wasn't his mommy either.

That thought was a sharp stab in the heart. Boone's mother hadn't bothered to feed him, what were the odds she cleaned up after him?

Slim to none.

Let it go, Sierra. Just for tonight. Bring up your expectations for house care, chores or whatever tomorrow.

I locked the doors and shut off the lights in the kitchen. Then I went to find my man.

Boone had fallen asleep sitting up on the couch. His head lolled to the side, his lips were parted and his arms were crossed over his chest. I had to smile that he'd kept the TV volume low.

I straddled his lap. I ran my fingers over his ropy forearms and up his biceps, trying to wake him gently. Then I framed his face in my hands, loving the feel of the dark scruff on his cheeks beneath my fingers.

He stirred. His confusion melted into happy eyes and a drowsy smile. "Hey."

"Hey, yourself."

"Did you get your article done?"

"Yes."

He placed an openmouthed kiss on the hollow of my throat. "I'm so damn proud of you." When he tipped his head back to look into my face, his eyes clouded. "What's wrong?"

Don't make excuses, make time to discuss this. It doesn't have to be now. "Remember those 'unspoken rules' I talked about at Kyler's that night? And you said you preferred no rules? Well, soldier, that is not working out so well for us. So starting tomorrow we'll have defined rules of the house. That way our duties and responsibilities are clearly spelled out. That way order is maintained and violations will be dealt with swiftly and immediately. Understood?"

Boone stared at me oddly.

"What?"

"You would've done great in the military. I feel like saluting and then polishing your boots."

I laughed softly.

He started to say something and I shook my head. "It can wait until morning. Let's go to bed."

25 Boone ♡

"T HE PARENT TRAP" was the codename my smartass girlfriend called the day I was meeting my dad in Flagstaff and she was attending her mother's wedding at the country club.

I suggested "Meet the Parents" but apparently that was too obvious.

I took comfort when I pulled into the motel parking lot that I wasn't alone in dealing with a parental shit show today. Sierra was stuck watching her mother pledge her eternal love and devotion to Bill's bills. Nope. No cynicism there.

I wondered why I agreed to this meeting with my father.

Maybe I should've asked over the phone if he'd recently joined a twelve-step program and had committed to acknowledging his past mistakes.

I didn't need that clarification. I already knew his mistakes; I'd lived with them.

After snagging my duffel from the front seat, I headed to the lobby to check in.

The room had a king-sized bed and that's all I cared about. I sent Sierra a quick text asking if being in room 113 was a bad sign.

What was a worse sign? Dad hadn't been in contact for a week. I'd be pissed if he had to cancel and hadn't bothered to let me know.

With nothing else to do besides sleep, I pulled out the two textbooks I'd brought for next semester and copied the proposed class list. Repetition helped my retention.

An hour passed. I'd started to get hungry. And antsy. I changed clothes and opened the door only to find my dad standing on the other side, poised to knock.

"Oh. Hey Dad. One of us has great timing," I said.

"Unlikely it's me." He ran his hand down his beard. "How's it going?"

"Okay."

I hadn't seen Dax West since I'd graduated from boot camp. Looking at him now...there wasn't a lick of a family resemblance between us. His hair, what was left of it, was an orangey gold shot through with gray. Seven years ago he'd had an inch or two on me. Now, with his shoulders slumped, I towered over him.

"I'm starved. You want to eat at the restaurant here?" I asked.

"That'll work."

We walked side by side down the hallway. "You're checked in?"

"Yep."

Christ. If this was how our talk would go tonight, I needed alcohol to get through it. Which made me blurt out, "Did you insist on this meeting because you're in a twelve-step program?"

"Nope."

Awesome. One-word answer again.

When we got to the restaurant and he reached for the door handle, his hand shook.

That sour feeling in my belly expanded.

The place was empty but he asked for a table in the back anyway. He took the seat in the corner, where he had a full view of the room and no one could look over his shoulder.

I studied the menu without seeing it.

"I ordered beer."

I glanced up at him.

He aimed his gaze out the dark window. "How pathetic is it that I don't know if my twenty-six-year-old son likes beer."

"I like beer just fine."

He said nothing.

The waitress poured the pale liquid—poorly—into glasses, leaving three inches of foam on top. Next round I'd forego the glass.

Yeah. I figured this would be a multiple-beer conversation.

We both ordered hot beef sandwiches.

That was one meal that reminded me of him. The few times he'd taken me out to eat, it'd always been to a truck stop café because that's what he knew and where he usually ate.

Neither of us was good at small talk. But we tried.

"While we're waiting on food, you wanna fill me in with what's going on in your life?"

I told him about being selected for the army's experimental program with the VA that resulted in me being in Phoenix to attend school. I talked about Raj, but didn't mention hanging out with my McKay cousins or my relationship with Sierra. He'd mutter about McKays, just because that's what the West family did.

He talked about a few of the more unusual items he'd loaded and driven across the country.

The food arrived. We each ordered another beer before we tucked in. I kept shooting glances across the table at him, searching for some familiarity. The harder I tried to rattle those memory banks, the more I realized there wasn't anything there.

But I did notice he wasn't shoveling in food like I remembered. He pushed his potatoes around on his plate. Set down his fork. Swigged his beer.

He's stalling.

As much as I wanted him to get to the fucking point of this meeting, I wouldn't push him. Whatever he needed to say...he had to work up to it.

That kicked those alarm bells in until my ears rang from them. I purposely slowed my eating pace to match his.

But he only ended up eating half of it. I hadn't seen that before either.

The waitress cleared our plates.

Dad turned his focus to picking the soggy label off the previous bottle of beer. When he finally started to speak, his voice was so low I had to lean closer to hear him.

"I don't gotta tell you I've always been a loner. That's why long haul works well for me."

"So you asked me here to talk about your career as a truck driver?"

His eyes met mine. Sometimes I forgot I'd inherited the color and shape of his eyes, so it spooked me to see such wariness in them now.

"No. It's just…I don't know where to start with this."

"You talking in circles isn't the way to start. Just rip off the fucking bandage."

"You're right. Lemme get through"—he looked away and cleared his throat—"the worst of it before you start asking questions."

"Okay."

Long pause. Then he said, "When I was a kid, I was sexually abused. But being a kid…you don't really know that it's wrong if that's how it's always been. If it's just part of the day or night…" He cleared his throat again. "My first memory of it was when I was three years old. And it's not one of them 'false' memories, where you see a picture and convince yourself you were there when you weren't. I know how old I was because there are pictures of my birthday party—the only birthday party I ever had. A picture of me with the plastic truck someone gave me as a gift, I remember holding it tight that night as he…when…"

I felt hot and cold, then that surreal sense of disbelief that accompanies shock.

"Like I said, I got a little older and I figured what he did to me and expected in return was probably wrong, since it was only just the two of us and he said I couldn't ever tell anyone."

I managed to choke out one word. "Who?"

"My dad."

My food threatened to come back up. I swallowed it back down, taking a healthy drink of beer, praying that helped.

"It went on until I was twelve. Over the last couple of years as I've started to deal with this, I tried to pinpoint why that's when it ended. Had my mother found out? Had I stopped looking like a child? I do know that's when my folks became born-again Christians. Was it the cause? Was it the effect? But it just stopped."

I waited and watched him working through this in silence.

"This is where it's fucked up, son. So fucked up I don't wanna admit it, but you need to hear all of it." He fiddled with his beer bottle. "After the abuse ended, I should've been relieved. But not only did the…physical contact end, all contact ended. For my dad it was like I ceased to exist. He ignored me. He wouldn't even look at me. I had no idea what I'd done wrong. No idea how to deal with such complete rejection. So I followed him out to the garage where all the stuff happened and I tried…"

My father seemed to shrink before my very eyes.

I felt so goddamned helpless. I reached out and put my hand on his arm and wasn't surprised when he flinched away from me. "It's okay. Take your time."

He nodded. Keeping his eyes closed he drained his beer.

I signaled the waitress for two more.

Finally he leaned forward again. "I followed him out to the garage and tried to do what he'd always made me do before. He…hauled me up off my knees and backhanded me. He beat the hell out of me, calling me a sick little pervert, claiming I'd been possessed by evil and he wasn't letting me lead him astray from the righteous path ever again."

Rage immediately supplanted that sick feeling.

"He sexually abused me and then shunned me. We didn't have a normal conversation after that until I turned fifteen. Now I can guess it was because I didn't look like a boy and the temptation was gone."

"And so did you just…block all of this out?"

"Yeah, for a few years. Especially those years I lived at home. I left as soon as I graduated. In those days if you passed the test for the Commercial Driver's License then you could be trained on the road by a company that hired you and not have to go to vocational school. I started out a secondary driver for long haul. I intended to get a fresh start someplace else." He looked me in the eyes for the first time since he'd started talking. "Then I found out about you."

What to say to that? My birth had forced him to keep a residence in Wyoming. So he couldn't cut ties with his family.

"I'm a shitty dad, Boone, I know that. I've always known that. I took one look at you when you were a baby and I felt sorry for you. You had a fucked-up mom and dad. I suggested adoption because you deserved better than you were gonna get, but your mom… She had visions of us bein' a family. Which I promptly crushed when I accepted jobs for logging hauls in Canada and didn't return to Wyoming until you were seven months old.

"At first I sent money because I promised I'd support you. But I heard she'd started doing drugs again, so I stopped paying and let her take me to court. At least with wage garnishment there'd be a paper trail of the support I'd paid instead of it going up in smoke." He sipped his beer. "During that time she left you with her sister for a few months..."

I frowned. "I don't remember that."

"That's because you were only two or something. One promise I had her make from the start was she was never, ever, under any circumstances to leave you with my parents."

"Did she ask why?"

"Not that I remember, but I wouldn't have told her the real reason even if she had. As far as I know, she didn't take you over there."

"But you didn't keep Chet and Remy from getting to know me. So I'll just ask this straight out; do you think they were abused?"

He didn't answer immediately. "My gut feeling is no. They were born so close together and they've always been inseparable, so it would've been harder for him to get one of them alone. I was the rule follower. Especially when it came to positions of authority, so I didn't ever question any of the stuff he did to me. I just did it or let him do it."

"Do you have any idea whether your brothers knew what was going on?"

"Nope. They had their own room, I had mine. They wouldn't have thought anything of Dad taking me out to the garage, because he always did."

The sick feeling returned.

"I definitely think they'd be shocked if I told them now." He stared at a spot across the room. "But there's always that part of me that isn't sure if they'd believe me, so..."

"What about your mother? How much of this did she know?"

"No idea. Could be when she found out, she stopped it. Could be she knew from the start and ignored it. Could be she'd sacrificed me, knowing he had those...tendencies and then he wouldn't go out into the community to pick a random kid and end up in jail."

"Did she treat you differently after your dad stopped...?"

He shook his head. "When I looked back at some of this stuff and tried to, I don't know, break it down, it becomes obvious. She was always about pleasing her husband. Everything she did was for him. I overheard her talking one time, about how she hadn't wanted more kids after me, that's why there's a gap between me'n Chet. Makes me think she knew what he was doing to me. And after an accidental second pregnancy she got knocked up again a third time with Remy—to protect them both."

"She should've been protecting you."

"Well, she didn't. I was already soiled goods so why not let him continue doing what he would be compelled to do anyway. And this is gonna sound sick as fuck, but she...she has the look, the body and the build of a prepubescent boy."

My head was spinning with all of this.

"If your next question is whether I plan to talk to my father or confront him or whatever, the answer is no."

"Why not?"

"He's in a nursing home in poor health. I haven't seen him or Mom in years. And with all that born-again stuff..."

"That's ten kinds of fucked up, Dad."

"Yep. It's also why it'd be pointless to address now." He closed his eyes. "I've seen the scenario a hundred times. I ask Dad why he did it, if he's even sorry he did it, and he doesn't answer. Instead Mom jumps in and reminds me that was a long time ago, he's asked God for forgiveness. Dad's accepted his past as a sinner and found redemption. He's been on a righteous path for years, so my issue with the past is just that; *my* issue. And maybe I should get right with God so I can move on too."

The odd thing was I saw that scene exactly as he'd depicted it, so I understood. Because in some ways...it was the same type of situation between him and me. Not the abuse, but the opposite; the complete detachment.

"Besides, as soon as you graduated I left Wyoming for Nebraska and I haven't been back. Haven't seen my brothers since you graduated from boot camp. Being away from there...it's been good for me. I don't see how going back would do anything but set me back. My counselor—"

"Wait. You're seeing a counselor?"

He blushed. "Weird, huh? But yeah. I met this woman and I really liked her. It was embarrassing to admit I didn't know how to be with her, because I hadn't done any of the normal...ah, dating stuff since I started driving trucks. She told me to deal with my issues because I'd been living half a life." He looked at me again. "That's when all this came crashing down. I checked into an addiction clinic in Omaha. Official diagnosis was exhaustion. My addiction was to work."

"When did that happen?" I demanded.

"Three years ago. It's taken me a while to come to terms with all of this, son. And I...hope you understand why I couldn't make the trip to see you when you were in Wyoming."

"I get it."

"There is another part to this. I'm gonna hit the can first." He stood and lumbered away from the table.

I took my phone out to see if Sierra had tried to contact me. Two text messages sent an hour ago.

> **SM:** *At least I have a third row seat to witness the wedding of the year – eye roll. Mom is acting strangely calm, so I'm assuming she popped valium before she arrived in her limo.*

> **SM:** *What is up with all the pastel-colored golf shirts? And plaid shorts? Do these dudes' wives purposely dress them like that in some kind of ugliest outfit contest? Anyway, four geezers were checking out my ass and I wished you were here, going all growly, sexy cave-man on them, letting them know who that ass really belongs to. ☺ My everything belongs to you. I miss you and I hope things are going well. Call me NO MATTER WHAT TIME YOU GET DONE. I need to hear your voice, Boone. Love you.*

I shoved my phone back in my pocket and closed my eyes. I knew it defined selfish, but I wanted her here, waiting in the room for me. I'd need her. I don't think she grasped how much I needed her.

I wondered how long it'd take Dad to get back into the swing of conversation after this break.

He launched in immediately after he returned to the table. "I already told you I was a shitty father. Not that it's news to you. What probably is news though is that it was intentional."

"Why?"

He was back to label-picking. "I didn't trust myself to be around you, Boone. My dad was a sexual abuser. I had no way of knowing whether that...trait, tendency, whatever the fuck you wanna call it, had been passed on to me. Back then, I didn't know half the stuff I do now, but a lot of this bad shit is learned behavior. It's a pattern. It's passed down. That sucks. I don't have any idea whether my dad was abused or who did it to him. To be honest I don't give a fuck. 'I didn't know any better' is never a valid argument. But one thing I did know?"

He looked at me with the most haunted eyes I've ever seen.

"Whatever fucked-up cycle of abuse I'd been born into would stop with me. I'd never do to you what my dad did to me. Never. And to ensure that didn't happen, I stayed away as much as I could."

My last sip of beer threatened to come back up. With all of the implications of what I'd learned in the last hour about my family? That hadn't crossed my mind. I never would've seen my dad as the perverted fucker who liked little boys.

Did you ever in your wildest imaginings believe your grandfather was a pedophile in an incestuous situation with your father?

No.

"Maybe this is the beer talking or maybe it's just that we've come this goddamned far in being able to talk about it. I can honestly say I never had any pull that direction. Ever. But I'll also admit I never put myself in a situation where it'd become an issue."

"Including spending time raising your son."

"Including that."

I counted to ten before I responded. "So while you fought with your demons, trying to keep me safe from sexual abuse, my *mother* abused me and neglected me. Starved me. Tried her best to turn me into a feral animal. And that was somehow fucking better? Than you stepping up to the plate and saying, 'I've gotta draw boundaries but here's how we can do it'?"

"I know that now. I didn't know that then. Back when your mom wanted you to live with me fulltime because she was pregnant, I couldn't do it. That makes me a shitty parent on a whole different level since I chose to leave you in what I knew was a bad situation."

"Yeah, you did. While I'm sorry that your past scarred you, now mine does too. That could've been prevented."

His eyes took on a hard glint. "Or you could be in therapy for the rest of your life after all the sick shit I did to you because I hadn't dealt with any of what had been done to me."

Jesus, fuck, this was so messed up.

"I did eventually bring you to live with me."

"Why did you bother? I mean, you were never home. Chet and Remy ended up looking after me. You just went on, business as usual. Things didn't change a whole lot for me. Except I didn't have my brother and sister underfoot—so I spent even more time alone. I still never had enough to eat. You never gave me money for anything. I had to get a fucking job at age thirteen. A job I had to walk four miles to. What lesson was the hardship supposed to teach me?"

"It got the job done, didn't it? You're no worse for the wear. Look at all you've accomplished."

I tuned him out. Fuck, I was tired of hearing that response. I was no "worse for the wear" now. I'd gone without then. That's what burned my ass. I was a child. I didn't have clothes that fit; I didn't have enough food or school supplies or gym shoes. Now if I needed that stuff I could get in my car that I paid for myself and buy what I needed, with the money I earned. But being a thirteen-year-old boy, without transportation, without money, without supervision…no wonder I stole a dirt bike and drove into town. Straight to the grocery store in Moorcroft, where I sat in the aisle and filled my hungry belly until the deputy came and hauled me away.

Had my dad come and picked me up and paid for the food I'd consumed?

No. Chet and Remy had.

Besides admitting I didn't know how to read at age nine, that'd been the most humiliating thing that had ever happened to me. The next day, my uncles took me to the local farm discount store where I ended up with jeans, gym shoes, work boots, T-shirts, socks, underwear and winter gear. I'd hated that they'd had to buy it for me even when I'd been so grateful to have it. That's when my uncles had started dragging me along to their jobsites after school and on weekends. "Keeping me out of trouble" they claimed, but mostly to make sure I wasn't starving and alone.

"Boone?"

I looked back at my father and didn't block the resentment from my eyes. Maybe he didn't need it, but he'd brought it up so he could just fucking deal with it. "What?"

"What were you thinking about just now?"

"All of this. You, me, the big reveal. Me thinking back and trying like hell to find one decent father-son memory." I leaned forward. "And I can't. Not one. You weren't a bad father; you weren't a father to me *at all*. You were this random guy who showed up sometimes. Your neglect and shirking your parental duties don't earn you the right to be proud of my accomplishments. I had no *choice* but to make it on my own. And it wasn't the lessons in hardship you 'taught' me that got me there."

"I told you I was a shitty dad."

"You didn't try not to be. The casual way you're admitting lousy parenting is almost a point of pride with you. Maybe that attitude deserves an additional conversation with your counselor. I believe they call that a self-fulfilling prophecy?"

That startled him.

I guzzled my remaining beer. Six beers. In roughly an hour and a half. And that didn't seem like nearly enough.

"I didn't want things to end this way. But I guess it's better than you being disgusted."

"I am disgusted by what I've heard. But I'm not disgusted by you. Jesus. You were a kid and didn't have any control over the situation."

"I...didn't know how you'd react. Because I don't really know you, do I?"

I shook my head.

"Is there a chance we might change that someday?"

"Someday. But not today."

Hurt flashed in his eyes.

"That answer is not because of anything you've shared with me tonight. If anything, you coming to me with this makes me hopeful that your counselor can help you get a clearer perspective on me."

"What about you? Does any of the family...cycle concern you?"

"That if I have kids I'll want to touch them inappropriately? Hell no. I'm one hundred percent sure of that right now. But knowing this about you, will have me looking at the past with a different...lens, maybe."

The waitress brought another round. I might as well drink the damn thing since I wouldn't be driving anywhere tonight.

And maybe if I had help easing into slumber I wouldn't notice that gnawing need in my gut to have Sierra close—because that's the only time I felt whole.

26 Sierra

UGH. I DID not want to watch my mother feed her new husband cake.

I turned away and heard laughter, which probably meant someone had a face full of frosting. I checked my messages and saw one had just come in from Boone.

B-Dub: *Hey. Back n room. Too many beers. Going to bed.*

I texted back:

Me: *Are you okay?*
B-Dub: *No*

My stomach pitched.

Me: *Time for a call?*
B-Dub: *I want to talk in person, k? Tomorrow.*
Me: *You can wait?*
B-Dub: *No choice. Drank eight beers or I'd be n my car on my way home to u.*

Before I responded, he texted back:

B-Dub: *LUV U – nite…*

Fuck this texting shit.

If he couldn't come to me, I'd go to him.

I left the reception—I doubted anyone noticed. I had to wait for the valet to bring my car around. As soon as I cleared the gated area I hit "start route" for the motel in Flagstaff.

THREE HOURS LATER I stood in front of Boone's hotel room door. I knocked loudly in case he'd fallen asleep and made sure he could see me through the peephole.

The security lock slid on the inside.

Boone opened the door wearing just his boxer briefs. He crushed me against his chest before I said a word.

My purse fell to the floor when I wrapped myself around him, touching as much of him as possible.

At some point we realized we stood in an open doorway.

Boone shut the door, locked it and sagged against it. "You came. I didn't ask you to."

I curled my hands around his face. "You didn't need to ask me."

He closed his eyes. "God. Sierra. I'm so fucking glad you're here." He hauled me against him, burying his face in my neck. "Can we just stay like this for a while?"

"Let's try this over here." I threaded my fingers through his.

Ten steps later we'd reached the king-sized bed. The bedding was a wreck. I kicked off my shoes, yanked the dress over my head and tossed all the pillows back onto the mattress. Then I situated myself in the middle and held my hand out to him.

It took Boone some time to settle in.

I ran my hands through his hair, down his shoulders and arms, trying to soothe those ragged edges because I knew my touch did that for him. It didn't surprise me that his breathing slowed and he fell asleep. I closed my eyes, relieved that I'd brought him some peace. Even momentarily.

Later, Boone's soft kisses peppered my jaw as he pulled me from a light sleep. He whispered, "Be right back," as if he expected me to leave.

Silly man.

The toilet flushed. Water ran. He crawled back in bed, snuggling his body behind mine. He rubbed his cool, damp face across my shoulder and his cold hand skated up the outside of my thigh.

"I thought maybe I'd dreamed you." He kissed the nape of my neck. "Thank you for coming. How was the wedding?"

"Boring. With a side of pompous. Everyone got gift bags. Like they were attending the freakin' Oscars or something. It was ridiculous. I did sneak a shot of the ceremony with my cell phone and sent the pic to my dad with the caption—'Freedom from Alimony!'"

I felt Boone smile against the nape of my neck. "Did Gavin see the humor?"

"Is it mean to say he always laughs at my mom?"

"No. Better laughing than crying or screaming."

"Thankfully those days are in the past. For both of us."

He started to move his hands all over me. More out of reflex than anything else. He pressed his lips into the back of my head.

Stalling.

Prompt him? Or let this play out on its own timeframe?

My concern for him won out. "What happened?"

"I don't even know where to start. Probably because I didn't know what to expect with him. I haven't talked to you about it because it seemed stupid to speculate. That doesn't mean I didn't. I'd half-convinced myself he'd been born again and wanted to share his personal journey to salvation. I had awesome zingers worked up for that possibility."

I snickered.

"I'd also prepared myself for the apology portion of the twelve-step program. Where he admits how he wronged me, swears he's given his life over to a higher power and accepted the change, needing me to offer him my forgiveness. The last two possibilities were either he would tell me he was gay, he'd been in a serious secret relationship for a few years and couldn't live the lie anymore. Or, he'd met the love of his life, decided to give up driving truck so he could marry this woman with four young kids that he planned to adopt and he'd be a stay-at-home dad." He rubbed his mouth across the top of my ear and his fingers dug into my hips. "I wasn't even fucking close to any of those scenarios."

I waited.

"This is so fucked up," he whispered. "I never imagined this stuff went on in my family. So he totally blindsided me when he said he'd been sexually abused from age three until he turned twelve." He paused. "By his dad, Sierra."

I rolled over and wrapped myself around him as he began to talk.

He'd stop and start, the shock still evident as he tried to process it.

My questions were slow in coming, mostly because I didn't know what to ask. Although Boone's grandparents lived in Wyoming, he'd never been close to them, which surprised me, given how I'd seen the other members of the West family act around their grandkids. Also given that Boone was their only grandchild. He wouldn't appreciate me saying he'd dodged a bullet with their apathy toward him. And I wanted to kick myself for thinking that when the conversation took a darker turn.

"I guess my dad's one edict to my mom was not to let me spend time with them."

"He considered that his way of protecting you?"

"Oh, he admitted his neglect of me was intentional. Because he couldn't be sure he wouldn't have those same tendencies as his father, so he left me with a drug-addicted and abusive mother...you know...to keep me *safe*."

The sarcasm was as harsh as a slap in the face. Boone was never sarcastic.

I raised my head from his chest and looked at him. "Boone. Are you serious? He *said* that?"

"What's worse? He justified it. Even now he acts like he made some big fucking sacrifice by purposely being a shitty father and staying away from me."

"What did you say?"

"What could I say? I lost my temper."

"I don't blame you. Did you get up and storm off?"

"No. I meant to say I didn't temper my responses. He took it in stride, but what other choice did he have?"

"Did...things end on decent terms?"

"We didn't hug it out, if you can believe that."

Even that flip answer hurt my heart.

"So yeah, it sort of ended on decent terms. With all the stuff he told me, I said I needed time to take it in. That wasn't a total lie." Boone traced my jawline. "You're clenching your teeth, gorgeous."

"Of course I am."

"Tell me what's going through your head."

"Filtered or unfiltered version?"

"Unfiltered." He leaned down and kissed me softly. "Always."

I glanced down at his chest and started toying with his chest hair. "Just because his childhood had been stolen from him didn't give him the right to steal yours. That's what he did. He can lie to himself and claim it was to save you, but it was to save himself the embarrassment of having to tell anyone what his father had done to him."

"I said the same thing. But it seemed really harsh to say."

"He didn't act like telling you his traumas should change how you view the past—your past? You know, all those years that you spent a lonely, neglected little boy? With no one hugging you or feeding you or giving a damn about you?" My voice broke and I tried to hide it because Boone didn't need to deal with my emotions—I was here for *him*.

"Hey." He tipped my head back. "I know this is ugly stuff."

"I can handle it. What I can't handle is you thinking you have to deal with any of this ugly stuff alone anymore."

"I sorta gathered that when you showed up at midnight." He traced the indent of my chin. "Thank you."

Then Boone idly stroked my arm so I knew something else was on his mind. I waited.

After a while he said, "Do you think love forgives everything?"

"For example?"

"I love you, Sierra. The longer we're together, the more I'm gonna love you."

"I hope so."

"Should my love for you forgive you for everything?"

"Are you asking me if there's an unforgiveable action that would allow you to—maybe *make* you—fall out of love with me?"

He stopped touching me for just a moment. "Yeah."

"I'm not being flip or saying this to make a bigger point, but if you found out that I sexually abused kids—ours or others—that's unforgiveable. I wouldn't deserve your love or anyone else's."

"But even if you stopped the behavior and sought help? Even if you had regrets and remorse? I shouldn't love you? I shouldn't believe you could change? I shouldn't stand by you and support you?"

I rolled slightly to look into his face. "What are you getting at?"

Boone paused again. "I was thinking about my grandmother. Say she didn't know about the sexual abuse. Say she found out and confronted her husband. Say he agrees to get help and stops the abuse. So at the darkest part of his life, she's supposed to walk away? When he needs her love and support the most?"

"Yes. He willfully harmed their child—physically and emotionally. He doesn't deserve love and support; he deserves to go to fucking jail. And from what your father told you, after the abuse ended, neither one of *them* gave *him* love and understanding. Your grandfather didn't show remorse. He's never apologized to his son for all the heinous things he did to him. Your grandparents just went on with their lives and left their son to deal with it on his own."

"Would you…could you forgive me? If we had a kid I abused? If I did all the right things afterward? Got help, asked for forgiveness, tried to mend my life and fix whatever sick compulsion that might be fucking genetic? Could you love me?"

My heart collapsed. That wasn't something he needed to worry about or focus on. "Boone. I can't imagine all of the things that are going through your head right now. Let's strip as much emotion from this as we can."

"What are you—?"

"Hear me out. You are a medical professional. You've taken the biology and psychology classes. Don't statistics overwhelmingly show that victims of sexual abuse usually become abusers themselves? I don't think you need to worry that you've got a gene that'll give you a higher chance than the rest of the population of becoming a pedophile."

"My dad worried about that."

I counted to ten. "Your dad was abused, so he had a reason to worry. He stopped the cycle."

"That's one thing he said to me. That I should be grateful I'm not dealing with what he is. He said my life, my childhood could've been so much worse."

"Stop." I kissed him. "Let's take a break from talking about this for a while. Try and stop thinking about it."

"I can't. Jesus. This is life-altering stuff. I wish I could just shut it down. Stop thinking about it, stop talking about it. I don't know how to say this... What I found out tonight, you won't talk about that with anyone else, will you?"

"Anyone else meaning...my dad? My sister? My McKay cousins? Or maybe I'd call up Aunt Carolyn or Aunt Kimi and go off on them about their brother being a sick man, an incestuous pedophile?" Infuriated, I wiggled free of his hold and climbed off the bed. "I cannot believe you even asked me that, Boone. Jesus Christ."

"This is new to me. I've never had anyone in my life I share everything with. So why are you acting offended? Like it's a given that you *don't* share what I tell you with anyone else, when I know damn well you've told Lu some of the things that have happened between us? Like us fucking in the foyer and the pool—I got an attaboy from Raj which did not make me happy. I have no idea how much detail you went into. You never asked if I minded that you discussed our sex life with your roommate!"

He shouted that last part and I cringed.

"So how am I supposed to know where you draw the line in telling secrets if I don't ask? I oughta assume you won't mention it even in passing to Kyler? 'Hey, Ky, no we couldn't make the party because we were in Flagstaff after Boone had a meeting with his father. That is one fucked-up situation with the West family—and I thought what Boone dealt with growing up was bad, but it's nothing compared to what his dad went through with his father. Some sick shit there. Not that I can tell you anything about it.'" He paused to slow his labored breathing. "Am I wrong?"

God. He pissed me off.

Mostly because he was right.

We'd talked about financial responsibilities.

We'd talked about household responsibilities—but it'd taken us a big goddamned fight to deal with that.

I didn't ever want to make a misstep and hurt him by my assumptions.

Maybe I already had.

I assumed because Lu and I joked around about sex that Boone and Raj did too. Had it been wrong to tell Lu that I'd finally christened the pool—with Boone—because it'd been a topic of conversation between her and me since I'd bought the house? Had it been wrong to tell Lu that Boone was awesome in bed? Even when I hadn't gone into details about our first time except to tell her where it'd happened and that it had been worth the seven-year wait?

We hadn't set parameters for what was private between us as lovers, between us as a couple, and as each other's confidantes.

I'd never had anyone in my life that I'd bared all to either.

I looked up and found my beautiful Brooding Boone staring at me, practically daring me to argue.

"I'm sorry. You're right. We should add this to those Relationship Rules as something that needs discussion and defined parameters. But to put our mind at ease, I promise what you've told me tonight won't ever leave this room. I promise everything you told me about your childhood will always only stay between us. I'm sorry you even had to question me about it, but you had every right to."

He blinked at me.

"So are we good?"

"Come here."

I took his hand and he tucked me against his body—after bestowing tender kisses that filled me with warmth, not heat.

I yawned, but Boone's entire body remained rife with tension. "Would a massage help you fall asleep?"

"No. But thanks for the offer." He kissed my forehead. "I don't know if I tell you often enough how much I love all the thoughtful things you do for me. I never understood the appeal of having someone take care of me. I love that you just…know what I need." He sighed. "I suck at doing that for you right now, but I promise I'm gonna learn how to give that back to you."

We were quiet for a bit. Then I said, "Do you work tomorrow?"

"No. I'm off until noon on Monday for the ever-popular noon to midnight shift. Why?"

I propped myself on his chest. "Have you ever been to Sedona?"

"Just what I drove through to get here."

"Let's spend tomorrow playing tourist. It's a gorgeous county and the weather is perfect this time of year. We haven't done anything like that yet. The two of us on a day trip with no agenda."

"You trying to keep my mind occupied, McKay?"

"Not as much as I want to show you the beautiful state I was born in. There's more to Arizona than Phoenix."

Boone smiled—my smile—for the first time since I'd shown up. "Sounds like a plan."

I peppered his chest with kisses. "We'll have so much fun! But we will have to hit a discount store first thing in the morning since all I have for clothes is the dress I wore to the wedding." I smirked. "Dude. Do you know what this means? I'll have my first walk of shame moment in Walmart! It's like a rite of passage. I'm totally Instagramming it."

That actually earned me a chuckle.

"Can we take selfies? So we have pictures of us as a couple to put up in the house and at work? We could even start a photo album, scrapbook thingy to document our adventures together."

His smile faded. "Sierra, why did you ask for permission? Because that wasn't what I meant when we talked about boundaries."

"I know. I asked because you wouldn't let me take pictures of you or us before."

"I'm not camera shy." He slid his hand around my neck. The tips of his fingers were rough and dry against the damp flesh at the start of my hairline. He brushed his thumb across my jawline. "I didn't want pictures of us because it would've been too fucking hard to look at them. For both of us."

"Oh."

"Besides, admit that if you would've had a pic of me, you would've enlarged that motherfucker and used it for target practice."

I laughed. "Maybe."

A KNOCK ON the door at eight a.m. had me scurrying over to slip the chain lock into place since I was still in my bra and panties. I said, "Come back later. We're not ready to check out."

"This isn't the maid," a male voice said. Then a pause followed. "This is Boone's room?"

Boone threw back the covers and stood to yank on his jeans and a tank top. "Hang on, Dad." He rummaged in his duffel bag and dug out a pair of athletic shorts and a T-shirt. He tossed them both to me. "Put these on."

"Or I could just hide in the bathroom."

He didn't even crack a tiny grin.

As soon as I covered myself, Boone opened the door. "Hey. I wasn't expecting to see you this morning."

"I thought maybe we could have breakfast before we went our separate ways." He craned his neck to see me better. "I didn't realize you'd met a…friend."

"Sierra is my girlfriend. She arrived last night from Phoenix and we're touring Sedona today. We were just about to head out."

I didn't fault Boone for using sightseeing as an excuse to explain my presence. I waggled my fingers at Boone's dad and said, "Hi," knowing that'd be the extent of our interaction. I tried not to stare, but I didn't see a family resemblance, either between him and Boone, or between him and his brothers, Chet and Remy.

Boone's father put me under equal scrutiny. As if he should know me.

That kicked me back to a memory I'd forgotten. I had seen Dax West one time. West Construction had been doing some remodel work for my dad. Because at sixteen I was obsessed with all things Boone West, I watched the construction from the upstairs window, hoping for a glimpse of my crush. That day a truck I hadn't seen before pulled in. The man opened the driver's side door and stood on the running board. Then he honked the horn twice and yelled something. Chet and Remy exited the barn with Boone following behind them. Boone of the slumped shoulders, with his hair obscuring his face, his hands shoved in his pockets and his focus on the toes of his work boots.

Boone's father pointed at his son and then the passenger side of the truck. I remembered thinking how odd it was that he never actually addressed Boone; the entire terse conversation had happened between Dax and his brothers. Then he'd gotten back in his truck and sped off.

So to watch this Boone, standing tall, looking his father in the eye and telling him no to breakfast because we had plans today, made me so freakin' proud. Boone had become his own man—no thanks to *this* man.

Boone said, "Safe travels," and shut the door. Then he faced me. "Better get your dress on for that walk of shame, baby."

SIGHTSEEING WITH BOONE ruined me for sightseeing with anyone else.

We spent the entire day exploring one part of the Red Rock-Secret Mountain Wilderness. He convinced me that instead of doing a drive through and trying to see all of the famous rock formations in one day, we should concentrate on a specific section. Setting a limit also provided us with an excuse to return because we'd barely scratched the surface of all the places to see.

He fell in love with the area, just as I suspected he would. Although the topography, rock coloration and vegetation was nothing like east central Wyoming, I knew it reminded him of Sundance and Devil's Tower.

We hiked the eight-mile Secret Canyon trail to Maroon Mountain. The gorgeous vistas included a dazzling display of scarlet and gold foliage from the maple and oak trees that grew in the upper section of the canyon where there was water year round.

I snapped tons of pictures with my phone and ended up with several great shots of us on our first day-trip adventure.

By the time we were back in the city of Sedona, we were both tired. Boone booked our reservation for the night and I didn't have any expectations—I just wanted a room with a shower and bed and him in it. So the luxury of L'Auberge de Sedona stunned me. We had a corner room with a four-poster canopy bed, a fireplace, a sitting area and a balcony overlooking Oak Creek.

After I showered, I slipped on the complimentary spa robe and wandered onto the balcony. I rested against the railing, watching the setting sun throwing light over the cathedral spires in the distance, when Boone came up behind me.

He latched onto my hips and placed a kiss on the side of my neck. "So? What do you think?"

His scent enveloped me and I closed my eyes. "I think everything about it is beautiful. You have excellent taste, West."

"Yes, I do." He swept my hair aside, using his teeth on my neck in that skillful and maddening way that weakened my knees. "I know what I need to taste right now," he growled against my skin.

"Right here?" I breathed.

"No. I want you naked and no one gets to see you like that but me." Boone steered me into the room, his mouth never leaving my skin.

Immediately I noticed a warm, woodsy scent filling the space. I twisted away from his marauding mouth for a moment so I could pinpoint the source of that scent.

Candles.

Boone had lit the candles scattered throughout the room. Every surfaced glowed from the flickering flames—reflected in the mirrors, the glass coffee table, the polished wooden side tables and glinted in the steel behind the mantel. The open balcony doors sent the sheer white canopy on the bed fluttering in the breeze. This fairytale setting disproved his claim about not being romantic.

My throat went tight. "Boone. What…is all this?"

"Me, taking care of you." He untied the sash on my robe, purposely dragging the fluffy, nubby fabric across my skin as he peeled it off my body. Then he murmured, "Sit in the chair by the fireplace."

Four fast heartbeats after my ass landed in the chair, Boone was on his knees, his hands spreading my thighs, his mouth on me. I let my head fall back and surrendered to his hot, wet erotic kiss that broadcast his hunger.

The first time I came it was fireworks and flames, colors exploding behind my lids in time to the pulsating in my clit.

The second time I came was even better.

Right after orgasm number two, while my breathing remained ragged and my entire body quivered, Boone had me on my hands and knees on the rug in front of the fireplace. His legs shook as he caged me beneath him. He kept one hand between us, his fingers teasing my drenched sex as he guided himself inside me. He paused, his hardness buried to the hilt as he fought for control.

Or else he was waiting to see how long I could hold out before I begged him to fuck me.

He nuzzled the side of my head, his lips traveling from my temple to the edge of my jaw. I lost my mind when he did that sucking-the-air-out-of-my-ear-rather-than-blowing-it-in thing as he began to stroke in and out of me. Each one a little faster, a little harder. Then he sank his teeth into the ball of my shoulder and surged into me.

His pelvis slapped my ass with every deep stroke. He placed his palm between my shoulder blades and pushed; a wordless lover's command to lower my chest.

I groaned as the rug abraded my nipples, shooting a zip line of tingles from those tight tips straight down my belly to my wet, desire-inflamed core.

Boone's sexy grunts as his flesh slammed against mine were almost enough to tip me over the edge. Almost. So when his clever fingers started a soft pinch and release on my slippery clit…that sent me bucking and arching as orgasm number three steamrolled me.

My head was still spinning; my sex was still spasming when Boone stretched over me completely, threading his fingers through mine and pressing his face into the nape of my neck. He pumped his hips in an erotic cadence, not fast, not slow, just mind-blowingly perfect.

When he started to come, in that dreamy, unhurried pace, I felt every hard jerk of his cock, every hot burst of his seed bathing my swollen tissues, every short exhale from his lungs as he poured every bit of his passion for me, into me.

Spent and sated, and unwilling to lose the connection, we stayed like that until not even the heat from the fireplace could warm the chill from our bodies.

Boone retreated, planting kisses down my spine as he moved out of me. He lifted me into his arms and carried me to bed.

We woke up two hours later, completely famished.

Rather than leave our romantic love nest, Boone ordered room service. But in a place this classy it wasn't food brought up on a tray. We had balcony service—a waiter arrived and set up the table with linens, a small bouquet of flowers and gleaming tableware. After popping the cork on the bottle of champagne, he left us to enjoy our romantic dinner in our robes.

So I nearly fell off the chair when Boone lifted the silver dome on the butler's cart to reveal...pizza. Gourmet pizza, to be sure, but it was still pizza.

I had to hide my watery eyes when he said he'd chosen pizza because it'd become a Sunday night tradition with us.

Later when we were curled up in bed, he sighed. "Back to the real world tomorrow."

"Today was perfect, Boone. Thank you."

"Thank you for...being there for me last night." He tightened his hold on me. "Did it bug you that I didn't introduce you to my dad this morning?"

"No. And not just because you didn't introduce yourself to my mom. Why? Are you wishing you had?"

"Fuck that. I knew he'd turn into an asshole when he found out your last name is McKay. But there was a nasty part of me that would like to see him squirm about that." He sighed again. "That nasty streak I inherited from my mom rarely wins."

I smiled.

"The reason I didn't introduce you is because he doesn't deserve to know you, Sierra. You are the best part of my life and something I never thought I'd have because of my fucked-up childhood. Since he was a good part of that misery, he doesn't deserve to see me happy. He hasn't earned that right. I suspect he never will. It's not me being petty. It's not me retreating because of what he told me about his abusive past. It's about me not letting my crappy past have any hold on my future." He pressed a warm kiss to the top of my head. "I love you. I know how to love *because* of you."

That was the first time I'd ever cried myself to sleep with happy tears.

27 *Boone* 💕

IT'D BEEN A long day, sitting in on conference calls, then writing up reports summarizing the calls. I'd scrambled to get everything finalized for our departure in the morning.

Sierra wasn't home from her PCE meeting. She warned me she might not be back until late. The clock inched toward twenty-two hundred and I hadn't heard from her.

After being inside all day, I opted to wait for her by the pool. I stretched out in a chaise, can of Coors on the table, earbuds in, but on low. I could sit out here for hours, watching the play of light, shadows and movement across the pool's surface. I figured this was as close as I'd get to a Zen experience.

I heard the garage door go up. It amused me that as soon as Sierra didn't have to present a business image, she dressed down—not that I'd ever complain about that ass of hers in yoga pants.

As I waited, I wondered if she'd eaten dinner—she forgot half the time. Especially on nights when she went directly from DPM to her meeting at PCE. She'd been on edge the past week, which meant she'd been on a baking spree. Anytime I asked if she wanted to talk, she claimed everything was fine. So tonight she deserved to unwind. From the small cooler, I pulled out a plastic cup and poured a can of premixed margarita over the ice. I even popped in an umbrella next to the straw.

The patio door opened and there she was. Her beautiful brown hair secured into a messy bun on top of her head, a loose cotton tunic that hit her mid-thigh and her feet bare. I got that one-two punch in the heart and the gut. My love for her just grew every damn day.

"I'm so glad you're out here. I'm sick of breathing recycled air in stuffy offices." Sierra smiled at me; the smile that was mine alone. Soft, sweet, sexy. Then she leaned over me. "Hi." She kissed me, starting out a tease, then she pushed her tongue past my lips and poured her passion into me, filling that empty space that used to be inside me, with...this. With everything. She took the kiss back down to sweet, gliding her damp lips across mine, and murmured, "I love coming home to you every night."

"I love this domestic stuff, baby. I love that I have it with you."

She sighed dreamily and stood.

I reached down and snagged her drink, holding it up. "For my hardworking corporate executive."

"God, I love you, West."

"Back atcha times a million, McKay. Have a seat."

Sierra lowered herself in the chaise next to me on her front side, her head by my feet. She sipped her drink and the dimple in her cheek popped out when she noticed the umbrella. "Nice touch."

"Only the best for you."

"Thanks for the blanket too."

The first week we lived together, I learned that the fuzzy blue and white blanket belonged to Sierra and she didn't share it. Ever. And the girl turned pissy if she suspected someone had been using it. I did not get her attachment to it, but I did respect it. I'd taken a chance bringing it poolside, and I breathed easier that I hadn't fucked up. "You're welcome." I ran my hand up the back of her thigh. "Take a moment to clear your head."

"Okay. But please keep doing that."

I brought my hand back down to her knee and let my palm slowly journey upward again. Over and over.

Only the right side of her face was visible, but I knew when she dozed off. I'd miss this in the next two weeks. After a lifetime of feeling adrift, this connection to her and proof of the life we were building together filled me with pride. I'd do everything in my power to keep this.

Sierra stirred after half an hour. The first thing she did in that groggy state was reach for me.

Fuck. I was just bursting with happiness over that one small thing.

She lifted her head and smiled at me. "Power nap accomplished." She readjusted herself so we were side by side and she sucked down half of her drink. "Guess I was thirsty."

"You wanna talk about your day, your meeting tonight? Or would you rather just chill?"

"Just chill. Except I will say the PCE meeting was the most productive we've had in months."

"Awesome."

"What crazy things did Sergeant West get up to today?"

"Phone conferences with the brass all morning and half the afternoon. Paperwork fun after that."

"I didn't know you had conference calls scheduled today."

"That's the thing; we didn't."

She looked at me. "Tell me."

"I have to go back to base tomorrow. Raj too."

Her face fell. "Really?"

"Yeah. It's just for two weeks."

"Two weeks!"

I raised a brow at her. "That's better than a month."

"I know that's supposed to put it in perspective, Boone. But dammit. Two weeks without you? That sucks."

I shifted my body, dropping my feet to the concrete and leaning over to touch her face. "It's part of the deal with me. You know that."

"Doesn't mean I have to like it," she retorted. "And if you say I should get used to it, I'm gonna punch you in the junk."

I laughed. "You're threatening to dick punch me when you won't see my dick for two weeks? Harsh."

"I lashed out. Sorry." She smirked and eyed my crotch. "You know I'd never do anything to hurt our cock."

"*Our* cock?" I repeated.

"Mmm-hmm. It's just as much mine now as it is yours." She slurped her drink and held a piece of ice between her teeth, her eyes glittering with devilment as she crunched down on it.

Fuck. Me. She'd tortured me with ice last week. I'd actually begged her to let me come.

"Besides, our cock likes me better because it knows that I make it feel good."

I laughed again. "That you do. So is it our pussy now too?"

"Nope. It's mine. Internal versus external thing that requires maintenance, that you as a man wouldn't have patience for. But you have unlimited lifetime usage rights to my pussy." She grinned. "I'll admit my pussy loves you way more than it loves me. Way more. So it'll expect a really long goodbye kiss before you take off. For two freakin' weeks."

"Deal." I looked at her. "And there's something else."

"What?"

"There's a retirement party a week from Saturday night." I scooped her onto my lap. "Would you consider flying to Fort Hood and attending it with me?"

Sierra tilted her head back to gaze at me. "It's important to you?"

"Yeah. A party isn't representative of military life, but it is a bonus. And it'd really be a bonus for me if you'd be there with me."

Her eyes softened. "I'd love to come."

I rested my forehead to hers. She had no idea what this meant. I'd never brought any woman to an event. The first—and only—one I'd attended, I'd gone alone. I'd been the only guy who didn't have a date. From that point on I'd avoided them.

She leaned back. "So it's formal formal. Like I have to wear a long dress and you wear...?"

"My dress uniform."

"I finally get to see you in uniform?"

"Any time you want to play soldier and spy, all you have to do is ask." My hands followed the outside curve of her thighs. "I've dreamed up a few interrogation methods that are all kinds of kinky." I opened my mouth on her throat and squeezed her ass.

She arched back with a gasp.

"Bed. Now." I wrapped her legs around my hips and stood, carrying her inside.

LATER, WE WERE entwined together, I'd started to drift off, when I felt her planting insistent kisses on my left pectoral.

"Sierra. Babe. After that last time I am wiped out. I have to be curbside at oh five hundred."

"I wasn't kissing you to tempt you into fucking me again, dumbass. I was just kissing your heart goodbye. I didn't want it to feel left out since I said a very thorough goodbye to our cock." Her next kiss was whisper soft. "I'm so focused on worshipping other areas of your body I forget about this one...and your heart is one of the best things about you."

God. What she did to me when she told me things like that. I swallowed the lump in my throat. "You don't have to tell my heart goodbye, because it'll be right here with you when I go."

28 Sierra ♥

THE FIRST COUPLE of days without my man hadn't been too terrible. Wednesday night after work I paddled around in my pool. Then I nursed three fingers of Crown and watched the weekend preview for college football. I paused the TV during the ASU profile to snap still shots of Ky's stats and then texted the images to him begging for his autograph.

He responded with PISS OFF and a hundred middle finger emojis.

Thursday night the McKay-kateers showed up to watch the football game. None of us gave a damn about the Eagles or the Rams, so the game served as background noise. I baked molasses cookies and had a lively discussion with Hayden about his business ethics class.

Friday night I attended my first pro hockey game. I loved it from the first drop of the puck—not just because I knew the Scorpion's star player. The atmosphere? Infectious. The fans? Maybe more rabid than football fans. Watching the players literally skating circles around each other was as entertaining as the fights. The first time I shot to my feet and yelled at the player from Minnesota for tripping Mase, Anton smirked at me and said they'd created a monster.

But home alone at night…I missed Boone like crazy. More than I anticipated.

Saturday, while Lu worked on her landscaping project, I watched the Sun Devils game on TV. Then Lu and I decided to test out the PS4 to figure out why our guys loved video games. We ended up playing *Grand Theft Auto* until two a.m.

I spent Sunday at McJock Central for football and Meat-topia. I'd baked three different desserts—which Mase almost singlehandedly devoured. Despite the killer brisket, Anton seemed as preoccupied as I was. When my dad called Sunday night to recap the weekend games, I avoided talking to him. I hadn't told him about Boone returning to base and I feared I'd blurt out the PCE offer just to gauge whether DPM would fight to keep me—that might make my decision easier.

Or harder.

Monday morning I was dragging ass. Even Griff from legal mentioned I looked tired.

Yes, I'm tired, dammit. I stayed up too late having phone sex with my kinky boyfriend.

Totally worth it though.

FRIDAY AFTERNOON, LU plopped next to me on the couch. She rested her head on my shoulder and sighed. "I miss Raj."

As much as I missed Boone...I realized I'd missed Lu too. She and Raj were shacked up at his sister's place, so last weekend was the first time just the two of us had hung out in ages. I missed heckling our favorite crappy TV shows. She hadn't updated me in weeks on how far she'd gotten with her senior design project. And she had no idea that I was considering taking a new turn in my career.

I loved her, but I couldn't chance confiding in her about the fulltime PCE offer. If she slipped up and told Raj, and Raj told Boone, Boone would go...*what the ever lovin' fuck?* Because I still hadn't said a freakin' word about it to him.

The timing had been off, especially after he'd dealt with his dad's stuff. Then he'd gotten recalled to base. After nearly two weeks apart...bringing it up this weekend wasn't a priority. With limited time together, banging the headboard held more appeal than talking.

"What are you fretting about?" Lu asked.

"If my dress for this gala thingy is too slut-tastic."

Lu lifted her head and batted her lashes at me. "Skanky-ass ho. Have you been shopping at the stripper's discount store without me again?"

"You're the skanky-ass-ho." I shoved her with my shoulder. "I'm serious. I do not want to embarrass Sergeant West, slithering in wearing the latest in ho-bag fashion or looking as if an Amish stylist chose my frock."

"Which dress are you talking about?"

"The backless blue beaded one."

Disbelief distorted Lu's face. "Sierra McKay. You haven't been *shopping*? You actually thought you'd *recycle* a dress from college? Dude. This is Boone, the man you're in love with. He deserves to see you in a dress that'll bring him to his damn knees."

"Omigod. You're right. What am I going to do? I leave tomorrow!"

Lu popped to her feet and grabbed my hand, jerking me off the couch. "Get your purse. We will get this fashion crisis handled tonight."

I'D OVER-PACKED FOR one and a half days in Killeen, Texas.

I didn't have to bring Boone muffins and cookies. But I'd baked plenty this week.

So I paced in the room, wondering why I'd chosen a hotel without a mini-bar and stopping at the window every time as if I could see him pull up. From the sixth floor.

Hurry up and get here, Boone. I was about to climb out of my skin. I'd never had a case of nerves like this.

Four hours had passed since I'd arrived. Boone's meetings didn't allow him to pick me up from the airport. Hailing a cab to his place wasn't an option because he lived on base and I didn't have an escort or a pass to get on a secure military installation.

Boone had texted me ten times—a new record for him. It ripped at his manhood that he couldn't fetch me from the airport. To kill time, I scrolled back through our text exchange.

B-Dub: *U here?*

Me: *I just got your text. I landed fifteen minutes ago and I'm waiting for my bag.*

B-Dub: *It kills me not to be there. I'm sorry*

Me: *I know. I'm fine. Just take care of your stuff.*

B-Dub: *I luv u*

Me: *Back atcha.*

Then half an hour later

B-Dub: *Hotel ok?*

Me: *It's good.*

B-Dub: *Be there at six-thirty*

Me: *I'll be ready ☺ will we have time for a quickie first?*

B-Dub: *U r miknag me hard.*

Miknag? What was that? Then I realized he'd transposed the letters. He was so anxious that he wasn't taking an eternity to type out a text.

Me: *I have to get ready. See you soon.*

B-Dub: *Can't wait. Luv u*

So sweet, that man of mine.

Darkness had fallen and I stared out at the city lights. Strange to think Boone lived here. He'd never mentioned loving it or hating it. Accepting it was more his way.

Had he ever driven by the military family housing and imagined coming home to a wife and maybe a kid or two? If we hadn't reconnected, would he have settled for someone else? That seemed plausible. Certainly more plausible than us ending up together. Then again, he'd come after me. The harder question was: would I have ever gone after him? When the word "no" echoed through my head, my heart and my stomach clenched with outrage. Now I couldn't imagine a life without him. But I could've easily gone the other way, ignoring Boone's attempts to start over. Thank heaven for the man's tenacity. Thank heaven for his faith in us—in this.

Four solid raps sounded on the door.

I raced over and flung open the door without checking the peephole first. "I thought…"

My brain stopped. My heart did too. I had the vague sensation I'd abandoned that whole breathing thing when I got my first look at him.

Boone was one hundred percent polished, from the tips of his shiny shoes to his belt buckle to the brim of his hat. Talk about heart stopping to see Boone West in that uniform.

I flashed back to the anguish in his eyes the night he'd told me he needed to leave Wyoming. He had to make it on his own. I hadn't doubted he could do it, even when I'd hated the decision he'd made. But it had been the best possible option for him.

"Sierra?"

My eyes met his. Such pride there. Such love.

"Look at you," I managed. "You're so…" I wished I'd had the foresight to grab a tissue. But the tears started regardless.

Boone followed me in. "What's wrong?"

I shook my head and kept walking backward.

"Sierra. Stop." He latched onto my upper arms. "What is going on?"

"I'm so proud of you. It just hit me, seeing you in uniform like you were born to wear it. And it makes me so ashamed that I was so selfish that I didn't want you to have this."

"Baby—"

"No, let me finish. I would've happily sabotaged your entire life and all your plans in order to make you mine. You were so much stronger than I've ever given you credit for. Maybe that sounds stupid, but I couldn't have made that choice. You did. For both of us." I sniffled. "So, I'm just…crazy in love with you, okay? Crazy in love and crazy proud that I get to be part of your life."

Boone studied me with an intensity that made me tremble. He didn't touch me, he didn't kiss me. Every inch of him, except his eyes, had gone still.

"Never has anything that anyone ever said to me meant as much as this."

I thought I was done crying.

I thought wrong.

But he caught the next tear, and the one after that, and the one after that, on his own cheeks as he kissed me.

I was utterly lost in him.

When he finally relinquished my mouth, he smiled. "That leaves us no time for a quickie."

"You can make it up to me later."

His lips grazed my bare shoulder and collarbone. "You look fantastic, by the way."

"Thank you." I'd chosen a red dress, simple in cut and design. I'd splurged on shoes, with distinctive red soles the exact same color as the dress. I'd debated on wearing my hair up, but I'd opted to leave it down because I loved how Boone swept my hair away so he could kiss my neck. I needed that familiarity.

"You ready?"

"I have to check my makeup." With my luck I'd have black streaks running down to my chin. I crossed to the small vanity and leaned closer. Not too bad. The waterproof mascara lived up to the name. I blotted under my eyes, added concealer, touched up my eyeliner and dusted powder across to seal it. Boone had done a number on my lipstick.

He moved in behind me.

I smiled. Which made it hard to put on my lipstick.

"I almost stopped and bought you flowers. But it seemed more important to get here, than to get here with a flower you probably wouldn't wear."

So freakin' sweet.

Keeping those dark eyes on mine in the mirror, he gathered a handful of my hair and delicately wrapped it around his palm. Then he pulled down hard, exposing the side of my throat. He dragged his lips up and stopped at my ear, sending chills through me. "When we get back? You won't know what hit you. I'm going to fuck you like it's my right. Because it *is* mine. *Just* mine." His breath fluttered across my damp skin. "All night, Sierra."

And…not so sweet.

THE BALLROOM SPARKLED as if we'd stepped into a fairy-tale castle.

Crystal chandeliers, enormous arrangements of fresh flowers. Tuxedoed waiters served champagne and beautifully crafted finger foods. The lighting was superb: dim enough to be intimate, bright enough that you weren't banging into tables in the dark.

Boone kept his hand in the small of my back. With any other guy it could be seen as gentlemanly behavior. With Boone, his continual touch was proof of ownership. If I could've dragged him off to a coat closet so he could fuck me fast and hard as a private testimonial, I would've done it without shame.

Warm lips touched my ear. "Care to share the dirty thought you just had?"

"How did you know?"

"Wouldn't it be worse if I didn't recognize it?"

"Point to Sergeant West." I tipped my head back to look at him. "This is some fancy gig."

"I had no idea it would be like this."

I frowned. "Haven't you been to a bunch of these?"

"One. I didn't bring a date. I had no idea that was expected. So I hid by the shrimp cocktail and stuffed my face until I could escape."

That image wrecked me. I discreetly drilled him in the stomach with my index finger. "That breaks my fucking heart. Stop trying to make me cry, douche."

He laughed.

A couple joined us.

The man offered his hand. "At ease, West. Good to see you."

I half-expected Boone to salute. He shook the hand. "Happy to have been invited." That "she's mine" hand on my back urged me forward. "Colonel Livingston, this is my girlfriend, Sierra McKay. Sierra, this is our commanding officer."

I had a momentary bout of nerves and fought the urge to curtsey and greet him in a fake British accent. "So happy to meet you."

Colonel Livingston offered his hand. "Very pleased to make your acquaintance. This is my wife, Bridget."

Bridget deigned a brittle smile and a limp handshake. "Yes, lovely to meet you."

I murmured something back. At least no one here had gone the kiss-kiss on each cheek route.

"Have you settled into Phoenix?"

"Day by day, sir. Things are done differently, but I'll adapt."

"You always do." The colonel studied me. "And where are you from?"

"Phoenix." I tacked on, "Sir."

"Ah. That's where you two met?"

"Sierra and I lived in the same small town in Wyoming. We recently reconnected in Phoenix."

Bridget paid no attention to the conversation. She appeared to be scanning the crowd for a more powerful—or at least more interesting—couple to speak with. She touched her husband's arm. "I see the Winchells have arrived. We should say hello."

"Of course. Enjoy the party," the colonel said.

"We will, sir. You also."

Boone didn't breathe again until the man disappeared into the crowd. No one else would've noticed it but I did.

"He seemed friendly."

"He is. Good man and great leader."

"He's your big boss? Or the semi-in-charge?"

"Big boss. Come on, I need a drink."

I'd been sipping the free champagne but Boone ordered a beer.

"So where are we sitting and all that jazz?"

"Assigned table numbers. At least I hope we sit with the guys from my unit."

We wandered through the room; Boone stopped to speak with a lot of people whose names I didn't catch. We ran into his group, four guys and their dates, in the far back corner.

"West, my man, why are you here?"

I saw Boone stiffen as if he feared the guy might do the half-hug, chest bump, back slap bro hug. He shifted slightly, using me as a buffer. "I'm here to contribute to the destruction of more trees in the name of a metric shit ton of paperwork."

They all laughed. My man personified charm.

"How are things in First?"

"Same old, same old." The stealth hugger cocked his head and smiled at me. "Sweetheart, whatchu doin' with him? The man is boring. Work, work, work, all the damn time. Gets off on making us all look like slackers."

"You *are* slackers."

"Wasn't talking to you, Sarge. I was asking your very beautiful date."

"Sierra, this rude gearhead is DT Sharp. DT, this is my girlfriend, Sierra."

"Girlfriend?" He whistled. "Man, you are coming up in the world." DT smiled at me. "Good to meet you. To say I'm shocked to meet you is an understatement."

"And why is that, Mr. Sharp?"

"Like I said. The man is all work. His off hours tend to be about…short pursuits."

Boone stiffened behind me.

Then all eyes were on me to see how I'd react. "Really? I beg to differ. Boone is very specific in his long term goals."

He kissed my temple.

"Besides, short is never a word I'd use to describe any part of him."

Everyone laughed. Then the insults flew and that loosened the tension.

But military speak confused me, so I let my gaze wander. Even with all the men in uniform, none of them looked as good as Boone. He carried himself with confidence and I loved seeing it since I knew it hadn't always been there.

"I need a drink of water," I said to him. "I'll be right back."

"I'll go with you."

"No, stay. I won't get lost."

At the hospitality table, I filled a crystal glass with ice water. Disappointing not to find snacks there, since the waitstaff had stopped circling with tidbits and I was starving.

"So you're Boone's *girlfriend*."

I slowly faced the woman with the sneering tone. "Yes, I am. Who are you?"

"Janell. I'm here with Cody. These guys don't bother introducing their dates."

But mine did. "Cody works with Boone?"

"Only in the broadest sense. It's a little freaky to see them all in dress uniforms. Usually they resemble bums when we're hanging out at Spike's."

The old "I know them, I'm part of the group" tactic to make me feel like an outsider. Hah. Too late. I already felt as if I'd stepped onto a movie set and it appeared I'd found the villain. "Boone hasn't mentioned Spike's."

"That's weird. That's where I met him. At least a couple of years ago."

Nice follow up with the "neener neener I've known him longer" shot. I said nothing.

So she kept on. "DT said they were all at Spike's earlier in the week. Boone went along but he didn't say *anything* about a girlfriend, which was why DT was so surprised tonight."

"Oh, right. When Boone called me Monday night he did mention he'd gone out for a beer with the guys. He didn't specifically say DT was there, so I don't know what they talked about."

"Did Boone mention Katherine being there too? She's been pretty close to him."

Why didn't she just hand me a list of the chicks Boone fucked? But now I was curious about her end game so I'd play...dumb at first. "I just met DT. We didn't talk long enough for him to say anything about a Katherine, so I don't know how close they are."

"I didn't mean DT and Katherine were close, I meant Katherine and Boone were close."

"Ah." I nodded. "I wouldn't know that either because Boone doesn't talk about his work in Fort Hood or who he works with." I waited for steam to come out of her ears.

"You're not the brightest bulb, are you?" she sneered.

"I'm perfectly bright. Here's a thought. Since you want me to know that you fucked Boone and your friend Katherine fucked him too, just say it outright instead of adding in all of the bullshit and expecting me to dig through it."

"Me and Katherine weren't the only ones," she retorted.

"Again, what is the point of this? To make me jealous? To make me mad? To get me to pick a fight with Boone about his past that has nothing to do with me?"

"Why don't you just admit you're not Boone's girlfriend? That you're just some random chick he brought as his date to save face."

"Why would he need to save face?"

Her eyes lit with triumph. "Because before he left for godforsaken Wyoming or wherever, he was complaining about having to attend this party, because he'd been told by the colonel he couldn't skip it. He said he'd just pick some random chick off the street as his date. I'm betting that's you."

I smiled with complete condescension. "If I'm a random chick, you think you still have a shot at him? Really? With all that you've told me about how very many women he's... *close* to?"

"You don't know—"

"Oh yes, I think I do. Boone fucked you once. You wanted more, even when you were aware he's the quintessential 'one and done' guy. Maybe you fantasized he'd ask you to this event. So it pissed you off that he admitted he'd rather show up with some 'random chick off the street'...than with you or any of the other base rats who've hit the 'one and done' threshold."

"You think you're so smart but you don't know shit."

"No, you don't know shit. So I'll let you in on a little secret, Janell. I *am* Boone's girlfriend. I was his first girlfriend and I'll also be his last girlfriend. See, we met in *godforsaken* Wyoming years ago. We lost track of each other. But we found our way back to each other. So I'll admit the irony that 'one and done' applies to me too—but it's like this; I'm his *only one* and he's *done* with everyone else. I don't care that you fucked him in the past. But I do care if you put your fucking hands on him now. Because if I see you lay a single finger on him? I will come after you with everything I have because he is mine. Get that? *Mine.*"

Not so ballsy, now, are you Janell?

I got right in her face. "Nod your head if you understand."

"Yeah. I get it."

"Good. Feel free to pass that around to any of your fellow base rats who have visions of Sergeant West's combat boots under their bed."

She practically ran away.

Right then I believed that blood could actually boil; mine rushed hot and fast and angry. My lungs were heaving. My heart raced.

I needed that glass of water. With a goddamned Crown chaser.

Strong arms circled me from behind, trapping me.

Boone buried his face in my hair. His body shook.

I turned my head toward his and hissed, "Are you laughing at me, you rat bastard?"

"No. Never. Jesus. I'm…" His lips found my ear through my tangle of hair. "I heard what you said to her."

"And?"

"And I'm so fucking hot for you right now that it's taking every 'deflect combat' maneuver I ever learned to stop me from dragging you the fuck out of here."

"Oh."

"Two hours. Then we're gone."

"Promise?"

"Promise."

"I ALMOST RENTED a limo to pick us up after the party," I murmured in Sierra's ear as she slipped the keycard in the door.

"Why?"

"That'd be a classier way to fulfill your car sex fantasy that you keep bugging me about."

Once we were inside the room, Sierra pushed me against the door and cupped my cheek in her hand. "What is going on in that head of yours, soldier? Why would you think a limo would matter to me?"

"Because sometimes I wonder if I'll ever feel worthy of you."

"How ironic. Because sometimes I wonder if I'll ever feel like I deserve you."

We watched one another.

"You deserve a man who celebrates everything about you that is uniquely you." I turned my head and kissed the base of her thumb. "A man who loves you like you are the sunshine that fills his days and the moon glow that fills his nights."

"How lucky I am that you are that man." She placed her hand over my heart. "I love that I'm the only woman you've ever deemed worthy enough to share this poetic, romantic, utterly sweet side of yourself with."

"I didn't know it was there until you brought it out in me."

"Show me without words."

No idea why my nerves kicked in. I knew what Sierra wanted in bed; I'd become an expert at giving it to her. Hard, fast, dirty, greedy. Sometimes sweet and slow. Sometimes funny but always frequent.

But maybe tonight, I'd give her what she needed. What we both needed.

I brought her mouth to mine for a long, exploratory kiss.

She swayed against me and I automatically righted her by latching onto her ass.

My hands were rough, so I kept my touch light on the delicate fabric of her dress as I skimmed my palms up her back. When I reached her shoulders, I ended the kiss and whispered, "Turn around."

Her teeth dug into her bottom lip as her eyes met mine. Then she faced the bed.

I slowly tugged the zipper on her dress down. I slipped my hands beneath the fabric as I peeled it away, planting kisses in a line down her spine until my lips connected with the section of skin between the dimples of her ass.

Then her dress was a pool of red fabric on the carpet.

She hadn't worn sexy garters and stockings, just a fire-engine red thong. So I could see every sexy inch of her. From the nape of her neck, to the curve of her ass, down her long legs to the backs of her heels, still encased in sexy black stilettos.

Fuck. She was just so beautiful.

Her body trembled. From the cold or my intense perusal...didn't matter. I'd warm her up soon enough.

I swept her hair off to the side, letting the hot wash of my breath choose the spot on her neck before my mouth descended. While I tasted her there, I continued to caress her with my fingertips, my palms, and the backs of my knuckles. Everywhere I could reach; her arms, the outside curve of her body from her rib cage to her hips, her belly, her breasts, her collarbones.

She didn't speak. She didn't have to; I was already attuned to her. I felt every quiver and every goose bump. I heard every ragged breath and every tiny sigh. I caught the scent of her arousal and breathed in the perfume of her skin.

This deliberate seduction of her was intoxicating me.

A sheen of sweat coated my skin beneath my uniform. My cock was painfully hard. My chest felt tight. I had to lock my legs to keep myself upright. I'd become lightheaded from all the tactile and emotional sensations bombarding me.

Then Sierra trapped my hand on her hip and turned back around to face me. She allowed one fleeting brush of her lips across mine before she began to undress me.

Her hands were reverent as she smoothed them over my uniform. She had me unbuttoned, unhooked and undone in no time. Then she stepped back and watched as I removed the last of my clothing until I was as naked as she.

We reached for each other at the same time.

We ended up on the bed. Not in a frantic tangle of limbs. But bare arms and legs slowly sliding and gliding together. I needed every inch of her skin touching every inch of mine. Rubbing on mine.

I spooned her from behind so my front side covered her back. Then we rolled across the sheets so I could feel the soft press of her tits against my shoulder blades as her hands mapped the front of my body from my face to my neck to my chest to my cock.

I rolled her onto her back and levered my body over hers. Not in a pushup position, but my weight on her, my passion-dampened flesh sliding on hers. Exchanging breath with openmouthed kisses.

She reached between us and guided me to her entrance.

I pushed inside her warmth, her heat, her wetness until I couldn't go any deeper.

I watched her face lost in pleasure, and part of the pleasure came from seeing her recognize the look on my face mirrored hers.

Our bodies arched and moved together almost of their own accord. I didn't lead. Neither did she.

We were in perfect sync.

The rising storm, the waves crashing and then hitting that crest, followed by the ebb and flow of passion, all clichéd, but true.

In that moment she'd reminded me exactly what it meant to belong to her, body, heart and soul. And I reminded her that her heart, her body and her soul were safe with me.

29 Sierra

WITH THE HELP of Red Bull, I survived my mid-afternoon Monday slump.

Which turned out to be a lucky thing because Phyllis Mackerley showed up.

Even when it was probably stupid, I remained behind my desk and had her sit across from me. I needed every confidence boost no matter how small. The tug of war between *take the job* and *decline the job* had started to feel like a stalling tactic to increase the perks.

That wasn't it at all—and I told Phyllis as much.

"You don't even need to clarify that for me, Sierra."

"Thank goodness."

"But what I am about to tell you will sweeten the pot." She grinned. "Or more accurately, will make the pot runneth over."

I squinted at her. "Did you and tequila have a reunion and a little afternoon delight?"

Phyllis giggled. Giggled. "I'll admit I do feel almost high right now." Okay.

"Ask me why." She fairly bounced in her chair. "Go on."

"Why are you so giddy?"

"I had a phone call from Pashma Wickersham this morning."

"Get out. Seriously?"

"Seriously. And *she* called *me*."

"Tell me, dammit. Was she headhunting you or what?" That wouldn't surprise me. Phyllis was brilliant and generous and exactly the type of leader that an organization like Women Entrepreneurs International—WEI—wanted on their roster. Pashma Wickersham, the president of WEI, had outstanding accomplishments in the decade she'd been at the helm of the organization. The founding members of PCE had used the WEI business model and we'd embraced Pashma's philosophies for business and life.

"No, dear, she wasn't headhunting me." Phyllis grinned. "She's headhunting you."

"What?" I must have misunderstood.

"Or more specifically, WEI has been watching PCE for the last year."

"They have?"

"Yes. And they would like to bring PCE in as a charter."

"No way."

"I absolutely would not joke about this."

"Omigod, omigod, omigod!" I pushed my chair back and jumped up and down a couple of times. I might've screamed.

Phyllis was laughing at me. "I knew you'd react this way! Isn't it just unbelievable?"

"Yes! This is huge. WEI doesn't have any charters in Arizona. And the cities that do have a WEI charter? The members have access to the WEI database, their speaker's bureau, their conferences, not to mention the whole financial side and the worldwide networking."

"I know. I'm in shock. This is beyond anything I could've ever hoped for, Sierra."

"Me too." I lowered into my chair. "But why us? Isn't the vetting process done by the CIA or something?"

She laughed. "No. But it is very thorough and like I said, they've tested PCE a few times."

"Tested. Like how?"

"From what Pashma told me, WEI sends a new potential member to PCE for guidance with a marketable product. How things are handled at each stage earns a rating. If the first test is failed, there are no others. If the first test is passed, then two more tests are conducted, a product with limited marketability and one that isn't viable at all. Evidently honesty earns the highest value points. PCE passed all three tests. We passed the requirements for a well-run, well-organized meeting that is welcoming to new members yet continues to be relevant to existing members. We show continued membership growth. We have a variety of mentors across age, race, cultural and educational backgrounds. In fact, PCE had the highest test values of any charter in the past four years."

I could scarcely wrap my head around all of this.

"And that is what brings me here, Sierra. If you accept the directorship of PCE, you will in effect also be the chair of the WEI charter."

"Holy fuck."

"Not a bad thing to have on your resume at age twenty-three."

All of a sudden I felt like I was suffocating. This was too much. This was the big leagues. The big, big leagues.

"Sierra," Phyllis said sharply, "look at me."

I raised my gaze to hers.

"You can do this. I never would've agreed to mentor you or offered you the directorship if I didn't believe that you're more than capable."

"Can I be brutally honest?"

She nodded.

"I don't feel like I've earned your confidence. I don't have that confidence in myself." I briefly closed my eyes. "I poured everything I'd become into PCE because of my early success. I wanted to make sure it'd been more than just a fluke. Or luck."

"Sierra McKay. Flipping six pieces of real estate and netting over a million dollars in profit is not a fluke. You invested in your friend's business and put her innovation into production. Yet you understood the finite timespan for ROI and adjusted accordingly. You still personally netted a quarter of a million dollars—which was thirty percent of the gross receipts—and then you turned around and leased the patent. That wasn't luck. You created a business model that worked."

"It worked from inherited capital," I reminded her.

Phyllis narrowed her eyes at me. "Because you inherited the money that somehow lessens the success you had increasing the principle? Because you didn't earn that cash waiting tables you're not allowed to put the money your family earned…to work for you?"

"God. I hate that you're so fucking logical."

She laughed. "Never discount your successes. Trust me; there are plenty of other people who are more than happy to do it for you."

"True. I'm just a little…torn."

"I suspected that. Can you be specific?"

"How can I hope to foster a productive work environment at PCE when I can't manage it here?" My cheeks burned with embarrassment. "If I can't achieve results here at DPM, why do you have faith that it'd be different for me at PCE?"

"Maybe you're stymied here by a number of factors that you aren't even aware of."

I'd heard that before. From Rory.

"But the reason I'll put all of my faith in you, Sierra McKay? *You* fostered the work environment at PCE. You didn't inherit it and all its problems from other managers. You built it, you nurtured it, you created it from the ground up. Maybe that's easier to do than stepping into someone else's vision, figuring out what's wrong and having to right it. I truly feel you cannot compare the two entities. That means you'll have different levels of success—one for each of them by default."

I burst into tears.

Phyllis let me cry. She tracked me down a tissue. She gave me the *there-there* pats I needed.

After I wiped my eyes and blew my nose, I looked at her. "It's overwhelming. In a good way. I've been beating myself up about this for a month and now I feel like a weight has been lifted. Thank you. You have influenced me more than any person besides my father. If I'm ever half as good of a mentor as you, I'll consider myself blessed."

She reached for a tissue. "Silver-tongued little thing. Thank you."

"So now what?"

"You're officially agreeing to take the directorship of PCE?"

"Yes."

That felt…good. Damn good.

"We'll announce it at next week's meeting. They'll put it to a vote, but you won't get any opposition because everyone admires you and sees you as the future."

"They do?"

"Yes. Last piece of business, and this is a biggie. WEI requires the director of the charter to go through an orientation process. To learn all aspects of WEI from the ground up. To network with every chapter. That is key. That global network is the glue that holds the organization together."

"Okay. That won't compromise my responsibilities running PCE?"

Phyllis smiled. "I love that you asked that first thing. No, it won't. You'll have a liaison while you're traveling and I've volunteered to do it for the year you're in orientation."

Everything inside me stilled. "Maybe you'd better go into a little more detail about this year-long orientation."

"Your schedule for the first year will be networking focused. That means a considerable amount of travel. I've been told not to expect you to be in the PCE offices more than five days a month."

"Only five days a month?"

"But just think where you'll be the other twenty-five days. Any-where from India to Pasadena. Doing everything from listening to tips on securing international financing to giving seminars on finding your niche in the marketplace."

I heard what Phyllis said, but above it in a high-pitched panic tone, I heard *Only five days a month? Only five days a month? Only five days a month?*

What the hell had I agreed to?

My brain immediately started a war.

This is the opportunity of a lifetime. One year is nothing.

No. She withheld crucial information about the travel schedule because she knows no sane person would agree to that.

No sane person with a life or a family or in a serious relationship.

Then it sort of clicked.

As far as Phyllis knew, I had none of those.

Except...now I did.

How could I tell Boone I was taking off for a year when he'd re-quested the Phoenix program because I lived here? Would he think I'd taken the job as some kind of revenge?

This is why you should've talked to him about it.

"Sierra?"

I refocused on Phyllis. When had she pulled out a contract? I glanced at it, then at her.

"It's just a statement of intent," she explained quickly. "Not a big thing."

"Then you won't care that I don't sign it until I've had my attorney look at it?" I said coolly.

That surprised her. "If that's what you prefer. But it is an unnecessary step."

"I always err on the side of caution. You taught me that."

"I also taught you to accept things at face value."

A standoff.

Not what either of us had wanted.

Phyllis gathered her things. "I'm so glad you verbally agreed to take the position, Sierra. I'll let the folks at WEI know and I'll be by later in the week for additional discussion."

I watched her walk out.

I'm so glad you verbally agreed to take the position, Sierra.

If I backed out and pushed my point that a verbal agreement isn't binding, I'd lose any credibility I'd earned.

If I backed out, I wouldn't be welcome in PCE—a business I'd poured my blood, sweat, tears, heart and soul into.

But I didn't want to back out. This was an opportunity any woman in business would kill for. This wouldn't ever come along again if I didn't take it now.

And what about Boone? Are you willing to sacrifice what you're just building with him?

If the situations were reversed he wouldn't worry and fret over taking the next step in career advancement and fulfillment. He'd just do it. He'd do it without asking for your opinion because he's done it before.

But things were different then.

The more I obsessed about it, the more I…had no freakin' clue what I should do.

Eventually I decided my only option was to talk to my dad.

In person.

I told myself I wasn't running from my problem when I booked a flight to Wyoming.

30 Boone

I HADN'T HEARD from Sierra in thirty-six hours and I'd started to get worried. Especially since she'd acted weird and distracted the last time we'd spoken on the phone.

Lu claimed she hadn't talked to her for two days either.

I didn't want to worry her dad so I didn't reach out to him. I just hoped her sister would answer a call at seven a.m. from an unknown number.

She picked up with, "This is Rory McKay."

"Rory? This is Sergeant Boone West."

"Ooh, don't you sound all official and big-time army guy. So why are you calling me, Sergeant Boone West?"

"Have you heard from Sierra?"

A pause. "You haven't?"

"Not for a solid day and a half and that's not like her."

"Well, I saw her last night as a matter of fact. She's in Wyoming. She's staying at the cabin."

Immediately my heart slammed into my throat. "What the hell is she doing... Dammit, did something happen to Gavin?"

"He's fine. She didn't tell you she was coming home?"

"No. I've been in Fort Hood the last two weeks. She flew down for the weekend and I took her to the airport on Sunday. I talked to her Monday night. Me and my roommate left at fifteen hundred yesterday and we've been driving straight through to Phoenix. Sierra hadn't returned any of my calls, but she didn't say anything this weekend about going to Sundance."

Rory sighed. "It wasn't something she planned. It was last minute."

"Why?"

"Why should I tell you?"

I'd expected her to protect Sierra; I just hoped I could convince her I only had Sierra's best interests in mind too. "I appreciate that you look out for her and that you're her sounding board. But if you've talked to her, you know that everything is good between us. I know that she's not running from me. You know that she's not running from me. So please tell me what she *is* running from so I can help her, okay?"

A beat of silence passed. Then she sighed. "Fine. You know she's having some issues at DPM. It's to the point where she has to make some hard decisions." She paused. "Did she tell you any of this?"

"Some. But I can tell by the careful way you're phrasing things I'm missing several pieces."

"You are. I don't know whether to be annoyed with her or you."

"Be annoyed with her. I knew something was on her mind but she wouldn't talk to me about it no matter how many times I asked her, so tell me what's going on."

"Did you know that Sierra was offered the directorship at PCE? Fulltime with pay and everything?"

I grinned. "She was?" Her face lit up whenever she talked about the work she did with the organization she helped found, so it would be a huge coup for her career. "Why would she keep that from me?"

"She's independent and feels it's her responsibility to make her own decision. I'd guess a lot of her attitude stems from her mom, but I won't play pop psychologist. But the other thing is Sierra hadn't said yes. I mean, she was wrestling whether to take the position. She's fiercely loyal to her father."

"Even to her own damn detriment," I muttered.

"Exactly. But she did make a decision and say yes to the PCE position—before she knew all the travel that it entailed. So now she's waffling. Big time. I suspect that's why she ran to Wyoming. If she has to look her dad in the eye to turn in her resignation, then she'll feel too guilty to leave DPM and it'll give her an excuse to back out of the offer to run PCE."

I briefly closed my eyes. Fuck. I wanted to talk to Sierra about this, not her damn sister. I hit the mute button. To Raj I said, "Change of plans. Take me to Sky Harbor."

"Seriously, dude?"

"Yeah, the airport exit is coming up."

I clicked the mute off to hear Rory say, "I'll be blunt, Boone. This decision will affect both of you, but mostly it'll have a lasting impact on *her* future. You want what's best for her, right?"

I understood what Rory didn't say. *But what's best for her might not be best for you.*

"Always."

"Then do the right thing."

"Which would be what?"

"Break up with her."

I laughed.

Which pissed Rory off. "Why is that so funny, asshole? You left her broken-hearted before when it served *your* purposes. I'm asking you to do it again so Sierra will take this amazing career opportunity instead of passing it up because she'd rather be home baking fucking *cookies* for you, beings she's afraid if she's not with you all the damn time you'll leave her." She laughed. "But you and I both know that you're going to leave her again eventually, so I'm just asking you to do it sooner, rather than later."

I curled my fingers into my palm, forming a fist and then slowly letting it out. "Rory. With all due respect, you and I are not going to see eye to eye on this, so I'm giving you two choices. You either listen to me and do exactly as I say, or you put Dalton on the phone."

"Why would you need to talk to Dalton?" she demanded. "Because he's a man and I'm far too emotional?"

"No. I'd talk to Dalton because he understands what's at stake when you finally go after the woman who has always fucking owned you—as I believe he did with you."

Silence.

Then Rory said, "All right, West, tell me what you need me to do."

I released the breath I'd been holding. "If the stars align...best-case scenario is I pull into Sundance eight hours from now. Keep Sierra occupied and from meeting with Gavin until she and I can talk."

"Done. I'll just tell him Sierra is on a rampage because the two of you had an epic fight. He'll avoid her at all costs."

Of course Rory would find a way to blame this on me. But if it worked I didn't give a damn.

"One last thing. If you fuck over my sister again? I'll come after you. I know how to use my husband's ax and I'll scatter pieces of you in the forest where no one will ever find you." She hung up.

Jesus. Sierra had some seriously violent friends.

Raj said, "What's up?"

After I finished explaining, I said, "You probably better pull over at the next gas station so I can get out of this uniform." We'd both been so eager to leave we'd jumped in the SUV ten minutes after shift change. We'd stopped only to fill up with gas and switch drivers.

"No way. You need the extra love wearing that uniform will give you today. I ain't telling you to do it all the time, but this is an emergency, amirite?"

"I guess."

He took the airport exit. "Which airline?"

"Southwest has the most frequent flights to Denver."

At the terminal, I hauled my duffel out of the backseat. "Thanks, man. And if you could do me one more favor…"

"Talk to my Lucinda Grace about keeping this on the down low. But you don't gotta worry 'bout Sierra hearing from her 'cause me and my woman are gonna be occupied."

I scored the last seat to Denver on the eight-thirty a.m. flight.

Since I was in uniform, I got a wicked military discount.

At the rental car agency in Denver, I groaned at seeing the long line.

A businessman around my dad's age, at the front of the line, motioned me over. "On your way home, son?"

"No, sir. I'm on my way to get my girl."

He let me cut in front of him with a pat on the back and a murmured, "Good luck."

A quick stop at REI for a winter coat and blankets and I was on the road headed home.

Not home to Wyoming; home to her. Home wasn't a place. It was a person. And she was mine.

31 Sierra

I'D GOTTEN TO the cabin late last night and had immediately burst into tears because Rory had fired up the wood-burning stove and stocked the refrigerator—such a thoughtful welcome home. She'd stayed for half an hour and listened to my dilemma before she'd gone back to my dad and Ree's house where she and Dalton were staying.

I'd been so physically and emotionally exhausted I just crawled into bed.

After a quick shower this morning, I made breakfast and checked my messages—eight missed calls from Boone. Four voice messages. He deserved at least a quick reassurance that I was all right. But how did I tell him I'd grabbed a last-minute flight to Denver to talk to my dad about the PCE/WEI job offer? When I hadn't mentioned anything about those offers to him?

So I did nothing.

I called my dad and let him know I had a few important things to discuss with him. But his reaction? Bizarre to say the least. Acting totally put out that I'd shown up in Sundance without warning. Then he'd informed me that he and Ree had plans they couldn't change and they'd be gone until early evening.

That sucked. I'd have to sit around and stew all damn day. I could've done that in Phoenix.

So then I thought, no biggie, Rory and I can catch up. But she had plans with Dalton's family and she hadn't invited me, assuming I'd be bored spending the day talking about cows and babies.

I wasn't keen on heading into Sundance. Guaranteed I'd run into some of my other relatives—oh, like Kyler's parents—and I'd have to keep a straight face about how far Ky had *come* in his studies with his tutors. Or any of Kyler's or Anton's siblings who wanted to know every single detail of their big brothers' lives at college. Or Hayden's mom, who always asked if her shy boy had come out of his shell, to which I could truthfully answer he still spent a lot of time in his bedroom—just not alone.

I prowled around the cabin, the urge to bake overwhelming me. The cupboards were devoid of any baking ingredients and that would require a trip to town. Then the perfect solution occurred to me. I picked up my phone and dialed.

She answered right away. "Sierra! How lovely to hear from you!"

"Hi Grams. Guess what? I'm at the cabin."

"You are? Well, this really is my lucky day."

"Are you busy?"

"For you? Never. What's up, sweetie? Is everything okay?"

No. "I'm just here doing some thinking. And I wondered...did you ever figure out that Almond Joy cheesecake recipe?"

"As a matter of fact...I did. Shall we test it out?"

"I'd love that."

"Be over with the stuff in a jif. And sweetheart, you know your grandpa is gonna tag along."

I smiled. "He's always welcome too." I missed seeing my grandparents. They tried to get to Arizona at least once a year to see me but it wasn't the same as Grams popping over and baking a cheesecake with me.

For the next three hours I forgot about everything—mostly—as I caught up on McKay gossip and laughed with Grandma Vi and Grandpa Charlie. The cabin smelled great, my belly was full and my grandpa had even loaded up the woodbox.

Immediately after they left my feeling of contentment vanished.

I missed Boone.

I wasn't being fair to him by ignoring his phone calls. He was back in Phoenix by now, probably pissed that I was ditching him, and I didn't blame him.

My phone dinged with a text message.

My heart jumped when I saw it was from Boone.

B-Dub: *I luv u. U know that, right?*

Me: *Yes. I love you too.*

B-Dub: *U trust me?*

Me: *Without question.*

B-Dub: *Meet me n the clearing n twenty.*

I got a funny tickle in my belly.

Me: *What clearing?*

B-Dub: *U know where. Dress warm.*

Me: *Boone, are you here?*

No response.

Dammit.

I bundled up, grabbed my keys and ran out the door.

THE WIND TWISTED snow flurries into shimmering ribbons that danced and spun across the sky and frozen ground.

I bumped over the cattle guard, pulled into the clearing and there he was.

Boone leaned against the driver's side door of an SUV. He wore an oversized coat and a knit cap. His booted feet were crossed at the ankle. His arms folded over his chest. He wore his everyday uniform.

Damn, I loved him in uniform.

I threw the car in park and bailed out, then I was running straight toward him.

His arms were open when I reached him. They closed around me tightly the instant our bodies connected. His cold lips landed on mine and he kissed me with the surety, passion and possession that reminded me who I was to him.

His life. His love. His everything.

Boone ended the kiss with a groan and stared into my face.

"You're here."

"Not because *you* called me and told me what the hell was going on."

I deserved that. "Who called you?"

"No one. I called Rory. You think I might've been a little concerned when I hadn't heard from you in thirty-six hours after I was gone for two weeks?"

"I needed to get some stuff figured out before I saw you."

His eyes searched mine. "And this isn't something I can help you with? Whatever decision you're wrestling with?"

"Boone—"

"Sierra. We're a unit now."

I snorted. "Unit. Military man to the core."

"Unless that's what this decision is about? You dismantling our unit?"

I hated the hard set to his jaw and the fear in his eyes. "No. No," I repeated. "I finally have the forever kind of love with you that I wanted. Which is why the thought of being away from you makes me ache, Boone. And…the decision I made? I have to undo it."

"What decision?"

"Phyllis offered me the directorship of PCE."

"I know. Rory told me. I wished you would've told me, but we'll table that part for now. When did Phyllis offer you the directorship?"

I looked down. "Uh. A while ago."

The rough tips of his fingers pushed my chin back up, forcing me to meet his gaze. "When?"

"The week you moved in." When his eyes darkened, not with anger, but with hurt, I clarified, "I hadn't decided, okay? Phyllis gave me time to think about it. Every time I thought I'd come to a decision, something happened either at DPM or personally that made me question it. For the first time in my career I was this wishy-washy version of myself and I didn't like it."

"That's why you didn't talk to me about it? You didn't want me to see you as less than a super-confident, super-badass business woman who had all the answers all the time?"

I allowed a smile at his vision of me because it was so freakin' awesome he saw me that way. "Partially. You were dealing with your own career issues and I didn't want to add to your worries. Then all the stuff went down with your dad...and the timing to talk to you about it never seemed right. So I kept putting it off. I'm sorry."

Boone stroked my jawline with his thumb. "What aren't you telling me? Because getting paid to run PCE is a dream come true for you. You started the organization. It's where your passion lies."

"I know. On Monday Phyllis informed me that WEI—Women Entrepreneurs International—has offered to bring PCE into their organization as a charter club. Which is huge. The impact would be...indescribable because there isn't a chapter in Arizona. They have worldwide reach. But as chapter director of a new charter I'm required to undergo extensive training." I locked my watery gaze to his. "I'd be traveling not only all over the country, but all over the world. For a year."

"A year," he repeated.

"Yes. And I've been warned little of that time will be spent in my chapter city. So you're committed to being in Phoenix for the next two years because you wanted to be with me. How can I possibly sign on for a position that will take me away from you for a year? You'd end up resenting me—"

"Never gonna happen." He framed my face in his hands. "Never. I love you. Without conditions. And baby, always keep that in mind when making any decisions, okay?"

I nodded.

"So you already took the position."

"Yes, it's a verbal agreement. But—"

"But what?" Those dark eyes bored into mine. "Are you here to give your dad your notice in person? Or are you here because you know you won't be able to hand in your resignation if he's looking you in the eye and asking why? So that'll enable you to go back and tell Phyllis that the CEO refused your resignation, allowing you to back out of your verbal agreement?"

My jaw would've dropped if he hadn't been holding onto it. How had he known?

"No."

"Excuse me?"

"I'm not letting you back out."

I filled my lungs with cold air. "You don't get to decide that! So many women base their career decisions on what the man in their life wants, instead of what they want. I swore I'd never do that."

"Sierra, you're basing this decision on fear, not what you want, not even what I want. You're afraid I'll get lonely and take up with someone else?" He got in my face even more. "Woman. Are you fucking serious? When will you get it through that stubborn McKay head that you're it for me? I've been waiting for you for *seven* years. You, being gone for one year for an amazing career opportunity? I'll stand beside you, wait for you, support you...that's what people in love do. There are no damn conditions or time constraints."

My belly fluttered. "You promise?"

"Yes." He rested his forehead to mine. "I will miss the fuck out of you. Every minute, of every hour, of every day. I'd rather deal with loneliness for a short time than your resentment for a lifetime. And keep in mind, I'm career military. This is the first separation for us, but it won't be the last. You don't have to choose, Sierra. You already have me. Take the damn job."

"Okay." Excitement and fear started a tug of war inside me. Could I really be lucky enough to have the dream guy and the dream job?

"Just...please don't tell me that you're leaving for Switzerland in the morning." He groaned. "Although, that'd be karma biting me in the ass for how much notice I gave you."

I laughed. "No. I have a month or so."

"Good. Because there is one guaranteed way to make sure you believe this is forever."

Those brown eyes shone with so much love I was nearly blinded by it. "How?"

"Marry me."

Holy crap. *Do not ask him if he's serious.* My mouth had gone as dry as the desert. I swallowed hard and attempted to keep a light tone. "If I said yes, would you stop calling me McKay?"

He shrugged. "I'll probably still call you that when we're at home, screwing around and stuff, because it's a habit. But I would expect you, as my wife, to share my last name."

My heart felt like it might pound out of my chest. "If I said yes, could we have a small wedding with just my dad and Ree, my grandparents, Rory and Dalton, with Lu and Raj standing up for us?" I frowned. "But the McKay-kateers would be ticked if they didn't get invited."

"No more than that," he warned. "I'd be thrilled if we didn't have a spectacle with the rest of the McKay family."

"Would you wear your dress uniform?"

Boone grinned. "Like that, do you?"

"You know I love it. You know when I see you in it I'm so...proud of the boy who left everything behind to make his life on his own terms."

His eyes softened. "Will you *please* say yes to becoming my wife?"

"Sierra West sounds pretty awesome, actually. But maybe you should talk to my dad first."

He leveled me with that I've-got-a-secret-smile. "I already did."

"When?"

"When I signed that damn stalking contract. I told him I was gonna marry you."

Cocky bastard. "What did he say?"

"He said, 'Son, I knew when you left her you had no choice. I also knew you'd be back for her someday. Guess that day is here.'"

My dad. Such an insightful, sentimental, awesome dork.

I felt my smile fade.

Boone was right there. "What?"

"It's going to be hard giving Dad my notice for DPM."

"It's going to be hard giving the *CEO* notice because he'll have a helluva hard time replacing his top executive and he knows it. Your *dad* will be so damn proud of his daughter for the impressive opportunity she's earned." He kissed me. "Keeping that distinction will make it easier for you."

"You're probably right." I grinned at him. "This is a much better outcome than the last time we were in this clearing."

"Agreed." Boone's eyes took on a wicked gleam. "But I would like to revisit that idea about fucking you in the wildflowers under a moonlit sky sometime."

I whapped him on the chest. "I believe I stated that much more romantically."

"You were a virgin. Now you know that down and dirty can be just as romantic as slow and sweet. I'll give you a detailed reminder of both ways later."

I shivered.

Boone rubbed his hands up and down the outsides of my arms. "It's getting dark. We should go."

"I'll meet you at my dad's house."

"Hold on." He crushed me to his chest and brushed his mouth across my ear. "I love you, Sierra McKay. I couldn't have said that to you seven years ago because I didn't know what it meant. Now I do. All because of you. So will you please agree to marry me before I lose my fucking mind?"

"Yes."

He smiled against my cheek. "A McKay marrying a West. That'll be an interesting twist for us to detail in the family archives."

EPILOGUE  Sierra

One year later...

"LADIES AND GENTLEMAN, we've begun our descent into Phoenix. Winds are calm so we should have you on the ground in twenty minutes."

I half-listened as the flight attendant blathered on with the same spiel I'd heard a million times in the past year. Okay, not quite a million, but some travel days it felt as if I lived on a damn airplane. I'd racked up so many frequent flyer miles that I usually got upgraded to first class. My favorite part of that perk wasn't the free booze but being one of the first passengers to deplane. It seemed especially urgent today. I'd already visualized how fast I could get my roller bag out of the overhead compartment—I never checked a bag anymore—so I could hustle off the jet bridge and through the terminal until I reached the main level where he'd be waiting to welcome me home.

Home.

Finally.

For good.

While the people I'd met, the places I'd been and the sheer array of knowledge I'd amassed had changed my life, my worldview and my goals, the travel schedule the last year defined brutal. I'd kept track of the number of nights I'd spent in my own bed. Sixty. Out of three hundred and sixty-five.

Three hundred and five nights apart from him.

No, that wasn't right. We'd spent a week together in Hawaii on our honeymoon. We'd spent another week together in Fort Hood.

Still...two hundred and ninety-one days apart was a lot of lonely nights.

We missed each other with a ferocity that could be gut-wrenching. But we'd survived it. We'd thrived because we never took a single moment of the time we did get to spend together for granted.

This last stretch had been the longest. I hadn't seen him in person for six weeks. Skype and FaceTime made it somewhat better; I could at least see his handsome face and hear that sexy voice. And the smartass always did an onscreen sweep of our house with his phone or his laptop to prove that he hadn't returned to his slovenly ways.

I was too damn restless to sit, so I made one final trip to the bathroom and combed my hair. I touched up my makeup and removed the remnants of my lipstick—that'd be history the second we were within kissing distance anyway. The plane dipped and I placed my hand on my stomach. The last thing I needed was a bout of nausea to ruin my first night back home so I returned to my seat.

The woman sitting next to me smiled. The other thing I liked about flying first class? The other passengers weren't chatty, so it surprised me when she struck up a conversation.

"I will be so very glad to feel the desert heat again after a week in New York in January."

"I've been in Scandinavia for three weeks. I won't miss wearing a parka, that's for sure."

That prompted a bunch of questions about the nature of my trip, so the last twenty minutes of the flight went by quickly. But as soon as we touched down, I wanted off the plane. I didn't text him to tell him we'd landed. I didn't call him. I knew he'd be waiting outside the arrivals gate like he always was.

I'd never deplaned so fast.

But I forced myself not to run. With my luck I'd trip in my heels, which were his favorite. I couldn't wait to see that molten look in his eyes when he noticed them. I couldn't wait to see what inventive position he'd put me in while I was wearing them. The man had a wicked streak as wide as the Grand Canyon.

There were more people in the terminal than usual and I got swept up in the mass exodus. I weaved through the throng but didn't get clear of them until I was well past the area where we usually met. My grip tightened on the handle of my roller bag as I scanned the waiting area.

Then I saw him.

My soulmate, my lover, my husband, my partner, my everything.

My heart started beating again. It seemed listless and mopey when we were apart.

Boone had worn his uniform. His everyday uniform, the faded-looking gray camo one that thousands of other men and women in the armed forces put on every day.

But he wore it better.

I saw anxiety in his eyes as he scrutinized the arriving passengers. Normally he saw me first, so I didn't get to see this—his anticipation, his complete oblivion of the admiring glances women sent him since he looked so fucking *fine* in his uniform, nor did he pay attention to the men who stood a little straighter as they walked past him because he epitomized a military man to the core.

And he was mine.

God. I was so proud that he was mine.

Our gazes connected.

The relief I saw in his eyes brought tears to mine. Sometimes I'd wake up to find him watching me as I slept as if he still feared he'd wake up and find the last year a dream.

Silly man. I'd give him seventy years to get over that.

And I didn't have to run to him because he was running toward me.

He picked me up, crushed me to his chest and held onto me, burying his face in my neck.

Then our mouths collided.

I melted even as I marveled at how exquisitely, how perfectly he expressed his tenderness, his love and his hunger for me with just a kiss.

Boone set me down. He cradled my face in his hands. The metal from his wedding ring pressed against my jaw. He wore that band with as much pride as he did his uniform. "Welcome back, Mrs. West. I missed you."

I smiled at him. "You love saying that."

"No. I love you. Missing my wife sucks."

"I love you too, darling hubby."

"You're really done? This was your last orientation trip?"

"Yes."

"Thank fuck."

I laughed. "You sure you're ready for me to be underfoot all the time? Messing up your routine? Baking when the mood strikes me? Yelling at you to turn down the TV? Hogging the blankets? Doing normal boring, married couple stuff?"

Those soulful brown eyes were filled with a contentment I'd never seen. "I've wished for that kind of life with you since the moment I saw you on the bus, McKay."

I brought my lips to his and whispered, "Wish granted, West. Let's go home."

AUTHOR ACKNOWLEDGEMENTS

To my kick-ass team—Lindsey, Kim and Meredith: This wouldn't have been possible without any of you. Thank you, not only for the hard work you do for me and Team LJ, but for rolling with the craziness that is me on a daily basis. Thanks for all the times you talked me off the ledge, for all the texts that made me laugh and cry, for all the times you encouraged me to get my ass back to work, and for those other times when you told me to take a damn break and stop working all the freakin' time. Thanks for being a security blanket and a cattle prod—and knowing when I needed one of those things over the other. Each one of you is a remarkable woman, a strong and positive influence, and a creative force to be reckoned with. I'm grateful EVERY DAY to have you in my life as friends and colleagues. (Now go post something in Wunderlist because I know much you love assigning me tasks and making me do stuff on *your* schedules. Yes, she can be taught!)

Thanks to the awesome authors I admire so much that agreed to read an arc!

Sawyer Bennett, who I met in Hawaii this year and is so generous with her time and talents, not to mention so savvy and productive that I want to BE her~

Abbi Glines, who shocked the hell out of me at RT in New Orleans and gave me one of the best compliments I've ever received as an author~

Elle Kennedy, who knows how much I adore her work, and responded with a "F*CK YEAH GIMME BOONE AND SIERRA!" (yes, in all caps) followed by, "Rielle isn't in this book is she? I'm still pissed off at her about Bennett."

Sarina Bowen, who lets me pick her brain anytime I ask, despite her crazy busy schedule and doesn't seem to mind when I go all fan girl on her~

And to my readers…FUCKING FINALLY, huh? The book is done and in your hot little hands after 4 ½ years of waiting for Boone and Sierra to grow up enough to earn their happily ever after! Thanks for sticking with me through the end of one series and for waiting somewhat patiently for the beginning of this series, and for the support of all my other series.

I say this with the utmost love and respect, but now you can QUIT NAGGING ME to write Boone and Sierra's love story…you'll see that it was definitely worth the wait ☺

OTHER BOOKS BY LORELEI JAMES

Rough Riders Series
LONG HARD RIDE
RODE HARD
COWGIRL UP AND RIDE
TIED UP, TIED DOWN
ROUGH, RAW AND READY
STRONG, SILENT TYPE (novella)
BRANDED AS TROUBLE
SHOULDA BEEN A COWBOY
ALL JACKED UP
RAISING KANE
SLOW RIDE (free short story)
COWGIRLS DON'T CRY
CHASIN' EIGHT
COWBOY CASANOVA
KISSIN' TELL
GONE COUNTRY
SHORT RIDES (anthology)
REDNECK ROMEO
COWBOY TAKE ME AWAY
LONG TIME GONE (novella)

Need You Series
WHAT YOU NEED
JUST WHAT I NEEDED (Aug 2016)
ALL YOU NEED (April 2017)

Blacktop Cowboys® Series
CORRALLED
SADDLED AND SPURRED
WRANGLED AND TANGLED
ONE NIGHT RODEO
TURN AND BURN
HILLBILLY ROCKSTAR
ROPED IN (novella)
STRIPPED DOWN (novella)
WRAPPED AND STRAPPED
STRUNG UP (Sept. 13 2016, novella)
HANG TOUGH (Nov 1 2016)

Mastered Series
BOUND
UNWOUND
SCHOOLED (digital only novella)
UNRAVELED
CAGED

Single Title Novels
RUNNING WITH THE DEVIL
DIRTY DEEDS

Single Title Novellas
LOST IN YOU (short novella)
WICKED GARDEN
BALLROOM BLITZ
(Two to Tango anthology)
MISTRESS CHRISTMAS (Wild West Boys)
MISS FIRECRACKER (Wild West Boys)